PRAISE FO

Praise for *How to Fake a Haunting*

"Christa Carmen delivers the goods in this twisty, clever domestic horror novel that Rachel Harrison fans will love! A twenty-first-century Amityville, haunted by marital strife and the meddling best friend we all need. Now I want the film version of this, immediately!"
—Christopher Golden, *New York Times* bestselling author of *The Night Birds* and *Road of Bones*

"*How to Fake a Haunting* is a poignant, frightening, and utterly original story about the ghosts that haunt families and the homes they create. By turns darkly funny, emotionally devastating, and memorably chilling, this book twists the horror genre in ways I never saw coming."
—Tracy Sierra, author of *Nightwatching*

"Christa Carmen joins the eerie echelon of Catriona Ward and Silvia Moreno-Garcia as one of the reigning queens of modern gothic. *How to Fake a Haunting* forgoes the fog and centuries-old castles for something far more frightening: the beguiling black mold insinuating itself within contemporary homelife. The gloom and ghouls may be prefab, but the ghosts lingering within this toxically haunted house are real all the same."
—Clay McLeod Chapman, author of *Wake Up and Open Your Eyes*

"Carmen is at the top of her game with this bewitching page-turner that pulls you in through its endearing characters, slowly creeps open, and finally rips you apart in a harrowing climax."
—Kate Maruyama, author of *The Collective* and *Bleak Houses*

"A table-turning thrill ride that chases you to the very end. Carmen puts a terrifying new spin on what it means to be haunted."
—Lindy Ryan, author of *Bless Your Heart*

"Relentless, heartbreaking, and unexpectedly funny in so many places, a deeply human work that I'll be thinking about for many months to come."
—Cassandra Khaw, author of *The Salt Grows Heavy* and *Nothing But Blackened Teeth*

Praise for *Beneath the Poet's House*

"Bram Stoker Award winner [Christa] Carmen weaves a captivating web of psychological suspense in her latest spine-tingler . . . For gothic mystery fans, this is a treat."
—*Publishers Weekly*

"*Beneath the Poet's House* is creepy and addictive. Carmen uses a gothic New England setting to explore art and magic and left me thinking that the things men do to women are far more terrifying than any conjuring."
—Jessa Maxwell, author of *The Golden Spoon* and *I Need You to Read This*

"*Beneath the Poet's House* is a brilliant, gripping novel filled with secrets and danger. Christa Carmen captures the haunted magic of Providence and introduces one of the most fascinating and singular characters I've ever encountered. The novel shimmers with questions of what is real and what is imaginary, helped by the extraordinary setting of a writer's house with a tragically romantic rose garden, a cemetery, and ghosts in love. Shocking, tender, and wildly compelling, *Beneath the Poet's House* will keep you racing through the pages all night long."
—Luanne Rice, Amazon Charts and *New York Times* bestselling author of *Last Night*

"With secrets as deep and dark as catacombs and lyrical writing befitting of its literary inspirations, *Beneath the Poet's House* is a truly eerie page-turner."

—Zoje Stage, *USA Today* bestselling author of *Baby Teeth* and *Dear Hanna*

"In *Beneath the Poet's House*, haunting history meets a riveting modern mystery. It's a spellbinding, beautifully told story about secrets, the supernatural, and ultimately, finding the strength to fight back against impossible odds."

—Jess Lourey, Edgar-nominated author of *The Taken Ones*

"With lush, haunting prose to rival any classic, *Beneath the Poet's House* twists patriarchal gothic tropes and gives new breath to old stereotypes in a story that is at once a historical reckoning, a desperate love story, and an intriguing mystery. Like a crooked finger beckoning the reader down a castle's winding staircase, Carmen's writing is impossible to resist. Mark my words: She will soon find her place among the gothic greats."

—Katrina Monroe, author of *Through the Midnight Door*

"Christa Carmen has cleverly resurrected the infamous Providence romance between Edgar Allan Poe and Sarah Helen Whitman in this thrilling novel set in modern times. What unfolds is worthy of a plot concocted by Poe himself. You won't be able to put this book down!"

—Levi L. Leland, creator of www.edgarallanpoeri.com and *A Walking Tour of Poe's Providence*

"Haunting and gorgeously told, *Beneath the Poet's House* brings new life to the tumultuous romance and compelling lives of Edgar Allan Poe and Sarah Helen Whitman, all within a modern psychological suspense with a riveting plot that will enthrall readers."

—Vanessa Lillie, *USA Today* bestselling author of *Blood Sisters*

Praise for *The Daughters of Block Island*

"Great fun for readers . . ."
—*Kirkus Reviews*

"This compelling and atmospheric thriller pays homage to classic gothic novels while still adding something fresh to the beloved genre. An easy sell to fans of the Brontës but also those who enjoy the creepy, psychological suspense of Simone St. James."
—*Booklist*

"Christa Carmen celebrates the gothic in this twisty, spooky tour de force that ticks all the boxes with panache and style! This love child of Barbara Michaels and John Harwood has written a chilling page-turner guaranteed to keep you up all night. *The Daughters of Block Island* is a top-notch read!"
—Nancy Holder, Lifetime Achievement Award Winner, Horror Writers Association

"The mystery leaves the reader feeling like they are trying to escape a twisted haunted dollhouse without knowing what is real or imagined. Lovers of gothic fiction should pick up this book that contains a wealth of nods to the genre, but also discusses personal horrors like addiction, abuse, and mental health."
—V. Castro, Bram Stoker Award–nominated author of *Goddess of Filth* and *The Queen of the Cicadas*

"A tantalizing love letter to gothic fiction, imbued with rain-soaked atmosphere and scandal-ridden mysteries that unravel to reveal the dark beating heart at the center of a mysterious island mansion. Readers of gothic novels will delight in nods to classic works and the way the past continues to haunt the present in White Hall. Filled with intrigue, this book is the perfect addition to your bookshelf, tucked in beside Radcliffe and du Maurier!"

—Jo Kaplan, author of *It Will Just Be Us*

"With its lush and exquisite language, Christa Carmen's *The Daughters of Block Island* honors and explores the great gothic novels of the past, but here the rules are rewritten. Be prepared to find yourself in White Hall's spider's web."

—Cynthia Pelayo, Bram Stoker Award–nominated author of *Children of Chicago*

"Offers an atmospheric, harrowing plight of ghosts and murder. Christa Carmen paints an island of vivid and unsettling imagery, where every claustrophobic twist leads deeper into an underworld of dread. A compelling mystery, with arresting characters ready to engulf you."

—Hailey Piper, Bram Stoker Award–winning author of *The Worm and His Kings*

"Christa Carmen has long been one of my favorite horror authors, and *The Daughters of Block Island* is further proof that she's among the most important voices in the genre today. A clever inversion and exploration of gothic tropes, this is a debut novel unlike any other. A true macabre masterpiece, this book is a must-read."

—Gwendolyn Kiste, Bram Stoker Award–winning author of *The Rust Maidens* and *Reluctant Immortals*

"Christa Carmen cleverly combines classic elements of the Victorian literary canon in a fast-paced island intrigue that is atmospheric and enigmatic. A tale to rival Ann Radcliffe's own *The Mysteries of Udolpho*, told in exquisite prose and embracing contemporary themes, Carmen's debut novel is a triumph of the modern gothic genre."

—Lee Murray, five-time Bram Stoker Award–winning author *of Grotesque: Monster Stories*

"Immerses the reader in the inexorable, chilling, uneasy atmosphere one hopes for in a Gothic novel. Classically genre-aware while still being inventive, Carmen has a compelling voice no matter which of the sisters is taking the lead. Generational trauma, true villainy, tragedy, loss and resilience collide in a rushing tide of a powerfully wrought story."

—Leanna Renee Hieber, award-winning author of *Strangely Beautiful* and *A Haunted History of Invisible Women*

"The gothic horror novel just received a massive shot of adrenaline to its bleak-but-beautiful-heart . . . In this debut novel, Carmen doesn't attempt to top the classics; instead, she subverts them in a unique manner. She embraces the tropes that made the subgenre what it is and forges an enthralling tale of two sisters, a strange town, and a cast of characters that would make the masters proud . . . If this is any indication of what Christa Carmen can bring into the world, readers will be smiling under candlelight for years to come. An exceptional new talent has arrived."

—*Cemetery Dance*

HOW TO FAKE A HAUNTING

ALSO BY CHRISTA CARMEN

Beneath the Poet's House

The Daughters of Block Island

Something Borrowed, Something Blood-Soaked

HOW TO FAKE A HAUNTING

CHRISTA CARMEN

This is a work of fiction. Names, characters, organizations, places, events, and incidents are either products of the author's imagination or are used fictitiously.

Text copyright © 2025 by Christa Carmen
All rights reserved.

No part of this book may be reproduced, or stored in a retrieval system, or transmitted in any form or by any means, electronic, mechanical, photocopying, recording, or otherwise, without express written permission of the publisher.

Published by Thomas & Mercer, Seattle
www.apub.com

Amazon, the Amazon logo, and Thomas & Mercer are trademarks of Amazon.com, Inc., or its affiliates.

EU product safety contact:
Amazon Media EU S. à r.l.
38, avenue John F. Kennedy, L-1855 Luxembourg
amazonpublishing-gpsr@amazon.com

ISBN-13: 9781662530746 (paperback)
ISBN-13: 9781662530753 (digital)

Cover design by Caroline Teagle Johnson
Cover image: © kevron2001 / Shutterstock

Printed in the United States of America

*For my parents, Jeanne and Rick,
for giving me a childhood so rich in excitement and imagination
that coming up with stories of spirits and specters is a piece of cake.
And to my grandmother,
the first one you get to read in heaven . . .
Oh, and for Nell, of course,
because they all are.*

Then

The satiny garnet petals of mid-spring irises are said to pacify even the staunchest detractors of red-hued blooms. The new house, white with black trim—and, aside from the irises, a complete absence of red—stood in the shadows, its roof, while suitably peaked, refusing to ascend to those heights reached by every other roof on the street. It looked upward at the adjacent house's third-floor wraparound deck, and at the intricate weather vane one house beyond that. Farther still, it gazed to where a hooded-eye-shaped window skewed the lines of the shingles around it, so elevated that it was occasionally obscured by the clouds.

I looked upward too, more for a reprieve from the chaos than from a desire to admire the architectural feats of nearby houses. When I looked back at the party, I saw that my friends and family members had been joined by caterers in navy polos, as well as a local bluegrass band preparing for their opening number.

"How *great* is this housewarming?" my brother-in-law, Cody, crowed, and I flinched. He held a plate of salad in one hand and an Aperol spritz in the other. "You and Cal must be so excited!"

I forced a smile. "It's great. And we're glad to be settled."

"How's Cal doing?" Cody asked. "I'll never forget the first two weeks after Sean and I moved. *Constant* trips to Home Depot. My nightmares will forever be steeped in orange."

My smile curdled. Cody *would* complain about having to run out for light bulbs after being gifted a 1700s waterfront farmhouse in

Avondale Circle. Though I supposed I couldn't judge; Callum had taken his parents up on their long-standing offer of land, real estate, or cash in the same way Cody and their older sister, Corrine, had. Callum and I had used our own money to build the house, but the lot had been given to us by Rosalie and Dustin Taylor. That it was down the street from the historic Gilded Age mansions where I worked was an added bonus.

"Callum's doing well," I said carefully. "Excited to join the Newport Country Club."

"Best course in Rhode Island!" Cody sipped his drink. "Though I'd venture to say Sean does more drinking there than golfing." He laughed in a way that made me think of a cartoon hyena. No wonder the hospital where he worked constantly fielded complaints about his gossipy nature, at least according to Callum.

I looked to where Cal had been taking shots with Monty but no longer saw them. I didn't bother telling Cody that lately, Callum hardly needed an excuse to drink or that the liquor cabinet was the first one he'd filled after moving into the new house.

"You don't drink, do you?" Cody asked.

I pulled myself back to the conversation, flustered by his directness. "What? No. I mean, I do, just not often."

Cody smirked. "Not big on losing control, huh?"

Before I could respond, a hand gripped my arm.

"Lainey, there you are! You're needed for an urgent hostess question in the kitchen." Adelaide Benson fixed Cody with a smile that didn't reach her eyes. "*So* sorry," she said. "I need to steal Lainey for a minute." Her gaze shifted to Cody's hands. "Isn't that salad delish? The prosciutto complements the dressing perfectly." Her smile widened as she pulled me away, leaving Cody staring after us, open-mouthed. "See you!" Adelaide called over her shoulder.

Her grip on my arm tightened as she led me toward the house. When we reached the porch, I gave up on stifling my laughter. "My mom made that salad!" I exclaimed. "There's no prosciutto in it."

"I know," Adelaide replied. "But I also know Cody's a performance vegan, and I wanted to see that faux-horrified look on his face." She grinned and opened the door on the empty foyer. The house was silent.

"What's this 'urgent hostess question' that needs answering?" I asked, confused.

"Oh, I don't need to ask you anything. I wanted to tell you"—she pushed a lock of lilac-colored hair behind one ear, relishing the growing suspense—"you're looking at the new assistant to the director of development!"

"Oh my gosh, Adelaide, you got it! That's amazing." I wasn't surprised; she'd impressed everyone with her talk of bringing the mansions—those eleven properties the Preservation Society of Newport County held under our stewardship as historic house museums—into the present by connecting them further with the past.

"All thanks to you, Director of Visitor Experience."

"Not *all* thanks."

"Oh, please. I never would've gotten in without your recommendation."

I waved a hand dismissively. "When do you start?"

"Monday. This party's my last hurrah before I have to be a responsible adult."

I laughed. "I'm not sure how much of a banger it'll be. But should we head back out?"

"I was kind of hoping you'd give me the grand tour."

"Of course! I should have offered." I gestured for her to come farther inside.

"I *love* the deck and pool," Adelaide said, wiping her shoes. "Were the trees here, or did you plant them? It's like a forest out there!"

"Funny story," I said dryly. "Cal's parents tried to help with what they called some 'amenities.' I said no to the backyard pond and pergola, but I accepted an increase in the landscaping allocation for the fast-growing arborvitae. Even our highest-elevated neighbors don't have a view into the yard."

We were about to turn into the living room when a noise came from above us, a grating shriek like metal on glass. Adelaide's eyes traveled to the ceiling. I cocked my head, listening. "Probably came from outside," I said.

As if in response, the shriek came again. Louder. Shriller. Followed by a low, disturbing thump. For a moment, there was silence except for the muffled sounds of the party. Then five pounding footsteps, loud enough to rattle light fixtures in their brackets. I stared at the freshly painted ceiling.

"Maybe someone's using the bathroom upstairs?" Adelaide offered.

"Maybe." I turned back toward the living room, but the grating sound came again. I sighed. "I better go see what that's about."

We climbed the stairs to the large room above the garage, but it was clear the sound hadn't emanated from here. "Might as well continue the tour while investigating the strange noises coming from some dark corner of my house." Adelaide laughed, and I shrugged. "This is my office," I said. She eyed the boxes waiting to be unpacked, the artwork leaning against the walls. "At least, it will be at some point," I added.

"This feels like a room I would've wanted as a kid. Off-to-the-side and quiet. A little hidden. A good place for scheming."

I gave a *Hmm* of agreement while studying Adelaide. We'd been friends for nine months, the same length of time I'd dated Callum before getting engaged. If anything, learning what made Adelaide tick had been more of a process than getting to know my husband, something Cal pointed out whenever he had to spend more than five minutes with her. Adelaide and Callum weren't each other's biggest fans.

Adelaide could be cagey and bossy and had a bizarre, albeit mesmerizing, style—a cross between a bohemian academic and a second grader obsessed with glitter, as evidenced by her evil eye–patterned sweater and fingernails painted ten different shades. She never ordered the same drink twice at a coffee shop, and her hair color changed only slightly less frequently than her nails.

I looked down at my own clothes: white shorts, white top, white tennis shoes. White was my thing. Clean. Cool. Easy. The polar opposite of the new assistant to the director of development. But as far as free spirits with devil-may-care attitudes went, Adelaide was the smartest and most responsible one I knew.

I closed the door, and we doubled back along the hall. "Guest bedroom," I explained when we reached the room at the front of the house. "And I guess maybe a nursery in the future."

Adelaide cooed. "You'd be such a good mom."

I shot her a look. "What makes you say that?"

"It's a vibe you have. In control. *Totally* in control. Selfless."

"Huh," I said. "Well, thanks."

We left the guest room, Adelaide closing the door behind us. The only room left was the primary bedroom. At the door, a string of muttered curses reached our ears.

"Callum?" No response. I turned the knob and stepped inside. The space was as I'd left it. Late-afternoon sunlight streamed through an open window. A hollow clang echoed wrongly from beneath the bathroom door. Anxious to figure out what the hell was going on, I crept toward it. Adelaide followed.

"Cal? What's going on?"

I tried the door handle and found it unlocked. "I'm coming in," I said, and pushed the door open.

Callum, red-faced, paced on the other side of it, a metal candleholder clutched in one hand. Vomit stained the white tile floor behind him. "Lain-ney," he slurred. When he saw Adelaide, he straightened, trying to appear more sober than he was.

"What are you doing?" I asked, and reached for the candleholder. He jerked away.

"I'm—" he started, then looked down, as if unable to recall why he was holding the piece of metal.

Adelaide nudged me. Her eyes were on the brand-new, intricately arched mirror we'd hung the previous weekend. It was cracked in one place and marred by three deep grooves in another; Callum had evidently dragged the metal across the mirror deep enough to carve out strips of its reflective surface.

"Callum," I said, not recognizing my own voice, the incredulity and uncertainty there. "What the hell is this?"

He looked down at the candleholder again and then up at the mirror. As he did, his mouth trembled. "I saw—" he stammered. "I saw a—"

White-hot rage coursed through me. Sure, Callum was stressed, and not just about finishing the house. Now that we'd moved in, there was no more planning, no more anticipating living up to the expectations of his parents. Now that Rosalie and Dustin had given Cal his "leg up," he would have to deliver on it. But I didn't give a shit how frightened Cal was of growing up; getting drunk and destroying our new house was unacceptable.

"If you trashed the mirror because you're shit-faced and, I don't know, you saw a spider or something, I'm going to kill you."

Callum shook his head, the movement slow. "Not a shpi—*spi*der. I saw . . ."

He locked eyes with his own reflection and raised the hunk of metal.

"No!" I cried, and leaped forward, but it was too late; Callum brought the candleholder down against the mirror's center. The sound was the shattering of a frozen lake beneath a monstrous oak. The cacophony filled the room—and my head.

For an instant, the explosion was beautiful, shards of glass like flakes of ice spinning through the air. But not before I saw my husband's face in the mirror at the moment of impact. Callum's face, but not quite his face. Twisted and distorted. Dark and shimmering and multipaned, like the iridescent eyes of a fly.

I dropped to the ground like falling glass myself, slivers of crystal piercing my arms and neck like stinging rain. A stark, desperate thought occurred to me as I crouched in the ruin, the beat of my heart like the hooves of a runaway horse:

This is for the best. This is for the best because after this, it will be over . . . After this, there's no way he'll ever drink again.

Now

Chapter 1

The rain fell in a steady drizzle, stinging my skin and wetting the white lace sleeves of my dress. I held Beatrix tightly against me, an action that'd been easy when she was two but was much more difficult two years later. She shifted in my arms and murmured something unintelligible, her lips soft and warm against my cheek.

"I know, baby, I know," I cooed. "We'll be home soon. Ten minutes. Then you can get in bed."

She nestled farther into me, and I forced myself to hold her steady, the taffeta of her dress making it even tougher to get a good grip. A car pulled into the circular drive of the stately mansion, and I squinted through the mist, heartbeat rising at the prospect of escape. *Don't be so dramatic,* I chastised myself. It was a sleek gray Porsche, not my dinged-up and dusty Subaru.

I spun around looking for Callum and caught sight of what appeared to be the sleeve of his suit jacket behind one of the clay-colored pillars. A figure stepped out of the shadows beside me. The jasmine and ambergris of her expensive perfume snaked down my throat, thick as smoke.

"Lainey," Rosalie Taylor said. She pursed her lips and glanced at a nonexistent watch. "Leaving so soon?"

I stared, a little incredulous, despite an intimate knowledge of Rosalie's tactics of manipulation. "It's after eight," I said. "I've got to get Beatrix to bed."

I hated the defensiveness in my voice, a by-product of my worry that I'd not done enough to ensure Rosalie and Dustin had seen their granddaughter over the course of the evening. No matter that I'd brought Bea over to their table several times, or that they couldn't be bothered to tear themselves away from their "esteemed" guests. The simple fact that Rosalie had insisted on a four-year-old's presence at the gala—held annually in honor of the Rhode Island Police Chiefs Association—was ridiculous.

"The night just started," Rosalie said. "We haven't even given out the scholarships." She sipped from her champagne flute, and I cringed.

Why did the Taylors have to hold the gala here, at the Elms? But I knew the answer. It'd been a little over a year since I'd been promoted from director of visitor experience to director of museum affairs and chief curator, a position Rosalie interpreted as my now holding power within the Preservation Society of Newport County. And power in my hands was to be met with a display of power in her own. *You may curate the mansions' contents,* her actions said, *but I can rally a small army to fill any one of them for whatever purpose I deem fit.*

I shifted where I stood, feet aching in my too-high heels, the muscles in my arms and neck burning. Still, I refused to put Bea down, filled with an irrational fear that if I did, Rosalie would snatch her up and disappear into the mansion like an evil fairy after delivering a changeling. I shook away the thought, noticing as I did that more partygoers had spilled from the Elms' cavernous front entrance. They mulled about, laughing and puffing on e-cigarettes. I had to refrain from yelling through the drizzle that there was no smoking allowed on Preservation Society properties.

Rosalie kept her attention on me, but I looked past her to where the suit-jacket sleeve was emerging from behind the pillar to reveal Callum. He was laughing with one of the valets, slapping the younger man on the back. Cal handed him something that winked silver in the misty gray. The man returned the palm-size item to an inside breast pocket. It didn't take a psychic to know they'd been sharing a flask.

Anger flared within me. Callum had been drinking martinis all night. The last thing he needed—as usual—was another drink. I patted a pocket in my dress, relieved to feel the bulk of my belongings beneath the lace: glasses, phone, wallet. *Looks like I'll be driving home,* I thought as the valet pulled up with my car. Callum reached us a moment later, grinning lazily at me and then at Rosalie.

"Good timing," he said. Beatrix stiffened at the sound of his voice.

"If you say so," Rosalie responded breezily. "I still think it's awfully early to be taking off."

I swallowed my retort and opened the back door, depositing Bea gently into her car seat. I secured the buckles with swift, practiced movements, aware that Callum still stood on the sidewalk and had not yet moved toward the car.

"Where's Love?" Beatrix asked.

"Right here, sweetheart." I plucked the koala from the seat-back pocket in front of her and nuzzled it against her cheek. "Remember, ten more minutes and we'll be home." I kissed her forehead.

"'Kay, Mommy." Bea nuzzled harder against the koala and closed her eyes. I straightened and shut the door. Callum had stepped off the sidewalk and was circling the front of the car.

"What are you doing?" I asked him, aware that Rosalie was studying me intently. Several of the partygoers had migrated toward us, shooting clandestine looks at Rosalie, eager to get a word in. Between their great personal wealth and their admittedly generous philanthropic efforts, Rosalie and Dustin Taylor were one of the most well-known—and sought-after—couples in Newport.

"What do you mean, what am I doing?" Callum asked, confusion rippling across his features. "I'm driving. Get in."

I froze, thoughts firing: *Damn the event's valet parking—the keys in the ignition, the engine primed and whirring.* "You drank tonight," I said, delivering the words without the judgment I knew would incite him to anger. "I'll drive."

Callum scoffed. "Don't be ridiculous. I'm fine." He took another step around the front of the car, and I moved in that direction as well, coming alongside Rosalie in the process. I felt her bristle beside me, an attentive fox in the undergrowth, all pricked ears and glittering eyes.

"Callum," I said through gritted teeth, cursing the revelers who'd moved closer, desperately hoping to avoid a scene even as I knew we were in the midst of one, "I didn't have anything to drink."

"Didn't you, though?" Rosalie spoke the words with enough pointed curiosity to make it clear it wasn't a question. "Surely you had at least a few glasses of wine." She laughed and gestured vaguely around her. "I mean, who didn't?"

My mouth fell open. "*I* didn't," I insisted, but she wasn't listening. She jerked her chin at Callum, indicating he should get behind the wheel.

"Get your family home." Her tone was final. She smiled and smoothed her dress.

These stupid people, I thought, panicking. *This sick, secretive family.* How deep their denial ran, how perfect and complete their delusions. Callum and his mother were so committed to the belief that he was "fine," that his drinking was "normal," that they were willing to put Beatrix's—and my—safety in jeopardy. Anything to keep from having to glimpse the truth, to keep the skeletons locked in the closet even as they rotted and discolored the floorboards.

Callum gave his mother a nod, mumbled "night," and slipped into the driver's seat. I shivered on the sidewalk, not just from the rain but from the rage that threatened to consume me.

"No way," I said, though Callum could no longer hear me. "He can't drive in his condition. I'm not letting him drive Bea."

The group of gala attendees had inched closer, and a scream was rising in my throat, a command for them to back off, to give us space. Rosalie leaned forward, the scent of her perfume overwhelming, her words like flames that curled into my ear, burning away rational thought.

"I cannot imagine they'd want someone so prone to drama in charge of things at the Preservation Society. Kathy would likely be very interested to hear about it. Or, you can stop making something out of nothing, and get in the goddamn car."

She pulled back with a shark's smile and nodded at the door. Lead-limbed, certain I was in a nightmare, I yanked the handle and practically fell into the car. Rosalie slammed the door and spun toward her guests without another look at me or her son, who had put the car in drive and was inching it forward.

With the smell of vodka permeating the air and the metallic tang of dread in my throat, we left the bright, festive lights of the Elms behind and ventured into the dark.

Chapter 2

I flexed my fingers to quell their shaking. In the intermittent glow of the streetlamps coming through the car windows, Callum looked ill, his sweat-sheened skin a sallow color, his eyes more bloodshot than I'd ever seen them. He was breathing heavily, jaw clenched, and the muscles in his arms twitched as if he were cold, despite the jacket.

I spun in my seat; Beatrix's eyes were half closed. Praying she would fall asleep, I turned back around and swallowed. "Please, Cal. Pull over and let me drive."

Callum glared. "Will you stop this?" he slurred. "I'm fine. We're already halfway home."

I forced myself to breathe. I needed to stay calm. "Pull over," I said flatly. "I'm not asking. I mean it." Callum didn't respond.

The rain was still a drizzle, but the night was foggy, dangerously so. I squirmed in my seat. My fear was a rising tide of arctic waters, numbing me. "You're drunk," I said. There was something in my voice now, a preface to hysteria. "I told you what would happen if you kept drinking." Despite the growing terror, these lines sounded scripted. Then again, I'd been repeating them—some taken verbatim from therapists—for as long as I could remember.

"I'm not—" he started, but I cut him off.

"Not what? Not drunk? Not *that* drunk? Not doing anything differently than you've done since Beatrix was born? Since we got married? You're right, you're not doing anything differently. That's what's so exhausting. But

I am. I told you there'd come a time when I reached my limit, and I have. You shouldn't be around your daughter like this. In fact, why don't you keep right on driving after you drop us off, since, you know, you're so *fine*." Sarcasm dripped from my words. "Don't stop until you get to Monty's. Let him help you in your hour of need."

Callum's expression hardened. "I have to work tomorrow."

"No shit," I said, matter-of-fact. "Because it's *Tuesday*, Callum, a night on which normal people don't get shit-faced."

"Give it a rest, would you?" He shifted back and forth in his seat, the movement making me nervous. He wasn't focused on the road, on *seeing* the road through the fog.

"I won't. Pull over, Callum." Anxiety swirled through my stomach, the same anxiety I'd gotten in the face of empty promises and passing years, ever since his behavior had stopped affecting just me and started affecting Beatrix, putting her in danger. I rubbed my temples, where a headache was blooming, and thought of Bea behind me, nuzzling her koala. The dam broke.

"I can't do this anymore."

Callum shot me a look, jerking the steering wheel in the process. The car lurched over the line, and I yelped. He straightened the wheel and returned his gaze to the road. "What do you mean?" His voice was slurred and whiny. It set my teeth on edge.

"This." I waved my hand at him. "All of this. You know you have a problem. How many times have you said you'll get the number for the Employee Assistance Program from your boss or go to a meeting? That you're going to change? A hundred? Five hundred? But you never do."

The car sped up. Callum's jaw tightened.

"Slow down," I begged.

"Not another word about my driving," he growled. "What do you mean, you can't do this? So what, you want a divorce? You're done with me? With us?"

"There is no us!" My tone teetered between a frenzied whisper and outright ferocity. I didn't dare turn around to see if Bea was still awake.

The idea of her listening to this hurt my heart. But I couldn't stop. This was too long coming. "There is no us," I repeated. "There's me and Beatrix. And there's you and your booze."

Callum accelerated again. The Subaru swerved like a wind-battered ship. A whimper escaped me. "Callum, stop it. Slow down. Please. You can't even see."

We were on a winding back road not far from Bellevue Avenue. Somewhere to our left was Seaview Terrace, a privately owned mansion never acquired by the Preservation Society that had fallen into tragic disrepair. Seaview was buttressed by a massive iron gate, but I couldn't see it. I couldn't see anything. There was only the blinding, billowing fog.

"There's no us?" Callum asked. It wasn't a question but a challenge. "Just you and Beatrix? You're fucking kidding me, right? She's my daughter too. You think I don't care about her?" The car swerved again, and I reached for the wheel. Callum batted my hand away.

"How dare you say I don't care?" he said. He sounded even drunker in his distress, and this spurred my terror. "How fucking dare you? There's not a person on earth who could fault me for what I did tonight. I didn't *do* anything. You think letting loose after work, at my parents' charitable gala, makes me a monster? You're deluded. Insane."

The car swerved again. My eyes locked on the dashboard. He was going fifty-eight. Now sixty. The speed limit was twenty-five. "Callum," I said desperately, *"please."* A vein pulsed in his temple. The fog swirled like a living creature. The wheels shuddered on the uneven road.

Callum's next words were remarkably clear: "I know you want Beatrix for yourself. Well, I've got news for you. You can file for divorce—I can't keep you from doing that—but you'll never get full custody of Bea. Never. There's nothing you have on me, no matter what you think, that would make me an unfit parent in the eyes of a judge. Nothing."

The fog was so thick, the car going so fast, I was certain we'd left the surface of the earth and were floating, careening through the clouds. Callum's final words cut like glass: "You'll get Bea over my dead body. Remember that, Lainey. *Over my dead body.*" The vaporous air shifted. Our untethered ascent ceased. We plunged back down to earth. Directly before us, the towering gate of Seaview Terrace materialized through the fog.

There was a violent collision and an explosion of glass, the sound like sanity bending. There wasn't breath to scream or time to duck, only the taste of glass, the smell of sky rolling in unfettered, the absence of color. I needed to turn, to see Beatrix, even as the impact was happening. The deadly sharp finials of the gate protruded through the windshield. They reached for me like skeletal fingers.

They stretched, iron points like spectral tongues intent on tasting skin. The longest one had sliced into the car and past my seat. I tried to turn, to see if it had reached Beatrix, but I was pinned in place by finials on either side.

In a burst of adrenaline, I reached below me for the handle that would adjust my seat's position on its track. My fingers grazed it. I strained forward, the gate's deadly points so close that my cheek brushed against the one on my left. Finally, I'd inched forward enough to wrap my fingers around the handle. I yanked, sending the seat backward, giving me just enough room to release my belt. I flung myself over the middle console and thrashed my way into the back seat. Bea was okay. She was unhurt. The longest finial had come within inches of her chest. When she saw me, her shocked expression gave way to sobs.

"You're okay, baby, you're okay." I scrambled to her, releasing her restraints and checking for injuries. It occurred to me after a moment that I could hear nothing beyond my own manic yammering and Bea's sobs. There was not a sound from Callum. Desperate to get out of the car—what if one of the finials had punctured the engine?—I pressed Bea to my stomach and vaulted out. Bea wrapped her legs around me like a tiny, terrified chimpanzee. Once clear of the wreckage, I picked my way through the glass to the driver's-side window.

"Callum?" I called. "Callum? Are you okay?"

No answer. I peered into the front window. The driver's seat was empty. Callum wasn't there.

I jumped back, blinking against the terror that was darkening my vision. Where was he? Had he been ejected from the car? We'd hit the gate hard, but not *that* hard, had we?

I heard footsteps and strained to listen, then started after them, following in what I thought was the right direction. After several seconds, Callum's form appeared through the fog like a ghost.

"Where are you going?" I called, my voice drenched in incredulity.

His response was muted and made no sense: "There was a crash. Yes. You will? Okay. Yes. I'm running out of here now. I think they're okay."

"I know there was a crash," I said. Was he in shock? Why was he walking so fast? "Callum, wait." I caught up enough to see that he was holding his cell phone to his ear. Darting forward, I grabbed the sleeve of his suit jacket. One arm of it had been torn into strips.

"Did you call an ambulance?" I asked. "How long did they say? Bea's all right, but she still needs to be looked at."

He gave me a wild, wavering glance before turning away. "I have to go."

"Huh? What do you mean? Go where?"

He didn't answer. Instead, he lowered his head and jogged away.

"Callum!" I shouted. Beatrix stiffened and whimpered. I pulled her against me more tightly. "Callum! Where are you going?" The sound of his footfalls quickened. I tried to follow, but Bea's cries increased, and I stopped, my head reeling, nausea roiling through me.

"Callum!" I called a final time, but he was gone. I turned toward the weak beam of the headlights. I had to find my phone, which was no longer in my pocket. I walked, the crunch of glass beneath my feet keeping tempo with the stuttering of my heart.

Once, before we reached the car, I turned back and thought I saw him, a dark figure cut into the surface of a silvery tableau. But it was just a disturbance in the mist, or else a psychosomatic projection of my betrayal, my disbelief and disgust turning shadows into specters.

Callum had left, encouraged to flee by whoever was on the other end of the phone. We were alone. There was only the gutted corpse of the nearby mansion and an endless sky of invisible stars. With rage smoldering in my stomach, I carried my daughter along the glass-flecked road, back to the splintered, smoking wreckage of our lives.

Chapter 3

I closed the door to Bea's room softly, my head pounding, and crept down the stairs. I found Adelaide in the kitchen, her fuchsia hair pulled into a messy bun, her lips a thin, grim line. She was pouring water over tea bags into two oversize mugs. The polish on her nails caught the light above the stove in a kaleidoscope of color.

She crossed the kitchen when she saw me and pulled me into a hug. I allowed her to squeeze me but found no comfort in the embrace.

"You don't have to stay," I said. "Thank you for picking us up, but it's late and—"

"Don't be ridiculous. Living room. Now."

I went, relieved to have her with me. Adelaide's support had been unwavering for the last six years, but never more so than tonight. After Callum had fled the scene, I'd found my phone wedged between the door and front seat. But I never got the chance to call 911. A tow truck had appeared, along with an off-duty policeman who introduced himself as Officer Gordon, still dressed in a suit and tie from the gala.

The officer hadn't asked who'd been driving or where Callum was because, of course, he'd already known. He spoke with the tow truck driver and asked if I had someone to call and pick up Beatrix and me. Adelaide was there in less than fifteen minutes. We'd learned from a social media post that Officer George Gordon had been this year's recipient of the biggest award given out by Rosalie and Dustin Taylor's nonprofit. From the post's time stamp, it appeared that Officer Gordon had commenced his acceptance speech mere minutes before he'd been dispatched to the scene at Seaview Terrace.

My body ached. My mind felt spongy, too tired to make sense of just how thoroughly the Taylors had manipulated events.

"Here." Adelaide handed me a steaming mug before setting her own down on the coffee table.

I took a sip.

She tilted her head, coiffed eyebrows raised. "What are you going to do?"

Tears stung my eyes, but I blinked them away. "I have no idea. I mean, he left, after driving us into a goddamn iron fence. And he got away with it. It all happened so fast."

"I know," Adelaide admitted. "Dammit! I wish we'd handled things differently. Callum was long gone when I got there, and the car had already been towed. What were we supposed to do? The goddamn hit-and-run was being covered up even as it was happening."

Adelaide fingered her feather earrings thoughtfully. "Remember a few months back, you told me that not only was Callum's drinking picking up again, but his body was reacting to the drinking in gnarly ways? Is that still happening?"

"I remember. And yeah, it is. Maybe because he's getting older? We're almost forty. But sometimes, when he's passed out on the couch and I try to wake him to go to bed, he jerks out of his stupor like a reanimated corpse, disoriented and with no idea where he is."

"How disoriented?" Adelaide pressed.

"Um, I don't know. I mean, I can tell him *why* I'm waking him up, point out that he's on the couch and I don't want him there when Beatrix gets up in the morning, and he looks at me like he doesn't even know who I am. This can go on for minutes; either that, or he'll finally recognize me and then pass out again right there. When I wake him a minute later, he's as disoriented as before. Why do you ask?"

"Got it," Adelaide said, ignoring my question. "Now, on a seemingly unrelated note, you said he's had night terrors in the past, right? And that he occasionally gets really creeped out by certain horror movies?"

"Yeaaah," I said, now even more unsure where this was going, despite her acknowledgment of the non sequitur. "The night terrors are maybe once a month? Sometimes less frequently. I think the more he drinks, the less he has them."

"But he *has* had them?" Adelaide reiterated.

"Yes. And to your other question, Cal has always liked scary movies, but he definitely gets freaked out by stuff fairly often. Things seem to stick in his subconscious more than they do mine. He'll dream about some nun with fangs standing in his closet and insist it was something from a movie we saw, and I won't have the faintest idea what he's talking about."

"You don't have to tell me twice about Callum getting freaked out while drunk." She made a face, and I knew she was thinking of the housewarming party, of the past-Callum's face flecked with glass, blood oozing from half a dozen cuts. While my money was still on some creepy-crawly, Callum had never revealed what caused him to smash the mirror, even after he sobered up. The incident instigated a brief period of sobriety, but Callum had started drinking again not long after.

"Okay, lastly," Adelaide said, "tell me again why you haven't filed for divorce."

Adelaide's question hung in the air, and I felt I might collapse from the weight of it. I reached for the tea but couldn't drink it. I stared past the soot-stained hearth, my vision slipping between the stones like someone searching for meaning on the surface of a rippling pond.

"Because," I said finally, sensing she was about to prod me for a response, "think about Callum's drinking. He doesn't drink in the mornings or at work. He's not living under a bridge." I stared hard at Adelaide. "Even after tonight, he hasn't gotten a DUI. He hasn't harmed anyone while drunk. He hasn't beaten or raped me. He hasn't put his hands on Beatrix. Any judge—especially in this town or even the state—who knows Callum's family would see this nonexistent track record and claim he doesn't have a drinking problem."

I gripped the mug harder to steady my hands. "But when you live with someone day in and day out, and they drink like he does?" My voice grew quiet. "It's a slow death, like someone carving out little pieces of you with a spoon instead of a knife." I managed a small sip of the lemony tea, hoping to ease the rawness of my throat.

"He's lazy, but only at home," I continued, feeling my cheeks heat up. It was embarrassing to admit what I put up with. "At work, he excels—yet another thing a judge would point to. 'What's the problem, ma'am? You've got yourself a good provider here.'"

"Rhode Island is a no-fault state," Adelaide pointed out.

"True, so maybe that won't come up during divorce proceedings, but it sure as shit will when I go for full custody of Beatrix."

"Right," Adelaide agreed. "Sorry, go on."

"When he drinks, he becomes the worst version of himself. His abuse isn't physical, it's mental. Spiritual. He consumes me. But no judge will listen to that. And even if they do, they won't *hear* it. And I'll be stuck having to hand my lovely, curious, intrepid, unique, spirited daughter over to a man who will consume her too, like a goddamn vampire."

I didn't realize I was crying until the tears fell onto my hands. "That's not even the worst part," I said. "The worst part is, despite how lucky he's been in the past, his drinking is dangerous. Look what happened tonight. If he had partial custody, I can't bear to think of what might happen."

I paused, laughing bitterly. "That's why I'm afraid to divorce him."

Adelaide's eyes were twin orbs of gleaming fire. "Let's recap," she said, and brought her hands together. "We've got a man whom you cannot merely divorce without potentially deadly consequences, who drinks to the point of complete intoxication and sometimes utter disorientation, and who is known to have, if not outright phobias, then at least certain superstitions that often manifest themselves through night terrors or nightmares with some hypnopompic hallucinations thrown in for good measure."

"Hypno-what?"

"Hypnopompic hallucinations. Seeing things—like Callum's fanged nun—upon waking. They're like dream leftovers. Regardless," Adelaide said, as if we were getting off track, despite my having no idea what track we were even on, "there's only one way to get rid of someone like this without relinquishing control of your shared child, short of killing them."

I jerked my head up.

Adelaide waved her hands, nails glinting. "I'm kidding."

"Okaaay."

"Well, no, I'm not kidding," Adelaide said. "I mean, we're *not* going to kill him, so I don't need to kid. Therefore, *this* is the only way."

I squinted at her, confused. I was drained from the drama of the evening and longed to crawl into bed beside Beatrix, to smell her lilac-and-honeyed scent and tuck wayward strands of curls behind her ears as she slept. The idea of being rid of Callum without my greatest fear coming to pass was intriguing, but where was Adelaide going with all this? "And the only way is . . ." I prompted.

Adelaide smiled. Her perfect teeth glinted in the glow of the overhead. She leaned in close.

"The only way is to stage a haunting in this house until he is so out of his mind with terror that he willingly walks out the door to escape it, abandoning you—and Beatrix—and coming across to any judge in the state of Rhode Island as a complete lunatic."

Chapter 4

I blinked at Adelaide across the coffee table. "*Stage* a haunting," I repeated. "What the hell do you mean?"

"I mean, you start small. Rotten eggs in the wall. Strange noises. Flies on the windowsills. Nothing over the top. It can't be something he could attribute to you; that's critical. No fake blood pouring down the walls unless you can hide the evidence. Everything needs to be done in a way that Cal can't accuse you of being behind the haunting."

Questions fired in my mind like fast-flipping pages, but what I landed on was, "Is this like the time you tried to get Kathy to hire Joe and Morgan Tallow?"

"What? No! This is nothing like that."

I said nothing, but the defensiveness in her tone made me nervous. Joe and Morgan Tallow were the Ed-and-Lorraine-Warren-wannabes of Rhode Island, a couple who'd pitched their "Haunted Newport" ghost tours to every employee at the Preservation Society, including CEO Kathy Barnes. No one gave them the time of day. Except Adelaide, who maintained even now that there was something to the Tallows' particular breed of "spiritualism."

"Seriously, Lainey," Adelaide insisted, "this is different."

"Okay, fine. Whatever you say. But couldn't Callum accuse me of leaving rotten eggs in the walls pretty easily?"

Adelaide shook her head, her eyes never leaving mine. "Not if you're right next to him when the smell hits. Or out of the house. We plan everything down to the smallest detail."

I wrinkled my nose. "How will the rotten-egg smell and strange noises happen if I'm out of the house or sitting right next to him?"

Adelaide sat back against the cushion with a grin. "That's where I come in."

"Why would you go to all that trouble?"

"You're my friend. My best friend. I wanna help you bury this asshole." She winced. "Not in the ground. I mean legally. Get him to where he doesn't have a sane leg to stand on. Full custody for you, visitation if—and only if—he gets his shit together. You'd be free. Bea would be safe. She could have the life you want for her. The life you both deserve."

I shook my head, unwilling to get too lost in this unattainable fantasy. "Why would Callum even buy the idea of a haunting here?" I ticked things off on my fingers: "The house is twenty-five hundred square feet, not some gothic mansion. We're not on a cursed burial ground. There wasn't a murder here. We built it, remember? There's no body beneath the floorboards."

Adelaide waved a hand. "None of that matters. What matters is convincing him something evil has taken up residence here."

"When did you even come up with this?" I asked. "We've tried all sorts of things, and if calling the police to alert them of a man 'driving erratically' and getting Cal pulled over didn't work, why would this?"

"I still can't believe that cop was Cal's dad's golfing buddy," Adelaide growled. "Though, after tonight, I'm hardly surprised." She shook herself as if to loosen the memory's hold. "As for when I came up with it, well, this has been affecting you—and by extension, me—for a long time. I figured to achieve something as implausible as getting full custody of Bea, we needed an implausible solution."

"An 'implausible solution' is putting it mildly. I don't understand how we could fake a haunting to the point where it drives him crazy. We're not Hollywood directors."

"We're not. But we're smart. And we've got something better than any Hollywood director."

"Desperation?"

"Motivation. If we do this slowly, like the death he's causing you, we can break him. If we get this right, we can stage a full-blown *Poltergeist* remake here in this living room, and he'll be so spun up over all the strange occurrences that preceded it, he'll probably check himself into a mental institution. What do you have to lose? Not time. As it stands, you're shackled to this guy and his rampant alcoholism until he dies . . . or you do."

I tried to picture it. Tried to picture Adelaide hopping ceiling beams in the attic, breaking rancid eggs by the air-conditioning vents and then slinking out of the house while Callum stood there, swigging from a beer can and scratching his head . . . or maybe his balls. I could call Callum from work, proving my location, while Adelaide, who was remote three days a week—like all of us at the Preservation Society—rearranged the furniture ever so slightly. That was all I could come up with. I wasn't exactly bursting with ideas, and said as much to Adelaide.

"Whatever you do, don't change your behavior," Adelaide warned. "Don't let Cal catch you binge-watching all three—or is it four now?—*Conjurings* to come up with ideas like you're cramming for a final exam. Don't search anything on the internet. And get in the habit of deleting our conversation history. I can communicate each stage of the haunting via text."

I scoffed. "Adelaide, do you hear yourself? This is ridiculous. There's no way we can pull this off. No way it'll work."

Adelaide's eyes narrowed. "How long have I known you?"

"Almost seven years."

"And in that time, I've watched you go from putting the pieces of your life together and not having much—except Callum—to having everything"—she looked hard into my eyes—"*except Callum.* You've worked tirelessly to have this wonderful life—amazing daughter, fulfilling career, gorgeous house, great relationship with your parents—and he's the one thing making you miserable. Are you going to let him torture you until you start drinking alcoholically too?"

Fear jolted through me at the thought. "That'd never happen."

"It could, after another six years of Callum jeopardizing your happiness . . . your sanity. No way we can pull this off? How does a man with low self-esteem and a beer belly, and whose parents gave him everything he has, take advantage of the smartest and most successful woman I know? Because his denial is so strong that he believes you will continue on like this forever."

Adelaide took my hands. "If you approach this haunting with radical acceptance and the unwavering certainty that it will succeed, no matter how crazy it is, you can have what you want. And we can go all in on this while we're trying to make it work, and it doesn't matter if we get caught."

I uncurled my feet from beneath me. "What do you mean?"

"Callum's behavior puts him at risk for consequences: say, if he got a DUI out of state, away from the protection of his parents, or hurt someone so badly that they couldn't cover it up. And he's never going to file for divorce from you. Abandon this cushy life and his in-home caretaker? Not happening. So there's no risk of having your behavior examined by someone who matters—say, a judge—because the only way you'd end up in court is if this plan succeeds and you initiate the proceedings.

"Prior to that, if Cal were to catch you propping up an iPad in a crawl space, ready to jack up the volume on a playlist of haunted-house sound effects, what's he going to do? Yell? Get mad?" Adelaide let out an exaggerated gasp. "Drink? Who cares? He's certainly not going to have his mother sic her fancy lawyers on you for trying to scare him. That should give us even more motivation to attack this idea with all the blind faith of a drunk behind the wheel."

Adelaide grew solemn. "Getting caught only matters if this works." She pursed her lips. "Once we send Cal over the edge, we destroy the evidence." She paused, giving me time to realize that the stakes were surprisingly low, while the potential gain was enormous.

"So"—Adelaide's eyes had that glint again, all fire and excitement—"what do you say? Shall we turn this place into a motherfucking haunted house?"

Chapter 5

I woke with Beatrix asleep beside me. While parts of the previous evening had taken on a dreamlike quality in my mind, the image of the iron finials smashing through the windshield, along with Adelaide's words—*The only way is to stage a haunting*—danced in my head on a loop.

I stared at the ceiling, torn between my desire to text Adelaide and tell her I was in, and wanting to forget the whole thing—and not just Adelaide's plan, but also my threats to Callum. How much easier would everything be if I didn't care so goddamn much? If I didn't want the best for Beatrix? If I could turn a blind eye—as I imagined so many partners did—to my husband's toxic drinking and complete disinterest in being a half-decent parent?

I'd considered leaving many times before I had Beatrix, but the things Cal did, the promises he broke, never seemed quite serious enough to give up on him completely. The drunken freak-out that resulted in a broken bathroom mirror and the weekend-long golf and drinking binges took on the air of an elder millennial's last hurrah. He was always apologizing, always pointing a finger at friends, at his brother and brothers-in-law, the allegedly worse and more frequent trouble they'd get into, always putting together short stints of sobriety, like a distance swimmer coming up for air. And he'd been more excited than I'd been at the prospect of starting a family. That excitement had coaxed me into making the ultimate mistake: believing that having a child would force Cal to grow up.

Four years later, and I knew the truth: Alcoholics don't grow out of their alcoholism, and babies don't make alcoholics any less alcoholic. There was no point in wishing I'd left before Beatrix was born. Now that I had her, I could summon only gratitude for every little decision that had resulted in my perfect daughter, who felt more like she'd been carved from my very bones than like she'd emerged from my womb.

Adelaide hadn't been kidding when she said I had everything aside from Callum. Well, aside from him and the drama his influential family and their obnoxious wealth created. I wouldn't be able to live with myself if I allowed Callum's behavior to harm Bea or permanently alter the trajectory of her life. I leaned over Bea's sleeping form and planted a kiss on her cheek. Then I crept from her room, where I slept whenever I wasn't hiding from my crumbling marriage in the daybed in my office, fighting against my foggy brain and burning eyes.

In the kitchen, I made myself an extra-large cup of coffee, surprised to find I was thinking about Adelaide's plan for the second time since waking. *You aren't really considering it, are you?* In the light of morning, it was even more ludicrous. I surveyed the bright and airy house, with its still-new-looking appliances, and tried to imagine something sinister happening within its walls. I was contemplating the logistics of wiring a coffee mug to subsequently yank across the room, *Poltergeist*-style, when I heard footsteps on the stairs leading into the house from the garage.

I got as far as sliding off my stool before a key clicked in the lock and the door into the kitchen swung open. Callum stood on the top step, energy drink in hand, blinking bloodshot eyes. He cleared the last step into the room and closed the door.

"Hey," he said, his tone free from the previous night's malice. "Bea still sleeping?"

I stared as he walked into the foyer and kicked off his boots.

"Is . . . Bea . . . still . . . sleeping?" I repeated, tongue slow, brain murky. He smiled, and that was when my disbelief turned to rage. "What the fuck, Callum? You crash the car last night and almost kill us, leave me to deal with everything, then stroll in now and act like nothing's wrong?"

He scoffed. "I didn't 'almost kill' anyone."

"You drove us into a fence of metal death-spikes and then took off so you wouldn't get arrested!"

He wrinkled his mouth, as if tasting something sour. "I took off because if the wrong kind of cop came, they would assume I was drunk once they found out we'd been at the gala."

I laughed wildly. "And what kind of cop is that? One that's not in your mother's pocket?"

"Are you done? I have to get ready for work."

Rage flared so intensely I thought I might double over from the force of it. "I told you I wasn't doing this," I hissed. "Not anymore. You're not going to keep drinking, then come home as if nothing happened. I—"

Cal winced. "Seriously, Lainey, not so loud. You'll wake up Bea."

This time I did double over; otherwise, I would have screamed. "And what about last night, Callum?" I asked, squeezing my hands into fists, "when Bea was trying to sleep after your parents' stupid party, and you shattered the fucking windshield? But you're right, me *talking in the kitchen* might wake her." I shook my head. "I'm not doing this. I want you out. Today. I told you to stay at Monty's."

He laughed. "Yeah, okay, Lainey. I can't *stay* at Monty's." He stepped around me, his eyes landing on the deck outside the kitchen window. He turned and gave me a lopsided smirk that reminded me of his brother. "Besides, if I stay at Monty's, how am I going to fix the broken deck rail?"

I seethed, made speechless by his audacity. I'd been asking him to fix the broken railing on the deck—the dangerously broken railing, suspended over a seven-foot drop—every week since the previous summer. I hadn't even let Bea out there by herself since the rail had splintered, and now Callum was treating the whole thing like a goddamn joke.

"I've got to shower," Cal said. "Oh, and in case you were wondering, the car's fine. They're replacing the windshield and the front bumper. It should be ready by tomorrow. You can take my car until then. I've got Monty's truck." I opened my mouth to reply, but he walked out of the kitchen. A moment later, his feet pounded up the stairs.

I returned to the counter with my now-cold coffee and fumed, listening first to the water in the pipes as he showered and then to the creak of the ceiling as he walked across his bedroom. He came downstairs a few minutes later and laced up his boots in the foyer. "Did you happen to see if my case of seltzer is scheduled to come today?" he asked.

I gritted my teeth. "I don't care about your seltzer. I care about you acknowledging your drinking problem."

Callum straightened, his face clouding over. "You want to do this right now? So we can both have the shittiest day possible?"

"All my days are shitty, Callum. I mean it. I'm not doing this anymore."

He narrowed his eyes to slits. "So we're back to what you said last night? You're divorcing me?"

I let out a groan. "Can't you take responsibility for your own actions instead of turning everything around on me?"

Why are you even talking to him? Last night was supposed to be the end of talking until I was blue in the face, the end of negotiations and rationalizations. He was going to keep doing what he always did. I *knew* that. When was I going to get the depressing knowledge through my head?

Now. You're going to get it through your head now. Walk away. Be truly done. Nothing you've said in six years of marriage, four years since Bea's birth, has made the slightest bit of difference. Why the hell would it matter now? Then another thought occurred to me: *There's another way to deal with this . . . to deal with* him.

The rage that'd been swirling in my stomach since Callum walked in dissipated like a tornado cut off from warm air. "Never mind," I said. "You're right. No sense fighting first thing in the morning. I've got to shower too, then get Bea up. See you later."

I strode toward the stairs, pausing on the landing to listen to him open the door and walk into the garage. In the bathroom off Bea's room, I turned on the shower as hot as it would go. I wanted to go numb beneath its stream, to be blessedly free from thinking about Cal and all his problems, at least for a few minutes. But first, I had a message to send to Adelaide.

I'm in.

I listened to the whoosh of the outgoing text and set the phone on the sink. Then, before the steam could obscure my face in the mirror—a mirror similar to the one Callum had smashed six long years ago—I smiled at my reflection. "Let's haunt this asshole," I whispered.

Chapter 6

I pulled into a cul-de-sac two neighborhoods from my own after dropping Bea with my mother on the other side of town. Sometimes it still hit me: the surprise of living so close to my parents. They'd settled in Newport after retiring. Not long after, my dad had suffered his first heart attack. I'd come after grad school, loath to be more than fifteen minutes from them should my mother need me. I'd met Callum at a fundraiser for the American Heart Association in Providence, thrown—unsurprisingly—by his parents. My dad had been doing okay over the last several years, though his commitment to exercise, cholesterol medication, healthy eating, and better sleep was still a bit shaky.

Adelaide was already leaning against her Prius, parked halfway off the road beside a grove of trees. "Cal's at golf?" she asked after I'd pulled in behind her.

"He teed off five minutes ago. We have a solid five hours to figure things out."

"Let's go, then." Adelaide walked toward the trunk, and I noticed the compact aluminum ladder leaning against it.

"What's the—" I started.

"Uh-uh," Adelaide interrupted. "Don't get going with your questions already. I have no idea how loud the ladder is when retracting or whether it will even reach your windows, but we'll figure it out."

Adelaide strode into the woods beyond the cars, carrying the ladder over one shoulder. I followed but couldn't help but ask a couple of questions.

"You're going to walk all this way every time you need to sneak in?"

"It's not like I can leave my car in your driveway while I'm creeping around your attic, haunting the shit out of Callum, now can I?"

"What happens when you need to get back to your car in the dark?"

"There are these things called flashlights, Lainey, believe it or not. I doubt your attic's that well lit, so I'll already have one on me."

"What if someone sees your car parked here every night and calls the cops?"

Adelaide gestured around us. "I like to hike in the woods."

"With a ladder?"

"I'm an avid birder." Adelaide shrugged and shooed a mayfly from her face. She grinned, but I frowned, and she relented. "Relax, okay? I'll dress in hiking clothes and wear a backpack; I'll be transporting whatever supplies I'm going to need on any given evening anyway."

Adelaide repositioned the ladder on her shoulder and zigzagged through the woods, following what couldn't exactly be called a path but was at least somewhat clear of brambles and branches. Less than ten minutes after we abandoned our cars, we came to a stone wall at the top of a hill that buttressed my neighbor's house to the north.

"Well, shit," I breathed. "I had no idea this is where we'd come out." Adelaide let out a little harumph, clearly pleased with herself.

We kept to the trees, following the stone wall down the hill on the other side, hopping over it into my yard at the bottom. "There's certainly enough tree cover for this," I said.

Adelaide repositioned the ladder again. "Which means I should be able to find a place to stash this so I don't have to lug it back and forth every time."

We cut behind the pool, obscured by the cypresses and arborvitae that separated my property from my neighbors' on one side and a stretch of fruit trees—and more arborvitae—along the fence on the other.

"Your yard couldn't be more well suited for secret missions," Adelaide mused in response to the greenery.

"I wanted trees that would grow so tall no one could see into our yard, remember?" We circled the far end of the pool and came within sight of the back porch. "Unfortunately," I added, "I think that's where the convenience factors end."

We regarded the house, with its second-floor windows: two in Bea's room—or what had been the nursery when Adelaide first saw it—at the front, two in Callum's room at the back. Bea's windows loomed over a gravel-filled rose garden, and Callum's over a small concrete patio we never used.

"There are windows on the other side of the house, of course," I said. "To my office. But they're over the driveway. And, well, the front walkway. You'll have to go in through Bea's room. It's the safest. That's where the entrance to the attic is anyway."

Adelaide shrugged. "Sounds good. But with how drunk Callum always is, and how heavy a sleeper, I could probably go in through his bedroom in a pinch." She leaned the ladder against the house, released the strap, and lifted each step, locking it in place as she went. When the top rung met the bottom of the second-floor window, she locked the last step in place and tested the base.

"It's pretty shaky," I observed.

"It's a twenty-three-foot telescopic ladder. Of course it's shaky. Look how far apart the steps are." Adelaide gave the ladder one final jiggle and started up. When she was halfway to the window, the ladder bowed beneath her. She continued her ascent. At the window's base, she placed both palms against the glass and pushed up, But the window didn't budge. "You left this unlocked like I told you to, right?"

"Of course," I called up. *This is way too dangerous. What the hell are we doing?* "Come down! This isn't going to work."

"Sure it will," Adelaide called back. She spit on her hands and rubbed them together, then placed them on the glass and pushed. This time, the window flew open, and Adelaide was thrown off-balance. She lost contact with the ladder, and the ladder lost contact with the house. Adelaide's arms remained out in front of her like a magician frozen in the act of unveiling a trick.

"Shit!" I cried, and pushed against the ladder's base. For a moment, nothing happened, and then the top of the ladder returned to the side of the house with a clatter. Adelaide drew in a shaky breath but said nothing. After pushing the window the rest of the way up, she crawled inside. When she turned and poked her head out, she was grinning.

"Come on," she called.

I grabbed the ladder and climbed, cursing under my breath. No way I could refuse to test the method Adelaide would be using dozens of times over the next few months—that is, if we got that far. Adelaide was the one taking all the risks. The least I could do was not shy away from the logistics at the plan's inception.

I made it up the ladder and through the window without calamity. It unnerved me to be standing in the familiar space of Bea's room after entering the house in such unusual fashion. Adelaide, however, had already crossed the room and opened Beatrix's closet.

She slid a handful of hangers to one side and peered down at a pink-and-turquoise dollhouse on the closet floor. "You'll need to clear this out in case I can't get to the ladder fast enough and have to hide."

I refrained from pointing out yet again the infinite ways this whole stage-a-haunting idea could go wrong. "Right." I forced an air of normalcy into my voice. "I've been meaning to donate that. She's got too much stuff as it is."

As soon as I said the words, a twinge pulled at my chest. Bea was already moving away from the interests and characters that had defined her toddlerhood: *Paw Patrol* and *Gabby's Dollhouse*, *PJ Masks* and *Gigantosaurus*. She was into horses now, and art, particularly painting and beading. Time went by so fast, trite though the sentiment may be, and would continue to fly as Beatrix grew older.

The thought of missing out on half of all the memories that remained to be made with Bea filled me with heartsickness and panic, though not as much as the thought of losing her completely to some horrible accident at the hands of her father.

"Lain, you with me?" Adelaide looked concerned. "You're not getting cold feet, are you?"

I swallowed, shoving down my fear for Bea and my anger at Callum. "Not at all," I said, my voice hard. "Let's get the hell on up to the attic and see what we're dealing with."

Chapter 7

Adelaide and I looked up at the trapdoor. The rectangular sheet of wood was painted white to match the ceiling, its surface smooth and unblemished.

Adelaide eyed the plastic dollhouse again. "Got anything sturdier than this"—she poked the dollhouse with her shoe—"and potentially stackable?"

I tried to picture the biggest items in Bea's playroom. A rocking horse? An easel? I frowned. "I don't think there's anything sturdy enough for you to stand on."

Adelaide stepped back, looking the closet up and down.

She's going out of her way to help. You can't be completely useless.

"I've got it," I said, excited to have come up with something. "I know I'm not supposed to change my behavior, like, watching horror movies and stuff, but I've been complaining about the lack of storage space in Bea's room since before she was born. I'll get a closet organizer. One that can double as a step stool to access the trapdoor. Cal will never realize it has a purpose beyond me finally having a system for keeping track of Bea's clothes."

"Great," Adelaide said. "I'll add it to the list."

"What list?"

"The list of things we're getting at Home Depot after we see how much of a disaster it is up there."

She strode from the room, and I heard her jog down the stairs. Half a minute later, she returned, holding a chair from the kitchen, and maneuvered it into the closet.

"Here we go," Adelaide said, looking more uncertain than I'd seen her since unveiling this crazy haunting business three days prior. I wanted to reassure her, but I didn't know what to expect either; I'd stored all the holiday decorations, unused exercise equipment, old books, and other bric-a-brac in the basement.

Adelaide shook herself and smiled. "Well, beam me up, then, as they say." She pushed up on the trapdoor until the wood lifted, then whisked it over to one side. Gripping the longer sides of the rectangular opening, Adelaide pulled herself up.

The kitchen chair wasn't high enough. I grabbed Adelaide's left ankle and hoisted her up the last few feet. When she had disappeared into the hole, first one foot then the other, a sense of disassociation settled over me. This experience was so strange, so different from any other I'd had in my house, that I felt I was no longer me. *I am not Lainey Taylor; I am a stranger, in this house and to myself.*

Before the feeling could cleave me in two, I stacked one of the small chairs from Bea's art table across the room onto the one from the kitchen, and climbed on top of it. In another moment, I was crouched beside Adelaide, the open trapdoor yawning beneath us—the dim, arid attic stretching away, toward the opposite end of the house.

We were each perched on one of the dizzyingly narrow ceiling joists that extended horizontally across the space. The room was haphazardly insulated and broken up by random pieces of plywood laid over select sections of joists. From the back wall at the center of the space, dingy light splayed out from a small hole between a wooden beam and the roof.

"This is worse than I thought."

"It's an attic, Lain. It's pretty much exactly how I imagined it."

Adelaide tested her height against that of the slanted ceiling and found she could stand without ducking, unless she were to move to one of the corners, where the eaves met the floor. The joists were sturdy enough, and she traveled across two before coming to the first section bolstered by plywood. I followed hesitantly to the attic's center.

"This isn't so bad," Adelaide said. She raised her eyebrows twice, as if daring me to agree.

"If you say so." I shivered, despite the lack of chill in the air. The attic was dangerous—an unlucky accident waiting to happen—but more than that, it was creepy. The color was off, as if I were viewing everything from beneath a soot-colored veil or through the gauzy haze of twilight after a storm. And the air wasn't just still; it seemed immovable. I had the distinct feeling that if I were to hoist a ceiling fan up here, it would refuse to function, the blades whirring uselessly, the air not only too heavy but too stubborn—too ornery—to be coaxed into a breeze.

Adelaide, on the other hand, appeared elated. "All right," she said, rubbing her hands together. She pulled out her phone and snapped a few photos. "We could definitely use some more pieces of plywood up here. I'll add them to the list."

"Have you decided that the first 'stage' will be the knocking?" I asked. "And are we using an iPad to play the sounds?"

"The less high-tech we go, the better. Even if we bought an iPad specifically for this and didn't pair it with any other cloud or devices, I'd be too worried it'd get random notifications."

"So, a voice recorder, then?"

"A few of them. I can space out the knockings on the various devices so that they play at different times above different rooms." Adelaide reached the mosaic-stone chimney and broke into laughter.

I jerked my head up from where I'd been inspecting a piece of torn insulation. "What's so funny?"

"I want to leave as little as I can up here between visits, and whatever I *do* leave, I'll need to hide as best as possible. But if I'm going to be creeping from board to board, hitting play on whatever recorder is closest to Callum at any given movement, it'd be nice to have some slippers. If I match the color to the insulation, I can leave them in plain view. Even if Cal got suspicious and stuck his head up here, he wouldn't know what he was seeing."

She laughed again, full-throated and infectious, and I shook my head, half amused, half bewildered. "You're unbelievable," I said. "I mean, I can't believe how cheerful you are about all this. Maybe *cheerful* isn't the right word, since I know you wish we didn't have to resort to this. But . . . low-key excited? Keen to take on the challenge?"

Adelaide had been making her way to the far side of the space, but at this, she stopped and regarded me. "It's nice to be doing something concrete for you for once. Something besides listening and offering useless advice."

"Your advice is never useless," I said.

"It's never worked, has it?" she challenged. "In my defense, neither have any of the suggestions from the Al-Anon groups or your therapists." She raised an eyebrow and gestured for me to join her by the chimney.

I made my way over joists and plywood. "Still," I said, "I can't believe you're willing to do this."

"Oh, please." She sounded bored, but I detected something beneath the boredom. "You know my last few relationships have been shit," she elaborated. "Work keeps me busy and fulfilled, but what else would I be doing right now if I wasn't helping you?"

"What about the ER nurse? Aren't things going well between you two?"

"We broke up."

"What? When? You were still together last week."

"I ended things three days ago. Conflicting personalities on top of conflicting schedules."

I winced. "Sorry."

She waved a hand. "Not the point. I *want* to help you with Callum. I want to help you help yourself. Does that make sense?"

My cheeks grew warm, not only in response to the things Adelaide was saying but also because she had the ability to say them at all. *Thank her! Tell her how much you appreciate her! You suck at showing your emotions.*

Intellectually, I knew this. The same way I knew nothing in life was helped by rigidity or a false sense of control, that life did not fit into neat little boxes of "good" or "bad." I reminded myself of this often, but lately I'd found myself discussing Callum with Adelaide, dissecting him with the sterility of a mortician, and this development worried me. My relationship seemed to have turned "bad" in my mind, keeping me from having any actual feelings about what was happening, my reactions as stunted as if I were relaying something I'd heard about on the news.

Callum had become a problem to solve, not a human being with whom I'd shared my life for the last six years and with whom I needed to find a path forward, one way or another. My inability to express gratitude to Adelaide was similar: My responses to what we were doing were devoid of emotion. Only with Bea did I find myself truly feeling things anymore. Unless, of course, the emotion I was experiencing was rage. Where Callum was involved, I had more than enough of that to go around.

Still, Adelaide was going above and beyond for me, was promising to *continue* going above and beyond in the coming weeks, maybe even months. I needed to tell her how I felt.

The sound of tires crunching over the driveway cut through the strange, heavy air and the lack of color, as well as the cavernous void created by all my myriad inadequacies.

"Shit!" I cried, my anxiety over thanking Adelaide displaced by all-consuming panic. "It's Cal! He must've come home early!"

Chapter 8

"Quick, what should we do?" I asked.

Adelaide was already making her way over plywood and joists like an Olympic hurdler. When she reached the trapdoor, she crouched before the descending roofline, then lowered herself onto a piece of plywood.

"What are you doing?"

"There's a vent here," Adelaide said, inching herself closer to the wall, "with a tiny opening above it. I think I can—" She paused, the toes of her shoes creasing against the plywood as she pushed herself forward.

My heart crashed against my rib cage. "Is it Cal? Can you see him?" Then, more to myself than to Adelaide, I said, "What the hell is he doing home? He never leaves the golf course early."

Adelaide pushed herself away from the wall, then worked her way to a seated position and scooted forward, dangling her legs over the hole to Beatrix's closet. "Did you forget about something?" she asked with a hint of irritation. "An appointment, perhaps?"

I scrunched up my face. "I don't remember any appointment."

"With Wildlife Extraction Services? You know, to get a bunch of dead animals so we can freak Callum out?"

"What? No. That was supposed to be on Monday. Mondays I work from home, and Cal's in the office."

"Well, the dude—what did you say his name was? Tim? Todd?—is here now," Adelaide said and leaned forward, ready to drop onto the perilously stacked chairs. "I'm going out there to talk to him. Take a few more pictures of the different vents, will you? I need to see what type of screwdriver we need to pry them open. Then come out and join us."

I started to protest, but Adelaide was already lowering herself through the trapdoor. A second later, she disappeared completely.

"Dammit," I said, my annoyance quickly replaced by unease and the sensation that insects were scuttling up my spine despite the preternatural stillness of the attic.

I picked my way over to a vent, snapped a few photos, crossed to a second vent, took a few more, then decided I'd had enough. That strange sense of stagnant air and an off-color patina persisted. I could take more photos later, after we talked to Tim-slash-Todd, though I was pretty sure a regular old Phillips head would do the trick in opening the vents.

I wondered how Adelaide was faring. Calling a wildlife relocation company under the guise of animal removal only to pull a bait and switch and ask whether they'd be willing to sell the carcasses of the opossums and raccoons they removed from other residences seemed an unlikely endeavor at best. *We'll tell them we're starting an Etsy shop*, Adelaide said when she'd presented the plan to me. *That we make jewelry out of the bones, claws, teeth, and hides.*

No way this would work. Though, if anyone could pull it off, it was Adelaide. I was halfway to the trapdoor when something happened to the air. It was no longer immobile—immovable—but shifty. Shifting. Breathing.

"Hello?" I said, which was foolish. There was no one up here besides me. Why, then, did I have the distinct, prickly feeling of being watched? I stood on the plywood floor, trying to keep my breathing steady. I listened, hoping that instead of another instance of the walls sighing around me, I'd catch a snatch of conversation from the driveway, some concrete reminder that Adelaide and Tim-Todd were not far off.

There was only silence. I risked a look behind me, and as I moved, something moved with me across the attic. My breath caught in my throat.

Adrenaline narrowed my vision down to slits. The figure stuttered, its movements jerky, like some fish-belly-white thing from a horror movie, all sharp angles and long, dark hair, a specter that pulled its way out of a stone well or a staticky television screen or a...

... broken mirror.

Staring at me from across the room was my own reflection, fragmented and distorted, caught in the jagged shards of the mirror that had once hung in the upstairs bathroom before Callum had smashed it with a metal candleholder in a drunken stupor.

I let out a shaky exhalation, the rapid retreat of adrenaline leaving me woozy. Why was the mirror up here? Even as I asked myself the question, a vague memory took shape: hauling the mirror into the attic the morning after the housewarming party. I'd wanted to get it out of sight as quickly as possible but had been strangely unwilling to throw it away.

I approached the broken remnants of the past warily, almost superstitiously, for hadn't this mirror foretold the future? Hadn't it seen what Callum would become before he had? Before I did? Or, perhaps not before he'd discerned his fate; maybe Callum hadn't seen a spider that day after all, but a glimpse of himself... the self he was destined to become.

The thought left me even more disoriented, and I abandoned the mirror to pick my way back across the attic, moving from joist to joist before dropping to my hands and feet and crab-walking to the trapdoor, and the escape offered beneath it.

I dropped onto the top chair with far less coordination than the move required. The makeshift structure jerked beneath me but somehow remained upright. I slid from Bea's art chair onto the closet floor, where I lay for several seconds, breathing hard and brushing dust and spiderwebs from my hair.

I realized I *could* hear Adelaide and Tim-Todd talking. I stood with a groan and hurried outside to see how she was handling our bizarre request.

"No, no, I understand," the man was saying. *Ah, so it is Todd,* I thought, reading his name, along with the words OWNER AND SOLE EMPLOYEE, WILDLIFE EXTRACTION SERVICES on the side of his truck. "But I'll need to check with the town to see if I'm licensed to do that," he finished.

Adelaide put a hand on his arm and smiled. "Todd, I totally get it," she said. "But this is a short-term thing, and I can pretty much guarantee you'll never be asked to do this by anyone ever again." She laughed as if they were sharing a secret. "Do you really want to jump through hoops, maybe even have to pay some sort of fee, all for what amounts to a quick favor for some local artists and a bunch of extra money in your pocket?"

Adelaide saw me and gestured for me to come over. "This is Lainey Taylor. My partner in this jewelry-making endeavor."

I shook Todd's hand. He was handsome, with thick brown curls and kind eyes. At present, however, those eyes were jumping around, searching for a way out of this interaction.

"Whatever you find," Adelaide said, apparently returning to some previous thread of conversation. "Woodchucks, beavers, squirrels. Hell, even a deer. A deer would be great. Lots of, um, material there to work with. And we don't even care how mangled they are," she added. "In fact, the more mangled, the better."

Pump the brakes. You're making us sound insane.

"Are you married?" Adelaide asked suddenly. "Girlfriend?"

Todd looked taken aback by the question, posed so soon after Adelaide's grisly proclamation. "Uh, yeah, a girlfriend," he stammered.

"We'll give you jewelry for her," she said. "It doesn't even have to be animal-bone jewelry. We make regular jewelry too." She smiled sweetly and nodded, as if she were a hypnotherapist goading a client along; he nodded back with wide, unblinking eyes as if the procedure had worked.

"So how often do you get calls for them? The dead animals?" Adelaide asked.

"Uh, once a week, maybe. I can drop them off here?" He shot a look at the house as if he wasn't quite sure how he got here.

"I'm going to give you a different address, actually," Adelaide said. "My place." She winked at him, and he blushed. "It's about five miles from here. Does that work?"

Two minutes later, Adelaide and I were standing by the front garden, waving as Todd drove away. When he'd gone, I turned to her. "Why do we need dead animals again?" It was the same question I'd asked two days earlier, when we'd been working through the details of stage one over the phone, and she'd prompted me to call the wildlife removal service in the first place.

"Cal leaves for work when it's still dark. What could be more disorienting than finding the smashed-up carcasses of animals stuck in your grille or smeared over your tires when you go out to your car early in the morning? At first, he'll wonder if he was too drunk to remember hitting them the night before, but eventually, he'll realize something is up. Something creeeepy." She drew the word out like she was hosting *Fright Night Theater*. "At the very least, he'll get a nasty little shock at five a.m., after what I aim to make a fitful and nightmare-disturbed sleep."

"And what exactly are you going to use to smear carcasses across his tires?"

Adelaide considered this for only an instant before her face lit up. "I'm not sure, Lain. But I bet they have something at Home Depot. Come on. Let's get that ladder off the side of your house and go for a ride."

Chapter 9

When Callum returned that evening, Beatrix and I were in her room, making our way through a pile of books. She appeared unscathed in the wake of the accident; by her account, she'd fallen asleep upon leaving the Elms and had only woken after the crash. Still, I'd spent every one of the last three nights spending as much time with her as possible. Over duck-watching and library-book hunting, Bea had opened up *and* burrowed into me, displaying both a resilience beyond her years and a fierce need for the security I provided. As I read, I kept looking over to her, tracing the cleft in her chin, tucking wisps of hair behind her ears, and marveling at the gray-gold of her eyes.

The sky was an obfuscous shade of sage, tinged copper around the edges. The first fat drops of rain splattered against the pollen-dusted windows. The smell of petrichor came in through the retractable screen, drifting up from across the yard where, one hour earlier, Adelaide and I had packed up the ladder after our first day of preparations. The last thing we did before she left was to glue felt pieces to the underside of the rungs to muffle the hollow-sounding *thwunk* the ladder made when retracted.

My muscles ached from our efforts. Building the closet organizer and hauling plywood through the attic's trapdoor had been no small task, and by the time we'd trudged through the woods and back to our cars, I'd been lightheaded with exhaustion. But the prospect of our efforts paying off, of seeing the plan put into motion that very evening, had kept me going. Now, anticipation and optimism were replaced by incredulity at our hubris, as well as a sick sort of dread brought on by Callum's return.

Waiting while he entered the house felt like listening to some storybook villain stomping through a castle: Each step brought a fresh wave of panic crashing into the shores of my heart. Bea tensed beside me, and though I continued reading, I felt she was attuned to the sound *beneath* the words—the hum of the garage door opening, the stomping, the creaking door, and now, the heaving breathing coming from the bottom of the stairs.

"The animals lead her out of Toadstool Forest to a cozy burrow," I read. "It's dark in the Witch's Garden now, and Eleanor is tired, but she misses her mother." I turned the page, and the door to the kitchen crashed open. A nervous tic animated Bea's lips, and I could see her trying to reconcile the emotions churning within her.

Over the last few years, Callum had made what he thought was a good show of playing the interested father, distracting Bea from his bloodshot eyes and the stench of vodka that hung around him like a shroud with over-the-top antics and no small amount of ice cream. But the older Beatrix got, the less these displays concealed her father's increasingly bizarre behaviors. Going to sleep earlier than she did, eating bags of the same fast food I prohibited, and disappearing outdoors to puff on e-cigarettes and slur into the phone (or down to the basement to swig from the handle of grain vodka he kept hidden beneath his rarely used workbench) had all accumulated to produce in Bea a notable air of distress.

Though my heart ached for Beatrix, allowing Cal his five-minute performance of paying attention to his daughter was less detrimental than the alternative. If I tried to bar Cal from seeing her, the drunken fireworks would upset Bea far more than Cal's droopy eyelids or jerky movements.

Tonight, however, Cal didn't even bother coming to Bea's room. I heard him stumbling around the kitchen. A moment later, the knocking began. After the Home Depot trip, Adelaide and I had recorded twenty minutes of rapping our knuckles against the drywall on one of the digital voice recorders she'd purchased. *These things have about fifty hours of battery time,* Adelaide had said. *Eventually, we'll use those hours to our advantage, but for now, we keep it simple.*

I forced myself to continue reading as I listened, grateful that Bea had picked a book I could practically recite. Aside from the knocking, the downstairs had gone silent.

I tried to picture Callum's reaction. Was he standing in the kitchen, one hand in a McDonald's bag, trying to determine if the noise was real or if he was hearing things? Another sound came then, a low grumble of thunder. Followed quickly by a streak of lightning across the greenish sky.

Bea pressed against me. "I'm scared of the storm." She cocked her head. "And what's that knocking?"

I stroked her hair. "Probably a loose board somewhere in the house. And it's okay, honey. Remember the *Little Blue Truck* book? Thunderstorms mean the thirsty plants are getting a nice long drink." Anxiety welled in my chest all the same. Was a storm a blessing on the first night of the staged haunting, or a curse? Would the weather heighten Cal's disorientation, or would it hide the sounds? As if in response to my worries, the next round of knock-knock-knocks reached our ears.

"How about I let you watch a show with your headphones for a few minutes while I talk to Daddy?" I asked. "That way you won't hear the thunder. How does that sound?"

Bea nodded, her cherubic face eager. I swallowed a pang of guilt that threatened to choke me. I never stuck Bea in front of the iPad before bed, not only because I thought the blue light screwed with her sleep cycle, but because it was our routine to spend that time together. *One night won't hurt. Better to keep her away from whatever is about to go down.* I worked my way out from under Bea's covers.

Another knock-knock-knock-knock came, followed by Cal's confused shout: "What the hell *is* that?"

I hurried to retrieve the iPad from the top of the bureau along with Bea's noise-canceling headphones. After setting her up with a show about an underwater unicorn I hoped was low-key and soothing, I went—in conjunction with two more booms of thunder—to find Callum in the kitchen.

What struck me was not that he was pressed against the wall, head cocked, mouth scrunched, clearly bewildered by the knocking coming from somewhere in the ceiling, but how incredibly shit-faced he looked. He swayed—the continuous movement nearly imperceptible to the untrained eye—and his eyes roved in two different directions at once. He licked his lips, the movement so spasmodic and involuntary it seemed to be tethering him to reality, to the present. When I walked all the way into the kitchen, Callum jumped, but the jerk of his body was off by a beat, the quintessential delayed reaction of a drunk.

Lightning flashed in the kitchen window, followed by an ear-splitting blast of thunder, and Callum actually whimpered. The knocking—and this was the first time I was hearing it up close through the walls—sounded both echoey and spectral, as if the noise was simultaneously floating around us and uncannily close.

"Cal?" I said, afraid to startle him again, which was absurd, for wasn't that the goal? "Cal? What's going on?" He appeared so out of sorts that it was easier than I'd anticipated to act as if I had no idea what was happening.

"Do you hear that?" His voice was strained. "That knocking. It's in the walls. It's been going on for ten minutes now, and it's driving me nuts!" At least that's what I thought he said. What came out was far more garbled, his words alien and distorted.

And utterly, undeniably scared.

I narrowed my eyes. "All I hear is thunder." As if we were actors, and I'd delivered the inciting line, more thunder erupted. The rain had turned from a steady onslaught to violent, driving sheets. The walls of the house strained against the force of the wind.

Still, Callum remained on the far side of the kitchen, his head mere inches from a photo collage I had made one year after Bea was born. It showed the three of us at various milestones: a trip to the ice-cream parlor after Bea had been sick, a day at the park in spring, a visit to the zoo for her birthday, Bea dressed as Raggedy Ann for Halloween. I heard the knocking beneath the pelting rain and Callum's muttering, but I continued to focus on his face.

"Are you okay?" I filled my voice with concern. "Why don't you go lie down? I've got to get Bea to bed soon, despite this." I gestured at the window to indicate the weather. Cal swayed on his feet, and the knocking came again. He pressed his hands over his ears. He looked dreadful, pale-faced and perspiring. The plan was working almost too well for the first night. We were supposed to gear up to bigger things. Start small. Build momentum. When he sobered up tomorrow, would he be suspicious?

Cal clutched his stomach and looked as if he were about to be sick. His eyes watered, and his skin shone with an almost translucent patina.

I was about to ask if he needed the sink when a crack of thunder as loud as dynamite detonated around us like the hammering of an implacable god.

I never got the words out. Because in addition to the thunder and the knocking, the thoughts swirling around my head and Callum's pathetic, plaintive whimpering, another sound burst through the kitchen like a scream. A nasal, disembodied voice, and acoustic guitars as loud as sirens. Minor chords off-key and off-kilter, and a cascade of drums like a runaway heartbeat.

I felt the blood drain from my face. *What's going on?* Neither Adelaide nor I had planned this. This sudden, thunderous explosion of song was not a part of our haunting.

Chapter 10

My heart shot into my throat. I turned in a circle, trying to find where the creeping, disconcerting music was coming from.

Callum had dropped to his knees and had his hands pressed to his ears. "Make it stop!" he shouted. "Please, Lainey, make it stop!"

I kept turning, but the music moved with me, along with the storm and Cal's frantic words. "Shut up!" I cried. "Shut up and let me think!" I glanced down the hallway, but Bea had not come to see what all the yelling was about. *Thank goodness for noise-canceling headphones.* I gripped the edge of the marble island and tried to focus. Lightning flashed. I blinked and gripped the island harder, staring at various spots around the kitchen.

My computer . . . off. The charging station . . . free from both our cell phones. The iPad was in Bea's room. Paper towel dispenser, knife block, fruit basket, ceramic canisters . . . nothing there that could play music. Toaster, refrigerator, coffee bar outfitted with espresso machine and Keurig . . . nothing there either. And yet, the music was coming from somewhere in the room.

Wait! My gaze shot back to the coffee bar. Besides the appliances on its surface, there was a rack for mugs, bags of coffee, some fancy bottles of syrup, and a small fern in a black cylindrical planter. But what was that beside the planter? I rushed across the kitchen and grabbed the object, which was also black and cylindrical. There were several buttons on top of it: volume up, volume down, mute, and a button with a circle on it . . . maybe record? I had no idea, but I thought I recognized the device.

"Stop," I said. The music didn't stop. I turned the device upside down, but there were no words, no instructions. "Alexa," I guessed, "stop!"

The music stopped. Though the rain continued, the silence after the grating guitars and eerie lyrics *(Open your eyes,* the singer had commanded. *See what's right in front of you. There are ways to see what's hidden in the dark.*) made my temples pulse with the effort of processing the relative quiet. It was only in that quiet that I realized the song hadn't just been disorienting; it had been familiar. But I wasn't sure why, couldn't place it, no matter how hard I tried.

I looked up, Amazon Echo in hand, and met Callum's gaze. His face contorted. "What the hell is that?"

Think. Adelaide must've put it here, so don't blow this.

"It's an Echo," I said, aiming for a tone somewhere between sheepish and abashed. Anything to keep from sounding like I was lying. Callum didn't look like he thought I was lying; he looked bewildered. *And angry.* "A smart speaker," I said.

Thunder boomed, but from much farther away. The storm was moving on. "I got it at work," I continued. "A colleague-recognition program they recently started." I stared at the speaker in my hands. "I never set it up, though. The Verizon guy must've seen it in the drawer"—I tapped my foot against the coffee bar—"and plugged it in when he was checking the router. Remember last week?"

Verizon had unequivocally *not* been to the house last week; Verizon hadn't come to our house since we'd moved in, but Callum didn't know that. Callum didn't know anything about bills or utilities or appointments. "It must have malfunctioned in the storm or something," I finished.

Callum picked himself up off the floor, his face a far angrier storm cloud than those still racing along outside the windows. He turned his thunderous expression first on the device in my hands, then a warier one in the direction of the wall from where the knocking had come. I hadn't noticed the knocking had stopped. I was too busy fuming over the fact that Adelaide had apparently gone rogue. And on the very first night. Should I have pretended not to hear the music? Or had my spontaneous reaction worked out for the better? I needed to talk to Adelaide, to ask her what the hell she'd been thinking, how she'd been hoping I'd react.

"I can't deal with this shit."

At the sound of Callum's voice, gravelly and hard, I jerked my head up. "Huh? Can't deal with what?"

Callum didn't answer. He walked to the counter, placed one hand on its cool marble surface as if to steady himself, and glanced down the hallway.

"Are you going to bed?" I asked.

Again, he didn't respond, just turned and looked at the spot where I'd found the Echo. His eyes narrowed. "That was fucking weird. And why would some Verizon guy randomly plug that thing in?"

His words were slurred, but I could still detect the unease behind them. "I don't know. But what else could it have been?" I waited for him to accuse me, to question me, but he didn't.

Cal grabbed his bag of fast food, stomped down the hall, climbed up the stairs, and slammed the door to his bedroom. I stood in the kitchen, feeling like I'd been thrown out to sea without a lifeboat. *What now?* The answer came floating down through the stairwell.

"I'm done watching my show!" Bea shouted.

I sighed. *Get Beatrix to bed. By then, Callum will be passed out, and you can barricade yourself in the playroom and call Adelaide. Find out what the hell happened tonight. What the hell she was thinking.*

A last low growl of thunder sounded, like a retreating wolf. I returned the Echo to the coffee bar. Seeing Callum freak out in his drunken stupor had been beyond satisfying.

Make it stop! he had cried. Adelaide had been right from the start: Cal would be far easier to freak out by virtue of his constant intoxication. The trick would be to raise the intensity and frequency of the episodes so consistently that even *he* would remember what was happening, cataloging each new fright, balancing them like dominoes along the already fragile floor of his mind, waiting until they were all lined up before Adelaide and I set the final one toppling.

Beatrix called for me again, and I hurried up the stairs. As I went, I couldn't help a small, contented smile. *I'll be goddamned, but this crazy plan of Adelaide's just might work.*

Chapter 11

After I'd gotten Beatrix to sleep, I sat curled on the leather love seat in the playroom. The room was separated from the rest of the house by French doors, and it was my go-to spot for phone calls—usually to Adelaide, sometimes to my mother, especially when I wanted to check in on my father—when Callum had fallen asleep for the night. I sat among half a dozen stuffed animals, twirling the shimmery tail of a plush dragon Bea no longer played with, and pressed send on the call.

Adelaide answered on the first ring. "You're only calling while Callum is home because he's already passed out, right?" When I agreed, Adelaide continued, sounding breathless. "Okay, I'm dying to know . . . did the music freak him out?"

"You jerk!" I said, but I couldn't help it; I started laughing. "When did you even set that up? And why didn't you tell me?"

Adelaide was quiet for a moment, then said, "I don't know, to be honest. I bought the speaker a few days ago and brought it in with the Home Depot stuff. I connected it to your Wi-Fi while you were assembling the closet organizer."

"How did you sync it to my Amazon account?"

"I didn't. I synced it with mine."

Another short laugh escaped me. "Should I expect to be at the mercy of your musical tastes again in the future?"

"Nah. At least not anytime soon. It's lost its element of surprise. But . . ." She trailed off, then said, "I think it may be best if you don't know everything coming down the pipeline."

"What do you mean?"

"Your reaction to that song playing out of nowhere was genuine, right? Genuine and extreme?"

I snorted. "Of course. But I thought the plan was to make *Callum* think the house is haunted, not me. Besides, if I don't know what you have planned, how can I protect Beatrix from what's going to happen?"

"I guess you're right." There was a pause, and then Adelaide said, "Still, you have to be willing to make allowances for a really great idea. If something occurs to me in the moment, I have to be able to do it. For the benefit of the haunting. Are you okay with that?"

I sighed, too tired to argue. "If you know for a fact Beatrix is out of the house before you go rogue, fine. But not if she's here. Not if it could scare her too. The plan is for me to gaslight Callum into believing the house is haunted, denying things whenever it's feasible, and when it's not, making him think he's crazy for thinking it's a big deal. Like the music tonight. And the dead animals, once we get to it. If he mentions something, I play dumb. Otherwise, I blame it on his drinking. But I never play dumb at the expense of Bea's safety. Got it?"

"Got it," Adelaide responded without hesitation.

I hope she realizes how serious I am about this.

Adelaide yawned. "I don't know about you, but I'm beat. I'm going to bed."

"Me too." I paused. *Say it. Don't get off the phone without letting her know how you feel.* "And Adelaide? Thanks. For all of this."

It was as much as I could manage, but it still felt strange, boiling down my gratitude for this thing we were doing into five short words. Still, I was glad I was able to finally say it. Seeing Callum cower on the floor then scurry off to bed like a frightened dog had made this whole thing very real. Real and far more gratifying than I'd anticipated.

I could hear the grin in Adelaide's voice. "No problem. Now get some sleep."

I said good night and hung up, relaxing farther into the love seat while I contemplated all that'd happened since that morning. I jerked awake sometime later, the overhead lights burning my eyes and my neck twisted uncomfortably on the love seat pillow. With a groan, I made my way out of the playroom and up the stairs, still half asleep.

Before I could decide whether to turn left toward Beatrix's room or go right and head to my office, a low retching came from behind Callum's door, followed by the clang of metal against metal. I stood for several seconds. More retching came, then silence. I longed to climb into bed and succumb to sleep, but I also didn't want Callum to choke on his own vomit. With a sigh, I shuffled forward. Gripping the door handle to Cal's room, I let myself inside.

He was asleep on the bed, and, to my relief, lay on his side. Beside the bed, a small metal trash can had fallen over and was leaking vomit onto the floor. I didn't bother trying to wake him; from the sound of his snores, it wouldn't have done any good. I stood over him, studying his face and frame. At thirty-eight, it'd be foolish to expect either of us to look the same as when we'd gotten married, but the changes in Callum went far beyond smile lines and a few gray hairs.

There were purplish-black circles under his eyes, and he had the unhealthy complexion of someone who didn't spend much time in the sun. He still had the same strong legs and muscly biceps he'd had when we'd dated, but he'd gained weight over the last two or three years, mostly around the waist. More, even, than I'd realized, since we hadn't had sex since the previous fall, my desire for him having become inversely proportional to his drinking.

He lay, slack-jawed and twitchy, and I found myself transported to another moment in which I'd watched him while he slept, four years ago in the hospital, a few hours after Beatrix had been born.

Things with Callum had been better then. Not great; I'd already been fed up with his drinking, but it would be a while still before I realized he wasn't going to grow up and get sober, not even for Bea. Not for the second child he said he wanted. And certainly not for me. I'd held our newborn daughter in my arms, rocking the tiny bundle and watching Callum, wondering what our lives would look like in five years. Ten years. Twenty. As I stood beside him now, the acrid smell of vomit stinging my eyes, I realized the first of those milestones, the five-year-anniversary of Bea's birth, was two months away.

My current reality—shackled to a man more concerned with drinking than his daughter, my dreams reduced to getting through each day, holding things together for Bea while practically falling apart myself—was so far from what the woman in that hospital room had envisioned. It was as if we were not the same person at all. She was a distant, separate entity, cleaved from me at the first of many forks in the road. Had every fork since then produced yet another fragmented self? Were there different, dead-eyed versions of me strewn along the highway of my life, like roadkill putrefying in the sun?

The thought of these discarded selves filled me with terror. Needing to move, I grabbed a roll of paper towels and a bottle of floor cleaner from under the bathroom sink. I mopped up the mess and threw everything in the shower stall for Callum to dispose of in the morning. While I worked, that previous sense of disassociation grew into something blacker and uglier, something that sprouted spines and teeth.

Coupled with my exhaustion from the long, stressful day, the intensity of it dizzied me. I stood before the sink in the muted light of Cal's bathroom, swaying on my feet.

I felt myself sinking deeper and deeper into a mire. Why, no matter how hard I tried to control things, did they spiral further out of control? What if Callum *had* choked in his sleep and Bea had wandered into his room in the morning and found him? The idea that nothing I did mattered filled me with dread as black as my rage.

As my thoughts whirled, so did my hands, which felt tacky with dried vomit and ammonia. The tackiness persisted, and I rubbed harder, suddenly frantic, and reached for the glass bottle of soap beside the faucet. I pumped three squirts of lemon-scented foam into my palms, then reconsidered and pumped another two.

I wrung and worked my hands, but no matter how much I scrubbed, I couldn't get them clean. I glanced over my shoulder, but Cal's snoring continued. When I turned back, I caught a glimpse of my reflection among the shadows. Clutched before me, my hands continued to try to rub themselves clean. But it wasn't the white foam of soap I saw there, worked into a lather.

My hands were coated in blood.

At the sight of all that red, I recoiled with a scream, knocking the bottle of soap with my elbow. It toppled off the vanity and shattered against the tile. Shards of glass hit my legs like stinging rain.

I froze. Callum moaned and rolled over, but remained asleep. I let out a long, shaky breath and looked down. There was no blood on my hands. It was—had to have been—a trick of the amber lighting. I raised my gaze, but my reflection told the same story: Not only was there no blood, there was hardly any soap left on my hands. The only thing in the wide expanse of mirror was my pale and startled face.

I stared at my reflection, until, finally, I looked away. Then I swept up the glass and went to bed.

Chapter 12

Three days later, Bea and I walked into the house after spending the afternoon out on her swing set. The elaborate wooden structure had been her big Christmas gift last year, and because it'd been a warm winter, we hadn't had to wait until spring to install it. Bea loved the teeter-totter and the swings, though she was still waiting for Callum to add the extra "big kid" swing in place of the baby one. Nothing, however, compared to the spacious clubhouse at the top of the slide.

Unlike most playhouses, this one had real windows and doors. The doors at the ladder and before the slide could remain open, but Bea liked to keep them shut, insulating the fort against the elements. She'd had me drag her beanbag, several blankets, half a dozen stuffed animals, and her tea set up the ladder. We'd then collected dozens of pinecones and hung them on different-colored lengths of yarn from the clubhouse rafters.

The kicker had been when she'd overheard me telling my mother I was curating a new exhibit for Marble House.

"That's one of your mansions, right, Mommy? That you collect things for at work?"

"It is, love."

"You know what I named *my* mansion?"

I'd looked around, thinking she'd drawn a picture or found an image in a book. When I saw nothing, I asked, "What mansion is that?"

"The clubhouse!"

"Oh, of course! What'd you name it?"

"Pinecone House. Like Marble House, but full of pinecones instead of marbles."

The fort had been Pinecone House ever since. I'd even found a gorgeous gold mirror to hang on the eastern-facing wall, a replica of the one situated above the mantelpiece in Marble House's impressive ballroom. Its intricately patterned border resembled the scales and prickles of a pinecone. Beatrix adored it.

"Where's Daddy?" Bea asked as we abandoned the outdoors for the quiet of the kitchen. She shivered. "It's freezing in here!"

As I looked around for Callum, I realized Bea was right; the kitchen was about fifteen degrees cooler than the warm spring afternoon we'd just come in from. "I'm not sure, love. Why don't you put your shoes in the basket and head to your room? I'll run you a nice warm bath."

Beatrix scampered up the stairs. I looked to the central air-conditioning vents, then up to the ceiling. *What trick do you have up your sleeve today, Adelaide?*

I'd given Adelaide a key to the house for those times when it made more sense for her to come in through the front door before Callum got home as opposed to setting up the ladder. Adelaide worked from home on Tuesdays, and Callum left his office around three thirty. To what extent might Adelaide have already tortured Cal over the three and a half hours he'd been here? Had he been guzzling vodka sodas the entire time to drown out the knocking and ignore the chill?

"Cal?" I called, rounding the corner, but the living room was empty.

I ascended the stairs, catching the faint whiff of something rotten at the top. Adelaide had said she would be experimenting with different stink-bomb recipes, everything from match heads mixed with household ammonia to raw eggs, milk, and vinegar. Had she deployed a stink bomb in the attic above Cal's room and I was smelling it from the hallway? Inside Bea's bathroom, I closed the door to be safe and fished her bath toys from under the sink. Then I went to help Bea out of her clothes. Once she was bathed and dressed in pajamas, I set her up at her art table with a coloring book, Disney songs playing on the iPad, and crept down the hall to Callum's room.

He'd never said anything about the vomit a few nights earlier or the broken soap dispenser. The door was closed, but when I placed an ear to it, I could hear the persistent knock-knock-knock, as well as the clinking of ice against glass. I took a breath and rapped firmly on the wood.

"Jesus Christ!" came Cal's startled shout. Then, "Lainey, is that you?"

I pushed the door open. Callum sat in the center of his bed, glass in hand. He was red-faced and tired-looking. I could smell him from the doorway, heady with the vodka he'd already consumed. He placed the sweating glass onto the nightstand and fixed me with a wild-eyed glare.

"Do you hear that?" He cocked his head, listening, but no sound came. I kept my expression neutral, but inside, my thoughts were churning: *Adelaide must be here now, manipulating the voice recorders herself, not relying on the prerecorded knocking.*

"I don't hear anything," I said truthfully. "What was it?"

"It's that fucking knocking again," Cal said, only *It's* came out *Ish*. "It starts then stops, starts then stops, over and over and over again."

I narrowed my eyes. "Bea and I have been here for twenty minutes, and I haven't heard a thing."

"It's not just the knocking." Cal's voice was low. "The house has been freezing all afternoon. Like someone turned on the air-conditioning." His gaze turned suspicious. "You didn't, did you?"

"What? No. I haven't been here all day. And why on earth would I turn on the air-conditioning? It's the beginning of May."

"And the smell!" he exclaimed, ignoring my comments. "The goddamn smell in the bathroom. It came out of nowhere, sulfurous, like rotten eggs, or maybe something dead!"

I twisted my features with what I hoped looked like pity and more than a little disbelief. I nodded in the direction of his glass. "Are you sure you haven't been drinking too much? I haven't smelled a thing."

He said something I didn't catch, then, more coherently, "What are we doing for dinner?"

I groaned. Typical Callum. Avoid and change the subject. "I have leftover pasta in the fridge for me and Bea." I spoke curtly. "You didn't want it last night, so I'm not sure what *you're* doing for dinner." I turned, then spun back to face him and narrowed my eyes again, this time going for concern rather than judgment.

"Are you okay?" I asked, making sure not to lay it on too thickly. Callum might not buy a jump from anger and impatience to full-on worry; I had to play this right. "You've been . . . on edge lately, I guess." I allowed a bit of the usual clipped annoyance back into my voice. "I mean, aside from what your drinking is doing to our relationship, our lives, have you thought about what it's doing to your body?" I raised an eyebrow. "Your mind?"

Callum stared at me quietly. Might he be replaying the last handful of incidents? The overreaction to the thunder and music? Tonight's mini-meltdown over the knocking and the smell and the frigid temperature? I let my words hang in the air a moment longer, then shrugged and bit my bottom lip. "I'm going to get Bea out of the tub and heat up the pasta. I'll order groceries tomorrow." I almost added, *Your best bet might be takeout,* but stopped myself in time. Let him make the decision to call somewhere himself.

I turned and stepped into the hallway, pulling the door closed behind me. As I was descending the stairs with Bea, I heard Callum on the phone ordering Chinese food. *Here we go,* I thought. *Let's see if Adelaide can pull this off.*

Chapter 13

Half an hour later, Bea and I sat at the table, eating pasta and playing Favorite Thing, a spin on the game played by the characters in her favorite TV show.

"It's your turn," she said.

"I'll go after you take another big bite," I countered. While she chewed, I stared at the six pillar candles in front of me. Adelaide had bought them at Home Depot and placed them in a circle on the island. Another six, identical candles remained in the bag to be brought home with her. *Leave these candles here,* she'd said cryptically. *So Callum gets used to seeing them.* She'd winked. *For a later stage of the haunting.*

"I finished the bite," Beatrix said, bringing me back to the present.

"So you did. All right, then, on with the game. *My* favorite thing that happened today was when I was driving home from work. I was stuck in traffic, and I saw some clouds up ahead of me, and—"

"Remember the rules, Mommy!" Beatrix interrupted, unable to help herself. "It's got to be funny *and* pretend."

"I know, I know," I said, laughing. "You didn't let me finish. Anyway, as I was driving, the clouds turned into a herd of white horses. No, not horses, unicorns! They swooped down on fluffy hooves, hoisted my car onto their backs, and carried me over the traffic, all the way to my exit. Then they placed me back on the road, whinnied, shot sparkles out of their horns, and returned to the sky." I smiled at her. "*That* was my favorite thing," I concluded.

Beatrix squealed in approval, clapping her hands and giggling. I gestured at her plate, and she ventured another bite of pasta, though I could see her formulating the next installment of the game even as she chewed.

Before Bea could open her mouth, footsteps sounded on the stairs. I saw Callum as he passed through the hallway, but rather than come into the kitchen, he went to the foyer and opened the front door. Bea and I exchanged a look.

"Where's Daddy going?"

"I think his food is here." No one had knocked on the front door, but then, I hadn't expected them to. I'd kept Bea in the playroom before dinner, giving Adelaide an opportunity to get out of the house and into the driveway without being seen.

Cal returned a moment later, a large paper bag in his arms. The bag was folded neatly at the top. Had Adelaide intercepted the driver? And if so, how had she managed to keep the bag looking so pristine? *Are you really that surprised? For all her unorthodox ideas at work, she never approaches a project unprepared.* I squirmed, adjusting to the idea that my life had morphed into a three-ring circus, with Adelaide at the center. I envisioned her in a gold-buttoned jacket, cracking the whip.

From the corner of my eye, I watched Callum remove the Styrofoam containers and packets of sauce from the bag. He rummaged in the drawer for a fork, and grabbed a handful of paper towels from the dispenser. Then, stacking everything precariously, he started back toward the hallway.

"Do you want to play Favorite Thing with us?" Beatrix asked him. There was equal parts excitement and trepidation in her voice.

Callum wavered, caught off guard. "Oh. Um. Okay, honey. Sure." He lowered the stack onto the counter and pulled out a stool.

"Hooray! You go first, Daddy. Remember, it has to be funny and pretend."

Callum opened the Styrofoam container. A mountain of fried rice, golden chicken, and unnaturally pink pork sent a fatty, fried aroma through the kitchen. I averted my eyes from the food and tried not to think about what might be in it.

"Okay," Cal said, tearing into a packet of duck sauce and drizzling it over the chicken. "Let's see." It came out *lezz-see*. "My favorite thing today was seeing your face." He shoveled a forkful of rice into his mouth.

Beatrix frowned. "That's not funny or pretend," she said.

Callum chewed, squinting at her criticism. "Oh. Right, sorry."

"Come on, Cal," I said. "Can't you play the game right for her?"

He ripped a hunk of pork off the skewer. "Okay, so, my favorite thing was, um . . . at work, all the guys wanted to order lunch but I said, 'Forget ordering lunch, let's have the magical elves come in and make us something.'"

He took a second pork skewer from the container. I couldn't help it; my eyes flicked toward his place setting. Had Adelaide done it, or did Callum's meal consist only of the food he had ordered?

"What did the elves make for you?" Beatrix asked.

"Huh? Oh, well, uh, those crazy elves, they didn't know what they were doing. We couldn't eat any of it. There were dogs in the hot dog buns . . . golden retrievers, I think. Actual bear claws instead of bear claw pastries. And real grasshoppers on the grasshopper pie. Those little buggers started jumping everywhere."

"Gross," Beatrix squealed, and looked at me, as if asking for permission to enjoy this. I smiled and nodded.

Callum reached for his fork, then reconsidered and went for another skewer.

Look at Bea, I told myself. *Look at the refrigerator. Look anywhere but in that container.*

I heard him take a bite, chew, bite, chew, then pause. Beatrix fidgeted beside me. I forced myself to spin another forkful of pasta and raise it to my mouth, but I couldn't eat it. Callum was still frozen beside me. Slowly, I turned to look at him. The skewer was in his hand, but his gaze was directed downward. His eyes were full moons eclipsed with storm clouds of terror.

"Cal?" It took everything I had to keep my voice even. "What's wrong?"

He let out a choking sound, then actually choked. A half second later, he was spitting into the Styrofoam, eyes watering. He jumped to his feet, sputtering and swearing, sweat beading at his hairline.

"Callum!"

"What's wrong?" Beatrix's voice was fearful.

I scooped Bea from the chair and set her down in the direction of the playroom. "Go play, hon," I said, and ushered her out of the kitchen with a pat to the bottom. Bea scampered away, glancing over her shoulder with concern before disappearing between the French doors and pulling them shut behind her.

I turned back to Callum. He was retching, saliva hanging from his lips, his face so red it was nearly purple. Finally, he gave the Styrofoam container a violent shove and ran for the downstairs bathroom. A moment later, I heard him vomiting.

I grabbed the container of food and ran on silent feet for the living room, where I hoisted open the window. I took Cal's fork, still inserted beneath the mound of fried rice, and slid it beneath the head of the decapitated rabbit. One black eye looked out at nothing, while the other was an empty pink socket. The stringy tendon and gristle hanging from its neck was the same color as the spareribs.

I maneuvered the rabbit head through the open window and tossed it into a nearby bush. I shut the window as quietly as I could, and was about to fly back across the living room when I shot a look at the playroom to make sure Bea had fully latched the doors.

A bloody handprint marred the doorknob.

Panic shot through me. Had Bea cut her hand? But a step closer told me the handprint was too big to be hers. Adelaide must have left it in another attempt to scare Callum. With no more time to waste, I sprinted to the kitchen and placed the container back where I found it, making sure to reinsert the fork.

Callum emerged from the bathroom, running his hands down his cheeks. He looked as if he were returning from war. His eyes, even more bloodshot than before, were still wide in horror, and he stared at the container as if it would launch itself across the counter right at his face.

"Callum," I said, and the second I spoke his name, I knew I'd gotten it right. The tone, Adelaide had warned me, would be critical for Callum to believe that, not only did I have nothing to do with this, but that I was convinced he'd lost his mind. "What the hell was that? Was there a bone? A bug?" I looked from Cal to the counter and back again, waiting for him to comment. For several seconds, all he could do was point, mouth stuttering in time to the wagging of his finger.

"There," he finally got out. "In there, Lainey. It's a goddamn head! A rabbit head. In my goddamn food. I ate off it. I ate—" He dry heaved and held a hand to his mouth.

I stared at him, feeling the feigned incredulity straining my features.

"Look!" he shrieked, and I jumped, then shot a glance over my shoulder at the playroom. When I turned back, Callum was pointing at the container again. "Just *look* if you don't believe me."

I gave him a final, worried stare, leaned over the container, picked up the fork, and dug through the spareribs. When I didn't react, didn't gag or run screaming, Callum ventured forward, first one step, then another.

"Let me see that," he said, and grabbed the fork, pushing meat and rice out of the way. Globs of food flew from the container and splattered the marble.

"Cal," I started, but he kept digging with the fork. His movements became frantic until it seemed he could take the macabre scavenger hunt no longer. He picked up the container and dumped its contents onto the counter.

"Callum!" I cried.

He stared at the pile of food, the chicken fingers and pork, the little piles of chopped vegetables, the smeared puddles of duck sauce, and shook his head. He was muttering to himself, something I couldn't make out.

"Cal!" I shouted with enough force that he finally looked up, finally saw me. I made my eyes go wide with a strange kind of pitying horror, the kind I imagined bipolar sufferers saw on the faces of their loved ones right before they went out on another manic tear.

"There's no rabbit head in your food, Callum." I said the words *rabbit head* as if they were interchangeable with *unicorn horn*.

He blinked. Swallowed. Were those actual tears, or were his eyes still watering from having vomited?

"I don't know what you saw," I continued. "But there's nothing there." I paused, then said it again. And again.

"There's nothing there, Callum. There's nothing there."

Chapter 14

I broke off a piece of my muffin but didn't take a bite. Adelaide and I were tucked into a back corner of a coffee shop, discussing the events of the previous evening. "You didn't get the rabbit from Todd?" I asked. "Oh, god, Adelaide, please don't tell me you yanked some poor bunny from its burrow and decapitated it yourself."

We were supposed to be working, but neither of us were expected in the office on Wednesdays thanks to the Preservation Society's post-COVID policies. Adelaide had messaged asking if we could talk before our nine a.m. meeting, and I'd agreed. Though I was surprised I'd even seen Adelaide's text; I'd been avoiding my cell phone all morning. Callum had called six times since leaving for work. I knew he was keen to start in with his bullshit as soon as I answered. But I had no plans to answer. Not that morning. Not all day.

I didn't want to hear his voice. Didn't want to be subjected to his whiney, hangover-and-guilt-fueled speeches that were never apologies as much as they were canaries in a coal mine, dropping lines about whether he should pick up the salmon I liked from the fish market on his way home or asking how Bea was when I'd dropped her at school, when he was really gauging the extent of my anger. Each new drinking episode was like a game to Callum; he made his mess, then calculated how long it would take—and how much groveling was required—to clean it up.

And speaking of cleaning things up, I'd realized something as I'd stared at Callum's drunk, deluded face while he blubbered and stared, wild-eyed, at the rice and pork littering the table, the knowledge solidifying as I dug a small hole and buried the rabbit head in the backyard late last night. I wasn't just mad or disappointed or bitter or resentful or tired. I was furious. Rageful.

My wrath at everything he'd put me through over the years was like a white-capped surge of sediment-heavy river water finally freed from its dam. Witnessing the terror the ghastly rabbit head had elicited from him was the first time in years Callum had been stripped of his power, left without the upper hand. Nothing I'd ever said or done had gotten as much of a reaction out of Callum. Haunting him was liberating. Vindicating. Delicious.

Adelaide was saying something about her luck in finding the rabbit carcass in the woods after Todd hadn't come through yet with something dead, but I couldn't concentrate on her words. My mind kept spinning, reeling.

I've never been a spiteful person, never delighted in another's misfortune. But I liked watching Callum suffer. I liked seeing him fearful and upset, even hurt. How many nights did he lie to me about when he'd be home? About not drinking? How many times had he disappointed Bea? Missed her horseback riding lessons? Avoided spending a moment with her over an entire weekend? Been oblivious to her needs, her likes, her cute—and inevitably fleeting—little four-year-old fancies?

The next thought came with all the force of a high-speed train: *I wish we'd gone further. I wish the rabbit head had been infested with maggots and he'd bitten into it, tasted blood and rot, as bitter as the disappointment I've swallowed for more than half a decade.* My fingers itched with the desire to push Callum headfirst into a downward spiral. Sure, I'd take him fleeing the house in surrender, losing custody of Bea, but might I like to see his complete disintegration too? His madness?

I interrupted Adelaide mid-sentence. "So what's next?"

Adelaide frowned, caught off guard. "Sorry?"

"What's the next thing we're doing to him?"

Her frown morphed into a smile. "Last night really did go well, didn't it? Okay, yes, let's talk next steps." She dug into her bag and pulled out a notebook.

"How did you intercept the driver, by the way?" I asked.

"I pretended to be you. Walked around the side of the house and into the driveway brushing my hands off like I was simply *buried* in homeowner chores. I told the delivery guy I'd take the food in, then put the bag on the ground. 'Just want to make sure everything's here,' I said to him. When I put my hands into the bag to open the container, I sort of rolled the rabbit head out of my shirtsleeve and covered it with the skewers. Then I said something like, 'Shoot, I forgot something around back. Could you bring it up to the porch for my husband after all?' and moseyed back around the house."

"What if the driver had said something to Callum?"

Adelaide shrugged. "We talked about this, remember? We have to go all out in the moment. Why don't serial killers get caught for decades?"

I tilted my head, considering this. "Well, up until fairly recently, I'd say it's because of limited technology. DNA testing being in its early stages, fewer surveillance tactics, more—"

Adelaide groaned. "Good grief, Lainey, *no*. It's because they had serial killer confidence. They were brazen as hell, taking insane risks that paid off. Everyone's luck runs out eventually. But in our case, by the time Callum figures out what hit him, he'll be living in some dumpy apartment by himself, and you and Beatrix will be free and happy."

"Maybe he'll be sober," I said. "If he loses custody of Bea. Maybe the haunting will have a positive effect in the long run."

Adelaide eyed me curiously. "Maybe," she agreed, but I could tell she thought that was about as likely as last night's rabbit hopping through the coffee shop. "But by then, it would be too late."

I took a bite of muffin. "So what's next?" I repeated. The idea of Callum getting sober was like a mirage, some wispy, intangible thing

I'd couldn't conceptualize. "More stink bombs? Increase the frequency of the knocking?"

"Hardly." Adelaide's eyes glinted. "Have I ever mentioned a Chris Matheson to you?"

"Maybe?" I tried to remember.

"He's a plumber. Just over the border in Connecticut." Adelaide drained the last of her latte. "But before we get to him, I've got to employ the flies."

Dread pooled in my stomach. Adelaide had mentioned flies during our first conversation about the haunting, but I'd been so frazzled by the idea on the whole that I hadn't questioned its individual parts. "What do you mean, 'employ the flies'?" I asked warily.

"I found this place online, the Critter Depot. They sell crickets, spiders, baby chicks, and food for pet snakes and raptors. And they sell black soldier fly larvae. Apparently they're great for compost piles. Anyway, you can take the larvae through the pupa stage to adult black soldier flies. I ordered a thousand at the pupa stage now. The adults will be ready for release in ten to fifteen days." She held up her phone, and I winced at the Google image of shiny wasplike insects congregated on a wide, flat leaf.

"A thousand flies ready for release?" I pushed the muffin away. "In my house? You know I hate insects, but especially flies. And what about Beatrix?"

"What about her?"

"Flies carry diseases! I can't simply coat the windowsills of my house with a thousand flies and let them have at it, even if it would freak the shit out of Callum. They'll get into the food! Into Beatrix's bedroom!"

"It's not like I haven't done my research. Black soldiers are one of the few fly species that transmit zero diseases. They're also super-slow fliers. Easy to catch. You can practically pluck them out of the air mid-flight."

"Uh-uh, no way. You should have 'researched'"—I made obnoxious air quotes—"that I'm against flies in my house no matter the species."

"But it's right out of *The Amityville Horror*," Adelaide said. "It might as well be written into the 'stage a haunting' playbook."

"I can't tell if you're joking or not. Either way, the answer is no." I shuddered. "I'm no more bug phobic than the next person, but a *thousand* flies? No, thank you. No way."

Adelaide pouted. "The larvae were delivered this morning. I'm looking forward to watching them grow. I already feel like they're my children." She batted her eyes then, seeing she was getting nowhere, changed her tactic. "Doesn't Bea sleep at your folks' house semifrequently?"

"She does," I said. "So?"

"Sooo, when's the next time she's spending the night?"

"Next Saturday."

Adelaide raised her arms as if to say, *Well, there you go.*

I let out an exasperated sigh. "I'll think about it. As long as every single fly is out of the house by the time Beatrix gets home on Sunday."

"Yes, yes, understood. Sticky ribbon, bait bags, the highest-voltage bug zapper; whatever well-reviewed fly-removal products exist on the market, I'll have them on hand."

I took out my phone and opened the Venmo app. "I'm sending you a hundred and fifty dollars to cover it," I said. "But that doesn't mean I like this." Before Adelaide could get too excited, I added, "Didn't you start this conversation by talking about your plumber friend? Chris something? What does he have to do with this?"

She raised her eyebrows. "He's more of an acquaintance than a friend. But, yes, we're going to plan a little field trip to get some advice. I hope Callum is ready for what we've got in store for him. Because after the onslaught of a thousand black soldier flies crawling across every door and windowpane, I have a feeling he's going to want to shower."

A wicked smile creased her face; with her fuchsia hair, she could have passed for a comic book villainess. "Problem is, when he gets into the shower, he's going to end up far less clean than when he went into it."

"What do you mean?"

Adelaide leaned forward and lowered her voice. "We're going to make your showerhead rain blood."

Chapter 15

It'd been a while since Bea had come to work with me, though she asked often, her love of princesses, castles, and lofty stories manifesting as wide-eyed wonder for the Gilded Age mansions that'd once dominated Newport's high-society scene. Relieved to have convinced Adelaide to push off the meeting with the plumber until Monday, I lifted Bea out of her car seat and straightened her green-and-gold dress.

"It's a good thing we came when the Breakers is closed to the public," I told her, my tone serious. "Otherwise, the tour guides would think you belong in the house. They might try to keep you from leaving. A real princess from the past, come to rule us all."

Beatrix stopped twirling and regarded my mother, who was climbing from the car. "Would someone really try to keep me here, Gram?"

My mother slung her purse over one shoulder and smiled. "No one could take you from your mother, baby. She loves you too much." She ruffled Bea's curls. "But when we walk through the halls and the bedrooms, check out the portraits on the walls. You'll see all the fancy women who lived here one hundred years ago. They'll have on beautiful dresses like yours."

"One hundred years?" Bea's eyes grew wide. She was still staring in astonishment when I took her hand.

"One hundred years," my mother repeated, taking Bea's other hand before turning to me. "Can I treat you girls to lunch when we're done? It's the least I can do after you invited me for this lovely afternoon."

I pushed my sunglasses onto my nose. "That'd be great. As long as Bea isn't too wiped." We walked through the parking lot and toward the great iron gate, the Breakers looming before us.

"I still can't believe you work here," Mom said, "even after all these years. You were always so enamored of the past, more likely to reenact Shakespearean plays than talk to your friends on instant messenger. Do you remember coming to the mansions when you were little?"

"Of course. Rosecliff and Marble House were my favorites. Still are."

"Marble House is full of marbles," Bea said. "Like Pinecone House is full of pinecones."

I laughed. "It's full of *marble*," I agreed. "But marble staircases and marble balustrades, not marbles like you play with."

Bea skipped, undeterred, as we strolled beneath the gate and into the front garden. Creamy roses and purple lupines had turned the grounds into something from an impressionist's postcard. As beautiful as it was, it reminded me that tourist season was around the corner. I needed to finalize the new exhibits in the coming weeks.

I followed Bea's gaze to the explosion of blossoms climbing a nearby trellis. "Don't pick the roses. If I know you, you'll be a worse thief than Peter Rabbit loose in Mr. McGregor's garden."

"Aww, shucks," Bea said, grinning. My mother and I laughed.

We strolled past the empty ticket booth and entered the mansion alongside its four Corinthian pilasters. In two weeks, the Breakers Third Floor Preservation in Progress Tour would be unveiled to the public after two years of painstaking work. The guide-led experience of private bedrooms, bathrooms, and recreational spaces used by the Vanderbilt family and household staff for more than a century would draw thousands over the course of the summer. Today, however, Mom, Bea, and I would be the only guests.

I watched Beatrix stare at the luminous chandelier in the massive foyer, transfixed. I leaned down and whispered, "Wherever you'd like to explore, we'll follow."

Bea continued to stare, the gray-gold of her eyes set off by the buttery warmth of the lights. "Who lives here?"

"No one, sweet pea."

"But people did?"

"Once upon a time."

"Are they ghosts now?"

I straightened, wondering what Adelaide would say if she could hear my daughter. No one at work wanted Adelaide back on her "Make the Mansions Spooky Again" kick, least of all me, but it was hard to argue with the idea that the average tourist—maybe even the average person—harbored an insatiable appetite for all things eerie and unexplainable. Ghosts' capacity to be about things other than themselves was universally appealing. Still, I wanted Joe and Morgan Tallow as far away as possible from the realism and accuracy of the properties we managed.

"Maybe they're ghosts," I said gently, returning my attention to Bea. "Maybe not. Why don't we walk around, and you can think some more about it."

We traversed velvet staircases and took detours through mirrored hallways and ornate bedrooms, my mother listening to self-guided audio tours while Bea chattered about tapestries she liked and the way the La Farge stained glass skylight threw kaleidoscopic patterns over our feet. In one cavernous bedroom, Bea pronounced the decor to be reminiscent of a pale-pink-frosted cake, and I watched her marvel at the marble-topped nightstand, the frilly pink pillowcases and rose-patterned wallpaper, and the gold-framed photo of a little girl above the bed.

"Who's that?" Beatrix asked.

"Gertrude Vanderbilt. This was her bedroom," I said.

"Where is she now?"

I hesitated. "Well, honey, she died a long time ago. She lived a long time ago. Her time in this house happened long before you or I or Gram were even born."

"So she *is* a ghost," Bea said, matter-of-fact. "Like the others who lived in this house."

My mother shot me a look.

I inhaled. *How the hell do I not say the wrong thing here?* "No one knows if ghosts are real, baby. The people who lived here, after they died, their bodies returned to the earth, but their souls could be anywhere. They could also be part of the earth. Part of the trees. The grass. The wind. Or, maybe they're still themselves, in the form of what we think of as 'ghosts.' No one knows. And so, everyone is free to believe whatever they want about what happens after we die."

Beatrix nodded, as if this made perfect sense. "Some kids at school said ghosts were scary," she said. "I said they weren't. They're like the characters in the books we read at Halloween-time. They teach us things, right?"

"Right, sweetheart," I managed.

Bea shrugged, as if to say, *Well, that's that,* and the gesture was so innocent and happy-go-lucky I wanted to pull her into my arms and never let go. Instead, I watched her run ahead to inspect an antique rocking horse, her curls falling forward and framing her face so that she looked like the portrait of five-year-old Gertrude Vanderbilt on the wall. My mother's headphones were still in her ears, but based on her pursed lips and the way she held her head, I knew she'd heard our conversation and was wondering what kind of books I was reading to Beatrix.

Did ghosts teach us things? Maybe. In Callum's case, I hope they'd teach him how to get the hell out. But I couldn't help noticing that, like Adelaide—and the Tallows—my daughter's inclination upon stepping into the mansions was to consider those who'd walked these halls before us. My job was to preserve the past, and yet all I could focus on was the future. Future guests. Future exhibits. Future profits that would lead to future artifacts.

A future life for me and Beatrix away from Callum.

I followed Bea and my mother into the hallway, stopping beside a large vase set into a recessed niche of the wall. Amid the vines and clusters of grapes decorating the vase were several small painted birds. I'd never paid them much notice before, but their white wings and black chests led me to think they were magpies. The magpie, a symbol of duality. Black versus white. The opposite of how I was meant to be thinking. It was dangerous to believe that, as long as I stayed in control, I could keep my life from careening off the rails.

Past. Present. Black. White. I went about curating museums—and staging hauntings—as if there was a "right" way to put the pieces back together.

As if I could forge the future by keeping the past—and my secrets—at bay.

Chapter 16

We came out onto the back veranda a half hour later. My mother and I sat on a carved stone bench while Bea frolicked through the grass, the sea backdropped behind her like an endless liquid mirror.

How many afternoons had Mrs. Vanderbilt sat in this same place? Her children were older when they'd started coming to the Breakers, but that didn't mean she didn't face difficult parenting decisions. She'd been forced to disinherit Cornelius Vanderbilt III, for goodness' sake. There was no way she hadn't sat on this bench and wondered if she was doing right by her children. I shifted against the unforgiving stone and sighed. Beatrix's talk of ghosts had made me contemplative.

What was a ghost, really? A dream? A wish? An illusion? A memory? Bea and I were living with myriad ghosts, layers upon layers of them, the past, present, and future folded in on each other like intricate origami, the shape of which I might glimpse but could never quite make out.

There was the ghost of who Callum used to be. The ghost of whom I was before I'd been forced to become Cal's petulant mother figure. The ghost of whom I wanted Beatrix to embody in the future—though that one was tricky, because I didn't want to impart a future vision of my daughter onto Bea. I wanted her to build her own. Then, and perhaps most disappointingly, there were the ghosts of all the people I could have been had I not married Callum.

It was an unfair thought—and a useless one. I was not a victim. And yet, feeling there was no way out without harming Beatrix, no way to stay without coloring my future, filled me with rage so potent I thought it might rip its way out of me and form an entirely new person. I watched Beatrix hold something to her face, inspecting it closely. An inchworm; she was forever enchanted by their slow-and-steady progress. All I wanted was to do right by her. But was this the right path? Haunting her father into submission?

"You're a good mother," my mother said suddenly, as if she could hear my thoughts.

"Why do you say that?"

She lifted her sunglasses. "Because you are." She smiled, her brown eyes darker than Beatrix's gray-gold ones, or even my own. "She's such a delight. So curious. So polite. Happy. Sensitive. All that's a testament to you."

"It's nature *and* nurture, Mom. So, developmental psychologists would beg to differ."

"Oh, please. You and I both know how much time you spend with her. The books you've read to her. The things you've exposed her to. The music, art, history, science, magic, the natural world."

Her face clouded over, eyes flicking toward Beatrix, who was not only still engrossed with the insect crawling over her fingers but was talking to it, singing a little made-up song. "How are things with Callum?" she asked.

I froze. How to navigate a conversation with my mother about Callum, convince her I wasn't sitting around doing nothing about our problems while obscuring the details of Adelaide's and my plan?

"They're . . . the same," I said. "We've been fighting a lot."

"Not in front of Beatrix I hope," she said.

"Of course not." *I'm torturing him with dead animals and freezing-cold temperatures in front of her instead.*

"He's still drinking?"

I nodded.

"I'm sorry, honey. I wish I could shake some sense into him." She pulled her gaze from Beatrix and looked at me again. "Have you thought about talking to that attorney whose number I gave you?"

I winced. "Yes."

"But you haven't called."

"I haven't."

Her gaze turned hard, but her tone was gentle. "What are you waiting for?"

"I don't know." As soon as the words left my mouth, I regretted them. "No, that's not true. I do know, but it's—"

"I know what you're going to say, but Lainey, this is life. It's messy, and shit happens. People get into this situation all the time: marriages that don't work out. Women—women with children—get divorced all the time. I want you to be happy, and I know you aren't. I don't understand why you're so unwilling to do something about it. At least talk to a lawyer."

"I'm *not* not doing anything about it," I insisted. "And . . . Adelaide's helping me with some things."

Her mouth turned down ever so slightly. "Are you sure she's the best person to be helping with your marriage problems?"

"You don't like Adelaide, do you?"

"Of course I do. It's just . . . well, she's a little dramatic, that's all. I don't want you enlisting the help of someone who *creates* more problems instead of solving the ones you already have."

If you only knew. What was I supposed to say, *Adelaide is preparing the black soldier larvae for Flypocalypse as we speak?* I settled for, "No matter what Adelaide suggests, I'll keep my perspective."

She took my hand and squeezed it. "I'm your mother, and while that will never change, I can't tell you what to do anymore. You're an adult. But your beautiful, brilliant daughter was just asking you about ghosts. And you, my dear, are haunted. Why not let go of the things that are no longer serving you? Trust the system, the lawyers, the judges, to do the right thing so you have a chance to get out of this misery before it's too late."

She paused, as if unsure whether to go on.

"Go ahead," I urged. "Don't stop now." I wasn't angry, merely defeated. "What do you want to say?"

"No one is prouder of you than me and your father"—she gestured at Bea—"with regards to your personal life. Your career. But we worry—and you know that's not good for your father's heart. We wonder if a big part of your success hinges on your ability to remain in control."

"I'm not in control of anything," I said, ignoring the twinge in my gut that came at the words, not to mention the reminder of my father's poor health. "I know that. I can't control other people, can't control what happens."

But haven't I exerted control over the very thing many people argue no one should get to control, ever? The image of myself in the bathroom mirror rubbing nonexistent blood from my hands came to my mind. I pushed the thought away before it could take root. "I'm not successful because I try to control things."

"I didn't say that. Not exactly. I'm just saying it might be worth exploring. Are you still seeing a therapist?"

I winced again, but Beatrix chose that time to screech, waving frantically at the hanging bough of a willow tree.

"Goodbye, Inchy!" she called.

I stood, giving my mother an apologetic smile, and walked toward Bea. "Are you ready, my little inchworm?" I leaned toward her. "Did I tell you I have the key to the gift shop?"

She grabbed my hand, pulling me toward the winding path. "Mommy, Mommy, I love the mansions. I love the little girl's room and her fancy rocking horse. Do they have horsie toys in the gift shop? Or horsie books? Could we get something to take home with us? To read at bedtime?" Beatrix spun around. "Come on, Gram. Hurry up! We're going to the gift shop!"

Beatrix continued chattering. "When we get home, I'm going to pretend to be a ghost, and I'm going to scare Daddy!"

My mother laughed, but I couldn't help but feel relief that Adelaide wasn't around to hear Bea's comment. The last thing I needed was her deciding Bea would be a welcome addition to the haunting.

Chapter 17

Phoenix Plumbing and Heating was a little over an hour away from Newport, which lessened my anxiety over our plan to speak to Adelaide's "acquaintance." Chris Matheson had close-cropped sandy-blond hair and a large tattoo of a phoenix on the back of his head. We'd agreed I'd go by "Theresa Cotes" in front of Chris; Rhode Island—hell, New England—was small, and it wasn't out of the realm of possibility Chris knew one of the Taylors. Still, I liked that the tattoo was so conspicuous; I would have remembered if Callum had ever mentioned a dude with fiery wings stretching across half his head.

Chris shook Adelaide's hand, then mine. "So, Theresa," he said, nodding for us to join him at his desk at the back of the shop, "Adelaide gave me a call. My old man used to be her grandmother's plumber; did she tell you that? Anyway, Adelaide said you two are working on a little science project of sorts?"

"Not a science project," Adelaide jumped in. "We're aspiring directors, working on a film about a haunted house." And she launched into a monologue about everything we'd "shot" thus far, turning the stunts we'd pulled on Callum into detailed descriptions of supposed horror movie scenes. She even managed to include an anecdote about freaking out one of our "actors" with a decapitated rabbit's head.

Chris perked up. "Right on, this sounds awesome! Have you guys ever entered the Lovecraft Film Festival in Providence?"

"No," Adelaide and I said in unison.

"But we're hoping to with this film," I added.

"Right on," Chris said again, nodding. "So, how can I help?"

Adelaide leaned forward in her chair. "We need you to tell us how to run pigs' blood through the water line so it comes out of the showerhead."

Chris stared back and forth between us for several seconds before booming with laughter. "Pigs' blood, huh?" He laughed harder. "Going full *Carrie*, then? I like it."

Adelaide smiled, but I could tell she was already irritated, wanting Chris to get on with it. Adelaide hated small talk and grew impatient easily. It was actually something Kathy had suggested Adelaide work on to better her relationships with the collections managers and conservators with whom we worked. It was . . . a work in progress, at best.

"Pigs' blood, cows' blood, whatever we can get from the butcher shop," Adelaide said. "Can you tell us how to do it?"

Chris's expression turned serious. "Why not shoot it with special effects? Add blood capsules to the showerhead that will burst when hit with hot water."

That actually sounded like it could work. But Adelaide was shaking her head.

"It can't be capsules. It has to be the real thing. Look like blood. Taste like blood."

Chris frowned. "Taste like blood? Why?"

Too far, Adelaide.

But she was two steps ahead, as usual. "Our actors, they've agreed to be kept in the dark for a lot of the scenes. We're trying to elicit the most organic responses from them as possible." She smiled. "You know, like with the rabbit head."

I tried to catch Adelaide's eye, to shoot her a look of warning, but she kept her gaze on the plumber.

Chris's frown deepened. "It would be a pretty complicated process."

"We're not afraid of complicated," said Adelaide.

Chris sighed. "No, I mean, complicated to the point of impossible. Hypothetically, it could be done. Hypothetically, pretty much anything can be done. But in reality, it wouldn't work."

"Why not?" Adelaide challenged.

"For starters, you'd have to plumb the blood into your water line, and whether that's city or well water, I mean, how would you even do that? You couldn't. Not without getting arrested for tampering with the city's water or corrupting your well. Here, look." He grabbed a notepad and pen and drew a diagram. "Even if you got blood into the water line, you wouldn't get straight blood from the nozzle. It would mix with hot and cold water from the individual lines and be diluted by the time it came out. You'd go to all that work to not even come close to the desired effect. Then there's the water pressure. You wouldn't be able to keep the eighteen or twenty pounds of water pressure you needed in order to—"

"All right, all right, we get it." Adelaide's eyes flashed with annoyance. She shot me a look, and I could tell she was still working through every little thing Chris had said, searching for a hole she could pry open. I squinted at his diagram but couldn't make sense of it; he'd labeled things, but his handwriting was terrible.

"So," Adelaide said a moment later, "there's no way to get into the hot water heater and fill that with blood? Even if it was temporary, wouldn't that make the shower run as red—and as hot—as we wanted?"

It was Chris's turn to look annoyed. No, not annoyed. Angry. "Listen," he said, "there's no way to do this short of something that will irrevocably demolish your system." He ran his hands over his head and leaned back in his chair.

"I don't want to sound like a dick," he continued, "but I can't let you walk out of here thinking you might be able to finagle something by messing around with shit in your basement. I went through five hundred seventy-six hours of training at a state-approved program and had to pass the journeyman plumbing license exam to do what I do.

"Most women"—he paused and corrected himself—"most *laypeople*, don't know the difference between a gas line and a water line. I don't want you getting carbon monoxide poisoning because you did something stupid, you get what I'm saying?"

"We get it," Adelaide said, because Chris was waiting for a response. The smile pasted on her face looked more like a grimace. "Thanks for your time and the expertise and all that." She stood. "I guess we'll have to look into the fake blood capsules after all."

Chris walked us out, insisting we could call him with additional questions. "Let me know when your movie is done," he said, all traces of his patronizing manner gone. "And good luck with the festival. I'll look for you. Maybe you can give me a shout-out in the credits." He winked.

Adelaide's grip on my arm grew tighter as she pulled me out of the shop.

Chapter 18

Adelaide strode to her Prius at a breakneck pace, and I hurried to follow.

"That guy was an asshole," I said once we were inside the car. "How do you know him again?" When she didn't answer, I added, "Today was such a bust."

"Maybe." Adelaide put the car into reverse. I couldn't read the expression on her face. "But maybe not. There's one other thing I have scheduled for today."

"What's that?"

Adelaide pulled out of the lot and stepped on the gas. "You're not going to like it."

My stomach tightened. "What am I not going to like?"

Adelaide stared straight ahead, not answering.

"Adelaide. What am I not going to like?"

"Well . . ."

Still, she said nothing, until I couldn't take it anymore. I grabbed her arm.

"Hey, I'm driving here."

"Tell me what I'm not going to like."

"All right, all right," Adelaide relented. "We have a meeting at your house at noon." She grimaced. "With Joe and Morgan Tallow."

My mouth dropped open, but Adelaide pressed on. "You know, to drum up some new ideas." She merged onto the narrow road that ran along the river, avoiding my stare.

"What do you mean, 'drum up ideas,' Adelaide? Ideas from Joe and Morgan Tallow? Are you nuts?"

"Hear me out, okay? We pretend we're reconsidering their proposal for haunted tours at the mansions and ask them what they see when they encounter haunted phenomena, how it manifests, et cetera. After we've gotten what we can out of them, we thank them, tell them we've decided we're not going forward with the tours, and send them on their way. After that, we'll have all new material, and we can come up with some really kick-ass hauntings!"

"You realize we cannot just meet with Joe and Morgan Tallow, right? I cannot tell them we're considering their proposal." I frowned. "And why my house? If Callum came home, we'd be screwed. Why not your house?"

Adelaide's cheeks flushed until they were almost the same color as her hair. "I sort of had company last night. He's still there."

I stared. "Who?"

"Don't worry about it. We're talking about the Tallows."

I was too mad to focus on Adelaide's unexpected confession. "We are talking about the Tallows. *The Tallows*. If Kathy found out—"

"She's not going to."

"But if she did, we'd be accused of putting the mansions' integrity in jeopardy."

Adelaide rolled her eyes. "Don't you think that's kind of bullshit in the first place? Spiritualism and the occult have their place in the history of the Gilded Age. Joe and Morgan are—"

"Joe and Morgan are going to take advantage of us. You have to call and cancel."

"Have I led us astray yet? No. So will you trust me? I've been reading their research online, and I think we can get some really great, really wild ideas from them."

The twisting in my gut wrung tighter. "You said yourself, with all the novels and horror movies out there, why would we ever want for inspiration?"

Adelaide's hands tightened around the wheel. "Because that's all fake. Everything we've done to Callum, I mean, who knows if that's how an actual haunting would manifest. It's just some shit Hollywood came up with to look good on camera. To elicit screams. We want to elicit madness."

She pried her eyes away from the road long enough to give me a discerning look. "If Joe and Morgan Tallow have witnessed even one thing that was real, and we can get them to tell us about it, imagine what that could do for our arsenal against Callum."

"Oh, I'm sure they'll *tell* us they've seen things that are real. And I'm sure it's the same shit they post on their YouTube channel to get followers."

The sun filtering through Adelaide's hair patterned the console red. She stared out the windshield.

"I don't think we should be bringing anyone else into this. First the wildlife guy, then Chris, now Joe and Morgan Tallow? We're casting too wide a net. It can only lead to trouble."

We rode in silence while I fumed. After what seemed like an eternity, Adelaide stopped at the last red light before my neighborhood. "Have you forgotten why we're doing this?" she asked softly. "The endless little deaths Callum subjects you to, your need to protect Beatrix? Think of this meeting with Joe and Morgan as one step closer to getting past all that."

Would it bring me one step closer to getting rid of Callum? Or one step closer to losing my job and having to rely on Callum's income to support my daughter? I resisted the urge to scream. Why was everything so goddamn difficult? We were on my street now. I stared at the lines of sage along the neighbor's property, their sky-blue blossoms bursting out from the waving stalks while resignation and dread swirled within me.

"Forget books and movies," I tried one last time. "Let's pretend something came up and go back to your place. We'll get online, look at the historical records of demons, possessions, that sort of thing. That makes way more sense than dragging two more people into—"

"We're already here." Adelaide checked her makeup, threw off her seat belt, killed the engine, and opened the door. "And so are they. Come on."

Panic clogged my throat like bloom-choked stems. The Tallows' dust-caked Mazda had pulled up beside Adelaide's Prius. Short of a black hole opening up beneath me, I was going to have to face them.

I climbed from the car, all the trust I'd put in Adelaide settling like a weight at the bottom of my stomach. Praying what we were about to do wasn't going to turn my career into the same sort of living nightmare to which we were subjecting Callum, I turned toward the Tallows and pasted something like a smile on my face.

Chapter 19

"Lainey Taylor, so nice to see you!"

Morgan Tallow glided across the driveway and took my hands. I allowed her to squeeze them for several seconds before pulling away.

"Hi," I said through gritted teeth, earning me a look of warning from Adelaide. *Be nice,* the look said. *They're here now, and you've got to deal with it.*

"Laineeeey," Joe Tallow crowed, as if greeting an old friend as opposed to someone who'd avoided him like the plague anytime he'd approached society headquarters. I tried not to stiffen when he pulled me in for a hug.

When I stepped back, Adelaide was halfway up the walkway.

"Come on," she urged. The Tallows followed. I brought up the rear as if I were approaching a guillotine. *Treat this like any other meeting on behalf of the preservation society. Polite and to the point.*

Ten minutes later, we were seated around the kitchen table. Adelaide had made tea. I took a sip and burned my tongue.

"Okay," Adelaide said. "Lainey, where should we start?"

"Wait," Morgan cut in, and Adelaide and I snapped to attention. Had Morgan already discerned there was something suspicious going on?

"Let me just say that Joe and I are thrilled you asked to meet with us," Morgan said. "I know we've been at odds over the years, but all we've ever wanted is to give the guests who come to your beautiful mansions and gardens access to experiences and stories they otherwise wouldn't have."

I froze, hands wrapped around the scalding mug. *Goddammit.* Why did Morgan have to be so nice? There was no chance Kathy was letting them do their campy tours; it felt wrong to lead them on like this, no matter the potential gain.

"Morgan, can I be honest—"

Adelaide cut me off. "Yes, can *we* be honest? We feel the exact same way." She smiled at the ghost hunters. My stomach dropped. *There goes that.*

Morgan returned the smile, glanced at Joe, and then turned back to us. "Okay, then. Glad we're on the same page. So, what would you like to know?"

Adelaide pulled a notebook and pen from her colorful cardigan and opened to a fresh page. "What types of things have you seen in your work, and what are the various ways hauntings have manifested for the two of you over the years?"

Joe and Morgan exchanged another glance. Morgan brushed a lock of glossy blond hair over one shoulder. "We'd be happy to tell you about things we've seen. But if it's okay, I'd like to tell you a little story first. About how we got started in this field and why I'm so keen to spend my life exploring the paranormal."

"Of course," Adelaide answered for both of us.

"Thirteen years ago," Morgan began, "not long after Joe and I got married, we started trying for a baby. Nothing happened for a while, until it did. Once I was pregnant, I started seeing a little boy. Like you, we live near the mansions, and that's usually where I'd see him. On the grounds of Chateau-sur-Mer. Along the Cliff Walk. In the cemetery between our house and the Breakers."

She paused, a faraway look in her eyes. "I saw him often in the cemetery. His black hair and big dark eyes. I'd call out to him, but he never responded. He was always just out of reach, out of earshot." She

How to Fake a Haunting

trailed off, but no one spoke. I had the sense that, while this was a well-trod story, it was not one often exposed to light, to the air.

"The baby I eventually gave birth to was stillborn," she continued a moment later. "I'd had early-onset preeclampsia that'd gone undiagnosed. My son's blue skin and silent lips didn't distract from his dark eyes and hair. He was ethereal in his paleness. Ghostly. But beautiful." Morgan smiled sadly, and something clenched in my chest.

"When the universe of my grief became a mere galaxy and I was finally able to get outside, to walk, to stand the sight of the trees, I searched for the little boy. In every cemetery, at every mansion. It didn't matter; I never saw him again. Except in my dreams. Dreams in which my son was defined by his realness, his presence, as he traipsed across garden paths and along sand dunes, as opposed to the void his death had torn open. Not long after, I told Joe I was quitting my job; I wanted—needed—to find ghosts for other people. Because the knowledge that I'd seen my son, even a finite number of times, even from afar—that knowledge saved me."

It was like a gong had been struck in the kitchen, the air molecules around us set into teeth-rattling vibrations. I forced my dry throat into action. "God, Morgan, I'm so sorry." *She's not a huckster after all. She's grieving.* All this time, I'd been judging her without knowing anything close to the truth.

Adelaide echoed my sympathies. "How awful for you both. I'm so sorry."

"I'm not telling you for your condolences. I'm telling you so you know that I understand—that I've always understood—your hesitancy in bringing us on board for tours at the mansions," Morgan said. "By virtue of my connection with the supernatural being so personal, so paramount to who I am, I don't expect others to forge that connection easily. Or ever. My own husband doesn't believe in ghosts, so why would I fault anyone else for their reservations?"

"Wait," I croaked and looked at Joe. "*You* don't believe in ghosts?"

Joe laughed. "What can I say? I'm a skeptic. Can't believe in anything I haven't seen for myself. But I love my wife, and I understand her need to do this." He shrugged. "What else am I going to do, if not support her, after everything she's been through?"

"But what about the EVP recordings on your channel?" Adelaide asked Joe.

"Apophenia, cross-modulation, expectation, or wishful thinking," Joe answered matter-of-factly.

Adelaide was nonplussed. "Apo-what?"

"Apophenia. The tendency to perceive a connection or meaningful pattern between unrelated or random things. Seeing patterns in meaningless data, detecting shapes in unexpected places. It's a psychology term, used to describe the human tendency to see connections and patterns that aren't really there."

"And cross-modulation?"

"Without getting too technical, cross-modulation is the intermodulation distortion caused by multiple carriers within the same bandwidth."

"In English, hon," Morgan prompted.

"Basically, it's the EVP recorders picking up unwanted frequencies."

I looked to Morgan to see how she would react to her partner, with whom she'd weathered the loss of a child, dismissing her beliefs to a series of scientific—and, from my perspective, perfectly reasonable—explanations. But Morgan gazed affectionately at Joe and said, "He keeps me honest. Honest and hungry." I stared back and forth between the two of them, enthralled by their dynamic.

Morgan turned to me. "So, back to why you asked us here. What sorts of phenomena do you want to know about?"

"Oh, um . . ." *Shit, think of something!*

Adelaide jumped to my rescue. "When you've been called to investigate a haunted house, what signs are usually reported?"

Morgan nodded, as if she'd expected this question. "There are a few things we see over and over again," she said. "Pressure on a person's chest, auditory hallucinations, or, and this is probably the most common, the simple feeling that something is wrong. Most of our calls are from people who feel besieged by an overwhelming sense of dread."

"And what have you uncovered as the cause of these signs?" Adelaide asked.

"Carbon monoxide poisoning," Joe said without hesitation.

"Carbon monoxide poisoning?" Adelaide and I exclaimed in unison.

"Yep. Prolonged exposure to a gas leak can manifest as apparent psychic phenomena. Carbon monoxide was even found to have caused one man's vision of a strange woman dressed in black rushing toward him from another room. Chronic exposure can lead to the kind of hallucinations often associated with a haunted house."

"But," Morgan broke in, "for every case caused by a chemical leak, we've had half a dozen others not solved by a call to the gas company. Not to mention all the other paranormal experiences people have recounted. Black flies swarming the windows. Feeling as if they've been covered by a heavy blanket. Foul odors. Children's toys moving around the house. Footsteps in the basement, the creak of doors in the attic, shoe- and footprints left in carpets where no earthly person had walked, warping floors and walls and ceilings."

"The warping floors are almost always attributed to a hidden water leak," Joe pointed out.

"Almost always," Morgan echoed, and winked.

"Have you come across any instances where the phenomena had been faked by the house's occupants?" Adelaide asked, and I forgot my dismay at the Tallows' increasing likability. This question was way too close to home.

Joe and Morgan exchanged a look. "Yes," Morgan admitted. "But only once was it good enough to fool us."

"Five years ago," Joe jumped in, "a woman called, claiming she and her husband had a poltergeist. Our first visit was amateur hour: taps left on in the bathrooms, a burning smell permeating the house, faces in the family's framed photographs scratched out with a knife, claw marks dug out of the walls. Anything that was easy for someone to stage, this couple had done. We were confident it was a hoax."

"But they insisted something was going on," Morgan said, "and they begged us to come back." She cast her eyes downward. "I convinced Joe to give them one more chance."

Joe put a hand on Morgan's arm. "She can't say no to people in need."

"That's when they hit us with the Prince Rupert's drop."

"What's a Prince Rupert's drop?" Adelaide asked, and I leaned forward, engrossed by their story in spite of myself.

Joe's hand remained on his wife, as if tethering himself to the present. "It's a bead created by dripping molten glass into cold water, causing it to solidify. The solid droplets can handle extremely high residual stresses, which give rise to counterintuitive properties, such as the ability to withstand a blow from a hammer or a bullet on the bulbous end without breaking, while exhibiting explosive disintegration if the tail end is even slightly damaged."

"In English, hon," Morgan said.

"Right, sorry. It's a piece of glass that looks like a tadpole. You can smash the thicker part, the tadpole's head, with as much force as you want—I'm talking sniper bullets—and nothing happens. But if you break, or even scrape, the tail, the whole thing explodes."

"Whoa," Adelaide said, and I suppressed a groan. She sounded like a kid who'd just found out what happened to ants when you directed sunlight at them through a magnifying glass.

"So, this couple invites us in, gives us a couple of cold drinks, and while we're standing there, sipping lemonade and listening to how they're being assailed by physical disturbances, large objects moving, chairs stacking themselves, et cetera, my glass explodes in my hand like I'd been holding a firecracker. The sound was electric. At first, I didn't even realize what had happened."

Morgan paused, looking stricken. "Glass went everywhere. One of the shards tore through Joe's eye and damaged the retina." Her voice grew low. "They couldn't save it. His eye."

My gaze flicked from one of Joe's eyes to the other. Now that I'd heard what had happened, I thought the left eye might be the glass one, but it was impossible to be sure. "My god," I breathed. "How terrible. Joe, I'm so sorry."

He waved his hand. "It's all good. Like I said, this was years ago."

"Now he says the scariest thing in any house we're called to is him," Morgan joked. She brushed light fingertips along the corner of her husband's left eye.

So I was right about which one was the glass one. Still, it was remarkable how unnoticeable it was.

"How'd they do it?" Adelaide asked. "How'd they make the glass explode?" I froze. Would the Tallows think it strange Adelaide wanted to know?

But Joe merely smiled. "Morgan figured it out. Tell 'em, hon."

"While Joe was in the hospital, the couple swore what had happened was the work of the poltergeist," Morgan said. "I went back, desperate for answers. While I was taking EVP readings in the basement, I came across a package for a glassworks company in the recycling bin. After googling the company—and seeing their most popular product—I figured out what they had done pretty quickly."

"Gotta hand it to them for originality." I was surprised to see that Joe looked like he actually meant this. "Turns out, the husband had inserted a Prince Rupert's drop into a boba straw. One of those extra-fat straws, you know? For bubble tea? When I bent the straw's top portion, the drop exploded, along with the drinking glass, giving a pretty darn convincing impression of paranormal activity. Well, I imagine it would have looked convincing, if I hadn't been losing my eye at that exact moment."

Adelaide looked too appreciative of the hoax, and I kicked her under the table. She rearranged her expression into one of sympathy.

"Anyhow, that was our most impressive 'fake haunting,'" Morgan said.

"Though there've been plenty more along the way," Joe added. "Morgan usually has a feeling from the first call of how legitimate they're going to be."

"Yeah?" Adelaide asked. There was something in her voice I didn't like. She glanced at me long enough to smile widely, as if to broadcast that what was coming next was entirely innocent, a real spur-of-the-moment idea.

"Joe, Morgan, this has all been so fascinating, but could I turn the tables a bit? Could I ask . . . What's your professional opinion about this place? Any ghosts?"

Chapter 20

I forced myself not to react. What the hell was Adelaide doing? Why turn the Tallows' attention to the house when we'd been getting all we needed from a good old-fashioned discussion?

Morgan looked around, but not before fixing me with a discerning stare.

I don't need to believe in the supernatural to know this woman has razor-sharp powers of perception. She knows we're not being straight with her. She knows things aren't what they seem.

"*This* house?" Morgan asked.

"Yeah, you know, just for fun," Adelaide said.

"Oh, I don't think—" I started, but Adelaide cut me off.

"We wanted to learn more about ghosts and the supernatural. Why not see Joe and Morgan in action?" She turned to face them. "I mean, if that's okay. I'm sure lots of houses have psychic energy, right? And, if there's nothing like that here, at least we'll get to see how all your fancy equipment works."

Adelaide turned back to me. I could practically see the gears turning in her head. "Think, Lainey," she said. "If we did want to incorporate anything into our programming—I'm not saying ghost tours, but maybe the history of spiritualism as it relates to the Gilded Age, or something along those lines—it would be great to have a modern benchmark to work up to."

Adelaide's gaze had turned penetrating, entreating me not to mess this up. So, she wanted to get Joe and Morgan moving around the house, operating their equipment, in order to generate ideas with which to haunt Callum later? I supposed we did need new concepts. While I could scratch out Callum's face in framed photographs easily enough, I couldn't exactly slide a Prince Rupert's drop into a straw. No matter how badly I wanted Callum out of the house, out of my life, I didn't want anyone losing an eye.

"Okay," I relented. I tried to smile at Morgan but feared it came out a little pained. "As long as you have your equipment with you and everything, it would be nice to see how one of your investigations plays out."

"Normally, I would ask a series of questions," Morgan said, sounding somewhat perplexed. "You know, age of the house, its current condition, any previous inhabitants or on-site deaths, what had happened to make the current inhabitants think it was haunted." She looked around. "The house is fairly new?"

"It's six years old," I responded.

"You built it?"

"Yes."

"From a professional perspective, if someone asked me to run an investigation on a six-year house with only one set of inhabitants, I'd decline, as all tests would likely turn out negative," Morgan said.

Even as she said it, I saw her squirm beneath Adelaide's penetrating gaze.

"But since it's to see the equipment in action and to"—she stared hard at me—"further our working relationship, I'm happy to oblige. Joe, hon, want to grab everything out of the car?"

Ten minutes—and one clandestine text to Callum ensuring he was still at work—later, and the living room was full of various bags and camera cases. An hour after that, Joe was compiling spreadsheets of data from digital thermometers and Geiger counters. Morgan sat across from him on the couch, cataloging files. She'd recorded several minutes of audio in each room, as well as video footage while standing in front of every reflective surface in the house.

"Joe and I will review everything in the studio," Morgan said, and shrugged. "But that's basically it. If we were to find anything in the data we collected today, we'd give you a call and schedule a time to return."

Joe finished zipping the laptop into a briefcase. "Did you ladies see everything you needed to see?" he asked.

How do I know if I saw what I needed to see when I don't know what I'm supposed to be looking for in the first place?

Adelaide wasn't so indecisive. "Yes, thank you. *So* interesting. Lainey and I have a lot to talk about." She stared at me pointedly. "Don't you think we could sell Kathy on an exhibition featuring spiritualism throughout the Gilded Age? We could highlight the progression in ghost-hunting tools from the mid-nineteenth to the early twenty-first century."

I nodded dutifully, but even if I'd wanted to come clean to the Tallows now, the afternoon had left me exhausted. I wanted everyone—even Adelaide—to leave so I could lie down for a few minutes before picking up Beatrix.

"Yes," I forced myself to say when Adelaide continued to stare. "Thank you, Joe, Morgan. I guess we'll be in touch with any additional questions."

Joe shouldered a duffel bag and the briefcase before reaching for Morgan's hand. "And we'll be in touch with you if Morgan finds anything unusual in your files." His tone was jokey, but I guessed he was making fun of the fact that Adelaide and I had convinced him and his wife to investigate a house even *we* didn't believe was haunted.

We offered to help with the bags, but Joe declined, so Adelaide and I walked the two of them to the front porch. We smiled from the doorway as Joe loaded up their car, and waved as they pulled out of the driveway. Between the Tallows and their equipment, and Todd's Wildlife Extraction Services truck, it was a good thing there were so many trees between us and the neighbors. I could imagine their puzzled glances, the questions, the *Something odd's going on over at the Taylor place* comments. *This was the last time*, I thought. *The last time I let Adelaide bring someone else into this.*

When the Mazda had disappeared down the street, I closed the door and walked to the living room, where I collapsed onto the couch. Adelaide sat opposite me, tucking her feet beneath her.

"I told you I wouldn't steer us wrong," she said.

I gave her a weary, befuddled look. "Aside from learning the Tallows aren't the money-hungry hucksters I'd always thought them to be—and hearing about their awful loss—I don't see how that was the lesson in how to fake a haunting you wanted it to be."

Adelaide gaped at me. "Of course it was! I can mess with the frequency of the transistor radio Cal uses on the golf course. And that thing Morgan said about people feeling like they're being suffocated by a heavy blanket? I could pull Cal's comforter off him while he's sleeping, soak it with water, wring it out a bit, and lay it back on top of him. He'll wake up freezing and anxious from all that extra weight on his chest."

I started to interject, but Adelaide was on a roll. "And the stuff about children's toys moving around the house? That's genius. How have I not tapped into the entire subgenre of creepy kids in general? But the best thing we learned today? I mean, come on, do I even have to say it?"

She stopped her rambling and looked at me. "Do I?" she asked.

I groaned, sinking farther into the pillows. "Yes, you have to say it, because I have no idea what you're talking about."

Her eyebrows raised, then furrowed. She looked flummoxed I hadn't reached the same conclusions she had. "The Prince Rupert's drops, obviously. If one of those drops was enough to fool two people who've seen it all over the last ten years, it will be more than enough to freak the shit out of Callum."

I sat up, blinking at Adelaide. "Did you somehow miss the rest of Morgan and Joe's story?"

Adelaide's look of disbelief didn't waver.

"I can't believe I have to voice this, but we cannot initiate an explosion of glass in my house, whether it will give off *Poltergeist* vibes or not. Did you not hear what happened to Joe? He lost an eye!"

Adelaide waved a hand. "That hoaxer dude probably didn't think things through. But if you and I plan everything down to the last detail, we can make it go off without a hitch."

I forced myself to take a breath. Adelaide had given up weeks of her life to stage this haunting. She was probably desperate to speed things up. Still, was she really suggesting we detonate a tiny glass bomb in my kitchen?

"We cannot use a Prince Rupert's drop to scare Callum," I said, relieved to hear the evenness in my tone. "I have to protect Beatrix. Bringing her into this haunting in any way would mean the end no longer justifies the means. As much as I want to protect her from Callum, I also don't want her to witness him blowing off half his face or several fingers, or for Callum to get seriously hurt. There are plenty of other things we can—"

"But we have to—"

"No, Adelaide! Just, no."

"Maybe if we put a handful of boba straws in your cabinet now, Callum will get used to seeing them. That way, if you change your mind—"

I jumped up, exhaustion morphing from lethargy and a desire to be left alone into a blistering migraine and all-out rage. What was she not understanding here?

But even as that rage roiled through me, another part of me understood her ambition. When Adelaide had first proposed the haunting, I never believed it would work. Not really. I'd only agreed to it as a distraction from my problems as opposed to having any real hope that it would result in Callum leaving. But now that we were in the thick of things, I felt differently. Very differently. We'd accomplished so much in a few short weeks. We could pull this off, and we could probably pull it off faster if we went with an impossible-to-ignore type of stunt like the one Adelaide was proposing. Despite this, I still couldn't get over my fear, or my anger.

"I'm not going to change my mind," I said. "In a way, I wish I could, or that the Tallows had given us another viable option, but I'm still pissed you set up a meeting with them in the first place, no matter how well you think it went. You're making decisions without me, and it's not cool, Adelaide. It's my house—my family—that these things affect. I'm not letting you bring your fucked-up *Paranormal Activity* vision anywhere near my daughter."

I took a breath, but it didn't calm the anger and confusion shooting through my blood and churning my stomach. I threw a hand in the direction of the door. "I've got to pick up Bea soon. You should go. I've got to clear my head of this fucking haunting for five goddamn minutes, and I—"

I was about to say more, but Adelaide stood. Without a word, she turned and walked across the living room. I heard her clear the foyer and open the front door, slamming it behind her as she left the house. The silence that followed was pronounced, amplifying my confusion as to whether I'd done the right thing in being so dismissive.

I stared into the black mirror of the television screen until my eyes burned and my brain buzzed, with no idea what to do next.

Chapter 21

Adelaide didn't call or text for several days, and I was grateful not to have to pretend I wasn't still mad. She was so stubborn, so convinced that her way was the only way. *Serves her right, thinking she could bring the Tallows in without consequences.* I distracted myself by going about my days, taking care of Bea, tiptoeing around Callum, and throwing myself into my work. It helped that Adelaide was assigned to a project that required her to be away from Preservation Society headquarters. Outside project notwithstanding, Adelaide still was hard at work on the haunting.

A grating shriek rang up from the stairwell every morning when Callum left for work, fulfilling some stage of things to which I hadn't yet been made privy. The walls and ceilings thumped with strange noises, and rancid smells wafted from the rafters. I managed to shield Beatrix from most of these "symptoms" with well-timed trips out to Pinecone House to play. The screen-free audio player I'd recently purchased was essential too; on it, she could choose a selection of stories, music, and educational content.

One afternoon, however, Callum cornered Bea and demanded to know if she'd been moving a teddy bear around the house to mess with him. Confused, Bea shook her head, but Callum complained about the bear the rest of the weekend and demanded that Bea keep her toys where they belonged, resulting in an epic, if out-of-character, tantrum from Bea in which she threw everything off every shelf in the playroom.

It was odd knowing Adelaide was around, skulking around corners, jumping from joist to joist in her fuzzy slippers. I couldn't decide if I was touched by her commitment or annoyed she wasn't giving me any space. Still, I had to hand it to her; she was preternaturally good at sneaking around the house, orchestrating all manner of creepy happenings.

One evening, several days after the meeting with Joe and Morgan, Bea and I came home to an ice-cold house. Bea reacted to the inconvenience of the chill uncharacteristically and, in light of my fatigue after work, intolerably, whining and stomping her feet, doing everything she could to push my buttons. Callum was camped out on the couch under a blanket, drink in hand, on the phone with the heating company.

I was worried they'd send a service person out, but whoever answered must have heard the slur in Cal's words. He broke into a stream of curses when they hung up on him and lurched down the hall, blanket dragging behind him. He spent the rest of the night in his room, tipping from drunkenness into full-on annihilation, if the overall timbre of chaos and mayhem was any indication.

The next evening, knock-knock-knocks sounded from behind the walls, and the creepy twang of a guitar drifted down from the ceiling. Beatrix commented on neither the music nor her father's absence, but was moody and sullen, and though I went to bed when she did, I woke short-tempered and foggy-headed. By the time Beatrix and I made our way to the kitchen for breakfast, Callum had already left for work.

The night after that, having returned from taking Beatrix to her horseback riding lesson—during which she was so irritable her pony picked up on the negative energy and nearly threw her—I found Callum in the living room again. There was no glass in sight, but he was clearly drunk, standing at the room's center and staring into corners like a man in a dream, shaking his head and talking to himself.

"Things keep *moving*," he said, his tone incredulous. "The furniture. The couch. The tables. The tilt of the television. When I got home, everything was slightly off-kilter. Three inches or so. Maybe four. I went to make a drink, but I had to go down in the basement for the extra case of seltzer, and when I came back, everything was worse. Six inches off. Maybe seven. The couch was so far away from the television, it was actually sticking out past the doorway there. I am not making this up. It was obvious. *Obvious.*"

Though this was the exact reaction from Cal that Adelaide and I had wanted, I was annoyed by the intrusion of his words, and grateful Bea had asked to play in Pinecone House rather than coming straight inside. "Ohhhhkay," I said, pretending to examine the location of the couch.

"I took a shower to clear my head," Callum continued. "I thought, you're out of it, Cal. In need of a reset. When I came into the living room again, everything was back to normal. Not one goddamn thing out of place."

He scrubbed the side of his head, as if trying to wash away the memories of the bewildering afternoon. "Then my boss called, so I went outside to talk to him. When I came back, everything had moved six inches *in the opposite direction.*"

He gestured toward the TV, and while his mouth was pinched and his shoulders were hunched, his eyes held no anger, only fear.

I glanced out the kitchen window. Bea was there, climbing the slide into her clubhouse. "Remember when I asked you if you thought the booze was messing with your head?" I started, "Do you think—"

"That has nothing to do with it!" Callum exploded. "You're not listening! Something has been going on here."

His words hung in the air. I waited, but he remained silent. I'd seen enough movies to know how deliciously reversed our roles were here. It was always the wife whose fears were being downplayed, the husband almost willfully ignorant to her observations: *I don't know what you're talking about . . . Nothing's going on here . . . Everything's fine . . . Perhaps you should lie down, you're not making any sense . . . You're hysterical. Hormonal. You're acting crazy.* Or, in our case: *Of course I haven't had anything to drink, it must be you.*

I put a hand to my chest, making a show of realizing that Cal was—somehow—trying to implicate me, and pitched my tone to contain a suitable amount of outrage. "What the hell does that mean, 'Something has been going on here'? I just got back from Bea's lesson, which was stressful as hell, in case you were wondering."

Amazingly, this broke through Callum's fixation with recent events, and he scoffed. "I still can't believe you let her ride a horse when she doesn't know how to ride a bike."

Inside my rib cage, poisonous petals unfurled. "Do you have a broken leg I can't see?" I growled. "*You* could teach her to ride a bike, you know. And what do you think, I made our daughter skip her favorite part of the week so I could hide in the goddamn fireplace and move the furniture a couple of inches every time you turned your back?"

I sneered, and something inside me recognized the ugliness I felt and that I was reveling in, warned me not to give in to it, not to give in to the stress. But give in I did. "That's crazy," I said, my tone full of all the vehemence I felt toward him, that I'd felt growing like a weed the past six years. "You understand that, right? That that's absolutely fucking insane?"

"I know how it sounds, but it's true."

I looked around. "News flash, Callum, everything is—"

"I know, everything's back to normal. So it must not have happened, right? I've lost it? I'm—"

"You're drunk, Cal. That's what you are. You're drunk, and I'm going outside with Bea. Why don't you do something productive like fix the deck rail instead of standing here staring at the furniture like it owes you money?" I stormed out, and when I returned almost two hours later—the afternoon had remained warm enough for Bea and me to restring some of the pinecones that had fallen from the clubhouse rafters—Callum was passed out in bed.

While Bea was in the tub, I climbed to the top of the closet organizer and peeked into the attic, ready to call out to Adelaide if I saw her. But she was gone, leaving behind no trace.

The following evening, Beatrix and I went out with my parents for pizza. I'd texted Callum, offering to bring him home a couple of slices—old habits die hard—but he hadn't responded. When we got home, he was in his room, shades drawn, lights out. There wasn't even an empty glass on the bedside table. I figured Adelaide had taken the night off—Lord knew she probably needed it—and I gave Bea a quick bath and got her into her pajamas, read her a handful of books, and got her to sleep relatively early.

I usually stayed in bed with Beatrix, watching movies on the iPad or reading on my Kindle. It'd been ages since I'd ventured into the living room to join Callum in front of the television. Even when he was sober, Callum wasn't big on movies or TV series, as he tended to fall asleep within minutes of choosing something to watch. I'd had the brilliant idea a few months back to attempt to watch something while ignoring Callum passed out on the couch beside me, but it was impossible to hear through his snoring.

Tonight, there was nothing stopping me from claiming the living room as my own. I checked on Bea and grabbed a pint of ice cream before crashing on the couch. Clicking through the latest Netflix offerings, I felt unexpectedly carefree.

Adelaide had warned me to stay away from horror movies, but Callum was dead to the world, and not watching one felt like a wasted opportunity. While I still felt Adelaide owed me an apology, I didn't like that we were fighting. Maybe if I found something in one of these horror films that we could use, it might reopen the channels of communication between us. It was worth a try. I scrolled through the seemingly endless options parading across the screen.

At first, when the thump came, I thought a trailer for one of the movies had started. But when the thump was followed by a grating shriek, like metal on glass—as if someone were dragging iron across a mirror deep enough to carve out strips—I knew it was coming from inside the house.

Then came the bloodcurdling scream, and my entire body went weightless with terror.

Chapter 22

I shot up from the couch, my mind a chaotic screen of static in my fear for Bea. But then the scream came again, and I realized it was Callum.

After taking the stairs two at a time, I skidded down the hall and flung open the bedroom door. Nothing looked out of the ordinary. Callum appeared to be in bed, the blankets a tangled mess. Beyond the bed, the windows were open. The bright-white lights of the solar-powered deck rails floated in the blackness like tiny spaceships. I turned my attention back to the bed.

The mattress was shaking, the entire bed rattling in its frame, and from it came a quiet, breathless keening.

"Callum?" I called softly.

"Is it out there?" He sounded desperate.

"Is what out where?" I looked around. What had Adelaide done? Like the windows, Callum's closet was open. "What's going on?"

"Is it out there?" he asked again.

"There's nothing out here." I didn't have to feign my irritation.

Callum flung the covers back, and I stifled a gasp. He looked positively haunted—gaunt-eyed, sallow-skinned, his face streaked with tears. "I woke up," he explained shakily. "Something . . . there was something in my closet." His voice rose in pitch. "It was some sort of demon. A goddamned monster."

"Beatrix is sleeping," I hissed. "Keep your voice down."

"I don't care that she's sleeping!" Callum shouted, jumping out of bed with surprising speed. "If there's a monster in the house, we need to get her out of here."

I sucked in a breath. *This is it. The most important performance you've had to give thus far.* I raised both hands and smacked Callum in the chest, stopping him in his tracks. "Knock it the hell off. Do you hear yourself? Are you really about to wake up our child right now, babbling about monsters? Have you lost your fucking mind?"

Cal threw my hands off him and stalked toward the closet. He flipped the light on and examined the closet's interior as if expecting something to jump out.

"What is it you think you saw?"

"A ghoul. A demon. I don't know. It was terrifying. White face. Sunken eyes."

I gestured at the door to the bathroom through which a strip of mirror was visible. "Are you sure you didn't see yourself?"

Callum shot me a look of incredulity and betrayal. "Asshole," he whispered. "You dumb, self-righteous asshole. I'm standing here telling you that something was in our house, and you're too stubborn to listen." He dropped to his knees and searched under the bed.

I looked across the room to the open window. Adelaide wasn't kidding about adopting the recklessness of a serial killer who snatched his victims in plain sight. From what I could gather, she'd come down from the attic dressed like some grave-worn wraith, stood in Cal's closet, scared the shit out of him, and disappeared out the window while Callum quaked and unraveled not five feet away.

I drew closer to the window and peered out. Adelaide had gotten away with it, telescopic ladder and all. I squinted and thought I could make out a flash of movement circling the pool fence by the garden. Adelaide, maybe, heading for the woods.

"You left the windows open," I pointed out, turning back to Callum. "Maybe something got in? Like a raccoon? You said it had dark eyes. If you woke up from a deep sleep and saw it, maybe you got confused?"

Callum's expression was thunderous. "A fucking racoon? Do you think I'm a moron?" He was screaming now, and my vision tunneled, shrinking down to him and only him, eliminating the open windows, the dark night sky, the yawning closet.

"You're going to wake Bea—" I started, but it was too late.

From the other room, Beatrix cried out, "Mommy!"

My darkened vision yawned back open, prisms of white light exploding at the corners, so all-consuming was my rage. "Prick," I spat. "Selfish asshole." Even as I said it, I knew my brain had buried the fact of Adelaide's trick; I was not acting, not playing a part. I meant every word, was ready to end him, to punish him for his reaction to something I had helped to orchestrate, the haunting allowing me to express the rage I'd kept bottled and carefully shelved for far too long.

"Worthless piece of shit," I continued. "*You* are the monster. Don't you see that? *You* are the one I need to protect Beatrix from, not some figment of your damaged imagination. It was bad enough when you were just a drunk, but now you've dragged us into the darkness with you. You're seeing shit in the shadows. Hearing noises. Smelling things. Imagining the furniture moving and the temperature dropping. You're sick, Callum. You need help. You're—"

Beatrix called out again. I sputtered, "Shut the windows. Go to bed. I wish I didn't have to hear another sound from you ever again, but at the very least, don't let me hear your fucking voice before morning."

I slammed Cal's door and rushed down the hall to Bea's room, taking her in my arms the way I had when she was a baby. "It's okay, love. It's okay. Daddy had a bad dream, that's all."

"But . . . but . . ." She could hardly talk for all her sniffling. "What did Daddy dream?"

"Don't worry, love. It wasn't real."

"But Mommy, I had a dream too. I saw something. I saw it there." She pointed at the dresser mirror, which was angled toward her closet.

Goddamn it, Adelaide! How could you have let Bea see you? "I promise you, my love, there's nothing to worry about."

"But I saw a woman. Her hands were red. And she didn't have a face! Well, she did, but it was funny and hard to see, like a mirror inside a mirror."

Was Adelaide holding something that was red? A flashlight, maybe? "Why didn't you call out for me when you saw it? I would've come right in."

Bea rubbed at her eyes. "I *did* call for you, just now. I was scared. Her face was there, and then it wasn't. It went all shimmery." There was more, but I couldn't understand it, Bea's words reduced to chest-hitching sobs.

I stroked her face and rocked her. She was so adamant, so frightened; I didn't dare challenge her story a second time. But she couldn't have called for me right after seeing Adelaide because by the time Beatrix yelled out, Adelaide was already gone, her dark form disappearing around the garden. I looked across Bea's room to the mirror. The string of fairy lights around it looked like unlit fireflies against the frame.

I stroked Bea's cheeks until her breathing calmed. Eventually, she fell asleep in my arms, and I nestled her onto her pillow and tucked her in. I stared at her tousled hair and the way her eyelashes fanned out beneath her closed eyes like tiny butterfly wings and vowed to ream out Adelaide for letting herself be seen.

But Adelaide wasn't here, a voice in my head whispered. *She was already gone.* And yet, Beatrix insisted there'd been something in the mirror.

In four years, no dream had ever followed my daughter into the waking world, no fabrication of such a nature had ever fallen from her lips. Which left only one real question . . .

What the hell had Beatrix seen?

Chapter 23

Each morning the rest of that week, I woke to the sounds of Callum in the driveway discovering yet another dead animal around his truck. On Tuesday, he scraped the mangled remains of a racoon from his grille and stared at it, dumbstruck, before going to the shed for a shovel to wrench it out. On Wednesday, the fat brown body of a woodchuck was wedged against his windshield. Again, Callum stared as I peered around a curtain in my office. I could see him trying to work out whether there were any associated memories that would explain the woodchuck's carcass and coming up empty-handed. On Thursday, another animal in the grille, this time a bloody mess of once-white feathers; I knew it was a seagull, but I didn't think there was enough left of it for Callum to come to that conclusion.

On Friday, I jolted awake the moment I heard the trill of Callum's alarm through the wall. As I lay in bed, listening to the sounds of the shower, I thought back to the night Adelaide had hidden in Cal's closet. I'd confronted her at work the next day, insisting I was no longer mad about the Tallows but wanting to know how she'd gone about getting Callum to lose his shit. She'd admitted to donning a ghoulish costume and makeup but was distracted throughout our conversation, answering texts on her phone with a strange little smile. The one time she looked up and gave me her full attention was when she insisted there'd have been no way Beatrix could have seen her.

"I stood in Cal's closet after sneaking in," she'd said. "He was sweating and whimpering in his sleep, so I knew freaking him out was going to be a cinch." She shrugged. "I whispered his name until he woke up. While he lost his mind and hid under the covers like a toddler, I shot across the room and disappeared down the ladder. And that was that."

"But Bea *saw* you," I'd said again. "Were you holding something red? Maybe a flashlight?"

"I wasn't holding anything. And I swear I wasn't in her room that night. I never went up to the attic. It was probably a run-of-the-mill nightmare. Kids dream weird shit all the time."

In the end, I was forced to concede that Adelaide was probably right. Still, I didn't like it. Bea was feeling the effects of the haunting even with me doing everything I could to shield her from them. *Soon*, I told myself. *Soon this will be over, and Bea and I will be free.*

The shower turned off. Drawers opened and closed. Cal's footsteps sounded on the stairs. A minute later, the garage door groaned beneath me. He never could just walk out the side door; he had to leave the house in the loudest way possible, despite not parking in the garage in the spring and summer. So predictable, the sounds of a marriage, the little nuances and idiosyncrasies of one's partner going about their day. In another life, another version of this one, I might've met the culmination of Cal's morning routine with a shared cup of coffee in the kitchen. Instead, I was waiting for him to open his car door and kick-start a scene that'd be at home in some backwoods horror movie.

I jumped up from the daybed, crept to the far window, and peeked over the sill. For several moments, nothing happened, and then Callum strolled out into the quiet haze of the morning, his shoulders slumped and his head hung low.

He gave the vehicle a wide berth, puffing his e-cigarette and staring at the grille as if something might jump out of it. Then, satisfied that the grille was clear, he fished his keys from his pocket and climbed into the cab.

I held my breath. Three seconds passed. Then another three. The driver's-side door burst open, and Callum fell out onto the pavement. His chest heaved as he scrambled backward, crab-walking away from the car. I tried to adjust my position, but I couldn't see inside the truck. I'd have to imagine the decapitated deer head perched on the front seat with its black, unseeing eyes, its fur ruined by whatever collision, bullet, arrow, or disease had killed it. If Todd-the-wildlife-guy had told Adelaide how the deer met its end, Adelaide hadn't shared that information with me. And if Callum came to me with the carnage, I needed only to accuse him of getting into yet another accident caused by his drinking. The dichotomy between Callum's memories and the horror of the deer head would hopefully increase his sense of reality disintegrating beneath him.

Callum managed to get to his feet and sprint away from the truck. If I strained my neck, forehead pressing into the glass, I could see him in the dewy grass of the silent backyard. He stared at the driveway, still breathing hard. I looked at my phone. He had about two minutes to make a decision before he was late for work. I waited for the squaring of the shoulders, the set of the jaw. Waited for Callum to march into the shed, as he'd done three days prior, and return with shovel and garbage bag. Instead, his lips formed the words *Fuck this shit*. He moved close enough to the car to slam the door before disappearing back into the garage.

I then heard all the noises of that morning but in reverse: garage door shutting, footsteps on the stairs, across the hall, and into Cal's room, drawers opening and closing, the spray of the shower. Finally, I heard the squeak of the mattress as Cal's body returned to it, heard the rustling of the sheets, then Callum's voice, muffled, but loud enough to hear the shakiness and uncertainty in every word:

"Steve, yeah, it's Callum, I must've come down with something. I'm not coming in today. Okay . . . okay . . . yup, got it. Yeah, hopefully I'll see you tomorrow, but for now, I'm . . . I'm in a bad way. No, don't call to check in. I'm going back to bed."

Callum's phone clattered to his nightstand. I picked up my own phone, opened my messages app, and sent off a quick note to Adelaide before returning to bed:

Operation Bambi = success

I lay there for almost an hour, thinking of all the progress we'd made in the last two weeks: the dead animals, the moving furniture, Callum's call to the heating company that'd been met with apathy and derision, the ghost that'd appeared to him in the night. At this rate, Callum would be gone before we'd gotten too far into summer.

It was only when I was drifting off to sleep that something occurred to me, sending a jolt of anxiety through my body that rendered sleep all but impossible. In all of Adelaide's explanations for how she'd pulled off her ghost-in-the-closet trick, she'd never relayed the source of the metal-on-glass sound I'd heard right before Callum screamed.

∞

I dropped Bea at school and was pulling into the driveway when I remembered that Callum had called in to work. *Goddammit.* No way I was working from home with him here. I'd get what I needed and get the hell out.

But Callum's car was gone. Maybe he'd gone in to work after all? Or gone somewhere to dispose of the deer head? I refrained from opening the garage in case he was sleeping upstairs, and walked toward the front door instead. I was halfway up the walkway when I saw the flash of blue, an envelope, in the jamb of the front door.

I jogged up the porch stairs and plucked it from the doorframe. Examining the envelope told me nothing. It was unaddressed, a plain expanse of pale blue, and unsealed. Probably a local business that went door-to-door, getting eyes on their gutter-cleaning services or low landscape prices by tricking homeowners into believing they'd received a personal letter. Still, I pulled the single piece of paper from inside and unfolded it.

> I know everything. What you're doing. What you're going to do. What you did.
> The question is: How much is my silence worth?

I read the words three times before dropping the paper, only breaking free from my shock when a breeze threatened to take it, and I had to stamp down with my foot to keep it from blowing away. I bent to retrieve the paper, my fingers trembling. Then I read it again.

Chapter 24

I clutched the letter so hard, the paper creased beneath my fingers. Someone knew about the haunting. *Or do they know something worse?* a voice in my head asked. *Another secret you've been keeping?*

No. No way. Adelaide was the only one I'd told, and she'd understood my reasoning, the ramifications if anyone ever found out. Understood that I'd pushed what had happened into the farthest reaches of my mind, never to be thought of, let alone spoken of, again.

The letter had to be about the haunting . . . so what should I do with it? Rip it to shreds? Run it to my car? Burn it in the sand beneath Bea's swing set? But there was no time to decide because the door opened, and there was Cal, squinting in the midmorning sun.

"What are you doing?" he asked.

"I'm"—I returned the letter to the envelope and slipped it into my back pocket—"not doing anything," I said coolly. "I decided to go into the office, so I came to grab my computer." I gestured over my shoulder. "Where's your car?" I leaned closer, my fear that he would discover the note replaced by shock at his appearance. "Jesus, are you okay? What's wrong?"

Cal's eyes were bloodshot and sunken, and he appeared to have lost ten pounds in half as many days. I'd seen him leave for work every day this week from my vantage point in the office, but I hadn't noticed he'd let his beard grow long; his hair, too, was in need of a cut.

He wrung his hands continuously and shifted where he stood, his neck jerking and then correcting itself, as if he were tempted to keep looking over his shoulder. He looked a decade older than his thirty-eight years.

"Callum," I said, and my shock wasn't feigned, "what's going on? Why aren't you at work?"

"I took the day off to bring the car to the shop. I, uh, spilled something on the seat and needed to get it detailed. I guess it's good I took the whole day because I'm not feeling well."

"How'd you get back to the house?"

As if in response, the door opened wider. Rosalie Taylor stood beside Callum in a camel-colored pantsuit, her hair perfectly coiffed and her lips a very bright shade of pink. "He called me," Callum's mother said.

"Rosalie," I choked out. "How are you?"

She smiled in her indifferent, regal way and gestured me into my own house. "Come in."

As I crossed the porch, I had to stifle a gasp. A bloody handprint was wrapped around the door handle, marring its metallic finish. Was this the work of Adelaide, knowing Callum was home? Or had the blackmailer left it as some sort of threat? At any rate, neither Callum nor Rosalie had noticed, and I breathed a small sigh of relief.

Composing myself as best as I could, I followed them to the kitchen. If Adelaide had something else planned, Rosalie *could not* be here. I scanned the room quickly but found nothing out of place. There were also no bottles or glasses on the counters, and no rings of condensation glinting in the sunlight coming through the window over the sink. I searched Callum's face, but it was impossible to divorce the signs of intoxication from whatever I was seeing there . . . acute stress reaction from extended haunting?

I was still stressing about the possibility of Rosalie seeing something related to the haunting when she said, "I can only stay a minute, Callum. I have a hair appointment, and then your father and I are having lunch with the D'Agostinos at the country club." I relaxed, if only slightly.

She walked to the cabinet above the refrigerator and removed a bottle of bourbon. Rage exploded inside me, as potent as if I'd thrown back my own shot of whiskey. "You're not feeling too ill to join me for a cocktail, are you, Callum?" Her eyes flashed. "You know I hate to drink alone."

"What time is it?" I asked, knowing it was nine thirty but unable to help myself.

Rosalie smiled stiffly, exchanged the bourbon for champagne, and pulled the orange juice from the fridge. "Better make it a mimosa."

I was swallowing a scoff when Callum surprised me by shaking his head. A wild thought occurred to me: Maybe Callum wasn't drinking. Maybe the haunting would have the opposite effect of what we'd anticipated. Maybe instead of drinking to the point of insanity and running out on Bea, reality falling to pieces all around him would get Callum to *stop* drinking. Get him to an AA meeting or a mental health center, to examine his own head and heart.

What would I do, if that were the case? Would I end the haunting, stop pursuing divorce and sole custody? Would I stay with the man whom I was actively pushing over the proverbial cliff into madness? I considered Adelaide. In her eyes, the haunting was only a success if it reduced Cal to a shell of himself, stripped him of everything. I wanted that too, so far as it meant triumphing over Cal in a courtroom. But the only thing that *really* mattered was Beatrix's safety. If I could be guaranteed that, guaranteed of my daughter's happiness, I'd happily accept a sober Callum, if not as a husband, then as a co-parent.

"Can I get by?" Cal asked his mother, stepping past her as she mixed her drink and pulling me from my thoughts. Rosalie moved forward to give him more room.

"Cal," I said, and stopped. I had no idea what I was going to say. Maybe that I was sorry he didn't feel well? Which was the truth, in a bizarre way. *I'm sorry you pushed me to do the things that have you feeling so miserable.* But Callum opened the freezer and removed the bottle of vodka, and any chance of saying anything fled with my sympathy.

"I'm not sure where that bourbon even came from," he said, his tone conversational, as if he were discussing a box of crackers and not the very thing that was tearing my family apart. He filled a glass with ice, and stuck a straw—one of Beatrix's twisty ones—into the glass with the unconscious movements of a sleepwalker.

"What adult drinks with a straw?" Rosalie asked, raising an eyebrow.

Callum rolled his eyes. "We keep them in the house for Beatrix, so I use them. Big whoop."

I watched him take the first sip, my cheeks burning. How could I have been so stupid? How could I have felt sorry for him, even for a moment? There was only one person to blame for the state of things, and it was not me. I would *not* be sorry for doing this to Callum, for haunting his thoughts, his life, his dreams. His dreams were supposed to be my dreams. *Our* dreams. Dreams for our family, for our daughter. He'd made his bed. He could fucking lie in it. Drown in it.

Die in it.

"You shouldn't drink if you're not feeling well," I said woodenly. *You weak, selfish piece of shit.* Then, far more loudly and emphatically, in a voice neither he nor his mother could ignore, I said, "In fact, you shouldn't drink at all. Not with your history. Not with everything that's been going on."

It was like I'd set off a bomb in the kitchen. Callum's face went white, with the exception of two small splotches of color in his cheeks. Rosalie lowered her glass from her mouth and stared at me as if I were a spider she'd just found in her salad.

"What is that supposed to mean?" Rosalie asked.

Don't back down from her. "It means we all know Callum has a drinking problem. I'm sick of being the only one who tries to do something about it. In fact," I said, and even though I wasn't backing down, was about to do the *opposite* of backing down, my voice wavered slightly, "I've told Callum that if he doesn't stop drinking, I'm going to see a lawyer."

Rosalie's eyes took on the gleam and hardness of galvanized steel. "Huh," she said. "Well, isn't that interesting?" She looked at her son. "See a lawyer for what?"

"For a divorce," I said, forcing my voice to remain steady. "And custody of Beatrix."

"Huh," she repeated. "Callum, you've never mentioned this before."

"I didn't . . . I don't . . . I mean, I didn't think that if—" he stammered, but she cut him off.

"If you *had* mentioned it, I would have told you not to worry. We have lawyers too." She turned her steely gaze back to me. "The best in Rhode Island. I imagine you'd get a vastly different outcome from what you desire, so that's something to think about." She didn't say how she'd go about making this "vastly different outcome" a reality, but from the look on her face, I didn't doubt she could accomplish it.

She drained the rest of her mimosa and set down the glass beside one of the pillar candles Adelaide insisted I leave on the island. "I've always thought you were a good mother, Lainey," Rosalie said. "But so am I. And a good mother does what's best for her child, no matter the circumstances."

Every inch of my body thrummed with adrenaline. Panic squeezed my heart, and I pressed my toes against the bottoms of my shoes to keep from sprinting out of the kitchen. Still, I held her eye, refusing to look away.

Rosalie stared back at me another moment, then walked out of the kitchen. She left the house through the front door. I heard the engine of her Mercedes start a moment later. She'd parked on the street, which explained why I hadn't seen her car. I turned to face Callum. He looked indifferent to his mother's little speech. A moment later, he picked up his glass and followed the same path Rosalie had taken out of the kitchen. He walked up the stairs and into his bedroom, shutting the door behind him. The house fell into silence.

I stormed through the kitchen and slammed the front door behind me so hard the birds in a nearby bush tittered in alarm and scattered to the sky. I remembered the bloody handprint at the last second before I stepped off the porch and spun to face it, my hand already going to my bag for something to wipe it with. But the bloody handprint was gone. *Nice, Adelaide,* I thought distractedly.

I walked to my car half blind with rage and shaking with fear. Fuck going to work. Fuck Rosalie Taylor. Fuck the blackmailer. None of them were going to ruin this for me. No one was standing in the way of my future with my daughter.

I was going to find Adelaide, and we were going to do some experimenting. It was time to raise the stakes. We wouldn't just illuminate the crypt of Callum's mind, where ghosts brooded over drinks and guarded the grime on the windows. We were going to explode it.

We were going to raise this haunting to the next fucking level.

Chapter 25

Saturday morning dawned cool and stormy. Callum had planned to host several work colleagues at the golf club, but after more than an hour of torrential rain, he started making calls.

"I know, I know." His voice was gravelly. "I'll cancel the tee time. If it was a drizzle, that'd be one thing, but it's supposed to pour the next five hours." There was another minute of small talk and complaining about the weather before Callum hung up.

"No golf today?" There was an edge to my words, as sharp as the teeth of a coil-spring trap.

Callum stared for a moment, as if surprised I'd spoken to him at all. "Yep," he finally said. "Too wet out. Think I'll play video games for a bit."

I bit my bottom lip. If it was too wet to golf, there was no point bringing up the deck rail again. I'd be lucky if the damn thing got fixed before Bea left for college. "I'm going to get Bea ready," I said through gritted teeth.

"Ready for what?"

"She's going to my parents' house, remember?"

Stupid question. Of course he didn't. In the past, I'd have followed this by baiting him, asking if he wanted Bea to stay with him instead, get some daddy-daughter time on the books, knowing he didn't want to. He'd play along for a minute but would default to his usual selfishness. It used to make me feel guilty, but after the last few weeks, guilt was no longer within my repertoire of emotions when it came to Callum. Neither, apparently, was the ability to even consider leaving Beatrix with her father.

And that was saying something, seeing as I'd never forgotten the time I'd left the two of them alone for the weekend to go to a museum curators' conference in Boston. When I'd returned, I discovered Callum had refused to speak with Bea for an entire day because she'd dumped paint into the Yeti cooler he took with him to the golf course. My almost-forty-year-old husband giving my then-three-year-old daughter the silent treatment because she'd pulled an—admittedly destructive but ultimately harmless—attention-grabbing stunt.

"You didn't tell me Bea was going to your parents'," Cal said.

As predictable as the decay of a precious artifact. "I did," I said, and set my coffee cup in the sink. "I'm going to drop her shortly. Then I have to run out to do some errands."

Callum nodded absently, not yet reaching for the controller. When I stopped on the landing, I heard him go to the kitchen and make a drink. I also heard him grumbling about his phone being dead despite having charged it, and couldn't help but smile. Adelaide and I had agreed we needed to take measures to keep Callum from compiling evidence where we could; I'd been creeping into his room every night since to pack dust from the dryer vent into his phone's charging port.

Before continuing up the stairs, I drafted a text to send to Adelaide when Bea and I left for my parents.

> C not golfing. Bea and I are leaving now. Can initiate Flypocalypse earlier than planned.

I was slipping the phone into my back pocket when it rang. The number on the screen wasn't one I recognized. I hurried into my office to accept it with a terse, "Hello."

"Lainey?"

The woman's voice on the other line was familiar, but I couldn't place it. "Yes."

"This is Morgan Tallow."

"Morgan, hi." *Why the hell is Morgan calling?*

"Is this a good time?"

"I have a few minutes." I sat down on the daybed.

There was silence on the other end of the line.

The silence persisted long enough that I had to look down and make sure the call hadn't dropped. "Morgan?"

"Yeah, sorry, Lainey. I'm, well . . . I'm trying to figure out the best way to say this."

My grip around the phone tightened. "Say what?"

Another pause, and then, "When Joe and I analyzed the data we got from your house, we saw some anomalies."

"Anomalies?" Already, the skepticism had crept into my voice, along with a hint of anger.

"Cold spots, radiation spikes, dips in lighting, jumbled sounds among radio frequencies, disruptions in electromagnetic waves."

"You found all that." It was a statement, said in the same tone used when questioning the number of drinks Callum had consumed in my absence.

"None of the findings were all that significant on their own. Honestly, they weren't even significant when taken together. It was when we looked at *where* in the house the anomalies occurred."

"Oh yeah, and where was that?"

Morgan was quiet for a moment, picking up on the coldness in my voice. I didn't care. I'd let my guard down, allowed them to distract me with their friendly demeanors and personal stories. I'd been warned to avoid Joe and Morgan Tallow from the day I'd started with the Preservation Society, and now here I was, listening to Morgan Tallow get ready to tell me my house was haunted.

"The anomalies occurred in those exact areas where I shot video: the reflective surfaces. The greatest variances occurred directly in front of the mirrors, specifically, the ones in the bathroom, foyer, and primary bedroom." Another pause, during which I almost told her where she could stick those video recordings, but Morgan started speaking again. "And that was before we watched the actual footage. Lainey, there are *things* in the mirrors. Shapes. Not accounted for by you or me or Adelaide."

"Shapes." Again, it wasn't a question but a declarative confirmation of the word, of just how gullible she thought I was.

"I know how you feel about all this stuff, that's why I was afraid to call you. Joe made me call you, actually. One part of the footage . . . well, there's a—"

"Morgan, I have to go," I said. "Thanks for coming by the other day, but I've got all the information I need."

"Wait, Lainey, hear me out. We're worried that—"

"Goodbye," I said, and hung up.

I sat there for a moment, keyed up, my thoughts flying. Should I tell Adelaide I was right, that the Tallows were, in fact, the hucksters I'd always thought them to be? I was actually awestruck at their nerve. Had their story of losing a child even been true, or was it all a ploy to foster sympathy and forge a connection? I stood, shaking off the call.

There was too much going on to harp on Joe and Morgan's bullshit. I needed to get Bea out of here and occupy myself for the afternoon while Adelaide worked through the next stage of the haunting. I saved Morgan's number in my phone. If she called back, I wanted to be sure I knew to reject it.

I found Beatrix in her room, playing in the fairy garden I'd given her for her third birthday. The garden had been a surprise, handcrafted and sneaked into her room while she'd slept. When she'd woken to the sight, along with the half-dozen tree decals I'd adhered to her walls, she'd gripped my arm and exclaimed, "Something magical happened!" It was one of my favorite memories, and one Callum had slept through, waking to watch her open the other gifts I'd picked for her and contributing nothing but disappointment.

"Hi, hon. What's happening in the fairy garden today?"

"It's a ghost garden now." She opened the door to a small wooden house. Inside was a tiny mirror, no bigger than a thimble, and opposite it, a brightly painted butterfly. "The butterfly knows the ghost-girl lives in the mirror."

Ghost-girl? "Is that so?" I said with forced nonchalance. "How does she know that?"

"The same way the tortoises know that the gnomes turn into horses at night." She shrugged, as if to say, *Duh*, and I took the opportunity to change the subject.

"You ready to go to Gram and Papa's?"

Bea turned away from the raised planter, her face breaking into a huge grin. "Can I wear my dragonfly dress? The one with the shimmery skirt?"

The word *dragonfly* bounced in my brain like a fly against a windowpane. *Fly. Adelaide's flies. We need to hurry.* But no, I hadn't sent the text; Adelaide wouldn't release the flies until we were out of the house. I found Bea's dress in the closet and laid it on the bed. "You get dressed. I'm going to let Daddy know we're about to get going."

"Okay, Mommy."

I scooped Bea's bag off the floor and headed for the stairs, the beeps and trills of the video game floating through the house. The day's rapidly evolving plans—from Callum's rained-out golf game, to the unwelcome call from Morgan, to Beatrix's strange comments—had me feeling a little queasy, and I walked to the kitchen for some water.

At the sink, I filled a glass but set it on the counter and pulled my phone from my pocket. I still wouldn't hit send on the draft to Adelaide—not when Bea might drag her feet getting into the car and delay our departure—but I wanted to text my mother and let her know we'd be there soon.

I tapped out the message, sent it off, and picked up my glass. I was drinking deeply and feeling a little better, a little more in control, when something bobbed in and out of my periphery. A small shadow, floating up and down . . . a line of black that zipped through the air like a falling star.

I turned and saw it instantly. A fly. It crawled along the windowsill. As I watched, it crawled in the opposite direction and then flew up to the vent in the wall. It disappeared momentarily, and when it returned, it was followed by a second fly. Then a third, black legs like black thread skittering over the wall, its narrow body and papery wings making my skin crawl.

At first, the flies came from the vent slowly enough that I could make out each one as it emerged. In five seconds, there were five. In ten seconds, there were twenty. Then the individual bodies were swallowed by a writhing wall of black, as if the vent were ejecting an endless sheet of crepe that ripped into a thousand different directions as it fell. There was a tiny tempest of buzzing that grew to a crescendo, like cicadas hidden in the trees. The buzzing quickly became a black cloud of panic that descended over my brain.

I never sent the text! The flies shouldn't be here!

I had to get Beatrix out of the house.

Now.

Chapter 26

The counterthought came a moment later: *If you go sprinting out of here to escape the flies, it will ruin everything! Callum's the one who needs to be scared, not you. And certainly not Beatrix.*

I forced myself to look away from the growing horde so I could concentrate, working desperately to decide what to do. The first step still had to be to get Bea out of the house. I couldn't pretend not to see the flies if Bea was standing right beside me, witnessing the horror. So, get Bea out, then figure out how to play things with Callum.

I walked quickly but calmly to the base of the stairs and called up, "Bea, are you dressed? Want to play in Pinecone House while I pack the car?"

Her reply was instant . . . and music to my ears: a mad dash for the stairs. A moment later and she was before me, and I had to commit to this impromptu plan.

"But isn't it raining?"

Shit. "Uh, yes, but if you get right up into your fort and shut the door, you'll be fine. In fact, I bet it'll be extra cozy."

"Okay!" She looked up at me, eyes gleaming. "Do you wanna play Favorite Thing?"

"Oh, um, not right now, sweetheart. But how about a different game? How about I bet you can't walk through the kitchen, into the playroom, and onto the deck with your eyes closed and your ears plugged," I challenged, speaking so close to her my lips brushed her ear.

"Sure I can!" she exclaimed.

"Okay, then. Let's go!" I scooped her up by the armpits and carried her quickly along the route I'd set forth. Callum remained with his back to us as we passed the living room, still oblivious to the flies. In the playroom, I yanked the slider open and shooed Bea onto the deck.

"Stay away from the broken rail," I warned, nodding at the safe path toward the stairs. When she reached them, I said loudly, in case Callum was listening, "Five minutes in the fort, then we're off to Papa and Gram's."

She sprinted through the rain, and I closed the slider door.

I turned toward the kitchen, my heart sinking; the number of flies had grown. The buzzing was a sick, savage grating against my skull. Black bodies and papery veined wings marred every inch of the crisp white paint. The buzzing was so unnerving and disordered it was otherworldly. Flies buzzed past my face, crawled over my neck. Hadn't Adelaide said she'd purchased a thousand? This seemed ten times that number, maybe more.

My fingers itched to grab my phone, to check if I'd somehow texted Adelaide by mistake. If not, why had she unleashed the flies when we were still in the house? I could only hope Bea didn't decide she needed me for some made-up game or to push her on the swings. I couldn't leave before Callum discovered the descending plague, could I? I might as well hold a sign above my head with the words I'm Behind the Flies in neon, blinking lights.

But he *hadn't* noticed them yet. I blinked and wiped perspiration from my hairline. The sound of the flies crept over me, filling my ears. I had made the snap decision to grab Bea's overnight bag and make a run for it when a disgusted shout came from the living room.

"Ugh, Jesus Christ! What the hell *is* this?"

There was a clatter, as if Cal had jumped from the couch in such a frenzy that the controller had gone flying. I heard him rush across the room and fling open a window.

"Get out of here. Get *out*! Lainey! *Lainey*! You need to get in here! And check on Beatrix!"

He actually thought of Bea, I thought as I ran to the living room. Well, the flies *were* like something out of the Old Testament; hell might as well have frozen over.

I skidded to a halt before rounding the wall between the living room and the foyer. Interacting with Callum after he'd seen Adelaide's "ghost" had been tough, but acting as if I didn't see ten thousand flies covering the walls, the furniture, the mantel, was on another level. I swallowed, preparing myself for what I was about to do, not even remotely confident it was the right move, terrified, actually, that the idea was too brazen, that it would undermine everything that had come before it.

Serial killer confidence, I reminded myself. *That's what I'm supposed to have.* Serial killer confidence and an earnest prayer that Callum was drunk. I took a breath and walked into the living room.

"What's wrong?" I asked. "What's going on?" I made a show of looking around while keeping my face neutral. There were fewer flies here than in the kitchen, or maybe it was just that the room was bigger? "Why do I have to check on Bea? Is she hurt?" I curled my toes against the unbearable, unholy buzz as a fly whizzed past my ears.

Callum stared at me from the middle of the living room, slack-jawed and horrified. A fly crawled over his cheek; several more dotted his forearms. When the fly on his cheek inched toward his mouth, he lost it, sputtering and slapping as if he were being assailed by wasps.

"What is it?" I asked again. "What happened?" I closed my mouth tightly after speaking. The flies were definitely less dense here, though they still pinwheeled and dive-bombed through the air.

"*What is it?*" Callum's voice was a siren. "Are you blind? Look at the fucking flies!" He reached for his cell, but it was still dead. Disgusted, he chucked the phone onto his chair.

I did look, but not at the flies. I looked at the glass next to the couch. To my eternal relief, it was empty. The vodka bottle was beside the coffee table, which meant he'd already had a refill.

"I don't see any flies," I said. I made a show of scanning the room.

A fly grazed Callum's cheek again, and he batted at it so hard, he smacked himself in the face. My own face contorted, and suddenly, I was no longer acting. It was as if a switch had flipped, a switch that meant I no longer remembered Callum *wasn't* losing it, that he was reacting to something I was responsible for having set in motion. The *Are you fucking crazy?* look I gave him could have convinced a hungry bear to think twice before pulling down a bird feeder.

Without warning, Cal turned and sprinted from the room. I took off after him, making a conscious effort not to swat flies as I rushed up the stairs in case he turned around. I caught up to him at the door to his bedroom. He tried to shut it, but I shoved my way inside.

There were hardly any flies here, which would make gaslighting him even easier. I walked across the room and looked out; through the tiny window of Pinecone House, I could just make out Beatrix.

"Now do you see there's something going on in this house?" Callum shouted.

I whirled back around to face him. "What the fuck are you talking about?" I gestured across the room. "What the hell is wrong with you? We're back on the whole 'There's a ghost in my closet' bullshit?"

"There *was* a ghost in my closet!" Callum roared.

"Riiight!" I shouted back. "And now there are flies in the living room? News flash, Callum, you're the only person seeing these things. Odors, cold spots, noises, ghosts . . . no one has smelled or felt or heard these things but you!"

Callum's mouth dropped open, and I resisted the sudden, wild urge to punch him. Rage was building, noxious and all-consuming, making it hard to keep my thoughts straight.

"You think I'm making this up?" Callum asked, incredulous. He laughed, sounding unhinged and manic. I recalled something Adelaide had said to me on the phone earlier: *How do you think the haunting is going overall? How far away are we from him completely losing his shit?* Callum was one intake form away from the psych unit.

"Tell me, Lainey," he continued, "Miss Fucking Perfect. Miss Always Right. How in the fuck do I make up this many flies?"

I spun in every direction and gesticulated wildly. "There are no flies, Callum!" I screamed. "You've completely lost your mind."

He shook his head, his eyes closed, swatting the air around his head even when flies weren't in his immediate vicinity. "I've been telling you for weeks." His voice was quiet now. "Maybe a month! This house is fucking haunted."

"Oh, shut up. Shut the fuck up. Can you please, for once in your life, act like an adult? The house is not haunted! In fact, our house being haunted is the most ridiculous thing I've ever heard. We built it, remember? How do you propose our house became haunted? There's no cursed burial ground or body beneath the floorboards," I added, echoing something I'd said to Adelaide when she'd conceptualized the haunting. I gestured between myself and Callum. "There's only us."

Callum mumbled something that sounded like, *"Maybe that's enough."* The idea that I was somehow contributing to the fucked-up energy in this house made the rage-fire inside me blaze all the brighter.

"If there *were* flies here," I said, my voice dangerously low, "it'd be because of something *you* did. Did you buy a bag of grinders for your golf buddies and leave them in the garage?" My voice was hoarse from all the yelling, and I lowered it further, feeling my expression twist, turning as ugly as the rage in my heart. "Or maybe you drove shit-faced and hit something worse than a wrought iron fence. Perhaps there's a body in the basement?"

I hadn't planned on saying this, but when I did, Callum's face went pale, his eyes full of something like understanding, like recognition, of perhaps the dreadful sense of possibility. Adelaide's idea to stuff Cal's grate full of roadkill every morning had paid off, albeit a bit differently than we'd expected. I turned toward the door. "I've got to go. Have fun playing video games by yourself in between your drunken hallucinations."

"Wait," Callum said, suddenly panicked. "You can't leave me here. I can't stay in the house with these—" He cast a worried glance toward the door. The flies' elongated bodies wove in and out along the woodwork. Though I could have sworn that some of them, many of them, didn't look like the pictures of the black soldier flies Adelaide had shown me.

"Yes, I can," I said to Callum. "And that's exactly what I'm doing. My parents are expecting Beatrix, remember?" I eyed Callum, and the words were on my tongue, but I couldn't speak them. Not yet. Even with Adelaide's little stunt today, we hadn't gone far enough, hadn't pushed Callum *past* the breaking point, and so I didn't dare say, *Why don't you go to a hotel?* Anything a judge could take as grounds for abandonment, Callum had to come to on his own.

"Goodbye, Callum."

I pushed past him and out the door. Callum followed me down the stairs, swatting flies and pleading.

I didn't stop, didn't look back. Didn't even, in that moment at least, wonder how in the hell Adelaide and I would get rid of all these goddamned flies. There'd be no "plucking them out of the air, mid-flight," as Adelaide had prophesized. But that was a later-problem. The now-problem was to get out of this house. And away from Callum.

I didn't even stop when Callum said, "Please, Lainey, you've got to help me. I swear to you. I swear it. Something really isn't right with the house. The house is haunted. You've got to help. I'll go to an AA meeting. I'll get my boss to send me to an EAP program. Or outpatient counseling. Don't leave. Don't take Beatrix. Don't leave!"

His words devolved into a chant that stayed with me as I collected Bea from Pinecone House, and we walked to the car: *The house is haunted. The house is haunted. The house is haunted.*

As long as you're there, I thought, *it will be.*

Chapter 27

I was pulling into my parents' driveway, wondering how I was going keep up the charade with the flies, when the answer arrived via text:

Leaving for Monty's...staying till Monday, when I'll call an exterminator. I'm not staying in a house full of fucking flies, even if you don't believe they exist.

If Callum were leaving now, that was perfect. I could drop Bea and call Adelaide, tell her to meet me at the house with the arsenal of flytraps and cleaning products she'd already purchased. Our original plan was to set up everything in the house while he slept, but that was when the number of flies was far less. Now I had another burning question for Adelaide, in addition to why the hell she'd unleashed the flies early: Were we going to need twice as many traps to make them disappear?

Inside, my mother had everything with which to bake cookies spread out on the counter, and I lost Bea to the pull of sugar canisters and chocolate chips within seconds. I kissed her cheek and told her I'd call to check on her later. My mother waved me off and told me to take whatever time I needed to go about my errands.

"Get a pedicure if you have an extra half hour," she said with a wink. "You deserve it. We'll be fine here, won't we, Bea?"

"Sure will, Gram," she said through a mouthful of chocolate chips. I blew them a kiss as I slipped out the door.

Back outside, I didn't even wait until I was in the car to call Adelaide. The phone rang and rang; I got her voicemail.

"Call me back as soon as you get this. Cal was freaked out enough to leave, at least temporarily. I'm heading home now to rid the place of as many flies as possible, but Adelaide, what the fuck? Why did you release them so goddamn early? And why were there about ten times more than we'd originally planned?"

It occurred to me that I was leaving a voicemail full of incriminating evidence about the haunting, but it was too late now. I'd have to make sure Adelaide deleted it. I backed out of the driveway and kept talking:

"Call me back, okay? I'll stop at your place on my way home to see if you're there."

I hung up and headed in the direction of Adelaide's. I called several more times on the way but got no response. Where the hell was she that she wasn't picking up?

Five minutes later, I pulled up in front of Adelaide's pastel-purple Victorian, a house as over the top as Adelaide, left to her by her maternal grandmother. I called her cell again. There was still no answer, but Adelaide's Prius was in the driveway. Annoyed, I threw the car in park and stomped across the yard.

Adelaide never used the front door, so I circled around to the side. But when I got within sight of the side door, I saw there was someone else here. A truck, pulled all the way to the top of the slightly curved second driveway. A truck I recognized. A truck with WILDLIFE EXTRACTION SERVICES emblazoned across the sides.

What the hell was Todd doing here? Adelaide was done with the dead-animal portion of the haunting. Maybe the extra flies had come from him? Questions pinged around my brain as I reached for the door.

Through the open blinds over the door's top pane, I saw them, the jerky movements of their bodies, before I realized what I was seeing. Todd, leaning over Adelaide on the parlor love seat, hips moving rhythmically, his hands woven through her fuchsia hair. My own hand flew to my mouth, and I stumbled backward, embarrassment tempered by shock. Without thinking, I dropped to the ground and crawled away from the door as fast as possible. Todd's truck blocked my path, and I rounded the front bumper.

I stopped, breathing hard. What the hell had I just seen? Was this a new development, or had Adelaide been sleeping with him for a while? I thought of the day we'd met with Joe and Morgan, and the reason Adelaide hadn't wanted to go to her house. That explained why she'd changed the subject so fast when I asked her who the guy was. Why hadn't she told me? I couldn't wrap my head around how this had come about, and what this meant for me, for her, for the haunting.

I had convinced myself that, at least for now, Adelaide and Todd didn't matter—I had to rid the house of evidence while Callum was out of it regardless of Adelaide's present circumstances. I was climbing to my feet beside Todd's truck, mentally cataloging the supplies I needed at Home Depot, when something caught my eye. I stepped closer, blinking through the steadily falling rain. I adjusted my position, leaned closer to the window, and saw it.

There, on the console, was an open box of notebook paper. Plain sheets. With matching envelopes.

In a very distinct shade of pale sky blue.

༄

I arrived back at the house with flytraps, bleach, and paper towels in tow to find that not only was Callum gone, so were a great deal of the flies. Sure, some remained, mostly centered around vents and doorframes, but the majority had been reduced to handfuls of crinkly, desiccated bodies jamming up the windowsills like sticks in a dam. I kept spinning, looking for them, listening, but no swarm materialized. There were flies on the floor, and while the corpses were plentiful, their numbers were far more in line with what Adelaide had purchased than with the multitudes that'd descended a few hours earlier.

Still, I hung traps and dumped dustpans and paper-towelfuls of flies in the garbage, all while thinking of what I'd seen at Adelaide's house. I wiped the walls and doorframes with bleach, mopped the hardwood floors and vacuumed the carpets, wondering if I'd imagined the distinct shade of blue paper in Todd's truck or if he truly was the blackmailer. Could he and Adelaide be in on it together? I was vacuuming the kitchen a second time when a sound came from above me, chasing away my dark and distrustful thoughts.

I shut off the vacuum and listened, but there was nothing. Probably my imagination. But as I was about to switch on the vacuum again, something moved above me. Not quite a groan but a scrape . . .

It sounded like it was coming from the attic.

I froze, straining to hear from two floors below. There was nothing for a while.

Then the scraping came again.

"Well, I can be pretty damn certain that's not Adelaide," I said aloud, but my stab at sarcasm didn't make me feel any better. I made my way to the stairs on silent feet.

I'd missed a swath of dead flies in a corner and could see their vein-threaded wings glinting like the droplets of rain on the windows. I paused, listening. The sound came again. But this time it was farther away, still in the attic, but on the other side of the house.

I climbed the stairs and crept partway down the hall, peering into the shadowy chamber of my office. Desk. Bookcases. Daybed. Nothing out of the ordinary. The scraping came again, from behind me this time, rising almost to a shriek, like steel wheels along steel tracks. Bea's room. I crossed the hall and pushed open the door.

The ceiling fan whirred and the closet stood open, but Bea's room was empty. What the hell was going on here? What was that damn sound? Had an animal gotten trapped inside the walls and was trying to get out?

I walked to the closet and looked up; the trapdoor was closed. Another scrape, short and dull, like a brick skidding against concrete.

Then, from far off, three short, twangy guitar notes, like a trio of ghosts, floated to me on the air from behind the plaster. It was the familiar song again, the one from the night of the thunderstorm, the one I couldn't place.

"That's it," I hissed, and climbed on top of the organizer. I pushed the trapdoor open and pulled myself into the attic.

Wriggling forward on my stomach, I peered around the now-quiet space. Like my previous time up here, I was overcome with the wrongness of the color, the immovability of the air. Today, that immovability felt even more intense, as if the air were a blanket of gauze . . . or as if I were viewing everything through the membranous wing of a fly.

Aside from that, the attic was empty. Still. Abandoned.

I pulled myself all the way up, vaguely aware that this was a bad idea, that if Callum came home to grab something, saw my keys and phone on the table, and went looking for me, he'd find the closet ajar and wonder what the hell I was doing. Still, I needed to know, to discover the source of the scraping; when taken with the guitar notes, I had to assume Adelaide had set up additional layers to today's haunting beyond Flypocalypse. I stepped forward onto the adjacent joist and looked around.

I found the voice recorders first, one at either side of the shallow alcove where the roofline converged with the floorboards. But the recorders were off. There must be another device stuffed down into the walls, set to play intermittent notes of music, or grating shrieks reminiscent of the opening of Michael Jackson's "Thriller." I navigated the treacherous sheets of plywood to the midway point of the attic, but what I found behind the pile of insulation were Adelaide's fuzzy slippers.

There was also a bottle of water, a cordless iPhone charger, and a small, thin blanket. I recognized it as the blanket Adelaide took to the beach with her in the summer. So this was where Adelaide relaxed while up here, if a word as strong as *relax* could be used. I grimaced at a pile of rodent droppings in the corner.

I crept closer to Adelaide's things. Light streamed up from a small hole where the wall met the closest ceiling joist. Dropping to my hands and knees, I crawled forward. When my face was a mere inch from the hole, I realized I could see through it into the house. I wasn't sure what I was looking at; the room was in shadow, and there was something reflective across the bottom of my view, at a right angle to a darker vertical line, like a slit in a doorway.

That's what the vertical line was: a slit in a doorway. Specifically, the closet doors in the primary bathroom, Callum's bathroom, containing the washer and dryer. The horizontal, slightly reflective object was the lip of the washing machine. If the closet doors had been open, I thought I might be able to see a good way into the bathroom, left of the toilet, thankfully. But Adelaide had an unobstructed, if small, view of the mirror, which would allow her to glimpse far more of the bathroom than what she could have seen without it.

Why hadn't Adelaide told me she had this window into our lives? I thought she'd been acting on sound alone, listening to where Callum was in the house. But this midway vantage point opened things up, literally and figuratively. I pushed myself to my feet and walked around the rest of the attic, then turned to find myself face-to-face with the broken mirror from the housewarming party six long years ago.

An inescapable chill caused me to shift on the joist. The mirror was in a different position from the last time I'd been in the attic, wasn't it? As I was trying to figure why Adelaide might have moved it, a sound came from behind me. A rustling, followed by a repeat of what I'd heard several times downstairs:

Scrrrrrrrape. Scrrrrrrrrape. Scrrrrrrrape.

I spun slowly, certain I was about to confront something horrible. But what I saw surprised me: Nothing. No wraith with sunken black eyes, and no Adelaide having come to her senses and sent Todd packing before getting her ass over here to help. The noise came again, and I realized I was seeing nothing because the sound was coming from beneath me, at the midway point of the attic.

Directly below the peephole.

I retraced my steps to Adelaide's little alcove, pushing her blanket and water bottle aside, and pressed one eye to the hole in time to see the closet doors of the bathroom swing open. My limbs turned to lead. Callum must have come home after all. He would catch me up here, rendering everything that had come before today—all our efforts and sneaking around—futile. *Why* had I returned to the house so soon, let alone come up to the attic?

But the figure in the bathroom didn't look like Callum. It floated past my vantage point like a train in the distance, steel gray and fast moving. I pushed my eye to the hole a little harder. The figure had walked out of view. I listened, but nothing further came.

Please, please, please don't let it be Callum. My recklessness made me queasy; had I really forgotten that Bea's safety, Bea's future, *my* future with my daughter, rode on not screwing up the haunting? The possibility of this thread that held Bea's fate unraveling over the next few heartbeats made me feel like vomiting.

I shifted, moving back slightly from the peephole, and as I did, my perspective changed. Now, I could see the bottom half of the bathroom mirror. And in that reflective portion, a figure moved from right to left. Smaller than Callum. Slight. A woman? Had Adelaide taken leave of Todd after all? I made my breathing as shallow as possible and tried to avoid shifting again, out of position.

The figure was dressed in loose, dark clothing. A hood covered its hair. I looked for a telltale strand of fuchsia but could make nothing out. I considered saying something, but what if Callum *had* come back and I gave away my location? The figure dipped in and out of sight. Between my light breathing and the aching of my muscles as I tried to hold my position over the peephole, I was getting dizzy. Maybe that's why the figure seemed less than corporeal, going hazy then sharpening, hazy then sharpening. The figure disappeared, drifting left and out of sight.

Thirty seconds passed. Then another thirty. I was starting to believe I'd imagined the whole thing and was about to tear myself away from the peephole when something blotted out my vision entirely. I blinked, heart rate skyrocketing, and shoved down the gasp careening up my throat. Another few blinks and I was able to parse the image beneath me: It was the figure, standing in front of the bathroom closet and a little to the left, facing the mirror. I was looking at the back of the black hood and the hunched shoulders, but the figure was *too* hunched to see its face. The mirror captured only the top of the head, the dark fabric there, with no hint at the shade or length of the hair underneath.

I heard myself breathing as if from far away. Who was down there? Why did I feel, in some deep, primal part of myself, that this wasn't Adelaide?

The figure raised its head slowly, stared directly into the mirror, and I saw, with growing horror, that there was no face at all. Just a shimmery surface, like a pond after a pebble has been thrown into it, or a mirror at the moment of impact, in the first nanosecond after it shatters.

As I watched, paralyzed with terror, the figure without a face raised its hands and wrung them, over and over.

Like Lady Macbeth in her staggering guilt, they were covered in blood.

Chapter 28

I jerked away from the peephole, falling to the side and rolling over the plywood, stifling a scream that felt less like it was struggling to escape my lungs than that it was engulfing my entire body. Despite my efforts, a strangled cry exploded up the scratchy corridor of my throat. What the hell *was* that? And why didn't it have a face? Had there really been blood on its hands, or had I imagined it, squinting through the peephole as I'd been?

My questions were interrupted by the fact that I was dangerously close to a gap between the plywood and the nearest joist. I threw my hands out and pressed them flat against the wood, earning a needle-sharp splinter for my troubles. Still, the tactic worked, and I avoided falling through the joists. My problems weren't over, however; as I struggled to quell the yammering of my heart, a door slammed somewhere beneath me.

I shot to my feet and darted across the attic, making it to the trapdoor quicker than I thought possible. If that was Callum downstairs, or someone with him, I needed to get out of this attic, and fast. I dropped to the top of the organizer shelves. After pulling the trapdoor back in place, I fell to the floor of the closet like a stone. I had climbed to my feet and was starting to feign interest in the dresses and sweaters hanging from Bea's closet when footsteps pounded across the upstairs hallway. A moment later, the door swung open.

Adelaide stood before me.

"Jesus," I said. "It's you."

Her smile widened. "Who were you expecting? Jeff Goldblum from *The Fly*?"

"Seriously, Adelaide, it's not funny." I paused, and for the first time, it occurred to me that what I'd seen between her and Todd had been brand new, maybe even the first time, and that in the next moment, she'd tell me all about it. "Why didn't you answer the phone when I called?" I asked.

Her expression wavered. "I was busy."

"Oh?" I saw she was wearing a loose-fitting black sweatshirt. Its large hood hung down her back. The figure from the mirror flashed before me, and I narrowed my eyes. "Were you in Cal's bathroom?"

She scrunched up her face. "Yes. I mean, no. Not really. I popped in and out of all the rooms looking for you." She took a few steps toward me. "I got your voicemail. What were you talking about? Something about too many flies?"

"Yes, there were too many flies!" I exploded, aware that I was jumping to anger before giving her a chance to explain herself. About Todd, about the flies. And not just anger but fear, after what had happened in the attic. "There were too many flies, *and* you funneled them into the vents when Beatrix and I were still home! What the hell were you thinking?"

She huffed out a breath. "You texted me! You told me Callum wasn't golfing and to go ahead with Flypocalypse earlier than planned!"

I yanked out my phone and opened my texts app. There was the message I'd drafted, still unsent.

"No, I didn't, Adelaide, it's right—"

She didn't wait for me to finish. "And secondly, Critter Depot isn't in the habit of sending their customers more product than what they paid for. I ordered a thousand flies. A thousand flies is what I got, *and* what I released."

I shook my head emphatically. "Uh-uh. No way. It was fucking biblical. They were everywhere, Adelaide. *Everywhere*. And I *didn't* text you! You're lucky I got Beatrix out when I did. Why would you do that? You promised you wouldn't do anything that'd put her in danger."

Adelaide dug her phone from her sweatshirt pocket. "I'll show you the goddamn text," she said, jabbing at the screen. Her expression turned disbelieving. "It was right here. There was a text from you, I fucking swear it. I even sent a reply, just to confirm, but I don't see that one either. What the hell is going on here?"

I glared at her from across Bea's room, my mind racing. What the hell was her angle? "Is this like the Echo?" I asked suddenly. "Did you decide to go rogue to make things more dramatic? No way this was a spur-of-the-moment idea. It was a *horrible* fucking idea, since I had to pretend I didn't see ten thousand flies crawling over every surface of my house! By some goddamn miracle, I managed to get out of there before they started crawling on me."

It was Adelaide's turn to shake her head. "There's no way there were ten thousand. It's not possible." Her dismissive tone made me want to throttle her. "You must have gotten caught up in the drama of it—fighting with Callum, trying to shield Beatrix from everything."

Another surge of anger coursed through me. "I know what I saw." *And speaking of seeing things . . .* "Why are you even here right now?"

Her eyebrows rose. "Why do you think? To help you clean up. I told you, I got your voicemail."

"I saw you." *Fucking Todd,* I thought but didn't say. "In Cal's bathroom. Through your own little peephole, ironically. What was on your face? Your hands?"

Adelaide gave me a look that I imagined Callum was used to seeing on my own face lately: incredulity bordering on concern. She reached into the pocket of her sweatshirt and held out a strange, reflective object. "Is that what you're talking about?" she asked.

I opened my mouth but nothing came out.

"It's a mirror mask," Adelaide explained. "I got the idea from my cousin. She wears something similar when she deejays." Adelaide held it up, and I shuddered. It was angular, entirely reflective, almost bovine in its angles. Was this what I'd seen from the peephole?

"I figured I'd wear this mask—like I wear all black—whenever I come inside. If Callum ever saw me, he wouldn't see my face, and it wouldn't be game over for the haunting."

I thought of Bea's words the night Adelaide had hidden in Callum's closet: *She didn't have a face! Well, she did, but it was funny and hard to see, like a mirror inside a mirror.* I fucking knew Adelaide had let herself be seen that night.

"What about your hands?" I pressed. "Why was there blood on them?"

She looked at me strangely again and turned her hands over, first one way, then the other. "There was nothing on my hands."

"Fine," I said, attributing what I'd seen to squinting through the peephole for too long, like the random bursts of shapes and colors you experience when rubbing your eyes. Or . . . could it have been some sort of stress-induced hallucination? Was it possible I'd only thought I'd seen blood, like the night I'd shattered the soap dispenser in Callum's bathroom? "Why didn't you tell me you had a direct line of sight into the house?" I asked so that I wouldn't have to ponder whether I was going crazy any longer.

"I can see into a linen closet," Adelaide said dryly. "That hardly counts as spying. And even if it did, it's a strange thing to get mad at me for, seeing as spying is what you've asked me to do from day one."

"Well, maybe I don't want you to do it anymore." The words were out of my mouth too fast. "It's just—"

"Just what?" There was challenge in Adelaide's eyes. *I dare you,* those eyes seemed to say. *I dare you to keep going. To say the words that will end this for me, for you.*

But I didn't care. Maybe we *needed* to end this. At the thought of all our efforts to drive Callum out going to waste, rage unfurled its poisonous petals along the walls of my stomach and up my throat. Rage that I consistently swallowed down and let fester while showing the world a smile, while playing the part of the dutiful wife to a husband who did nothing but make things worse. I knew I was about to unload on Adelaide, but I couldn't stop myself.

"It's *just* that you're not fooling me, Adelaide," I said, my tone thick with venom. "I'm not an idiot. You *said* you wanted Flypocalypse to be like something out of *The Amityville Horror*, so I know you purchased more larvae than you said you did. They weren't even soldier flies. Not all of them, anyway. Remember *black soldier flies*, the ones you said didn't carry diseases? Now I can only hope the house doesn't need to be fumigated or that Bea doesn't get sick!"

I shuddered despite my anger, remembering the feel of the flies' legs on my skin, their bodies—both heavy and strangely weightless at the same time—crashing into my face as I ran down the hallway. "Who does that?" I demanded. "Who goes from offering to help to making things worse?"

"I *am* helping!" Adelaide shouted, her tone somehow both defensive and bewildered. "At least, I'm trying to. I didn't release extra flies, and I don't know what happened to the text, but it was there."

"*Stop lying!*" I shouted back, breathing hard, my eyes so wide I thought they'd pop from my head. Why had Callum's haunting morphed into something different from when we'd started out? Why did it suddenly feel as if I were being haunted too?

When I'd gotten my breathing somewhat under control, I looked at Adelaide. "I saw you," I said.

"Yeah, you keep saying that."

"No," I said, eyes boring into her until she met my gaze. "I saw you . . . with Todd."

Chapter 29

Adelaide stared out the window, her mouth pressed in a thin, bloodless line.

"Adelaide," I pressed, "how long have you been sleeping with him?" She didn't answer. "He had a girlfriend," I said, recalling that first day, talking with him in the driveway. "We were supposed to give her some of our nonexistent animal-bone jewelry."

Adelaide shrugged. "They broke up."

"You told him about the haunting, didn't you? You told him the truth about why we needed the animals."

I thought there might be a chance she hadn't, and if she had, I never expected her to admit it. So when she sighed and nodded, I didn't know what to do.

"Did you tell him about November?" I finally managed. "About what I . . ." I couldn't finish.

Adelaide's face twisted in outrage. "Jesus Christ, Lainey, of course not! I would never tell anyone about that. I swear." She looked hurt, as if the accusation had wounded her. "I barely told him anything. Just that it was a 'teaching your husband a lesson' kind of thing. But, Lainey, he's not going to say anything. He's actually really cool."

"Did you two laugh about it?" I asked. If Adelaide had betrayed me so easily, how deep did the betrayal run? "Did you talk about how ridiculous I am? How pathetic? You're the hero in the story, right? The one with all the wild and hilarious tales of deploying stink bombs and hiding in closets. And I'm the wife who's too weak to leave her husband and too weak to stay without roping her best friend into something crazy. Did you write the note together too?"

Her forehead crinkled. "What note?"

"The fucking blackmail note! What I'm trying to figure out is, did you decide the whole haunting thing was taking too long, that you were sick of hanging around my attic every night when you could be getting it on with a guy who removes dead animals from under people's porches for a living?" Adelaide recoiled as if she'd been slapped. "Or was it Todd's idea?" I continued. "Maybe he found out who Callum's parents are and thought—wrongly, of course—that I might be able to get some of their money for the payout?"

"Wait, seriously? You got a blackmail note?" Adelaide's tone was unreadable.

"Cut the act. I walked past Todd's truck in your driveway. Inside was the same light-blue stationery as the note I got." I studied her face. She looked dazed, maybe even a little ill. "Let's say you weren't part of it," I offered. "Even if you started sleeping with Todd the day after you met him, it's been, what, a couple of weeks? How well do you really know him? Enough to know he wouldn't use what you told him to his own advantage?"

Adelaide shook her head, but she didn't look so sure anymore. "He wouldn't . . . There's no way—" she stammered.

Suddenly, I was so overcome with exhaustion I wanted to cry. No, I wanted to sleep, preferably curled up beside Beatrix, where I could hold her and pretend everything was as wonderful as she was and that the future—*our* future—would be okay.

I wanted many things, but what I wanted most was for Beatrix not to get hurt, for her to be happy and safe. And if that was what I truly wanted, then I knew what I had to do . . .

"We need to take a break from the haunting," I said, and though the idea of giving up filled me with unbridled terror for Beatrix and misery for myself, I knew as soon as the words were out that I'd meant them, and that I'd feel more comfortable if Adelaide's elaborate plans were no longer unfolding behind the scenes, if there were no further opportunities for me to stumble upon masked figures in the mirror or hear about creepy teddy bears migrating around the house.

Adelaide looked rattled. "No. No way. We're so close. You can't do that, Lainey. You can't give up. We have too many things in the works. We have—"

"There's no 'we' in this scenario. Not anymore."

"But what about Bea—"

"This is for Bea. I can't traumatize my daughter to get rid of her father." I sighed. "Maybe it's time to call the number of that lawyer my mother gave me."

"But Cal's parents—"

"Will do everything they can to help him. Rosalie made that perfectly clear. But it's not like they're the Kennedys or have ties to the Mafia. I would have to make sure any lawyer I retained knew what they were dealing with." My voice had a shrill, defensive quality to it; even *I* didn't believe the things I was saying. Still, I stood there stubbornly, refusing to cry no matter how helpless things were. Why couldn't Callum just fucking leave of his own accord and make all my problems go away?

Adelaide shook her head again. "I watch him sometimes, Lainey. Did you know that? From doorways. Windows. The peephole in the attic. He stands in front of the mirror and berates himself. Screams at himself to stop drinking, then goes into the kitchen and makes a drink.

"At first, I felt sorry for him. You know men. They don't want to show their emotions. To admit to weakness. He only shows how he really feels when he thinks there's no one around. But then I started watching him more closely, watched how he's been responding to the haunting. And I'm convinced he's dangerous. Unstable. Erratic. To be honest, I don't know how he still has his job. But if he had custody of Beatrix . . ." She trailed off. Just when I thought she wasn't going to say anything more, she said, "It would be a travesty. And quite possibly, a tragedy."

Now there *were* tears in my eyes. "Even so," I said, "I've got to find another way."

Adelaide stared at me, the challenge and concern in her expression giving way to something I didn't recognize. "Do you know why I want to help you?"

"Huh?"

"Why I want to help. You've never asked. Or, you did ask, but you never pushed." She waited, and I sighed.

"Why do you want to help me?"

"Because I *was* Beatrix. I was a little girl with a shitty alcoholic father. I waited years for my mother to do something about it. My entire childhood, really. But she never did."

I stared, dumbfounded but also annoyed. *She's telling me this now?*

"He died. Cirrhosis. And his alcoholism killed my mom too. Three months later. The stress from years of living with him, of letting his demons run her life."

"I'm sorry, Adelaide. I really am. And I wish you'd told me sooner. But I can't keep doing what we're doing."

We were both quiet for a long time. Finally, Adelaide asked, "You're sure?"

I swallowed. "I'm sure." I glanced at the door behind her. "I need some space. To process everything. You should probably go."

Adelaide glanced out the window, to where the cloud-covered sun had shifted in the sky, the flies littering the sills now in deeper shadow. "At least let me help you—"

"I'll be fine. Seriously. I'll finish cleaning up. We'll talk later or something."

Again, she looked around the room helplessly. I sensed she was waiting for me to say more, but I stayed quiet. Eventually, she let out a small sigh. *You're making a terrible mistake,* it said. All I could do was hope she wasn't right.

And with that, Adelaide walked out of Bea's room, down the stairs, and out of the house, leaving me, what was left of the flies, and all my problems in her wake.

Chapter 30

It poured as I drove across town, a chaotic deluge against the windshield that matched the cacophony in my head. Had I really put a stop to everything we'd been working toward? But each time I wondered if I'd been too hasty, I thought of the blue stationery tucked inside my bag. That, coupled with the memory of Bea—eyes scrunched tight, tiny hands covering her ears as I ran her through the house before she could be assailed by flies—was enough for me to know I'd made the right decision.

I got to my parents' house a few minutes before nine, my exhaustion exacerbated by the chilly rain dampening my clothes. Without an overnight bag of my own, I changed into a dry sweatshirt and sweatpants of my mother's and climbed into bed beside Beatrix. I thought my bone-deep weariness would win out and I'd be asleep the moment my head hit the pillow, but my mind was an endless loop of questions without answers: Was Todd the blackmailer? Was Adelaide in on it? Could she alone be responsible? And, worst of all: Did I make the right decision about the haunting?

I tried to push everything out of my head and focus on Beatrix, but that didn't make things any better. When was the last time we'd spent quality time together? Not in the last month, that was for sure.

But the haunting was over now. No more distractions. I'd resume my role of the parent who was there for Bea no matter what. We'd go on all our favorite adventures—the library, the bookstore, the zoo, the children's museum. We'd explore lighthouses along the coast and hiking trails tucked away in small Rhode Island towns, and bird-watch and paint rocks and spend more time at the barn before her horseback riding lessons. We'd tell ghost stories under the covers and do crafts and write our own picture books.

You were starting to lose yourself. Things were getting crazy. You *were getting crazy. You still need to find a way to make things better, but haunting Callum wasn't it. Starting tomorrow, you'll be better and find a way to get through this that's best for everyone.*

I took comfort from these thoughts, but then another voice—deeper, darker—piped up from somewhere inside me:

You'll find the way that's best for everyone? How'd that work out for you before? How many great—but ultimately futile—ideas did you come up with over the last four years? There's a reason you're feeling down about pulling the plug, and that's because haunting Callum was the final option. Remember how Rosalie looked at you when you said something about Cal's drinking? Like you were a spider that'd fallen into her fancy lunch. And what do powerful people do to inconsequential creatures that step out of line? They squash them. If you try to take out Callum, his family will come for you with lawyers far more cutthroat than the one whose number your mother gave you. Don't forget that.

My dreams were full of giant arachnids that Beatrix and I tried to escape by hiding out in Pinecone House. Instead of fangs or pincers, the giant spiders had teeth made of shards of glass. When I looked harder, I realized the shards were broken vodka bottles.

∞

I woke to an excited Beatrix kissing my face.

"Mommy, Mommy! I wanted you last night. I missed you at bedtime."

"I know, pumpkin. I missed you too. Did you have a fun sleepover?" I kissed her baby-soft cheek. "What would you like to do today? We can do whatever you'd like."

"Anything?"

"Anything. What are you thinking?"

Beatrix chewed her lip, and I bit back a smile. Her face lit up. "I'd like to go to the mansions again!"

"Oh," I said, taken aback. I knew she'd had fun on our last trip, but the preservation of Newport's architectural heritage wasn't high on a lot of four-year-olds' to-do lists. "Are you sure, sweetheart? We could go to the children's museum or the bike path or—"

"You said whatever I liked," Beatrix said, not impetuously but curiously, as if confused as to why I was pushing back.

"You're right. I did say that." I ruffled her sleep-tousled hair. "The mansions it is, then. Shall we go to a different one this time? Maybe the Elms? Or the Carriage House? You could see where they kept the horses."

"Could we go to Pinecone Hou—" she started, then realized her mistake. "I mean, Marble House." She blushed. "Since it's where we got the idea for our fort?"

"Not only can we go to Marble House, but guess what I saw in the gift shop the other day? Handmade ornaments, including . . . pinecones! As well as carved birds, angels playing flutes, all sorts of cool stuff. If we can't find something new to hang from Pinecone House's rafters, I *know* we'll get ideas for some new crafts."

Beatrix's eyes lit up, but I could tell there was something on her mind, something she was yet to relay as far as how she wanted the day to unfold. Probably she figured if she mentioned ice cream now, it would become an unalterable part of the "plan." Still, I would tread lightly, and pray she hadn't seen more of Flypocalypse than I'd realized.

"Is there something else?" I asked. "Something more you want to say?"

Bea nodded but remained silent.

"Go ahead, honey. You can ask me anything."

"Not this."

A tiny knife pierced my heart. "Of course you can." I wanted to say more but didn't want to force her into telling me. Better to stay calm and quiet until she was ready.

"Umm, well . . . if we're going to go to the mansions and have a nice family day together, I want Daddy to come."

I inhaled so sharply I started coughing. "Your dad?" I said after I could breathe normally, stalling for time. Beatrix nodded.

What should I say? Where was this coming from? Was her request really that surprising? Beatrix was sensitive, discerning, diplomatic, and overwhelmingly sweet. Even with everything I'd done to shield her, not just from the haunting but from her father's behavior, there was no way she hadn't observed, maybe even *absorbed*, some of the chaos. Bea needed to feel safe, and what other way to ensure a four-year-old she was safe than to surround her with the known, the familiar? I couldn't rip apart Bea's fantasy.

"Well," I said, "that would be nice. Let me call Daddy and see what he says." I lifted Bea off the bed. "I hear Gram downstairs. Why don't you use the potty, then run down to see her? I bet she'll make you a waffle and maybe even some bacon."

"A waffle with strawberries?"

"If you ask politely."

Beatrix scampered toward the bathroom. A minute later, her footfalls pattered down the stairs.

I forced my fingers to wrap around my phone, despite feeling like a concrete block was weighing down my arm. Was I really about to do this? Would he answer? If he answered, would he say yes? What were the odds he'd come sober and not embarrass me or disappoint Beatrix?

I looked down at my phone. No point putting it off. I navigated to my favorites, where Callum's name and number still occupied the top listing. Taking a breath, I pressed send on the call and listened to it ring.

I was about to hang up when Callum answered, sounding tired and out of breath but surprisingly sober.

I didn't bother with hello. "Beatrix wants me to take her to the mansions, but she asked if I'd call and see if you wanted to come with us."

Suddenly, the phone was trilling with a request to accept a FaceTime call. I watched my expression on the screen, saw my lips curdle into a frown as I hit the button to accept.

"Why FaceTime?" I asked.

"I wanted to see if you were messing with me."

I rolled my eyes. "I'm not messing with you, Callum." I swallowed a rude retort. "Like I said, Bea asked me to call you. Do you want to come or not?"

"Yes," he said without hesitation, and my eyes widened in surprise.

"You're not golfing?"

"I was supposed to play yesterday, remember? I didn't have a tee time scheduled for today, and it was too late to get one."

"You're not playing another course?" *Or going to the bar?* I added in my head.

"Nah." He said it in a way that made me think he couldn't get a last-minute tee time at another course either, but I kept that to myself.

"So you'll come? This is happening?"

"I'm coming," he said, and adjusted the phone, giving me a glimpse of what was behind him. In an instant, I remembered he was at Monty's, and the reality of what was actually going on coalesced into a cold, unpalatable truth.

"Are you coming because you want to spend time with your daughter or because you think the house is haunted and don't want to go back there today?" *Are you sure you don't want to not go back there at all?* I thought ruefully. *Like, forever?*

"Can't it be both?"

"Jesus Christ, Callum, no, it can't be both, because the house is not fucking haunted." *Not anymore, anyway.*

Callum pursed his lips "It is, whether or not you want to believe it."

"Like when the furniture kept moving but stopped right when Bea and I walked in?" I asked sarcastically.

"I'm serious. But either way, I said I'm coming. What's the plan? I assume you're at your parents'?"

"Bea and I will pick you up in an hour. And Callum? If you're drunk when we get there, don't bother coming out. I won't let you in the car. You got that?"

Callum's lips pursed again. "I got it."

I hung up before he could say anything more.

◦ ∽ ◦

I pulled into Monty's driveway an hour later to find Callum dressed and—at least for now—sober. He stood before Monty's open garage, and I saw the random detritus associated with single-guy living. The storage bins and bags of old video game controllers, the dented surfboard and air hockey table, the cornhole boards and Wiffle ball bats leaning against the dusty walls.

A memory surfaced without warning: Callum, in his apartment, asking me to move in with him. I'd looked around the space skeptically, noting the unhung football championship banners and stray golf clubs, a gym bag exploding with clothes and kitchen gadgets still in boxes.

When I'd tried to point out—gently—that there was hardly room for me, let alone my things, Callum had begun grabbing random items and throwing them onto the front lawn—a beanbag chair, several fishing poles, a potted spider plant more dead than alive, and hand-me-down records that lacked a turntable—insisting he'd always make space for me in his life. The earnestness of the moment had given way to hilarity as more things ended up on the lawn. He'd been about to throw a winter duvet into the pile when I grabbed it away from him and laid it on the floor. We'd spent the rest of the night there, giggling, making love, and talking. The next day, I moved in. We'd lived together, if no longer sharing inside jokes, ever since.

I shied away from the thought, away from the memories, and turned to regard Beatrix. There was an air of nervous excitement around her, and I was overcome with relief that Callum was sober, glad he hadn't immediately put me in a position where I had to burst Bea's bubble. He paused at the passenger door, and I tightened my hands around the wheel, believing he was about to make a fuss about wanting to drive.

He reconsidered and opened the door. "Hi, girls."

Hi, girls. Just like that. Like everything was fine. The nerve Callum possessed shouldn't surprise me, not with Rosalie Taylor as his mother. But then Bea's happy, albeit tentative, smile beamed out at us from the back seat, and I knew if someone was going to ruin her day, it wouldn't be me. Cal would go back to drinking tonight or tomorrow or the next day, that much was sure, but I could join him in his denial for one day if it meant giving Bea a chance to feel normal.

I parked in the lot near Marble House, and we walked across the pavement toward the stately building. I refrained from giving them the tour-guide spiel.

"Why are all these people here?" Bea asked.

I laughed. "Last time we came, the mansions were closed to get ready for a new exhibit, remember, sweetie?"

Callum opened his mouth then closed it, but I knew what he'd wanted to say. He wanted to ask when we'd come, maybe even why we hadn't invited him. He wanted to ask if we'd had fun or if Bea had missed him. He was probably also keen to know what else we'd been up to without him in the recent months, or even the last few years. Instead, he said nothing, but I could tell it was a struggle to swallow it down, the shame and regret, the annoyance and anger.

Maybe I was giving him too much credit. Maybe he wasn't experiencing anything close to these emotions. Maybe he never did. Worse to contemplate was that maybe he never would. I could only hope there was something left of the person I used to know, the person I'd fallen in love with, not because I wanted to mend things with him but because I wanted, *needed*, him to help me do the right thing for our daughter.

So he said nothing. And I said nothing. And Beatrix chattered on. We walked toward the mansion like we were walking into the past, Callum and I each holding one of Beatrix's hands.

Chapter 31

I dumped pasta into the boiling water, humming along to the song drifting from the Echo on the other side of the kitchen. In the two weeks since I'd told Adelaide the haunting was over, the smart speaker had become a welcome addition to the house, providing us with everything from the day's weather to songs that inspired impromptu dance-offs. Even Callum seemed to have forgiven the device for its initial—albeit manipulated—volatility, asking it to set cooking timers or reminders to take out the trash.

I hunted for a jar of marinara sauce in the cabinet and set the table for one. Bea was exhausted from an afternoon at the aquarium and had requested an early dinner so she could rest with her stories in bed.

I was tired too, and had asked Callum if he wanted to order takeout after Bea fell asleep. He'd offered to cook instead, citing the pizza dough in the fridge that he wanted to use before it went bad. He was down in the basement now, searching for a pizza oven I'd given him for Christmas several years ago and that he'd never unboxed. I stirred Bea's pasta and tried to take things one minute at a time. Even two weeks later, it felt strange to sit with Callum at the dinner table.

Attributing the sense of tranquility that had settled over the house to the culmination of the haunting felt trite, but against every expectation I'd had, Callum had not had a drink since the day of the flies. We'd been talking regularly, even civilly, and while I maintained he still needed help, needed to put actual safeguards to his sobriety in place, I'd been feeling my mindset shift from "waiting for the other shoe to drop" to cautious optimism. *Extremely* cautious optimism. Still, being able to discuss the idea of outpatient counseling or our need for groceries without the conversation devolving into a fight was a new and entirely welcome development.

I set Bea's bowl of pasta on a place mat and was about to call for her when Callum's footsteps pounded up the basement stairs. When he pushed open the door, he looked perplexed and a little annoyed.

"It's not down there." He scratched his neck.

"Really? Are you sure?"

"I looked everywhere. I think it might be up in the attic."

Every muscle in my body went still. "No," I said, hoping I sounded merely certain as opposed to cagey. "I wouldn't have put it in the attic."

Callum raised an eyebrow as if to say, *Are you sure?* and my stomach sank further because he was right; if the oven *was* in the attic, it wouldn't have been him who had put it there. Had I dragged it through the trapdoor after surmising Callum was never going to use it? I racked my brain, trying to remember if I'd seen the pizza oven on any of my excursions into the attic, but all I could picture was the broken remains of mirror and Adelaide's belongings centered around the peephole.

I swallowed around the hard, painful lump in my throat and tried to sound convincing when I said, "Seriously, Cal, there's no way it's up there."

"I'm going to check." He pulled his sneakers from the closet.

"Let me do it." I wiped my hands on a dish towel and wrangled my hair into a ponytail.

But Callum shook his head. "Get Bea fed. I know how tired she is. Besides, I saw that new organizer you got for her closet. That's a pretty convenient stepladder into the attic." He finished tying his shoes and started down the hallway. "Be right back."

I hadn't been in the attic—or spoken to Adelaide—since the day we'd ceased the haunting, but the recorder batteries would be dead by now, and Adelaide's slippers and blanket wouldn't stand out among the piles of insulation. I would have removed her things, but the idea of then having to contact her to return them was beyond what I wanted to deal with. And I still didn't want Callum up there, worried that the moment he pulled himself into that space, some bubble of safety would be popped, and all the negative energy and toxic melodrama that'd occurred during the haunting would be released back into the house, flowing along the same channels that the guitar chords and rotten smells had.

Since there was no way to stop him, I did the only thing I could do, which was to call after him, "Send Bea down for her dinner." Then, on numb feet, I went to butter Bea a slice of bread to go with her pasta, my hands shaking more than I cared to admit.

Bea chattered cheerfully as she ate, and I strained to hear not just to the second floor, but to the attic. Aside from Callum's muffled footsteps—he was heavier than Adelaide and unable to navigate the plywood and joists with anything close to the stealth she'd managed—I heard nothing. No grunts of displeasure or confusion, no cries of surprise or dismay. Only a full minute of silence from above us, during which my brow and lower back pricked uncomfortably with sweat.

"Want to play Favorite Thing?" Bea prompted.

"Oh, um . . ." I mumbled. "One second, honey." I continued listening for any sound that meant Callum was returning, but no such sound came. "Let me get you something to drink," I said, so I could avoid the game in lieu of the reprieve walking to the fridge and retrieving a can of seltzer would afford me.

It worked. By the time I was turning back toward Beatrix, I heard Callum drop from the attic to the floor above us. I waited for his feet on the stairs, but there was only more silence. Had he seen something of Adelaide's? Something of mine that made him suspicious? What was taking him so long? I opened Bea's seltzer and sat on the stool beside her. Finally, Callum came downstairs.

He stepped into the kitchen, the overhead lights illuminating his face, and I saw his slack jaw and pallid complexion. Steeling myself for the answer, I forced my mouth to form the words: "Did you find it?"

Callum shook his head.

"What's wrong?" If he'd seen something related to the haunting, I'd expect anger or disbelief, not this cold contemplation and quiet dismay. "Callum?" I pressed. Beatrix had yet to notice anything was amiss and was licking butter off her bread with gusto.

"Do you remember"—he paused, swallowed, blinked—"the mirror?"

"The mirror?" I parroted, stalling for time. I could understand if Callum were surprised at seeing the broken mirror again; likely he'd believed it long gone. But why would he care that, rather than putting it out with the trash the morning after the housewarming party, I'd squirreled it up to the attic? Why did he look as if he'd seen a ghost?

"The mirror." Callum's voice was monotone, even robotic, as if repeating something he'd been turning over in his head. "The mirror from the housewarming party. The one that . . ." He trailed off, his eyes darting around the room as if looking for something in the corners.

"Yes," I said, still not understanding. "The broken one. I remember." I searched his arms, his hands. "You didn't cut yourself on it, did you?"

Slowly, almost as if it caused him great pain, Callum shook his head. "I saw . . ."

Beatrix tossed what was left of her bread onto her plate. "Do you want to play Favorite Thing, Daddy? Remember the rules: It has to be funny and pretend!"

"I saw . . ." Callum said again. He closed his eyes and chewed his bottom lip.

"What did you see?" I pressed.

He blinked as he stared past me. Finally, he focused on my face. "Remember the figure in the hallway? The one I told you about? I opened my door and there was someone standing right there. But it wasn't an intruder; it was like my own shadow had separated from the rest of my body and kept on walking, down the hall, where it disappeared into the darkness." He continued to stare, his eyes pleading. "Do you remember?"

I tried to keep my expression neutral but knew I was failing. "You never told me that," I said. Then, because Beatrix was looking at him with a mixture of worry and fear, I nudged him. "It sounds like a really wild case of Favorite Thing, though... Maybe you want to tell Beatrix the part where it gets funny? Since you already have the pretend part."

Callum blinked again and licked his lips, his eyes coming to rest on Beatrix, who was looking at him expectantly. As if breaking out of a trance, his eyes lost their glazed-over quality, and he shook himself like a great, pensive bird.

"Right," he said, still looking at Beatrix. "Sorry. Right, my Favorite Thing. So, after I saw my own shadow"—he thought for a moment—"I jumped out the window and followed Peter Pan, Wendy, and the Lost Boys into Neverland. We flew around for hours, fought Captain Hook and, um, a ticking crocodile, and had tea with Tinker Bell. And that," he said with theatrical finality, "was my Favorite Thing. Was that a good one?"

Beatrix clapped her hands. "Yes, Daddy. *Great*."

Callum nodded, but he still looked distracted.

"Do you want me to check the garage for the pizza oven?" I asked.

He shook his head. "Maybe ordering takeout is a good idea after all. Chinese okay? I'll call." His gaze slid sluggishly toward the short hall to the staircase. "I know you wanted to shower. I can help Bea finish dinner."

I still didn't like the way he looked, but I *had* wanted a shower since coming home from the aquarium. "Yeah. Okay. Thanks." I looked at Beatrix "When you're done, have Daddy help with your pajamas, okay?"

I kissed her cheek and started from the kitchen, but turned by the coffee bar and regarded Callum again. He was staring at nothing, eyes glassy.

"Cal," I said, "seriously, are you okay?"

He nodded weakly, then seemed to pull himself together. "Sorry," he said again. "I must be hungrier than I thought. I'll call for the food."

In the shower a few minutes later, I tried to relax but couldn't get Callum's strange reaction to the attic—no, the *mirror*—out of my head. I recalled how he'd trailed off in the kitchen: *I saw* . . . And then that bizarre story about seeing someone step out from his own body and into the hall. What the hell had he seen? Some sort of dream? And why had he thought he'd told me about it already?

Duh, Lainey, I said to myself as I turned off the water. *Because alcohol.*

Alcohol.

I froze. Had seeing the mirror all these years later reminded him of why he'd smashed it in the first place? Of what he'd seen on that long-ago spring day? Or—and this was a thought too dark to comprehend—had he simply been confronted with the history of his alcoholism at a time when he was still too vulnerable to properly cope with it?

I hurried to get dressed, throwing on the same white leggings and white sweater as before. I was reaching for the bathroom door when I heard it: a garble of voices coming through the bathroom window, floating up from the back deck.

Heart thudding, I went to the window and peered out. Callum, swaying on the deck, a tall, glistening glass in his hand. Beatrix, riding her bike in jerky, wobbling circles, her stuffed koala poking out of the basket.

As Bea rode around, looking increasingly out of control, she lifted her head and said something to her father. He said something back and waved his hand. Their words were lost to me through glass and distance, but Bea's fear was not. Nor was the horrifying reality that she wasn't wearing her helmet.

I didn't wait; I turned from the window and sprinted from the bathroom, down the stairs, and through the kitchen, blood whooshing through my ears. At the door to the deck, I could still see them, still see *her*, little feet pumping, handlebars jerking wildly. I didn't want to call out too soon and startle her. She was too close to the deck rail. *That damnable broken deck rail!*

I gripped the door, my body as cold as if I'd plunged through ice and into arctic water. As I slid the door open, Callum again spoke to

Beatrix. In response, she cut left, then tried to overcompensate and cut hard to the right.

I tried to scream, but the words lodged in my throat, and even if I'd been able to, I wasn't sure Bea had the reflexes to squeeze her brakes that quickly. She was careening toward the splintered rail like a runaway railcar, the curls of her ponytail bouncing along behind her. The thing I'd been fearing for the past year was going to happen right in front of me, unless I did something to stop it. On legs that felt weighed down by concrete blocks, I willed myself to take two giant steps forward. Then I launched myself into the air in a desperate bid to reach Bea's back tire.

If I'd managed two more inches, my fingers would have jammed into the spokes and stopped her, mangling my hand in the process. I would have taken a hundred mangled hands if it meant stopping the horrible thing set in motion. Instead, my fingers grazed the rubber of her back tire as the front one cleared the lip of the deck and dropped forward. The rest of the bike—and Bea—barreled through the railing as if it were paper. Again, I tried to scream, landing on the deck with a crash that sent shock waves through my rib cage and the air shooting out of me. I crawled forward, silvery stars exploding across my vision, and peered over the edge of the deck.

Six feet below, Bea lay on the ground, her body crumpled and unmoving. The earth tilted on its axis and so did the deck, spilling me over its side to the dirt. Again, I hit the ground with a bone-jarring thud, but this time, instead of getting the wind knocked out of me, the pain spread, sharpened, angry and vicious.

I pushed myself up on one elbow to find a large splinter stuck deep into my left wrist. It must have gone straight into the vein, for blood gushed from the wound. I pushed the pain away and rolled onto my side to place my good hand on Beatrix.

I knew I couldn't move her in case she had a head injury, so I cradled her as best I could, pulled my phone from the side pocket of my leggings, and dialed. I ignored the sound of movement above me. Asking him for help, letting him anywhere near her, would be like asking the man with a can of gasoline hidden behind his back for help putting out the fire.

    I waited while the clouds and the fern fronds in the breeze and the kazooing of a mourning dove's feathers streaked away like paint chased from the bottom of a sink. In a world without color or sound, my blood hit the dirt, my fingers stroked Bea's cheek, and my eyes saw everything and nothing at once.

Chapter 32

The beeps and whirs of the machines disoriented me, tricking me into thinking I was hearing the mind-numbing trills and sonic booms of Callum's video game. If I kept my eyes closed, I could travel to the place inside me where those noises lived, to the living room of my mind. From there, I could make my way up the stairs to Bea's room, find her leaning over a raised planter, her hands wrapped around the painted body of a wise-looking wooden tortoise, a smile on her sweet and trusting face.

In the house in my mind, where all my hopes and dreams for my daughter lived and grew, I believed Bea to be as insulated from the dangers of the outside world as if she were in an actual fairy garden, protected by magic. But then, as I watched, the faces of friendly trees and wise owls grew pinched and twisted. Toadstool cottages moldered around the gnomes within them, and animals lay in discarded heaps of glass and plaster. Above the poison garden, the little girl who'd once watched over them was gone. Even in my mind, the place in which I kept Bea safe was haunted.

I opened my eyes, and the vision disintegrated, not gently like dandelion seeds but like dust motes before a vacuum. Bea lay in a hospital bed, her face as milk-white as the bedsheets shrouding her body, her dirt-marred koala bear tucked beside her head. A purple cast cocooned her left wrist, and her head was wrapped, mummy-like, around the bumps and cuts she'd sustained. What the wispy gauze wouldn't help, the doctor had informed me, was the concussion Beatrix had suffered in the fall.

Speaking of the doctor, how much time had passed since I'd seen her? In the stillness of the room, time was like wax that pooled around a lit candle, accumulating and persisting as much as burning away. I felt as if Bea and I had been deserted at the bottom of the ocean after being thrown overboard by a cruel and negligent captain.

I shifted where I sat, the gauze around my wrist tight and uncomfortable. The nurses had tried to convince me to remain in my own hospital bed across the hall but had decided to "expedite discharge proceedings" when it became clear I wouldn't accept being away from Beatrix. I wouldn't even use the bathroom in the back corner without leaving the door open, too worried about who might storm into Bea's room if I wasn't there to stop them.

It wouldn't be Callum, of that I was certain. Callum wouldn't come to the hospital until he was sober enough to pass a breathalyzer, which would be late tomorrow morning at the earliest. He'd told the EMTs he'd be right behind the ambulance in his truck, but that, of course, was a lie, and everyone present had known it. This time, sleeping it off wasn't only preferable, it'd be legally necessary. I wasn't sure how Callum had gotten so drunk in such a short amount of time, short of some frat party–worthy guzzling . . . or something supernatural. No, it wasn't Callum I feared would materialize in Bea's hospital room doorway . . . It was someone whose motivations I dreaded far more.

Sometime after the last of Bea's neurological tests had concluded, Bea's door had opened again, revealing a young woman in colorful scrubs. The woman had been jumpy and on edge and had looked down the hall both ways before closing the door behind her.

"Lainey. Lainey Taylor, right? I'm Veronica Schumann."

At my blank expression, she added, "Adelaide Benson's ex-girlfriend. Listen, I'm not supposed to be in here, and I can't stay. Joey de la Cruz, one of the EMTs who brought you in, he called in a report to

DCYF against your husband. Joey spoke with the doctor who saw you in the ER to let them know it had been done."

"DCYF?"

"Sorry, Department of Children, Youth, and Families."

She must have realized I was still having a hard time following, because she asked, "Lainey? Do you understand what I've told you so far?"

I nodded, but my brain was both on fire with questions and numb with fear. Was this good for my long-term plan to divorce Callum or bad for Beatrix overall?

"Okay," Veronica continued, "because the next part is very important. About forty minutes ago, your mother-in-law walked into the hospital. She disappeared into a room with the ER doctor who treated you and Beatrix when you arrived, and when she came out, she looked as high and mighty as ever. Gossip spreads in an emergency room like nowhere else, and from what I've heard, Rosalie forced the doc to give her the name of the EMT who called in the report." She stared hard at me, letting that information sink in.

"I don't know what's going to happen next," she said, looking over her shoulder to the door, "but if I had to guess, I'd say Joey is going to find himself embroiled in some sort of slander case. Either that, or the whole thing will disappear like it never happened."

And with that, Veronica turned and put her hand on the door.

"Wait," I said, my voice panicked, "why did you tell me all this? What am I supposed to do?"

She paused, hand still hovering over the door handle, and sighed. "Dating Adelaide is a one-way ticket to Crazy-town, but she's a good person, and she thinks the world of you. I don't know what you're supposed to do next, but this is as far as I can go. Maybe Adelaide can help you think of something. We all know what a goddamn evil genius she is when it comes to solving problems."

I sat beside Bea's bed, Veronica's words echoing in my ears, and picked up my phone for what seemed like the hundredth time since the doctors removed the spike of wood from my wrist. I kept telling myself it wasn't the right call, not yet, but with each new weighing of the pros and cons, I was landing less on the side of caution and more on the side of *It's the only way.*

Bea stirred, and I jumped, the stitches in my wrist tweaking painfully. Her eyes fluttered, then opened. I slid forward on my seat and readjusted my grip on her hand.

"Mommy," Bea said.

"I'm here, baby. Are you okay? Are you in pain?" I started to stand, to look for the call button, but she gave me a half smile.

"Nothing hurts. I'm tired."

"Okay. Okay, that's good, baby."

She looked down at the cast on her wrist. "I like the purple, Mommy." Her voice was soft, somehow more babyish than the way she usually sounded.

"Do you, my love? I picked it out for you while you were . . ." *Unconscious.* ". . . asleep."

Her eyes traveled down to the gauze around my wrist. "We have matching Band-Aids."

"We do, sweetheart. And we're both going to be fine."

She looked around the room, and I sensed her question before she asked it.

"He's not here," I said.

Her gray-gold eyes held mine, and she nodded.

"And when you're discharged, I'm taking you to Gram and Papa's." I smoothed the curls poking out of the bandage around her head. "At least for now. So I can figure out what to do about him." This was the closest we'd ever come to talking about her father's problem, but we couldn't be the family that shied away from the truth. Not anymore. Callum had crossed a line—again—that there was no coming back from. There'd be no more pretending, not just on my part, but on Bea's, that he was a capable, if uninvolved, father.

"He made me ride my bike," Beatrix said, and I froze, both needing and not wanting to hear what she was going to say. "I didn't want to," she continued. "I wanted to put my pajamas on and get in bed, like you said. He said that it was his fault I could ride a horse and not a bike and that he had to teach me."

Her beautiful eyes filled with tears, and my heart seized, the sensation so sharp I drew in a breath. "Oh, honey, it *is* his fault, but not in the way he thinks. He couldn't make up for all the time he hadn't spent teaching you to ride a bike in one evening. And it was also his fault that he didn't fix that railing. But I don't want you to worry about the things that are Daddy's fault. Daddy has to worry about Daddy. I need to worry about you."

I stood and pulled Beatrix to my chest. Her cast knocked painfully into my arm, but the pain felt good, awakening the dark and ugly things within me, clearing my mind of everything but love for my daughter and a fierce, primal need to protect her.

Bea's eyes were drifting closed. I leaned down and kissed her. "You sleep, honey. The next time you wake, we'll be almost out of here."

She sighed in the way she did at home before sleep took her. "When we get to Gram and Papa's, can they sign my cast?"

"Of course," I replied. I kept thinking she was asleep, but each time I responded, her eyes fluttered open again.

"And then what?" she asked.

"And then . . ." I paused, and realized I knew what would come next. Had known since the moment I'd watched Adelaide storm out of Beatrix's room the afternoon of Flypocalypse. Because there'd been no moment over the last two weeks during which I truly believed Callum was on the path to somewhere better. There'd been only a breathless, pregnant waiting for him to return to the path on which he'd always been.

Pausing the haunting hadn't been an end to Adelaide's grand plan. It'd only been a way to regroup, to catch our breath before a storm for which we'd need all our skill and cunning. That Callum had hurt Beatrix during that period of waiting was something for which I'd never forgive myself.

"Then what?" Beatrix asked again, her voice small in the hospital room, and I leaned down and pressed my cheek to hers.

"Then Mommy will make everything better."

Bea drifted off in the wake of my answer. Grimacing through the pain in my wrist—and my heart—I pulled my phone from my leggings and found the number I needed.

She picked up on the very first ring.

Chapter 33

I awoke to my phone's vibrating alarm in the middle of the night but lay there for several minutes, listening to Bea's comforting, rhythmic breathing. When I knew I could delay no longer, I gritted my teeth against the pain in my wrist and slid from the bed. The mattress in my parents' guest room was new and mercifully quiet.

I dressed—in all black as opposed to my usual white—and crept down the stairs, shoes in hand, then went to the window at the back of the house. Sliding it open and climbing through it onto the deck took no more than thirty seconds. After that, it was another minute to the road. Two minutes after that, headlights spilled over the rain-slicked pavement, and Adelaide pulled up beside me.

She was dressed in a vinyl rain slicker, strands of fuchsia hair poking out from beneath the hood.

"Hey," she said.

"Hey."

We didn't say much after that. Everything had been said on the phone when Bea and I had still been in the hospital. Apologies. Explanations. Plans. Goals.

"I have to tell you something," Adelaide said suddenly.

So maybe everything hadn't been said. "What's that?"

"It's about Todd."

I turned to look at her so quickly, the muscles in my neck twinged. Adelaide saw the anxious expression on my face and shook her head.

"*I* had nothing to do with the note. But I decided I couldn't say with nearly as much certainty that he had nothing to do with it either. So, I ended things with him. I wanted you to know."

I sighed and stared out the windshield. "I thought it'd feel good to hear you say that, but it doesn't. Not entirely. Maybe it's because without Veronica, and the fact that she obviously has a ton of respect for you, I would never have known that Rosalie was already on her way to squashing the DCYF report." I glanced at Adelaide. "It took guts for her to do that. I'm sorry things didn't work out between the two of you. And I'm sorry things didn't work out with Todd. Maybe he was great too."

"Maybe he wasn't," Adelaide countered.

I stayed silent.

"Do we need to go over the plan again?" Adelaide asked.

I shook my head. "I don't think so. I don't want to overthink things. Besides, we're at the cul-de-sac."

"We can talk in the woods."

"No way. Too risky. We've got this," I said, more to convince myself than her. She handed me a pair of plastic bags and two rubber bands, and we went to work covering our sneakers. Adelaide swapped out her rain jacket for a thin black sweatshirt and donned a backpack. I pulled a second backpack over my shoulders.

Trekking through the woods at two in the morning should have been tough, but Adelaide was beyond proficient at navigating the route in the dark. We made it to the fence behind my pool in under ten minutes. We were both in all black, but it hardly mattered. There were no lights on around the garage or over the deck, nor were any of the ground-floor interior lights on inside the house.

We rounded the back of the property, Adelaide holding the ladder over one shoulder. Aside from the soft rustling of the bags around our sneakers, I don't think any nocturnal creature could have been any quieter.

Adelaide propped the ladder against the house below Bea's bedroom and agilely climbed the rungs. Once inside, we removed the bags from our sneakers, stuffed them to the bottom of the trash can in the corner, and took off our shoes. We slipped off our backpacks and unzipped them. From mine came two towel-wrapped bundles and a small insulated cooler. The six candles at the bag's bottom I left for removal downstairs. Adelaide also left supplies in her backpack, but she did unearth one item, obscured with a towel, and placed it by the doorway. Then she climbed up the organizer in Bea's closet and disappeared into the attic.

She was gone for less than a minute, and when she dropped back into the closet, her movements as natural as a cat's, she gave me a thumbs-up.

"Let's go down," she mouthed.

I picked up the cooler. At the top of the stairs, I left it by the banister.

We crept downstairs and into the kitchen, where we again shrugged out of our backpacks. Adelaide checked that the Echo was plugged in and the volume was all the way up. I swapped the six candles from my bag for the six candles that had been sitting at the center of the island for the last month. Adelaide removed another towel-covered item from her backpack and walked it into the playroom. In the living room, I found the remote and followed the instructions on a frayed piece of notebook paper.

I met Adelaide in the kitchen, where she returned the towel—now free from the item beneath it—to her backpack. We consulted the checklist on the other side of the frayed paper and found it complete. Adelaide took a lighter from her back pocket and lit the candles. Then we crept back upstairs.

At the top, we exchanged a look. This next part would be the most difficult. I took a breath. Adelaide raised an eyebrow.

"Serial killer confidence," she whispered.

"Serial killer confidence," I whispered back, and picked up the cooler.

Quieter than flies, quieter than disappointment or suppressed rage, we tiptoed past Callum, asleep in his bed, and into his bathroom. I climbed onto the vanity. Onto the wall above the mirror I pressed three small adhesive-backed hooks. Adelaide gave me a thumbs-up to let me know they were obscured by the light fixtures. She reached into the cooler and lifted out the bag. I held my breath, praying the thin material of the bag wouldn't burst. I managed to take it from her hands and lift it above the mirror, where I suspended it from the three small hooks.

It was large enough to hang down slightly below the top of the mirror, but that was what we wanted. Once I was confident with its position, I gave Adelaide my own thumbs-up. She went to the closet and reached above the washing machine for the line of fishing wire she'd threaded through the peephole earlier. She walked it the short distance across the bathroom and handed it to me.

I attached the tiny adhesive at the end of the polyethylene line to the bag above the mirror. Its trajectory from the peephole to the bag was perfect. Not loose enough for Callum to notice, and not taut enough to break the bag. I gave everything a once-over, including pressing one last time on the adhesive of the hooks, then climbed down. Adelaide switched the flashlight off. We tiptoed out of the bathroom and walked down the hall into Beatrix's room.

"Ready?" Adelaide mouthed.

I wasn't, but it was now or never.

"Ready," I mouthed back to Adelaide.

Chapter 34

I crouched at the far end of my office, open backpack at my feet and eyes on my phone. This was the part I didn't like, but Adelaide insisted we needed to be connected for this to work. I made sure the brightness of my screen was all the way up and my volume was a little above a full mute.

A moment later, the FaceTime call came through. I answered. The screen was dark, but I could make out Adelaide's face, as well as the cereal boxes and cans of soup on the pantry shelves behind her. The orientation of the camera changed, and now I was looking at the door of the pantry. The door opened a crack, and Adelaide held the phone to it.

"Can you see everything you need to?" she whispered. "Kitchen, living room, playroom through the French doors?"

"Yes," I whispered back.

"Okay. It's showtime."

The FaceTime screen went gray, and I knew she had opened her Alexa app, still connected to the Echo in my kitchen. My heart beat wildly. A moment later, the same song that had unexpectedly blared from the smart speaker that first night of the haunting hit my ears, both through the phone's speaker and up through the walls of the house in a disorienting, echoey wail.

For two and a half minutes, I hardly breathed. Might Callum be so drunk he would sleep through the music? Or so scared he remained in his bed, hiding under the covers and rendering all our preparations moot? But then I heard his door open across the hall followed by footsteps on the stairs. Blood thrumming in my temples, I raced out of the office, across the hall, and into Callum's bedroom. I positioned myself at the center of the room, above the island in the kitchen, and took the last two items out of my backpack. A few seconds after that, I saw movement in the frame of Adelaide's phone. Bright light from the overheads joined the weak candlelight, and Callum stood in his boxers, hand still on the switch, his eyes wide and watery.

He stared at the Echo on the coffee bar as if a wild animal had gotten into the kitchen. The song was nearing its conclusion when Callum finally lurched toward the smart speaker and ripped the cord from its side. The house was plunged into silence. No, not silence; Callum's heavy breathing whooshed through the phone.

He turned and, for the first time since coming downstairs, seemed to notice the flickering candles on the island. He stomped in that direction, and I said a silent thank-you I'd set the timer two minutes later than I'd initially planned. Callum was blowing out the final candle when the television blared to life in the living room. Again, the twangy, eerie guitar floated from the speaker and through the floorboards simultaneously.

Where the hell do I know that song from? I thought. *And why is it always the one Adelaide chooses to play?*

Callum whirled away from the island, and I saw the terror and uncertainty on his face as he turned toward the hall. A second later, the screen went dark. Again, I held my breath. However long it took Callum to get to the living room and find the remote was as long as Adelaide would have to exit the pantry, relight the candles, trip the sensor on the object in the playroom, and return to her hiding place, all without being seen. Time bloated into an abstract thing. The song stopped as abruptly as it started.

The picture on the screen jerked, and I was looking back through the sliver in the pantry door. Callum stood in the entrance to the kitchen from the hallway, staring at the relit candles with abject horror. Before he could decide if blowing them out a second time would be prudent, a guttural chanting started from the playroom, whispers layered upon screams layered upon whispers, the language strange and indecipherable. The chanting was not loud enough to hear from one floor away, but it was chilling enough through the speaker alone.

Adelaide tilted the phone as Callum batted at the light switch beside the playroom, but the angle wasn't quite right, and I still saw a tilted view of the kitchen. I knew Callum was face-to-face with one of two identical, recordable teddy bears with light-up eyes, the other of which was in my backpack, but I'd yet to see them for myself; Adelaide had programmed the bears with a track from some horror sound-effects channel on YouTube, set the track to begin after forty-five seconds of silence, and wrapped the stuffed animals in black towels to cover their sensors, all without me being present. From the sound of it, Bear Number One was doing its job.

I was so fixated on Callum's high-pitched screams, I almost forgot it was time to employ the magnets. Hastily, I lifted the two high-powered cylinders, pulled the protective caps off their north poles, and slammed them into the floor. The sound of the six candles with magnetized bottoms shooting up to the ceiling was like a series of firecrackers. I knew hot wax had to be shooting all over the kitchen, but the house not going up in flames—and pulling this off without getting caught—were far more important. Adelaide had sworn the flames would go out as the candles rose, that they'd done so on a test run, but who could know for sure?

I left the magnets in place while I listened to Callum's primal shouts of fear. Then I turned, placed one foot on the footboard of Cal's bed, and used my body weight to knock first one magnet, then the other, onto its side, severing the attraction to the south-pole magnets in the candles. I heard the candles crash to the ground, but there was not a second to waste. I recapped the magnets and stuffed them into the backpack along with my phone, then pulled out the towel-wrapped bear.

There was a clatter of pots and pans, a sudden cacophony beneath me. Ignoring it, I sat the stuffed animal at the center of the bed, pulled off the towel, and stepped back, waving my hand in front of its face to activate the sensor. As I did, I got my first real look at the bear.

It had fuzzy chestnut fur, pink paw pads, a shiny black nose, and a pink satin ribbon around its neck. It was both the most nondescript stuffed bear in the world and so familiar that I choked on the memory. Every decibel of sound in the house whizzed away, replaced by a long, rising howl that took over my brain.

It's not the same bear. It's not the same bear. A brown bear with pink paws is probably the first thing that comes up in a Google search. This rationale didn't help. Neither did the fact that, while Adelaide knew about the bear's connection to my secret, I'd never told her what it looked like. *But you told her where you buried it. Might she have dug it up?* I pushed the thought away, ridiculous as it was.

I don't know how long I would have stood there, staring at the past, head roaring, if Callum's footsteps on the stairs hadn't roused me from my stupor. I spun from the bear. Grabbing my backpack, I sprinted into the hallway. I slid over the last two feet of hardwood and onto the carpet in Bea's room as Callum cleared the final stair. I heard the track of the bear on Cal's bed rise from silence into the demonic whisper-scream of hellish chanting as I lifted myself off the closet organizer and into the attic.

Now I just had to hope the wretched thing was enough to drive Callum into his bathroom.

I moved as fast as I could across the joists to Adelaide's blanket by the peephole. Kneeling, I found the small rock, positioned on the ground where I couldn't accidentally kick it, weighing down the end of the fishing line. I picked it up, unwound the line, and leaned forward, placing one eye against the peephole.

It took no more than three seconds for Callum to practically fall into the bathroom. He slammed the door, flipped on the light, stood with his hands on his knees, and hung his head, panting and crying.

"What the fuck?" he cried, over and over. "What the fuck? What the fuck is going on? What the fuck is happening?"

At least I'd forgotten my fear at seeing the teddy bear. The only things that existed were the twine in my fingers and the position of my husband below me in the bathroom. He hadn't looked up, hadn't looked anywhere but at the floor as he tried to catch his breath and come to terms with self-lighting candles and televisions that turned on and off on their own, with floating objects and talking toys.

He straightened, still looking down, wiping tears and snot from his face. He dug his fists into his cheeks and groaned, rocking back and forth on his heels.

Come on, motherfucker, I thought. *Look up. Look up and get the final shock of the night.*

And then he did.

I yanked the fishing line in a perfect trajectory along the bathroom ceiling, pulling the adhesive from the quarter-millimeter-thick membrane and exploding the bloated bag of pig's blood like a firework against a stark and starless sky. Blood shot out over the bathroom mirror, the vanity, the sink, in a trail of brilliant crimson bursts. The shock of red against white was like waking after an extended, monochromatic dream to a bright and blazing sun.

I saw Callum's face for a split second before the blood covered the entire surface of the mirror, but it was enough. Enough that I couldn't imagine the haunting needing to continue beyond tonight.

Callum fled the bathroom as if it were on fire. I listened to his footsteps on the stairs. In another moment, his car peeled out of the driveway. The blood dripped down the mirror, and I watched, hypnotized.

And maybe *I* was hypnotized, eye still pressed to the peephole like it was, because in the next instant, I saw something that couldn't possibly be.

I saw it in the mirror. In the thin slick of clinging blood. A figure, hunched and hooded, scrubbing blood from between her fingers like Lady Macbeth. The figure froze. It lifted its head.

To reveal the rippling pond, the shattered glass, the staticky screen, where there should have been a face.

Chapter 35

With Callum gone, ridding the house of evidence took less time than I expected. We tackled the blood in the bathroom together, wiping it away before it could dry. Downstairs, I scraped spatters of wax from the walls and floors while Adelaide swapped out the magnetized candles, cleared the television settings, shut the pantry, and packed up. The magnets, cooler, and stuffed bears went into the backpacks, and the trash into a garbage bag. We left the house as we'd found it, minus Callum sleeping in the bed upstairs.

On the return trek through the woods, Adelaide shouldered the telescopic ladder while I carried a trash bag of fishing line and blood-soaked rags. She pulled the Prius over at the same place she'd picked me up, on the corner of my parents' street.

"I'll get rid of everything tomorrow," she said. "You better get some sleep."

"Ha," I said. "I've got enough adrenaline pumping through me to not sleep for a week."

We stared at each other for several seconds.

"That was—" Adelaide started, as I said, "I can't believe—"

We both stopped. A moment later, we broke into uncontrollable, eye-watering laughter.

"I can't believe it," I tried again. "I mean, I really can't believe we pulled that off."

"I'll be honest," Adelaide said, and ran a hand through her hair. I noticed that, for the first time since I'd known her, her fingernails were absent of any polish. "I can't believe we pulled it off either."

I gasped. "Adelaide Benson. What happened to having the confidence of a serial killer?"

"Oh, I had it all right. I think that's the only reason we were successful. Still, I thought this was our 'Ted Bundy pulled over for driving a stolen car' moment. That our luck was up."

I nodded. "I almost didn't get the magnets onto the ground in time," I admitted. "And seeing that teddy bear kind of freaked me out." I studied her face, looking for any sign that she knew what I meant. I'd believed what she'd said in the car on the way over—that she hadn't had anything to do with the blackmail note. *But the bear looked practically identical to the one . . .*

I let the thought trail off. Of course it was ridiculous. Teddy bears all looked generally the same.

"They're pretty creepy, right?" Adelaide said. "The eyes give them a bit of that uncanny valley thing."

"The song, too," I said, unable to stop myself, though I still didn't know where the hell I knew it from. "That song gets under my skin, even though it's weirdly upbeat."

"I think it has something to do with how it's recorded on the stereo mix. One guitar is panned to the right channel while the other is panned to the left. Or something like that."

"That must be it." I paused. "Is that why you chose it?"

"What do you mean?"

"The guitars panned to different stereo channels. Is that why you chose the song?"

Adelaide shook her head. "That first night, I'd picked out a different song to mess with Callum. I can't remember which one now, but when I went to play it, the Alexa app glitched, and it randomly played 'What's Hidden in the Dark' instead." She shrugged. "Kind of weird, but it ended up working out. As for subsequent hauntings, I figured, why mess with a good thing?"

"Makes sense," I said, but it didn't. Not at all.

More sense than seeing a faceless figure in the mirror after Callum ran out of the bathroom?

I pushed this thought away too; we'd pulled off a multilayered, high-stakes juggling act in the middle of the night, and my brain had simply continued producing jump-scare content before fully calming down. Either that or my eyes had retained an afterimage of Adelaide in her mirror mask from the afternoon after Flypocalypse. Retained . . . and exaggerated it. I didn't linger on the idea that an afterimage retained this long was surely pathological in nature.

We stared out the windshield. The horizon was no longer fully dark but lined with a dull glow of hazy green. Not morning yet, but close. I looked at the clock and groaned: twenty after four.

"Here's to hoping Beatrix sleeps in for once in her life." I opened the car door and climbed out. "Talk later?"

Adelaide nodded. "Do you think you'll get a message from Callum saying he's never setting foot in that house before lunch or after it?" She grinned.

I grinned back. "The sooner the better. I'll let you know." I reached for the door, but Adelaide put a hand on my arm. I turned and saw she had taken something out of the middle console. A small cardboard box. She held it out to me.

"This is for if you *don't* get that message."

I stared at the box. "What is it?"

She gestured for me to open it. Sliding my fingers between the cardboard, I worked the top portion free. Beneath it was a thin layer of foam padding. And beneath that . . .

"A Prince Rupert's drop," I whispered, staring at the glass droplet with its long, delicate tail. From end to end, it measured about two inches. Joe Tallow's words echoed in my mind: *You can smash the thicker part, the tadpole's head, with as much force as you want—I'm talking sniper bullets—and nothing happens. But if you break, or even scrape, the tail end, the thing explodes.* "Why?" I asked her.

"If Callum *is* hanging on after tonight, he'll be hanging by a thread. This could be the straw that breaks the camel's back." She considered her words. "Or, rather, *this*"—she waved a hand over the droplet—"will be *inside* the straw that breaks the camel's back." She gave me a funny look. "Remember the boba straws I wanted to put in your cabinet? So Cal would get used to seeing them?" She shrugged. "Well, I did. In case you changed your mind. There were already a bunch of twisty straws there, so it was kind of perfect."

My annoyance at her nerve took a back seat to awe at her ability to think five steps ahead. "Of course you put boba straws in my cabinet," I said, and laughed, still staring at the droplet. It was hard to believe something this small and beautiful could be destructive. I'd been so mad when Adelaide had suggested we use this. Now, my fingers itched at the prospect of sending Callum packing once and for all.

"If he comes back tomorrow"—Adelaide looked at the clock—"or, I guess today, use this. Don't wait. We have to strike while the iron's hot. We started slow, but this is the grand finale."

I nodded. "All right."

"And Bea won't be there, so you won't have anything to worry about."

I nodded again. She was right.

I repackaged the droplet and tucked it under one arm, opened the door, and climbed out. Dew dampened my sneakers as I crossed the yard toward my parents' house. Sneaking in through the window proved as easy as sneaking out. I made it up the stairs and into the guest bedroom without waking anyone in the house.

I placed the cardboard box on the top shelf of the closet and climbed into bed, prepared to lie awake the rest of the morning, haunted by a face that shimmered like air above pavement hot enough to burn.

Chapter 36

Four hours later, Bea shook me awake.

"Mommy, I need to go to the bathroom."

"Right, okay." I groaned, and forced myself onto one elbow, studying her. "How are you feeling, sweetheart?"

"Great," Bea said, and smiled a thousand-watt smile. Already the cuts and scrapes on her head were healing, and the bruise on her temple had faded to yellow.

"Is this bothering you at all?" My hand trailed to the bulky purple cast on her wrist.

"No. I kind of like it." She held both arms out in front of her and rocked side to side. "It's my mummy arm." Her expression turned thoughtful. "Can I be a mummy for Halloween?"

I chuckled. Lifting her out of the bed, I nudged her in the direction of the bathroom. "Halloween's four months away, my dear. That cast will be long gone by then." I'd have to check my own wrist to see if I was ready to peel off the gauze.

The rest of the morning was as peaceful as possible, lounging around my parents' quiet, comfortable house. Bea and I colored and watched movies while my father dozed beside us on the couch. At noon, my mother insisted on making my lunch as well as Beatrix's, flitting in and out of the kitchen like a butterfly, bringing us lemonade and cut-up strawberries and bowls of popcorn. Dinner was no different, my mother catering to us both like we had matching concussions. At six o'clock, Bea started getting antsy. Subsequently, I was on edge.

"Do you wanna play Favorite Thing?" she asked, but her mouth was screwed up, like she expected me to say no.

"I think you're tired, my love," I said. "Why don't we go up and get ready for bed?"

"I don't want to go to bed. I want to go home." She said it dispassionately, as if it were any other Saturday evening.

"Oh, sweetheart, I want you to be able to go home too. But—"

"*No,*" she insisted, everything about her tone and expression saying it was critical I pay attention. "I want to go home. I know Daddy's sick, but I won't talk to him. I'll let you do whatever you need to fix him. But I want my room and my stuffies."

I scrambled to rearrange my face in a way that didn't show my shock at how astutely Bea had read the situation with her father, as well as my unfair annoyance with her stubbornness. Could I bring her home tonight? This last haunting had to have broken Callum. He'd fled the house as if the devil himself were on his heels. What had Callum said to Monty upon arriving? Had he asked him to stay long term? I glanced at my phone, but there was nothing I could text Callum without sounding suspicious. Besides, it was too soon, too dangerous for Bea to return.

"How about this?" I tried. "I'll go over and see how Daddy's doing. I'll bring back whatever books and stuffed animals you need." I smoothed her hair. "But I can't take you home until it's safe."

Her mouth turned down, and she balled her hands into fists, a difficult feat considering the cast. "I want my room. And my books. And Love is still dirty. You told me you would clean her." Each utterance grated on my already frayed nerves.

"I'm sorry I didn't clean Love yet," I offered. "I promise I'll take care of it soon. And I'll—"

"But I want to go home now!"

"Well, we can't, Beatrix, we just can't!" I exploded, then immediately felt terrible. To my surprise, Bea's face didn't crumble, but she held her ground, scowling at me, challenging me until I relented.

"Which stuffies do you want?"

She smiled, not a got-my-way kind of smile but a genuine, relieved one, and I felt more terrible still. "I want Waddle and Little Elephant and Asha and Wind and Hoots and Toby and Spike and Amaya."

"Oh," I said, trying to mentally match up the toys on her bed to the names coming from her mouth. "All right, then. I'll see what I can do."

She nodded and yawned, a bit of the poutiness coming back. "I'd like to get ready for bed now."

I swallowed an impatient retort and led her upstairs. By the time I'd started the second book, she was asleep. Healing cuts aside, the concussion was still taking a lot out of her; Bea hadn't gone to bed this early in a year. Of course she'd been a little tough this evening, what with all she'd been through.

I tucked the covers around her tightly and placed her water bottle at the edge of the nightstand where she could see it if she woke in the night. As I turned for the door, something stopped me. *If he comes back tomorrow,* Adelaide had said, *use this. Don't wait. We have to strike while the iron's hot. We started slow, but this is the grand finale.*

Without thinking through what I was doing, I went to the closet and pulled the Prince Rupert's drop down from the shelf. I slipped it into my bag, securing it in place with a sweatshirt. Then I tiptoed down the stairs to where my parents were watching television.

My mother sat up the moment I walked into the living room. "Did she fall asleep?" She saw my bag. "Where are you going?"

"To the house to grab a few things for Bea. And, well . . ." I sighed. "I need to see what's going on with Callum, whether he's willing to go into treatment or, if he's maybe leaving altogether."

I swallowed. I didn't want my parents to think I didn't have everything under control. *But do you?* An image of Callum's bathroom mirror covered with blood popped into my mind. That, and the faceless thing beneath it. *Stop it!*

"Honestly, I'm hoping this is the end of things," I added. "Callum and I . . . What he did to Beatrix. I can't do this any longer."

My parents exchanged a look.

"One of the EMTs submitted a report, right?" my father asked. "Someone will be looking into that."

"Absolutely," I lied. I hadn't told my parents what I'd learned from Veronica Schumann, hadn't wanted them to worry. If my parents—or anyone else who was paying attention—thought the DCYF report was still active, it would be all the less surprising when Callum finally left the house.

"Like I said, I'm going to see what's going on. I might stay the night, if things get heated. To be honest, I think he might have already left. But can Bea stay here until I know for sure?"

"Like you have to ask," my father said.

I pursed my lips. "It's not too much for you? You're supposed to get your rest."

My father waved a hand. "Nonsense. You know, I read something on the 'gram that says grandparents who see their grandchildren on a regular basis live an average of ten years longer than their grandchildless counterparts."

I walked to where he sat in his leather armchair and gave him a kiss on the cheek. "That's great news. And don't call it 'the 'gram.'" He smiled.

"We'll take good care of that little pumpkin while you're gone," my mom said.

"I know you will."

I walked out of the living room and into the foyer, where I passed a geometric mirror hanging above a small set of drawers. I stopped, something nagging at my subconscious, and as I did, I thought I saw movement to my left. In the mirror. As if my reflection had continued moving after I'd come to a halt.

My stomach gave a small but sickening lurch, and I turned toward the glass. But there was only me, pale-faced and tired-looking. There was no blood, no altered appearance. Just a woman hoping to be nearing the end of something that had gone on for far too long. Why, then, did I feel like there was something in the mirror I had missed? A portent? A whisper?

A warning.

You're as bad as Callum, I thought, and continued through the foyer and out the door.

Chapter 37

The first thing I processed upon returning to the house was the lights. Every single light, from porch sconces to foyer fixtures, from floor lamps in windows to floodlights over the garage, was burning, blazing, though it was only early evening. The second thing I comprehended was what these lights meant, the veritable gut punch of a realization that Callum had indeed returned.

One night? I thought desperately. *That's all Adelaide's and my efforts got us? Callum stayed away a single night?*

I parked in the drive and walked to the door with my bag over one shoulder, cocking my head to better discern what I was hearing. At first, I thought there were so many lights on that the place was actually buzzing. Then I realized there was music playing, so loud I was hearing it as a vibration, a rattling of appliances against hardwood and doors in their frames.

I walked inside, resisting the urge to bring my hands to my ears. "Callum?" I yelled. No answer. "Callum! Where are you? What the hell is this music?" It wasn't the twangy, vertiginous song that had played before, but some sort of death metal, and it was deafening. I ran to the speaker in the kitchen and manually jabbed at its buttons to lower the volume. The silence that followed throbbed in its stillness.

A dirty balled-up sweatshirt lay on the floor in the corner. A foul smell reached my nostrils, and upon peeking into the downstairs bathroom, I saw that Cal had neglected to flush the toilet. "Gross," I muttered, but it wasn't just gross, it was disconcerting.

I returned to the kitchen and set my bag containing the Prince Rupert's drop on the island—beside a sink of food-encrusted dishes—and listened, but heard nothing to indicate Callum's location in the house. No way he could have slept through that noise; maybe he was passed out, had gotten drunker than usual. I listened again, a memory from the day Adelaide and I had first gone into the attic coming to me, of looking up at the trapdoor in Bea's closet and having the distinct sense of not being myself. I had that feeling now, a mix of disassociation and déjà vu.

Something wasn't right in the house, some quality to the air, an energy of foreboding. It wasn't just the neglected sink or excessive light or absence of sound; my disquiet ran deeper. It was like the house was holding its breath. Like I'd come in on it in the middle of something and it wasn't happy to have been disturbed. Still, there was only one thing to do, and I set out to find Callum, flipping lights off as I went.

As I reached for the switch in the living room, the smart speaker exploded into blaring, raucous sound:

Open your eyes . . . See what's right in front of you.
There are ways to see what's hidden in the dark . . .

Dread pooled in my stomach like oil slick. That song . . . why did I keep hearing that fucking song? Then, without warning, the kitchen fell away, replaced by walls the color of ancient, patinaed marble, and I remembered where I was when I heard it, the exchange, the instructions. "Do you need me to repeat anything?" the woman had asked. *Closer . . . Let me whisper in your ear,* the song had teased from the overhead speakers, as it teased me now. "No," I'd responded, but I'd been distracted, had wanted to shoo the song away from my ears like a swarm of flies. "No, that's all right. I understand what I'm supposed to do."

I blinked, shaking the memory loose, my body thrumming with the emotion associated with it. This time I didn't bother with the volume button but yanked the cord from its side, as Callum had done the night before. Once again, the house was plunged into silence. No, not silence. A thump, on my right. From the playroom.

I walked to the French doors, pulled them open, and saw it immediately. The world tilted on its axis, and a lump of terror welled in my throat. The window was open, the screen pushed out, and sitting on the sill, posable arms folded in front of it as if it were praying, was the chestnut-furred, pink-pawed teddy bear. Again, a long howl filled every inch of my brain.

Had one of the bears gotten left behind last night? Fallen out of Adelaide's bag, and Callum had stuck it here? *Had Adelaide come back and left the bear herself? Or given it to Todd to do the same?* I stepped into the room, brain whirring with possible scenarios, but as I did, something crinkled beneath my sneaker.

I looked down and froze. It was a piece of folded-up blue stationery, lying two feet or so in front of the bear. The blackmailer—*Todd*, I thought vehemently, for even Adelaide had said she thought he could be behind it—must have placed the bear and the note on the windowsill, and the note had come loose and fallen to the floor. I picked it up and unfolded it, my fingers shaking as I read:

> I've got some questions for you, Lainey: Does Callum know where you went on Nav 11? Does he know you decided to play God? Did you take his feelings into account when you made a decision from which there was no coming back?
>
> Does he know what's buried in the backyard?

I was shaking so hard I could barely read it a second time. It was obvious, now, that this wasn't about the haunting. With the first note, I couldn't be sure, but this one left no room for doubt. The handwriting was terrible, and someone might have had a hard time making out whether the date read "May" or "Nov." But I didn't need to decipher the handwriting. I knew which date the blackmailer was referring to.

Todd knew my secret, my only real secret. The thing I kept not only from Callum, but from myself. How the hell had he found out?

I wanted to feel anger, to burn with white-hot rage at the idea of Todd prowling around my house, of knowing something he couldn't possibly know. Or *shouldn't* know. But all I could feel was a wave of fear that spread like ice over my muscles, leaving me trembling and numb.

"Why are you doing this?" I whispered. The bear stared crookedly from its post. "This isn't supposed to be about me. It's supposed to be about Callum." I squeezed the note in my hand. It was too much to be in this space, filled with the toys and games and crafts that Bea loved. Feeling sick, I stumbled out of the playroom and back to the kitchen.

For several long moments, I stood there, breathing hard and trying to decide what to do. Had Callum seen the note? I had to assume it was at least a possibility. Whether he had or hadn't, Todd was forcing my hand. I needed to end the haunting tonight. I needed to convince Callum, once and for all, that he was either completely crazy or the house was haunted.

And there was only one way to do it.

There was still no sign of Callum, the house sepulchral in its silence. I went to my bag and slid the cardboard box from it, then walked, as if I were in a dream, to the cabinet where Callum stored his various drinking accoutrements. There were wine and highball glasses, a decanter, and several stainless steel mixers, but I had eyes only for the pint glasses and what sat innocently beside them: a plastic cup of colorful straws, thicker-than-normal drinking straws with concertina-type hinges at the top for bending. The boba straws Adelaide had clandestinely sneaked into my house. *In case you change your mind,* she'd said.

I wrapped my hand around the contents of the cup, lifting out all but a single turquoise straw. I shoved the handful of straws to the bottom of the garbage can and covered them with paper plates and an empty package of English muffins. I took the remaining straw in one hand and the Prince Rupert's drop in the other. Very, very slowly, I inserted the drop into the top of the straw, tadpole head-side down, halting in feeding the drop through the plastic the moment its tail disappeared completely.

I stared at the straw. It was a good fit. Perfect, actually. The head was wedged in to where it wouldn't slip any farther down the opening, which would be crucial for this to work.

I opened the freezer. The ice tray was full, and a handle of vodka lay on its side beside a package of peas. I shut the freezer. Then, very slowly, I placed the straw back in the plastic cup and returned the cup to its shelf in the cabinet. Now all I had to do was wait for Callum to make a drink.

A crash came from the upstairs bedroom.

Chapter 38

A second crash came from upstairs, followed by a shout. An image of Callum at the housewarming party six years ago, candleholder clutched in his hand, flashed through my mind. I ran up the stairs, crossed the hall, and threw open the door.

Every light in the room was on, and the effect was like being on a stage. A glass was overturned on the nightstand. The comforter and sheets were pulled from the bed and strewn on the floor. The armoire doors hung open, and even the plants Bea had given Callum for Father's Day were knocked akimbo, soil ground into the cream-colored carpet.

This was nothing, however, compared to what greeted me in the bathroom.

Callum stood at the center of the room, his back to me. He was naked except for a towel, and his hands holding the towel around his waist were bloody. No, not just his hands. His whole body was drenched in blood, his usually light-brown hair dark with it. The white towel was stained red, and red-tinged water dripped onto the white tile. The shower curtain had been ripped from the rod and lay in a bloodstained heap in the corner. There were red footprints—and handprints—smeared across every surface.

"Callum?" I whispered.

Slowly, he turned to face me.

"Jesus Christ," I said, "what happened?" I scanned his body looking for a cut. "Are you hurt?"

Callum gestured weakly over his shoulder. "It was . . . there. It came from there." Against all that red, I saw that his teeth were more yellow than white, and he smelled awful even through the metallic scent of blood, all stale breath and rankness, as if the booze had pickled his organs and fermented in his veins.

"What came from where?" I looked around the bathroom. Was there a goddamn animal in here or something?

"The blood." He looked inquiringly at the shower, as if he still wasn't quite sure what had happened.

I stared, realization dawning. Realization but not understanding. "The blood came from the shower?" I asked. My mouth felt unbearably dry.

Callum nodded. "Well," he said, "that should do it, then."

I squinted. "What should?"

"That should do it for proof. If you needed any more of it, any other indication that the house is haunted"—he gestured around us—"the faucets, the shower . . . they're raining blood."

For a moment, I couldn't move, couldn't process what Callum had said, but then my brain connected his words with what I was seeing before me. Adelaide. Adelaide must have gone back to the plumber, and together they'd figured out how to splice the water line with pig's blood from the butcher. I remembered Chris's words: *There's absolutely no way to do this . . . most laypeople don't know the difference between a gas line and a water line. I don't want you getting carbon monoxide poisoning because you did something stupid.* So how had Adelaide done it? And why hadn't she told me?

The butcher-shop smell overwhelmed the unpleasant odor of my husband, and I swallowed hard against the sharp tang coating my nostrils and the back of my throat. I watched Callum, expecting him to do the same—to cough, gag, wipe at his skin frantically with the towel. But he only stood there, stunned into silence.

As he stood, I found my eyes drawn not to him, but to his reflection. Something was happening. The room had a strange sense of pressure to it, like the air had become corporeal. In the mirror, the air was tinged beige. No, lilac. No, it oscillated from one color to the other, like the curling, shimmering mouth of a conch shell. But that wasn't possible. Air didn't shimmer. But the mirror did. And as I watched, it shimmered until Callum was gone, replaced by the horrible figure I'd seen several times now, shoulders hunched, hands wringing, the place where its face should have been an open chasm of distortion reflecting into infinity.

I opened my mouth to scream, but the figure was gone as quickly as it appeared. I blinked. Had it been there at all? What the fuck was happening?

"Did you say something?" Callum asked me. He turned to stare at the mirror. Had he seen the figure too?

"I didn't say anything," I said dazedly. I needed to pull myself together; Adelaide must have gone to great lengths to pull this off. I pictured her rummaging through the basement, hefting buckets of blood, splicing water lines and patching everything together so it looked the same as when she'd started. How had she known what the hell she was doing? Hell, maybe she hadn't.

I don't want you getting carbon monoxide poisoning because you did something stupid. Chris's words rang in my head again. Carbon monoxide poisoning. Someone else had given us a similar warning. No, not a warning. An explanation. Joe. Joe Tallow explaining that prolonged exposure to a gas leak can manifest as apparent psychic phenomena.

Carbon monoxide was even found to have caused one man's vision of a "strange woman dressed in black" rushing toward him from another room. Chronic exposure can lead to the kind of hallucinations often associated with a haunted house.

Oh my god.

I kept my face neutral while thoughts sliced through my brain. Could Adelaide have nicked a gas line? Was there carbon monoxide seeping into the house? Our bodies? Had the faceless figure I'd seen in the mirror been a hallucination? But how could that be when the first time I'd seen it had been weeks ago? Bea had been frightened by it even before that. But one thing all the sightings had in common was that they'd occurred *after* Joe and Morgan Tallow had come to the house . . . after we'd heard—after *Adelaide* had heard—that carbon monoxide could cause phenomena consistent with a haunting.

A chill, like ice water, spread down my back. Was Adelaide systematically poisoning us? Was that why the haunting had become so effective . . . so real, not just to Callum but to me as well? We had carbon monoxide detectors, but how long had it been since I'd checked them? And if the leak was intentional, Adelaide could have disabled the devices.

Callum had turned from the mirror back to me. I forced myself to focus. The quicker I extracted myself from the bathroom and this surreal situation, the quicker I could call Adelaide.

"You had too much to drink, didn't you?" I asked, making myself sound as patronizing as possible to cover the fear and disbelief coursing through me. "You're drunk, and you cut yourself in the shower. It's as simple as that."

His expression curdled into an incredulousness that wasn't misplaced. With that amount of blood, the cut would have had to have been a stab wound. Still, I squinted at the bathroom with a sneer on my face. "Make sure you clean this up."

"I'm not cleaning anything." There was something in his voice I'd never heard before. Something like finality. Then, as if to drive home what I'd heard in his tone, he said, "I'm done."

"What do you mean, done?" My heart thundered in my chest. Was this really about to happen?

"I mean, I'm going to wash up as best I can and go to a hotel. I'm not sleeping here another night. Maybe not ever again." He put a hand on the door. "If you're crazy enough to stay here, have fun in this bloody haunted house of death."

I stared, unable to speak as he walked out of the bathroom and into his bedroom.

As soon as he abandoned the blood-spattered space, it was like the spell had been broken. I hurried out of the room and down the stairs.

I kept walking, through the kitchen and into the playroom, giving the bear still wedged in the window a wide berth, then slipped out the slider and onto the deck. Glancing up, I checked to make sure the windows in Callum's bedroom were closed. Then I walked to the section of the deck farthest away from the door—and the windows—before pulling out my phone.

I thought again about my theory. I didn't really believe Adelaide had been poisoning us for over a month, did I? And if I did, could I outright accuse her of it without irrefutable proof? No, better to act as if only the first part of my realization was true and that I was worried whatever she'd done to run blood through the water line had released gas into the house inadvertently.

The phone rang and rang. On the seventh ring, it went to voicemail.

I considered hanging up, then changed my mind. It would be easier to relay my suspicions in a voicemail. My words came out rushed and ragged in my ears:

"We did it, Adelaide. We fucking did it. He's leaving for a hotel. Tonight! First thing Monday, I'll call the lawyer. Maybe we'll even file. I'll get the locks changed." I was getting ahead of myself, but I couldn't help it. I forced myself to take a breath.

"I prepped the Rupert's drop," I continued, envisioning the elegant slip of glass waiting in the straw like a snake in tall grass. "I thought that was our secret weapon. Though, if he does make himself one last drink, a little poltergeist activity can only reinforce his decision. But it was the blood in the shower that put him over the edge. How in the hell did you do it? Chris said there was no way to rig the water line without going to the source."

I remembered how adamant Chris had been, how certain. *What had changed?* But the better question was, *What did it matter?* "I guess the blood in the shower was like the extra flies," I continued, "the less I knew, the better. I mean, how many times *did* you go rogue on me?" I started counting on my hands. "There was the mirror mask. The teddy bear." Something occurred to me, and I paused; if the bear was

Adelaide's doing, why had Todd left one with the note? I squeezed my eyes shut. It was hard to keep everything straight.

"The bloody handprints," I rattled off, returning to my message. "The metallic shrieks on hidden recorders that ripped through the house. And now the blood in the shower. Don't get me wrong, I'm not mad," I added quickly. *Unless you tried to poison my entire family.* "You were right all along. It was your brazenness that got us here, got Callum to leave when no amount of threats or begging would." I felt the tight, wry smile on my lips. "Your serial killer confidence knows no bounds.

"But"—I lowered my voice to just above a whisper—"remember what Chris said about messing with things in the basement? Is it possible that maybe something went wrong down there? That there could be a gas leak in the house contributing to Callum's . . ."—*and now my,* I thought but didn't say—"delusions?"

There were a dozen more questions I could have asked, but I needed to wrap this up. "Call me as soon as you get this," I said in a rush, then lowered the phone and ended the call.

I leaned against the house and closed my eyes again, thinking about being able to tell Bea she could come home, that she could *stay* home, with her books and her stuffies and her fairy garden and her swing set, and that she would be safe—after I made sure there wasn't a goddamn gas leak, of course.

I was wondering if I should have posed the question to Adelaide's voicemail as to whether I should be ridding the hot water heater of evidence, when I caught movement in the grass by the arborvitae. It was fully dark now, and while I couldn't make out any defining features, I could see that the figure was tall, too tall to be Adelaide. I backed farther into the shadows and watched the figure approach.

They came up the stairs to the deck, but instead of going to the door, they stopped and looked around. When no one appeared, the man—for I was sure it was a man now—crept to the window and grabbed the bear. He turned the stuffed animal over, looking for something.

The note.

Turn around, I thought. *Turn around,* Todd, *and let me see your face.*

And he did turn, but not toward me; rather, he turned toward the door. There was enough moonlight to see the back of his head . . .

. . . and the phoenix tattoo inked there, its black-and-orange feathers fanned out like fire.

Chapter 39

Chris, I thought wildly. *Not Todd at all but the asshole plumber!* I'd been completely off base that Adelaide's lover had used what Adelaide had told him against me. *Former lover,* I corrected myself, and all because I'd been convinced he was the one leaving the notes.

But how could *Chris* be the blackmailer? That would mean he'd uncovered my secret. My mind reeled, trying to make sense of what little information I had. Amid the lies and confusion, the various people who'd gotten tangled in this sticky web, there was one undeniable fact: Adelaide was the only one who knew about last November. The only one I'd told about the bear. If Chris knew about these things, he'd found them out from Adelaide, one way or another.

Adelaide had been sleeping with Todd and not told me. Might there be more to her relationship with Chris?

He'd reached the door and was raising his hand to knock. "Hey," I called out softly, "what the hell do you think you're doing?" He whirled around.

It occurred to me as he searched for the source of the voice in the dark that I may have gotten it wrong. Maybe he wasn't the blackmailer but was here because *he'd* been the one to rig the water line with blood in the basement. But then I saw his face, features tight, mouth pursed with anger. And he'd gone right for the windowsill, checked to see if his note had been found. Had Adelaide trusted Chris with what we'd really been up to, the way she'd trusted Todd? Could Chris be behind the blood in the shower *and* the blackmail?

Chris walked to where I crouched in the shadows, and I said a silent prayer that Callum was still struggling to wash up with a shower that was only spitting blood.

"Why did you leave the notes?" I asked, getting right to it.

His response was just as direct. "Money," he said, and shrugged. "You have a lot of it; I want ten thousand dollars not to tell your husband what you and that hot-ticket friend of yours have been up to."

I let out an incredulous laugh. "Callum and I don't have any money. Not like that. The only reason we live here and Callum golfs at fancy courses is because of his parents." I shook my head. "And you thought the way to get me to give you money for keeping quiet was to show up here *while my husband is home*?"

His face had gone pale at the revelation about Cal's parents, but he recovered quickly. "I came so you knew how serious I was after the last note. I was going to pretend you'd called for plumbing services. Make you squirm a little in front of your sad-sack husband. I knocked on the front door first, but no one answered." He gestured at my position against the house. "What the hell are you doing out here, hiding in the dark?"

I ignored the question. "The blue stationery, where did it come from?"

He gave me a funny look. "Huh?"

"Where did it come from?" I demanded.

He thought for a second. "The Rhode Island Small Business Coalition. They gave it out at their last networking event."

"Your office is in Connecticut."

He raised an eyebrow. When I made it clear I wasn't moving on without a response, he said, "I'm on the border, remember? I do business in Connecticut and Rhode Island." He shook his head. "*These* are the questions you want to waste your time asking me?"

I gritted my teeth, but there were far more pressing matters. "How did you find out?" I asked softly. "Did Adelaide tell you?"

"No. Why would she have? Adelaide's never liked me. I was surprised she came to me for help in the first place. It made more sense when I realized she wanted free advice."

"So how *did* you find out?"

"I golfed in a tournament with your husband. He played like shit and got ridiculed by his buddies the entire time. He started going off about how he hadn't slept in days and all the things going on at his house. Knocking in the walls, other strange noises, weird smells, cold spots. A rabbit head. What he said rang a bell. Adelaide had mentioned those exact same things when you were in my shop. Still, I didn't know what the connection was, at least not then. And the fake name you'd given me threw me. But only until I found out where he usually played and 'ran into' him again a week later. By that time, the coincidences were too many to ignore."

Goddamn small-state golf courses, I thought. *Everyone knows everyone.*

"This time, I heard about swarms of flies and moving furniture," Chris continued. "I remembered what Adelaide had said about not wanting fake blood capsules and realized that, for whatever reason, you two were trying to scare your husband."

I stared at him dumbly. "Scare . . . my husband? I don't understand." The blackmail notes had referred to my decision, to this past November. Was Chris going to stand here and tell me they were about the fake haunting all along?

He looked at me like I was an idiot. "What the hell else would it be about? Anyway, I didn't give a shit why you were trying to scare him. Maybe you had a new man. Maybe Callum beats you. What I did care about was that if you were doing this in the first place, there had to be a good reason. And if there was a good reason, I figured you'd pay to keep Callum from finding out."

I still couldn't wrap my head around what he was saying. How had the notes been about the haunting?

"But what about the reference to November eleventh?"

His forehead wrinkled in confusion. "Huh?"

I dug the note from my back pocket and held it out. "You wrote, 'Does Callum know where you went on November eleventh?'"

He snorted "That's an *m*. It says May. My handwriting sucks, what do you want from me? You and Adelaide came to see me on May eleventh. You two were playing God by fucking with Callum. I admit the whole 'decision there's no coming back from' thing was a little dramatic, but the poor dude was essentially getting forced into a breakup in a pretty gnarly way. I mean, we're talking some next-level psycho-bitch shit. As for what was buried in the backyard?" He shrugged. "I heard so much about the damn rabbit head, I took a guess as to how you kept him from finding it." He grinned. "Was I right?"

My head was spinning. I felt nauseous. "But what about the bear?"

"What bear?"

"You left the note with the teddy bear on the sill."

Chris's forehead wrinkled further. He looked genuinely confused. "I didn't leave any bear."

I was stammering out a reply when my phone lit up. A text message from Adelaide. I saw that I'd also missed a call from her. Chris started saying something about how I was crazy and Callum would be better off without me, but I wasn't listening. Adelaide's text paraded across my screen. The more I read, the more my head spun, until sentences were reduced to mere phrases, each more dizzying than the last:

... no idea what you're talking about ...

... the mirror mask was stupid ... I never ended up wearing it.

Bloody handprints?

None of the recorders were set to play a metallic shrieking.

. . . told you a hundred times, I didn't release extra flies!

And the bombshell:

. . . never went back to Chris . . . never went in your basement . . . gave up on the idea of blood in the shower a long time ago . . . I think you need to get out of there. I think the haunting might be real.

"You . . ." I started, my tongue thick and useless. "You didn't leave the bear with the note?" Still, my brain balked against Adelaide's text. *The haunting real? Ridiculous.*

"No." Another bewildered look from Chris.

"You didn't leave bloody handprints on the door?"

This time the look turned pitying, as if he thought I might be legitimately insane. "No."

"You didn't . . . you don't know about the abortion?"

The word hung in the air, as powerful as any of the knocks or shrieks that had sounded in the house over the last few weeks. Chris's face contorted. He appeared shocked, maybe even disgusted. "Jesus Christ. Abortion? No." He shook his head and started backing up. "If there's no money, then this is not fucking worth it. You really are crazy." He shot a quick glance up at the house, then a last, frightened look at me, as if he were afraid I might follow him. "I'm out of here. Good luck to your husband, man. He's going to need it."

With a final "Psycho bitch," Chris took off across the grass. I heard his truck start a moment later.

In the wake of his receding engine, there were only the sounds of the frogs and the crickets backdropping my own ragged breathing. I walked across the deck on legs that didn't feel like mine. Part of me wanted to keep walking, through the grass, into the trees, to disappear into the woods for the night, only returning when Callum was gone in the morning. When I could pretend that none of this was happening. When I could pretend I had things under control.

I turned, and for the first time since coming outside, I was far enough away from the house to see there were lights on in some of the windows. Including Callum's bedroom. A strangled cry escaped me. Callum stood, backlit by the bright orange light, a smudge of blood marring his neck. He looked down at me through the open window with an expression full of contempt.

Full of knowing.

Chapter 40

By the time I walked into the kitchen, Callum had made it downstairs. He stood across the island from me, skin ruddy from the blood, his expression somehow both horribly sorrowful and burning with hatred at the same time.

"I don't know what to ask you about first," Callum said quietly. There was a dangerous lilt to his voice. "The fact that you apparently *had an abortion* or that you were standing on our back deck talking to Chris fucking Matheson about it!" His eyes flashed. "Did you cheat on me with him?"

"Jesus Christ, no." This was not how I wanted to have this conversation. I'd never wanted to have this conversation at all. I exhaled slowly, but my whole body was trembling. "What exactly did you hear?" Had he heard that Adelaide and I had faked the haunting? Had I gotten within minutes of Callum leaving only to blow everything up?

"Something about bloody handprints. And the abortion. And how you were a crazy bitch and I needed all the luck I could get."

So he'd heard only the very end of the conversation. Thank Christ. Could I salvage this? Callum knowing about the abortion didn't negate everything else that had happened.

Then something occurred to me, something so revelatory I felt it physically, spreading from brain to body like medication through the bloodstream. I'd thought that by preparing the Prince Rupert's drop in response to the final blackmail note, I'd be spurring Callum to leave before my secret ever came to light. But what if the abortion had been the real trump card all along?

"I *did* have an abortion," I said. My words sounded flat. Frightening. "Chris Matheson had nothing to do with it. He actually came to see you, but I got confused. Something about how he had a fix for the problem you'd been experiencing and had told him about on the golf course." The lie rolled off my tongue, but what was one more in a sea of thousands?

"It shouldn't come as a surprise that I had an abortion," I continued. "Not really. Not after the last four years, how things have been between us. How you've been with Beatrix."

"I cannot believe you." Callum's eyes were full of shock and hurt, giving them a strange, depthless quality. "You selfish bitch," he said. "And you wonder why I drink?" As he spoke, he moved around the island, lessening the distance between us.

"What the hell does that mean?" I stepped away from Callum and gripped the marble countertop. "How the fuck are you going to turn this around on me?"

He laughed, the sound of it piercing my skull and causing me to grip the marble harder. "I've known this house is fucking haunted for the last month, but now I find out my goddamn wife, my supposed partner, went and got a fucking abortion behind my back, killed a baby that was half mine. It's like you *created* a ghost to haunt me. The ghost of our dead child. If you had told me you wanted an abortion, it might have been different. But to do it in secret? I will never get over this." His voice wavered. "I will never get over what you did to me. What you did to us!"

Something was growing in the air between us, some palpable aura or energy, mist-like but growing denser by the moment. "What *I* did?" I screamed back. "Look around you, Callum! I'm hiding Beatrix at my parents' house after you gave her a concussion and broke her wrist! I'm playing psychiatrist by day and fucking ghost hunter by night, getting sucked into your veritable lunatic asylum, and this is *my* fault? There is no us! There hasn't been an us in years, and it's all because of you and your stupid fucking drinking, your fucking immaturity and selfishness!"

Callum shook his head in some pantomime of disappointment, his eyes bloodshot, a vein in his forehead throbbing beneath the sweat-sheened skin. "You knew I wanted another baby. You *knew* I did. You did this to punish me."

"I did this for *me*!" I screamed. Blood thrummed in my temples as if my skull had been hit with a tuning fork. "I did this because the last thing I want is another connection to you! I want to *sever* what's between you and me, what little is between you and your daughter, and *I want to leave*. But you won't let me. Your parents won't let me. I can't stomach the thought of sharing Beatrix with you and your fucking family. You think I want to bring another child into the world and have to share them too?"

Callum took a step toward me, and I shrank back. I was almost up against the stove now. Callum was directly in front of the cabinet. *Pour yourself a drink,* I commanded. *Do what you do best, and pour yourself a fucking drink.*

"I told you you'd take Beatrix away from me over my dead body," Callum growled. "Now you've taken away a child of mine that I'll never even fucking see. Never get to spend time with."

The aura between us coalesced into something tangible, like the air in the attic. Immovable. Shifting. *Breathing.* "You don't spend time with your daughter," I spat, struggling to breathe through the stuffiness. "You don't deserve her. You don't deserve any child." I sucked in air, feeling like I was choking. "You know what you do deserve?"

Callum sneered and glanced over his shoulder. "I don't know about what I deserve, but I know what I fucking need." He pulled the cabinet door open and gripped a pint glass. Holding my gaze, he reached for the straw. "Is this it?" His tone was mocking. "Is this what I deserve, Lainey?"

Blinking through my tears, I nodded. I didn't trust myself to speak. The air between us was like smoke, but Callum didn't seem to notice. He was reaching behind him now, for the freezer. Forgoing ice, he opened the vodka and poured it straight into the glass. I thought he'd forgo a straw too, but then he slammed the freezer door shut and reached back into the cabinet. His fingers grazed the cup, then rose several inches and wound themselves around the straw.

"Is this what I deserve?" he asked again, and despite my anticipation, my growing horror, my rage reignited.

"Yes," I whispered.

Callum put the straw into his drink. "Say it," he said. "Say the words. What do I deserve, Lainey? What do you wish would happen to me?"

"You deserve to drown in your cups," I said, and now the tears spilled from my eyes because I meant it. I felt nothing for the person before me but a ceasing, searing hatred. "You deserve to be alone, to die alone. To have nothing but the pain you have caused me and your daughter."

Callum nodded. His eyes, too, were wet with tears. But I wasn't finished. "I want you to die," I said, and I was sobbing now, rocked by the bitterness coursing through me, not just for him but for myself, my lack of compassion. "Not for anything as opportune as insurance money or a clean slate. I want you to die because it would be easier for me and for Beatrix if you'd just . . . fucking . . . disappear."

The aura between us was swirling now, as if it'd absorbed my rage, his desperation, our mutual pain. He sniffed and laughed a strange, sad laugh, as if, somehow, he knew what was coming. He pinched the flexible portion of the straw.

And bent it.

There was the briefest moment of a pleasant-sounding tinkling, like rain on an aluminum roof, before the tinkling rushed into a crescendo of glass shattering against glass. The drop evaporated, and the pint glass morphed into a glistening cascade of a waterfall roaring into a plunge pool. Callum's hand shot back, and he yelped. A millisecond later, glass showered down onto the kitchen floor, the explosion devolving back into an almost harmonious tinkling.

I understood, now, what Adelaide had intuitively known after hearing Joe and Morgan's account of the Prince Rupert's drop, understood why she knew it'd be the turning point in the haunting. It was both beautiful and terrifying, an explosion otherworldly in its graceful devastation. My head—and eyes—hurt from the confusion of it. I'd both seen it and seen nothing at all, too fast and incomprehensible was the whole experience.

The blood, however. I saw the blood, viciously red and shockingly thick, covering Callum's hand up to his wrist. He howled the way Beatrix might have upon plunging through the deck rail, had she not been rendered unconscious.

At first, I thought the plunk-plunk-plunk was Callum's blood against the hardwood, or else a portion of the glass shards had somehow remained suspended in the air and were only now falling to the floor. But that was impossible. And . . . the sound was louder, somehow more ingrained, as if the very walls were speaking. Clink. Tink. Pop. Clink. Pop. *Tiiiiiinkle.*

Callum raised his gaze from where he'd been staring at his bloodied hand. Our eyes met, and despite the hatred still radiating from each of us, our simultaneous realization forged a momentary connection.

"The windows," I said at the same moment Callum shouted, "Get down!"

But it wasn't just the windows. It was the mirrors. Every glass surface in the house was popping and tinkling as if it were a frozen pond supporting the weight of one too many skaters. I had enough time to fold my arms over my head and duck before the glass exploded, one after the other after the other. The mirror at the other end of the kitchen sent glass shooting outward in every direction. The sound was like a ninety-mile-per-hour highway wreckage between a glass-lined limousine and a semi.

I thought the silence following the blowout had grown teeth until I realized there were tiny shards of glass in my ears. Gingerly, I shook them out. Callum had yet to move from where he'd slumped against the refrigerator. He held his bloody right hand in front of him, the fingers of his left hand wrapped around his wrist. I couldn't tell how bad it was, couldn't focus on his injury at all, my brain jumping from one thought to the next, making manic, disorganized connections.

The windows had exploded. *The mirrors* had exploded. In the exact moment after the Prince Rupert's drop had broken. There was nothing Adelaide could have possibly done to have instigated something of this magnitude. The words of her last text message wound themselves through my mind:

I think the haunting is real.

Chapter 41

I stayed pressed against the cool surface of the stove until Callum rose, visibly trembling, and lurched to the freezer. He grasped the neck of the vodka bottle with his uninjured hand and groaned as he unscrewed the cap, leaving a handprint of blood smeared across the glass. He lifted the bottle to his mouth, as if its contents were medicine—and, probably they were—but stopped short of drinking from it, a strange look on his face.

"Do you feel that?" he asked.

I wanted to say I didn't. I wanted to tell him not to talk to me. I wanted to point out that he should be gone by now, that the plan had worked, that Adelaide and I had haunted him into submission. But I didn't, because I *could* feel something. A rumbling, low but steady. As if the house's very foundation was shaking.

The candles on the island toppled over and shot up to the ceiling . . . the candles Adelaide had replaced after removing the magnetized ones. The entirely normal candles, made of nothing but beeswax and cotton wicks. The teakettle followed a moment later, water shooting from its spout and spraying over the kitchen. Followed by the paper towel rack, the fruit basket, and the knife block, along with all twelve of the knives housed inside it. When I took my hands from off my head and peered up, I saw that the knives were stuck to the ceiling by their handles, gleaming blades pointed down at our heads.

"What the fuck!" Callum shouted. "What the fuck is happening?"

But the knives were forgotten when the buzzing began a moment later. Flies poured in from the vents and out of the sink drain. They crawled in from the windows and beneath the doorjambs, flew past our heads and covered the picture frames, darkened the woodwork, joined the hanging objects on the ceiling.

The music exploded a second later, not from the smart speaker, which was still unplugged, but from the walls themselves. Or maybe it was in our minds:

Open your eyes . . . See what's right in front of you.
There are ways to see what's hidden in the dark . . .

The lyrics were distorted and discordant. A moment later, the acoustic guitars melted into horrible, tortured screams.

Callum had dropped to the floor when the knives had shot to the ceiling, but now he was up and turning in circles, staring at the horror unfolding around us. The rumbling started again, vibrating everything around us. There was a pounding in the walls, like something was trapped behind them and intent on breaking out.

I gripped Callum's arm. He looked into my eyes.

And that's when the creaking started from the shattered foyer mirror.

It was like the moment before the windows and mirrors exploded, those tinkling pops, the sense of stretching, of pushing a solid object to its breaking point. But there was something else, something that raised the hair along my arms. A metallic whine. A crunching scrape. Choppy. Intermittent.

Like something was dragging itself through the lingering pieces of glass.

"Callum," I whispered. "We need to go."

But it was too late. A blood-slicked hand emerged, fingers curling over the bottom frame of the mirror. The top of the head appeared a moment later, hooded with thick black fabric.

A second hand curled around the frame much in the way the first one had, pulling the thing forward so that the shoulders became visible, hunched and shrouded in the same dark fabric as the head. The thing crawled down the wall as easily as if it were crawling across a floor. When it was actually on the floor, it pushed itself to a stand.

Strands of hair hung from the hood, but it was impossible to make out the shade. Like the bathroom mirror earlier, its color shifted—blond, brown, pink, silver—so I couldn't tell what color it was. The thing lifted its head. It was the figure that'd been coming to me over the last several weeks, haunting me as much as we'd been haunting Callum.

It was the figure from Bea's nightmare, the face from the mirror. The shimmery, undefinable nonface. It refracted and folded in on itself, more like reflective flesh than hard angles of silver, nickel, and glass substrate. Decidedly human, if horrific. Specter-like . . . no mirror-mask trickery here. It raised its hands, and I saw there was something gore-soaked and gummy clutched between the blood-streaked fingers. I wanted to close my eyes but couldn't; it was as if they were frozen open. Silent tears of horror spilled down my face.

The creature glided over the floor, its feet silent on the shards of glass glinting along the hardwood. I shrieked, and Callum let out a strangled cry as we tried to get out of its path, but it didn't come for us. It was as if it couldn't see us. It paid us no more mind than it did the flies on the wall or the knives hanging from the ceiling.

As it traveled, the thing wrung its bloodied hands, Lady Macbeth having sealed both her fate and that of her husband. It floated into the playroom and through the sliding door, leaving a familiar bloody handprint in its wake. It descended the deck stairs and crossed the backyard until it reached the tree line. It fell to its knees at the edge of the property. A moment later, dirt flew up on either side of its body as it dug.

"What the fuck?" Callum said. "What's it doing?"

I didn't—couldn't—answer.

"What the hell is it *doing*?" Callum asked again.

"Who cares what it's doing," I finally got out. "What the hell *is* it? Where did it come from?"

As if in response, the figure at the back of the yard disappeared. A metallic whine came from the foyer mirror, followed by a crunching scrape.

We waited long enough to see the same bloodied hands, the same black hood, the same madness-inducing face-that-wasn't-a-face, the same specter on its mindless loop through our house, before we turned from the kitchen and ran.

Chapter 42

We got as far as the downstairs hallway before the sounds from the foyer were replaced by a low, dull scraping along the stairway wall and the tink-tink-tink of glass on wood. Callum and I froze beside one another, unable to stop staring at the thing coming down the stairs. A second figure, taller than the first, its face as abstract and amorphous, swayed on the top step of the first flight after the landing. Flecks of glass fell from its swirling, shifting clothes, and it held something in its right hand, something it was using to keep its balance. As it walked down the stairs, the glinting object dug against the wall, producing the horrible *scrrrrrrrape* that was like bone on bone.

The thing was too close to the bottom for us to move in either direction. When it cleared the final stair, it was a mere foot in front of us. This close, its shifting visage looked like a thousand insects undulating under an iridescent pool of oil. I felt Callum beside me, pressing against the wall, trying to disappear within it. The thing took another half step forward, and my mind shifted and bubbled like its face. There was something beneath my fear, beneath my abject terror. Something akin to understanding. But then the flicker went blank, as if my mind had seen the window through which it could glimpse the truth and quickly pulled a shade over it.

The thing swayed left, then right, as if looking at us through eyes we couldn't discern. I felt almost as if it were smelling the air between us and it. Then it lurched to the right and continued its unsteady progression through the house. Callum released a breath. My heart revved to life after having stopped in my chest.

"It came from upstairs," I said, breathless. "From the mirror in the bathroom."

"How many mirrors are there?" Callum asked.

I swallowed, counting in my head. "Five."

Callum's eyes grew wide. "Five? Why the hell do we have so many mirrors?"

Rather than answer, I held a finger to my lips.

"What are you—" Callum started.

"Listen," I hissed.

We stood, doing just that. From above us, in Bea's bedroom, more groans and creaks floated down through the stairwell. A similar assemblage of sounds came from the downstairs bathroom at the other end of the house. There was a mirror in each of these rooms. Did that mean there were two more specters?

I decided I didn't want to find out. Without waiting to see if Callum was behind me, I sprinted across the foyer, yanked open the front door, and all but fell onto the porch. Callum came crashing out beside me a moment later, but I kept running—down the front steps and into the grass—where I stumbled on the uneven ground.

Now that I'd put distance between myself and the house, the horror and impossibility of what we'd seen actualized, sticking in my brain like a dagger. I didn't waste time getting to my feet but half crawled, half scrabbled to the road. I lay on my back in the damp grass, breathing hard, the fingers of my right hand on the pavement, as if, by virtue of that physical connection to something outside the house, I was safe.

I stared at the star-strewn sky, moths flitting about my face, the trill of crickets and tree frogs filling my ears with the soothing sounds of the creatures of this earth, this plane of reality. What the hell had happened in there? What had been unleashed?

I rolled onto my stomach, pulled myself onto my elbows, and stared across the lawn into the house. I had a clear line of sight from where I lay, and the light above the foyer might as well have been a spotlight, but though I looked for several minutes, nothing pulled itself out of the foyer mirror and across the kitchen.

Could the beings not be perceived from outside? Did the walls and the places where the windows once hung act as some sort of barrier? I wished fervently that I could still make my carbon monoxide poisoning theory work, but there was dried blood on my arms from where shards of glass had sliced into my skin. Not to mention that having a horrific specter stare through you with nonexistent eyes from six inches away was a far cry from seeing a vague figure in black at the edge of your periphery.

"Do you see anything?" Callum asked. He'd come to crouch beside me. He stared in the direction of the house, squinting at the open front door.

"No."

"Why did you run? Shouldn't we be figuring out some way to get rid of them?"

I shot him an incredulous look. "Says the guy who was on his way to a hotel?"

Callum scoffed and said something I couldn't catch.

"What was that?"

He grunted. "Not for nothing, but I fucking *told you*."

I bit my lip. I knew where this was going. I knew that I could—probably *should*—admit to everything Adelaide and I had done. But I didn't want to. Let Callum have his moment of gloating. If there was some way to salvage things and get Callum to leave, I wasn't going to jeopardize that, real ghosts or not.

"You saw some flies," I said with a shrug, "and heard some knocking. I don't know what *this* is"—I gestured at the house—"but I'll figure it out." I stared past him, to the driveway. "You better get going. It might be tough to get a room at this hour." I stood and brushed grass from my pants.

Callum's expression twisted into something unreadable, but his eyes were red and watery, and I reminded myself that, even tonight, even in the midst of this nightmare, he was drunk. Or, at least, he had been before a ghost had pulled itself out of a broken mirror in our foyer, a sobering occurrence if there ever was one. Still, I couldn't forget my endgame: I needed him gone.

"You'll figure it out?" There was disbelief in Callum's voice. "So, you're staying? Why?"

I didn't answer. Anything I said might inadvertently cause him to consider what his leaving could mean for the future.

"There are fucking ghosts in there," he said, as if I might have forgotten. "*Actual* ghosts! You can't . . . stay!"

I started across the top of the yard to the driveway. When I reached my car, I opened the door and hit the button to open the garage.

"What are you doing?" Callum asked, appearing beside me.

I still didn't answer, just riffled around the large set of shelves along the right-hand wall until I found a cobweb-strewn bag. It was only when I followed Callum's gaze that I realized my hands, along with my entire body, were shaking.

"You're as scared as I am," Callum said, "but you're not going to leave." I didn't like what I heard in his voice, that note of revelation. His next words confirmed my suspicion: "You want *me* to leave. That way you can say I abandoned you and Beatrix."

"I don't know what you're talking about," I said, pulling the bag from the shelf.

"You don't, huh?" His tone had reached that same manic pitch it did when trying to convince me of the latest inexplicable thing he'd experienced around the house. "So if I leave right now and check in to a hotel, you're telling me you won't be on the phone first thing Monday morning with some dirtbag lawyer, filing a motion for divorce and loss of custody on abandonment charges?"

Bile rose in the back of my throat. Adelaide and I had done everything right, everything we could, and now actual fucking ghosts had to go and ruin everything? I turned away from Callum, rage growing inside me with the same ballooning pressure as had accumulated before the mirrors and windows exploded.

"Get out of my way," I said, trying to walk around him to another shelf.

He matched my stride.

"Seriously, Callum, get away from me."

He laughed bitterly. "If you want to get away from me so badly, maybe *you* should leave."

"I'm not leaving," I reiterated, and though the words made my stomach clench with fear, I knew they were true. A plan had formed in my mind, starting with this goddamn bag I hadn't opened in more than five years.

"What are you doing?" Callum asked.

"Not that it's any of your business, but I'm getting the camping equipment."

"What?"

"Camping equipment? You know, tents, sleeping bag, lantern, a pocketknife. Those things we used back in another life before your drinking kept us within a ten-mile radius of this house."

When he continued looking at me like I'd lost it, I sighed and waved at the door to the house. "You can go to a hotel or drink yourself into oblivion and pass out in there with the ghosts. But I'm sleeping in the backyard. That way, I'm still *here*," I said, gesturing again at the house to make it clear I wasn't abandoning anything or anyone, "but I don't have to lie awake all night listening to the sounds of glass tinkling and specters groaning."

I pulled the tent from the bag, but Callum grabbed the other end and tried to snatch it away from me. "What the hell do you think you're doing?" I demanded.

"Who says *you* get the tent?" he asked.

"It was my idea," I shot back.

"I was thinking the same thing."

"No, you weren't!"

"Yes, I was."

"We wouldn't even have this tent if I hadn't done all the research as to which one we should buy!" It was a ridiculous thing to say under the circumstances, but I was having a hard time dealing with this new reality of Callum no longer leaving. I needed him to remember how scared he'd been, to remember the blood-chilling scrape of the object against the wall as the second being had come down the stairs.

"Like that matters," Callum responded, tugging harder, but I held strong despite my still-injured wrist, glaring at him over the nylon.

"You don't even know how to pitch it," I growled, and that one indisputable fact was apparently enough for Callum to relinquish his hold. He glared at me, but I ignored him and pulled a sleeping bag and LED lantern from a pair of hooks on the wall. I left Callum in the garage, lugging everything across the top of the driveway and into the backyard, keeping one eye on the house . . . and anything that might come out of it.

Chapter 43

After traveling no more than a few feet, I stopped, staring at the place across the lawn where the menace from the foyer had traveled after walking off the deck. Was the ground out there further disturbed, or was it my imagination? Was the soil more disrupted than before? It was hard to tell with only the pale circle of lantern light and a waning crescent moon to see by. I pulled my gaze from the tree line and forced myself to keep walking.

I spread the tent at the center of a small area banked by massive oaks; between them, I would be far away from where Lady Macbeth—as I'd been calling her in my head due to the constant scrubbing of her blood-drenched hands—kept traveling to dig in the dirt.

She's digging awfully close to where something else is buried. The thought came unbidden, and I forced it away. I couldn't think like that now, entertaining madness and dredging up the past. Besides, I had a tent to pitch—and a phone call to make—before it got any later.

I worked as quickly as I could, relieved Callum hadn't followed. At one point, I thought I heard something scrabbling around by the arborvitae, but by then I had finished with the tent and was throwing my sleeping bag inside it. *An animal,* I told myself. *A racoon or an opossum.* I crawled in, holding the lantern, and zipped the front flap closed.

The second I was ensconced within the tent, I realized being inside was no better than being out in the dark, open yard. The lantern threw abstract shadows on the walls, and the night seemed to press in on me, the silence so loud I felt certain I wouldn't hear anything coming, let alone see it. I took a deep breath and pulled out my phone, keeping my eyes on the zipper in case it decided to start moving, then searched for the number I'd saved two weeks ago with zero expectation of ever dialing it.

It was after midnight, but Morgan Tallow answered after only two rings. "Lainey? What's going on? I saw your number and . . . Is everything okay?"

I was silent. What should I say? *The house is overrun with ghosts? I need you to come here and perform some sort of exorcism?* Ultimately, I went with something simpler: "About the mirrors . . . Morgan, you were right."

There was a gasp followed by silence.

"Are you there?" I asked.

"I'm sorry. I'm here."

I filled her in on what had happened, and was about to beg her and Joe to come, when I realized there was something else that needed to be said.

"I'm sorry. I'm so sorry, Morgan. I should have believed you. Or, if not believed you, then at least not been such a jerk. I should have listened to what you had to say."

Morgan sighed, but it was a sigh of understanding, not disapproval or frustration, as if she'd heard apologies like this before. "Remember how I told you my connection with the supernatural is personal, so I don't fault anyone for their skepticism? It's okay." She said it again, the kindness in her voice making me want to cry. "It's *okay*. What do you need us to do?"

"I need you to come here!" I exclaimed. I had thought that part would be obvious.

"Right. Okay. Where are you and your husband now?"

"I'm in a tent in the backyard. Callum is . . . I'm not sure where he is."

"And your daughter?"

"She's with my parents, at their house on the other side of town."

Of course Morgan wouldn't know why Beatrix was there, wouldn't know everything that'd happened in the last few days, or even the state of my marriage that had prefaced this awful evening.

"Okay, that's good. You need to keep her there. Do not bring your daughter into that house. Especially after Joe and I get there to do, well, whatever it is that we end up needing to do."

"So you'll come?" Those three words belied the flooding well of desperation inside me. I had kept it together in the garage in front of Callum, but inside my house right now was proof of the supernatural, and I didn't know how to deal with it. I needed Joe and Morgan if I was going to get rid of these things, if I was going to protect Beatrix.

"We'll come," Morgan said slowly, but there was a catch in her voice I didn't like. "But we can't get there until tomorrow afternoon. We're at my in-laws' in New York, but we're driving home in the morning. We can be at your place by three, four at the latest."

"Okay." That was good, or at least better than I'd expected. "Okay, tomorrow afternoon is fine. But what should we do until you get here?"

"From what you've told me, it doesn't sound like the ghosts are dangerous. In fact, it sounds like they might not interact with you at all. If they're engaging in the same actions over and over again, that's good. There may be some sort of residual haunting going on."

"Residual haunting? What the hell is that?"

"Well"—Morgan sounded less sure of herself now—"I don't want to speculate. I'll know more when I get there. But I think it would be okay for you and Callum to venture into the house tomorrow and see the state of things. The ghosts might quiet down overnight. They may disappear altogether."

"They could do that?" That sounded too good to be true. I figured any ghost worth its salt wouldn't leave until it got what it wanted or told the house's inhabitants something they didn't want to hear. Wasn't that how these things worked in books and movies?

"Whatever you do," Morgan cautioned, "be careful. We'll be there as soon as we can. I promise." I heard muffled words, as if she were covering the mouthpiece to speak to someone else. She came back on the line. "And Lainey? Joe made a good point. Until we get there, stay away from the mirrors."

"There aren't any left," I said, but she had already hung up.

I placed my phone beside the lantern and looked around. How the hell was I supposed to sleep? I pushed ghosts and mirrors from my mind, reasoning there was nothing I could do to fix this until Joe and Morgan arrived tomorrow, but the thoughts still swirled like mist, blotting out patience and reason. I had convinced myself to at least lie down when a noise came from outside. A shuffling sound, hushed but gritty, like something dragging in the dirt.

I held my breath and doused the lantern, plunging the tent into darkness. I tried not to succumb to terror as outside, someone approached the tent. I grabbed the knife and flicked open the blade. It was incredibly sharp, purchased for use in place of the small hatchets or machetes some hikers liked to carry. But what good would even the sharpest knife be against a ghost? The dragging footfalls grew closer, stopping in front of the tent.

Seconds passed. The figure stood, motionless. I realized I could hear somebody breathing. "Callum? Is that you?"

"Yeah," he huffed, "it's me. Come on, Lainey, let me in."

The fear went out of me like the tide, only to be replaced with a rushing tsunami of rage. I stabbed the lantern back on and unzipped the tent. "What. The. Fuck. Callum. No."

He was holding a garden rake, one of the metal ones with widely spaced tines. His face was utterly bloodless in the LEDs' glow.

"Lainey," he said in a breathless whisper, and it was only then I realized, in the lull of my own fear, how terrified Callum sounded. *Freshly* terrified, not the lingering fright from earlier, as if something had driven him toward me, pursuing him in the dark.

"Lainey," he said again, the terror in that whisper chilling the blood in my veins. "You've got to let me in. The ghost. The ghost from the foyer mirror . . . I can *hear her.*"

Chapter 44

Every inch of my body broke out in goose bumps. "What do you mean?" I asked.

"I hear her, moving across the yard. The one from the foyer."

"You said that already."

"I peeked inside, hoping they were gone, but they're not. There's another one too. It's . . . it's the worst one of all. It looks . . ." He trailed off.

"It looks what, Callum?" I hissed, terror making me impatient.

"It looks *dead*. It has a weird face like the others, but its body is disgusting. Rotting. It's a corpse, I fucking know it is. I ran, but not before I saw the one from the foyer too. The one with the blood on her hands. She's walking that same path from foyer to yard. From foyer to *right out here*. She's burying something. Over and over again. The sound of the digging is making me crazy. I was going to sleep in your car, figuring it was far enough from the house to be . . ." He paused. "I don't know. Not safe, but saf*er*. But I can hear her digging through the windows."

It was as he spoke this last sentence that I heard the slur in his words.

"Did you have something else to drink?" I asked, my voice rising. Could this night get any more unbelievable?

He stared, clearly trying to come up with some sort of retort. "I had some nips in the garage. What of it?" When I gave him a disgusted look, he added, "There are fucking ghosts in the house, Lainey. I think a better question might be, why the hell *aren't* you drinking?"

I jerked my chin at his rake. "If the ghost from the foyer is digging, maybe you should help her. Because you're not coming in here." And with that, I closed the flap and zipped up the tent.

The pleading started immediately. "Lainey, please. *Please.*"

"You would hear the digging just as well from in here. Better, even."

"But at least we wouldn't be alone."

"Sorry, Callum," I said coldly. "But if it's a question of being alone versus riding out a night full of ghosts with you, let's just say I don't regret bringing a single sleeping bag."

He said something I didn't catch, then turned and walked away. I heard my car door open, then slam shut. If he engaged the locks, I was too far away to hear it.

I shivered and tucked myself into the sleeping bag, the reality of my situation hitting with the hardness of the ground beneath me. This was crazy. Truly crazy. Staying in a haunted house to spite one another. Why hadn't I run back inside long enough to grab my keys and return to my parents' house? To Beatrix? Callum would never be able to accuse me of abandonment, the way I could him. Bea was with my parents because I was keeping her safe from her father.

But then I remembered what Rosalie Taylor had said about custody of Beatrix in my kitchen the day I'd found Chris's first blackmail note: *I imagine you'd get a vastly different outcome from what you desire.*

"What the hell am I doing?" I said aloud.

In the wake of my whisper, silence flooded the tent once again. No. Not silence. There was . . . something. At first, I thought it was the wind rustling the leaves in the trees, or else a far-off neighbor taking out the trash, the noise made more indeterminate by distance and fear. But the noise persisted, clarified into something far more horrifying and sinister. A muttering. Low and frenzied:

"No-no-no-no-no."

On the surface, it was arbitrary, a common word, a mere expression of disbelief. But I knew. I felt it hit some visceral part of my memory where things like absolute joy and absolute terror were stored. It was me, what I'd uttered, on the long walk from the bathroom to the backyard the night after the abortion, when the fetus had finally passed. It was me, out of my mind with a horror that I was prepared to repress had the blood and tissue not been expelled in such a violent, obvious manner. In such a violent, obvious, and *completely abnormal* manner.

It was me, knowing I hadn't made a mistake, but filled with horror for the experience, the secrecy, the shame of it, all the same.

Coupled with the *no-no-no-no* was the gritty rustling of digging. Manic. Maddening.

And as the long night wore on, growing closer.

And closer.

And closer.

When the first rays of sunshine finally slipped over the horizon, I pushed myself groggily from the ground. My back was sore, and I had the worst headache of my life. But at some point during the night, after the hours of muttering and digging had turned into an indecipherable whir, like white noise engulfing my brain, I must have fallen asleep.

The sun was a merciful haze through the fabric of the tent, but even with its glow sufficiently muted, the events of last night blared too loudly, too vibrantly, within me. I listened, but heard nothing, none of the sanity-stripping sounds that had scrabbled like talons in my ears and pressed like grit beneath my nails. Slowly, I unzipped the tent, wincing in the unfiltered light of morning, praying there'd be no signs of my and Adelaide's prank-turned-real, no evidence of ghosts that'd escaped from mirrors and turned my house into a feedback loop of horror.

I blinked.

And blinked again.

Then stared at the hundreds of shallow holes dug out of every available space in the yard, black earth exposed to the light like tide pools, like innards, like dark creatures pulled from hollows—from wombs—before they were ready.

With the smell of tilled earth stinging my nostrils, I stepped out of the tent and walked toward my very still, very silent, very haunted house.

Chapter 45

By the time I reached the driveway, Callum was opening the back passenger's side door of my car. He practically fell out onto the pavement, his eyes bloodshot and his face creased with sleep.

"Jesus Christ," he said, surveying the yard. "I knew that thing was digging all night long, but this shit is next level. Another day or two and the entire backyard will be one big pit."

"Things won't go on that long," I said, and continued walking toward the front of the house.

Callum perked up slightly. "Why do you say that?"

"I have some people coming today. People who should be able to help."

He hurried to catch up with me. "People? Who?"

"Don't worry about it."

"Lainey, fucking tell me!"

I stopped and sighed. "Jesus Christ. If you must know, it's Joe and Morgan Tallow."

Callum's forehead wrinkled. "Who the hell are they?"

I glared at him. He should know who Joe and Morgan were; I'd mentioned them enough over the almost ten years I'd worked for the Preservation Society.

As if to prove this point, the names finally clicked for him. "The Ed and Lorraine Warren wannabes?"

"Yes, the Ed and Lorraine wannabes." I was approaching the front walkway.

Callum seemed to realize the direction I was heading in and stopped, the expression on his face that of a frightened rabbit. "Where are you going?"

I didn't turn around. "Inside."

"Are you crazy?"

I sighed again but still didn't stop, worried if I paused long enough to think about what I was doing, I'd lose my nerve. "The Tallows are coming between three and four. Morgan thought it would be okay if we went inside before they got here. And besides, I'd like to see what we're dealing with. Who knows, maybe things have gone back to normal."

"You *are* crazy."

Now I did stop on the walkway, telling myself I wouldn't succumb to rage or participate in another circuitous argument. Instead, I looked up at the abstract patterns of sky filtering through verdant trees, the countless leaves fluttering on intertwined, mazelike branches. I'd been so hung up on haunting Callum, I was only now realizing spring had morphed into summer. Under a blue sky and warm sunlight, the idea of entering the house didn't seem quite as impossible as it had last night.

"I'm not crazy," I said, my face still turned upward. "I miss Beatrix and want her to be able to come home." I looked out toward the road, to the place where Bea and I had set out on so many of our "adventures." I wanted to pick wildflowers with her, take her to see the chickens at the farm down the road. I wanted her to be able to go to her room after one of our walks and lay the rocks and acorns and other treasures she'd collected inside her fairy garden and regale the wooden tortoises and butterflies with her made-up stories.

I swallowed. I felt like I might cry, but at the same time, my head hurt too much to produce tears. I wanted Bea to make up stories about scary and difficult things. *Stories*. Not be faced with those things in real life. She'd have to do enough of that when she got older. I swallowed again, finding there were tears in my eyes after all, and when I looked up, Callum was studying me. I huffed out a breath and resumed my trek across the walkway. I thought Callum would say something else, but he didn't, just fell in step beside me.

I gathered my nerve and climbed the steps to the front porch, gripping the rail and peering through the opening that'd once been a small side window. I could see glass littering the floor, but not much else. I resisted the urge to turn around and sprint in the opposite direction. I so unequivocally *did not* want to go in there. But I remembered what I'd said to Callum about Beatrix, and how I wanted to bring her home. I steeled my resolve and pushed the door open onto the disaster in the foyer.

Keeping one eye on the shattered mirror, I stepped inside, doing my best to avoid the glass. There was no sign of Lady Macbeth, no bloody hands cresting the bottom frame of the mirror, no dark hood crusted with shards like glittering diamonds. At least, there was no sign of her for now. I crept into the kitchen, stealing glances at the living room and playroom as I went. The objects that had hung from the ceiling the night before—the candles and teakettle, metal fruit basket and wooden knife block, as well as the accompanying knives—lay haphazardly on the floor. One of the knives was sticking out of an otherwise unblemished apple.

I backtracked from where I stood and almost walked right into Callum. "Jesus!" I cried.

"Do you see anything?" he whispered.

"No," I whispered back. "Now be quiet." I jerked my chin for him to get out of my way. I continued toward the staircase, but there was no ghostly figure wielding a blunt-force object like Jack Torrance dragging his axe along the halls of the Overlook. And there was certainly no "corpse specter," as Callum had reported seeing last night, darkening the threshold of any of the rooms.

"They're gone," Callum said, and while his voice was still hushed, there was glee in it, glee and relief.

"We don't know that for sure."

But as we went through the rooms a second, and then a third time, gaining courage, Callum even peering into what was left of the mirrors despite my admonishments, nothing out of the ordinary appeared. No shimmery-faced ghosts on mysterious missions. No tinkling glass or groaning stairs. After our fourth exodus through the house, I was forced to admit that, whether or not they were gone for good, they were at least gone for now.

And whether or not the house was haunted, it was certainly a disaster. Even if the ghosts were gone, I wouldn't be able to bring Beatrix home with glass covering the floors and peppering every surface. While Callum disappeared into his bedroom, I retrieved the broom and vacuum cleaner from the hall closet. With the coffeepot trickling, I set to work.

It was several hours later—plus a break for a shower and another pot of coffee—that it occurred to me I hadn't seen Callum since our last walk-through of the rooms. His description of the corpse flashed into my mind, and a jolt of fear shot through me. With trepidation, I called out, "Callum? Are you up there?"

No response. I cursed under my breath and started up the stairs. "Callum?" I called out again. Still no response. *Goddammit.* I went to his room, but it was empty. So was his bathroom, my office, Bea's room, and her bathroom. Had he gone outside? I hadn't heard him come downstairs.

Back on the first floor, I called out again, "Callum? Where the hell are you? Why aren't you answering me?" In the downstairs bathroom off the kitchen, I could see a sliver of glass from the shattered mirror I must have missed while cleaning, poking out from beneath the sink. The hairs on the back of my neck stood on end. A small squawk came from the direction of the living room. I made my way there, certain the horrible beings of the previous evening had returned.

But I was wrong. It was something much, much worse.

Chapter 46

Callum kneeled before the coffee table, a large piece of paper spread out before him on the light oak wood. It took me a moment to realize it was a stretch of easel paper from the roll in Beatrix's playroom. He had a fat black Sharpie in one hand and was frantically scrawling letters onto the paper while squinting at something on his iPhone, copying something from a web page.

Arranged in a circle around him were the candles I'd returned to the island two hours earlier, along with a collection of stones—mostly smooth, round gems like bloodstone and carnelian, but a few chunks of citrine and spears of selenite—from Beatrix's fairy garden. As I watched, Callum wrote the letters of the alphabet, stretched out across two lines and slightly curving, as if the letters were following the shape of a rainbow, thirteen per line. He scribbled numbers one through nine, followed by a zero, at the bottom of the page, then lifted his hand to the top left corner. He wrote "YES," then moved to the top right corner: "NO." Then, to the bottom of the page: "GOODBYE."

I should have realized what he was doing sooner, but it was so unexpected, so disconcerting, that I didn't figure it out until he'd finished.

"A Ouija board?" I said, incredulous. "A fucking *Ouija board*? Callum, are you out of your goddamn mind?"

He glared. "Do you have a better idea?"

I gawked at him. "Um, yes. Yes, I absolutely have a better idea. How about we don't fucking summon back the ghosts who have seemingly departed? What could you possibly hope to accomplish with this?" I waved wildly at his ridiculous art project.

Callum recapped the Sharpie and gripped the edge of the table. "What are *you* hoping to accomplish by bringing strangers into our home and asking them to solve our problems?"

"They're not strangers!" I exclaimed. "They're specialists. And I thought—"

"You thought," Callum echoed, his voice thick with sarcasm. "You thought it was no big deal to broadcast our marital problems to, oh, I don't know, the entire world?"

I leaned against the wall. "What the hell are you talking about? Broadcast our problems to the world? How do you get *that* from me asking the Tallows to come here?"

"They're ghost hunters, Lainey. *With a YouTube channel.* And we have actual fucking ghosts! You can't tell me they won't use us to make themselves famous. And at what cost?"

I closed my eyes, unable to believe the narcissistic nonsense coming out of Callum's mouth but unsurprised by his shortsightedness. "If you want to believe the Tallows are going to exploit us, be my guest, but I think we're in a pretty desperate situation and should take all the help we can get."

I didn't add—couldn't add, not without admitting to the staged haunting—that, contrary to what I'd thought about the Tallows for years, I didn't believe they'd mine our story for subscribers. Irrefutable proof of the supernatural seemed like it would strengthen Morgan's resolve as well as her and Joe's connection. I wasn't sure what I would do when the Tallows got here and potential details of their previous visit, of what Adelaide and I had done, came to light, but I would deal with that when the time came. Nodding at Callum's makeshift spirit board, I slid onto the end of the couch and crossed my arms in front of my chest.

"Let's see it, then," I challenged. "Let's see your brilliant plan to speak to ghosts." I was being flippant, but a chill passed through me.

"Fine," Callum said, but he already looked less confident. He picked up a lighter and lit the candles, rearranged the stones, and stared expectantly, as if he expected the "board" to flutter up from the table and shoot across the room, maybe burst into flames and fill the fireplace with crackling energy.

"I need a . . ." Callum searched for the name of the small heart-shaped piece of wood that was supposed to travel around the board revealing messages.

"Planchette," I finished dryly.

"Yes!" He jumped up from the table and disappeared. When he returned a minute later, he was holding a small clear glass.

"You *would* use a shot glass," I mumbled, but he ignored me and held it over the board.

"Where am I supposed to put it?" he asked.

I shrugged, and he shot me a desperate look. "For Christ's sake, Lainey, can you please look it up on your phone. I'm not asking you to participate in the séance, but a quick Google search isn't going to kill you."

When I still didn't move, he dispersed with another "Please!" and I let out a groan and pulled out my phone, more because he was obviously not going to start without consulting the infinite wisdom of the internet. It was almost two thirty, and I wanted to finish as much cleaning as possible before the Tallows arrived.

"*G,*" I said a moment later. "It says to start with the planchette on the letter *G.*"

Callum placed the glass over the center of the makeshift board, and I waited, biting my tongue to keep from saying something sarcastic. When he spoke, his voice was a great deal more authoritative than I expected.

"I'm speaking to the spirits who were here last night. Who"—he paused—"*escaped* from the mirrors. Who are you, and what do you want?"

I almost said, *They're the Ghosts of Christmas Past, Present, and Future, come to warn you about your drinking,* but I held my tongue.

Already, something seemed to be happening. The air felt charged, or else I was still on edge from the events of last night, my body primed for the slightest provocation.

Callum spoke again. "To the ghosts who were here last night, tell us why you came. What is it you want us to know?"

The house persisted in its silence. But . . . why did it suddenly seem too silent? I looked at the mantel to find that the clock there had stopped. Had that just happened, or had I forgotten to replace the battery? Outside the broken bay window, the air was absent of the birdsong I'd heard all day as I carried garbage bags of glass out to the bin.

"Stop, Callum," I said, half because the strange, layered silence unnerved me, and half because nothing was happening and I wanted to go back to preparing for Joe and Morgan's arrival.

"I'm not stopping," Callum said through gritted teeth.

A spark ignited in my stomach, and the rage that lived there rose up in my throat and caused my mouth to fill with heat. "Give it to me," I spat, scooting across the couch and snatching the planchette. "We're not doing this!" I got my fingers under one side of the paper and pulled, but Callum had taken hold of the other. The paper ripped apart in one long, smooth tear.

Instantly, the sky outside faded from piercing blue to a sinister gunmetal gray. Clouds like the arched eyebrows of angry gods surrounded the property at the top of the tree line. A moment later, the sky broke open and rain pummeled the earth. Puddles formed beneath the broken windows where I'd so recently swept up the glass. The temperature inside the room dropped to what had to be close to freezing, but as I wrapped my arms around myself, things went from bad to worse.

Thunder rumbled above us. I'd never heard thunder so loud. A second later, lightning streaked the sky. It pierced a tree alongside the house, which split. I screamed, fear shooting out from my core in every direction. One half of the large elm remained upright as if to protest the onslaught. The other half rushed toward us, both horribly fast and in agonizing slow motion.

The thick bark of the trunk helped slow its progression, and at the last moment, the split trunk caught. It hung there, suspended at a ninety-degree angle to the ground. One large branch, however, was lost to gravity and kept plummeting. It punched through the already shattered bay window, cracking the frame and sending the remaining glass shards flying. Callum and I both ducked. I felt a sliver of glass whiz by my forearm and looked down to see blood.

My ears were ringing. The rain kept coming. And something was happening on the coffee table. The candles wobbled as if alive. The wobbling grew more pronounced, and then the candles toppled over and shot to the ceiling. Hot wax sprayed across the room. Callum and I yelped and covered our faces.

We stayed like that for what felt like eternity, thunder rumbling and wind whipping through the house. Finally, the wind died down. The rain decreased from a deluge to a steady patter.

"Is it over?" I asked, and jumped to a stand. As I did, Callum's gaze flicked past me and to the wall. At first, he appeared confused, watching something behind me with unwavering intensity. But then his eyes grew wide as he pushed himself off the couch and stumbled backward.

"What?" I asked, afraid to turn.

Callum's eyes grew wider. He pointed. "The-there," he choked out. "Th-the shadows. The *shadow*." He tried to take another step back and almost stumbled over the hearth. "It's alive," he said, "and it's escaping."

Chapter 47

I turned so slowly I thought my heart would stop by the time I faced whatever was behind me. It wasn't a shadow, but I could see why Callum might have thought that; the figure was shadow*y*, as if light and dark fought within it. But it was a mirror-forged figure like the others, its face unknowable and ever-shifting, rising from behind the couch like a dark creature from an ancient sea.

I scrabbled backward to get away with it, but my retreat was stopped by the stone fireplace. "How?" I managed. "Where did it come from?" Even in my terror, I could see the guilt on Callum's face. "Callum?" I gasped. "What's back there? What's behind the couch?"

"The mirror," he said, his voice monotone. "The one from the attic."

"What?" I cried. Tears of shock and terror streamed from my eyes. "Why?"

He grimaced. There were tears on his face too. "After what happened with Beatrix, when she got hurt, I thought that mirror might have something to do with what was going on. It felt, responsible, somehow. Or, if not responsible, then like it knew something. Like the mirror was cursed. I only wanted to drink that night after I looked into its frame. I brought it down here. I meant to throw it away but . . ."

"But what?" I whispered. I hadn't taken my eyes off the figure. I had the sense that, beneath the undulating visage, it was trying to move its invisible mouth. It appeared to be in pain and was hunched and trembling. No, not trembling; it was rocking on its feet, as if it'd seen something it hadn't wanted to see.

"I got drunk and forgot. I slid it behind the couch so I wouldn't have to look at it."

As if in response, the specter opened a mouth we couldn't see and unleashed a wail of agony that shook the room. I shrank back, smelling gasoline and the unmistakable stench of alcohol and something else, something that I hoped wasn't burning flesh. The specter lurched forward, dragging one leg behind it. It winked out of sight for a second, as if being called back to its own world, but then reappeared and lurched forward, passing so close to where we were pressed against the fireplace that I could have trailed my fingers along its flickering body. It cried out a second time and fell to the floor, where it continued its progression across the room, dragging itself like a coyote whose back legs had been run over by a truck.

"What's happening?" Callum croaked from beside me. I couldn't speak. I was too gobsmacked by the horror. What *were* these ghosts, these mind-boggling, world-reshaping things? Was Callum right, and the mirror was cursed? Was there another world from which the beings were escaping? And why, somewhere deep inside my skull, did I feel as if they weren't as "other" as I wished them to be? Why did I feel like they lit up the same part of my brain that processed memory and dreams? Why did I feel like I'd always known them and always would?

There was Lady Macbeth scrubbing her hands over a sink. There was the specter on the stairs with the long, blunt object in its hand. The "corpse ghost" that Callum had seen. And now this. This mangled, tortured wraith. I felt like my brain was breaking. Seeing them was like watching a corpse rise from a slab after a jolt of electricity.

The creature dragged its mangled body to within a few feet of the French doors before it stopped, laying down its head. With its last bit of strength, it stretched its arms out, reaching for something, for someone. I watched its skin and the fabric of its clothes swirl and dissipate—like storm clouds, like smoke—without blinking, my eyes watering with shock and fear. The apparition's body sank through the floorboards and disappeared.

The lights flickered on and then bled back out to darkness at the same time the hunched and tortured ghost rose again from the back of the couch. It crept forward, dragging its leg, following the same path forward, emitting the same agonized wail as before. As I stared, movement on my right caught my eye. Lady Macbeth loomed in the doorframe, wringing her bloodstained hands. She passed the mangled ghost on her way to the broken slider as the room filled with the smell of alcohol and charred flesh. She floated onto the deck at the same moment the mangled ghost sank into the floorboards.

The cycle started again: mangled ghost rising from the mirror behind the couch, Lady Macbeth floating in from the kitchen. This time, however, they were joined by the shadow from the staircase. It lumbered through the living room, using its blunt instrument against the walls to hold itself steady.

I bent at the waist, pressing my face between my knees, desperate for the feel of the fabric against my cheeks, the smell of the denim, anything to bring me back to reality. It didn't matter. Rain fell. Thunder rumbled. Ghosts wandered, returned, wandered, floated, and crawled again. The massive tree branch protruded through the open frame like a monstrous hand hoping to snag hood or hair.

The accoutrements from Callum's short-lived séance were still glued to the ceiling, wax hanging down in stalactites. Dark shapes burst from a hollow in the tree branch, and I stared, dumbfounded anew, as bats swooped among the candles and selenite spears. I'd read once that humans could not naturally hear their sounds, but I could hear *these* bats, their demonic clicks and chilling squeaks as unnerving as the mournful cry of the tortured ghost that was once again sinking into the floor of my living room. Everything—colors, sounds, smells, the tacky feel of blood dripping down my arm—was turned up to eleven, augmented and amplified by the merry-go-round progression of the specters.

A groan came from beside me, and I turned to find Callum curled into himself, rocking back and forth on his heels. *Do something,* I wanted to shout. *Don't just stand there.* But I, too, was rooted to the spot.

I opened my mouth and closed it, opened it again, closed it. I wanted to collapse, to give in to the madness threatening to consume me, to drop to the floor and scream. This wasn't supposed to happen. *How* was it happening? At first, I thought another sound was joining the cacophony, but then I realized that the voice, *Adelaide's* voice, was in my head:

What do you say? Shall we turn this place into a motherfucking haunted house?

Had *I* done this? Introduced a toxicity, a negative energy, or at least added to what was already here? If we'd never staged the haunting, would any of this have happened? Had I opened a portal, given the ghosts a way to come in?

But then there was a noise, an actual noise, not another accusation or question in my head. Loud enough to discern through the rain and the thunder, the bats and the wails, the moans and the scraping of the staircase specter's object against the wall. It was heavy. Lumbering. Like Frankenstein's monster in an old black-and-white movie.

Footsteps.

In the bedroom upstairs.

Chapter 48

The footsteps traveled across the upstairs bedroom. Through the hallway. Down the staircase. Into the kitchen. The other three apparitions continued their well-trod movements, but I could no longer pay attention. I could only stare toward the hallway, dreading what was about to emerge from it.

And then the dread, the *terror*, became too much, and I was sidestepping along the wall one tentative shuffle at a time. When I was halfway to the playroom—and the door to the outside world—I looked back. Callum's eyes were on the yawning doorframe; he'd yet to notice my sideways progression. When I reached the French doors, I found the floor beneath the single step into the playroom with the ball of my right foot, unwilling to turn my back on the mind-bending spectacle in the living room, a tableau I felt no human brain should be forced to imagine let alone experience.

The footsteps had stopped on the other side of the wall between hall and living room. Whatever was out there, it was waiting. I reached out and took hold of the once-glass-fronted door, but Lady Macbeth whooshed through, so close I felt the frigid air of her encompass the right side of my body. She didn't slow, just continued on to the deck and down the stairs. I reached back out to grab the door. I slowly pulled the open door to me; it met its mate with an audible click.

Two things happened in the wake of that click: Callum jerked his head in my direction, and the fourth and final specter took the final two stomps it needed to reach the living room.

"What are you doing?" Callum yelled. His eyes had a desperate, disbelieving look I had never seen before, not even at his worst, not even when he'd done the unspeakable, hitting the gate outside Seaview Terrace, abandoning Beatrix. And maybe that was the cause of all this, that we'd both done unspeakable things and were paying for them. And surely, to lay eyes on the thing that had just walked into the living room could only be called divine retribution.

Callum had not been wrong to call it a corpse. Though its face was as shimmery and undefined as all the others, its flesh was a pallid, putrid green. Rigid limbs kept it upright, and tattered clothes clung to its frame. I couldn't see its mouth, but somehow I knew it hung open around a bloated tongue and too-prominent teeth.

Though its clothes rippled and swelled like a disturbed sea, I could tell, the way I could tell Lady Macbeth wore some sort of hood, that this corpse specter was clothed in a burial suit. I glimpsed a desiccated flower hanging from its pocket square the way you might catch sight of a clump of seaweed as it tumbled through a wave.

Revulsion turned my muscles to lead. My brain went blank with fear. And then the undead thing lurched forward, one hand reaching out for Callum. Callum screamed and tried to scramble away, but it wasn't just the corpse; the other three ghosts were each engaged in their circuitous routes. The one from the staircase was on Callum's left, the mangled wraith on his right. By the time he decided he should take his chances with the wraith, and dived in that direction, the corpse specter was on him.

The thing was roughly the same size as Callum, but instantly he was covered by it, as if the aura of death and rot swirling around the corpse was corporeal, obscuring Callum as effectively as if he were beneath a king-size blanket or a grizzly bear. He crumpled against the living room wall, struggling against his assailant. The thing pummeled him, went for his neck. When I caught sight of Callum's face, his eyes appeared to be covered with blood and what looked like a mixture of phlegm and vomit.

I shouted for Callum, but the sound was lost to the driving rain and rolling thunder, and to the bats, which flapped and dived crazily. More objects shot up to the ceiling and hung like vines—terra-cotta planters, the coffee table, a lamp without its shade, remotes, and coasters. The lights, however, were back on, showcasing the never-ending procession of ghosts that floated and lumbered around us. Three twangy guitar notes rang out, and then the band's singer was wailing from the walls, the sound rattling the French doors in their frame. I grabbed the ice-cold knob. Despite my terror, I had to do something, had to try to help Callum.

I pushed. The door didn't budge. Lady Macbeth floated through the jagged shards of glass, the crisscrossing sash bars, as if to mock me. I pushed again and again, batting at the knob, but to no avail.

Callum writhed on the floor, his eyes squeezed shut. The corpse specter gnashed and flailed on top of him. It grabbed his wrists, and even through the music I heard the snap, like a brittle branch cracking beneath a boot. Callum howled and tried to grab for his wrist, but the putrid thing lowered itself onto him again.

I let go of the door and backed against the wall. The house took up Callum's howls, and the squeaking chorus of bats rose to a crescendo. Over it all, I could hear Callum. My husband. The husband I'd started all of this to get rid of. To divorce and keep away from Beatrix. I could hear his horrified cries devolve into words, anguished and accusatory:

"Why? Why is this happening?"

I sank to the floor and hugged my knees. I ducked my head, and closed my eyes.

Then, finally, I screamed.

Chapter 49

Someone was shaking me. I screamed again and raised my arms, my eyes flying open. Morgan Tallow stood over me, her face etched with concern.

"Lainey! Are you all right?" Morgan's voice was shocked, but I couldn't focus on her question. Could only look around me in a panic. Where was Callum? Where was the corpse specter? The music had stopped, as had the rain, but the sky was still an unnatural gray. I leaned forward and peered through the doors into the living room. The ghosts were gone. All of them. Joe was helping Callum to his feet.

"Did you see them?" I asked. "The ghosts?"

Morgan shook her head. "No, but we heard you screaming. Joe wanted to call the police. I told him that was a ridiculous suggestion. Seeing as you were expecting us, I thought it would be okay to let ourselves in and see if we could help. We got to the door there"—she pointed to the living room entrance—"and we saw your husband. He was waving his hands at something, but we couldn't see it." She looked up. "We did see the bats, but I don't think that's what he was fighting."

She held out her hand, and I took it. "Was it the ghosts you told me about on the phone last night? The two that emerged when the mirrors exploded?"

"There are four now," I said. "And, no offense, but you weren't exactly right about them not being dangerous." I looked over Morgan's shoulder to where Joe was leading Callum down the hall and toward the kitchen. "I think the corpse specter was trying to kill him."

"Corpse specter?" Morgan frowned, her eyebrows furrowing. "Why don't we go into the kitchen? You can catch us up with everything that's been going on."

Five minutes later, we were seated around the table much the way Adelaide and I had sat with Joe and Morgan three weeks earlier.

"So," Morgan said, "these ghosts emerged last night along with"—she looked at the broken windows, the shattered remains of mirror—"an explosion of glass?"

I nodded, but my stomach churned with anxiety. To say all this started last night with the broken glass was the understatement of the century.

"Was there anything that prefaced the breaking glass?" Joe asked. "Any noises or changes in temperature?"

"Yes," Callum said, perking up. He had an ice pack on what was hopefully only a sprained wrist. Morgan had wrapped a piece of gauze and a large bandage around the cut along my forearm.

"I was holding a pint glass," Callum continued, "and it exploded in my hand. It was like, I bent the straw to take a sip, and the fucking thing burst into a thousand fucking pieces."

Joe and Morgan exchanged a look.

Shit, shit, shit, shit! "Yeah," I said, "about that . . ."

But Callum went on talking. "There were lots of things before last night too. Knocking in the walls. Strange smells. Furniture moving. Flies by the thousands."

"Is this why you called us, Lainey?" Morgan asked. "Back in May?"

Callum looked confused. "You called them in May? But you didn't believe me about the house being haunted. You didn't believe any of it until last night."

I picked at a corner of the bandage. What the hell should I say? There was no way out of this now, not to mention that I didn't want the Tallows basing their plan to help us on a foundation of lies.

How to Fake a Haunting

"Yeah, um." I bared my teeth in a pained, sheepish grimace. "I didn't believe you because I caused it." Now all three of them tilted their heads at me, bewildered.

"You caused it?" Morgan asked. "The ghosts?"

"Not them. But everything before it. Well, almost everything," I clarified.

Callum's eyes were still wide. He looked confused, but as I watched, realization dawned, and his eyes narrowed. "What are you talking about?" he demanded.

Wishing the house would engage in some useful haunting activity and open up a sinkhole next to the table that I could jump through, I sighed and started talking.

"Everything up until the shower rained blood last night and the mirrors and windows exploded? It wasn't a poltergeist or demonic activity. It was me. Or, more accurately, it was me working through Adelaide." I looked at Callum. "If I couldn't divorce you without giving up fifty percent custody of Bea, I figured it was worth a shot haunting you out of the house."

All the bewilderment and curiosity curdled on his face. I watched as he worked to make sense of what I'd told him, thinking through events, recalling incidents in a different light. "No," he said after a moment. "No, that's not possible."

"It is possible," I said. "Way more possible than the nightmare that's been going on around us." I gestured at the ceiling. "The knocking in your bedroom? Recorders in the attic. The creepy sounds and music? Same. The rancid smells were stink bombs Adelaide cooked up. The ghoul in your closet was Adelaide after a particularly successful makeup tutorial."

I contorted my face into that half-apologetic, sheepish grimace again. "Adelaide was in and out of this house a hundred times over the last month, courtesy of a felt-lined retractable ladder and your perpetual drunkenness, which made her all but invisible."

"No, no, no." Callum was shaking his head now. "No. There's no way." He brought his hands up to his face, then winced as the movement tweaked his injured wrist. "The candles shooting up to the ceiling?" he asked.

"Before last night, the candles shot to the ceiling because Adelaide and I glued magnets to the bottoms of them."

"And the teddy bears?"

"Adelaide and I were hiding in the house that night. We staged them, propped them up. The bears were recordable; Adelaide set them to play creepy sound effects from a Halloween YouTube channel."

We went through half a dozen more instances, and with each revelation, Callum grew angrier and more incredulous. Finally, his head jerked up, something like an epiphany on his face.

"What about the glass exploding in my hand? That happened before the mirrors!"

I felt Joe and Morgan's eyes on me. *Yes*, their expressions said. *Tell us how that happened.* "It's called a Prince Rupert's drop," I said haltingly. "A type of toughened glass bead. I put it in your straw. When you bent the straw, the bead exploded, which broke your glass."

At Callum's stunned expression, the dark thing inside me that reveled in hurting him reared its ugly head. I wasn't alone in my feelings; Callum looked like he was going jump across the table and choke me.

"You," he spat, "and your friend from work have been . . . haunting me? Making me think that I was crazy?"

I scoffed defensively. "And you've been drinking yourself to death, to insanity, in front of our daughter," I shot back.

Callum's expression twisted with resentment. He'd thought Joe and Morgan were going to sensationalize our story, had wanted to stick to ghosts in the mirrors rather than reveal the skeletons in our closets. But the idea that the ghosts weren't random, couldn't be attributed to a haunted artifact or building a house on a Native American burial ground, was gaining traction with every passing hour. There was a reason we were being haunted, and Joe and Morgan wouldn't be able to help us until we took the whole picture into consideration."

"I wish I were surprised," Callum said. "I wish I were mad. I *am* mad. I'm fucking livid. But I can't possibly care more about you and that psycho-bitch's crazy plan to haunt me than about your far worse, far more selfish betrayal."

He shook his head, staring hard at me, as if trying to find the reasons for my actions somewhere on my body. "*You* started this, Lainey." He spun on Joe and Morgan. "You're here to discover the big mystery? The reason our house is full of destructive, evil energy? Why don't you ask her how she can sit here with a straight face and say she needed to haunt me out of my own house when she had an abortion and kept it a secret?" He lunged at me. "How dare you turn me into the villain? This isn't my fault!"

As he spoke, I'd been growing lightheaded, rage climbing up my throat like ivy, making it hard to breathe. But with this last sentence, my vision sharpened with laser-focus precision. "It *is* your fault," I said, too raw and tired and fearful to hold back. "Your drinking must have been like an open invitation for all things evil to come into this house."

"Maybe we should—" Joe started, but Callum interrupted.

"My *drinking*," he said, incredulous. "You think my *drinking* is the problem, something that, oh, I don't know, eighty percent or more of people everywhere do on a regular basis, but your *abortion* has nothing to do with the ghosts crawling all over this place?"

Morgan tried to temper the shock with which she turned on me, but I still saw it there, in the parting of her mouth and the way her eyes creased as if she were in pain. Every detail from the story she'd told me about wanting a child and delivering a stillborn baby rushed back to me, and I hung my head.

"It was my choice," I stammered. "And I didn't make it because I don't like being a mother." *I made it because you are not a good father,* I thought but didn't say. Insulting him wouldn't help; I needed to steer the conversation back to the quartet of ghosts in the house if we were going to make any sort of progress. But first, I needed to try to explain.

"I didn't have an abortion because I don't like being a mother," I repeated, "but because Beatrix has always felt like a blessing I didn't fully deserve. When I got pregnant again, I was terrified. Whether or not I deserved Bea, I had her; why would I upset that sacred balance? Why would I take away a single resource or divert my attention from her for even a second when my greatest purpose in life was to be her mother . . . hers and hers alone?"

Callum didn't say anything. Joe shifted in his chair, looking uncomfortable. But Morgan reached out and took my hand.

"There is a lot to unpack here," she said, her tone patient. "Resentments. Secrets. Broken dreams and unrealized expectations. But I think we can help you." She looked across the table to Joe, and he nodded. Then she pushed back in her chair and looked down the hall. "The first mirror's down there?" she asked.

I nodded, and all four of us stared in that direction as if waiting for a repeat performance. But nothing emerged, no bloodstained hands or shimmering skin, no splatters of blood or unearthly wailing from a face as blank as an empty mirror, featureless, without focus.

Joe and Morgan stood and walked to the floor beside the island. Joe lifted a duffel bag onto the marble surface and unzipped it, then pulled out some of the equipment from the first time they'd been here: thermometers, night vision goggles, camcorders, a Geiger counter.

"What's happening?" Callum asked. "Do you have a plan?" Neither Joe nor Morgan answered. "What are you doing?" he pressed.

"I don't think *why* you're being haunted matters," Morgan said. "I think what matters is *who*. We have to find out the identities of the apparitions." She lifted a camcorder out of the bag. "Each and every one of them."

Chapter 50

"When we talked last night," Morgan said, "something occurred to me. You said the ghosts only emerged when the mirrors broke, and that they're shadowy, slippery, almost as if they're made of reflective material themselves."

I nodded, and Morgan slipped both hands back into the duffel on the counter. A moment later, she came out with an oval mirror, gold-framed, about a foot tall by a foot and a half wide. It looked like something that would hang over the sink in a tiny bathroom. "It's from our downstairs bathroom," Morgan admitted. "It's small, but I think it'll work."

Without realizing it, I recoiled slightly. Callum did the same—as if the mirror might shatter by virtue of being in our house.

"Work how?" I asked. "I mean, what's your idea?" I hoped Morgan didn't plan to break it, to summon the horrifying specters back.

Still holding the mirror, Morgan shot a quick glance at Joe. He nodded, urging her on. "I . . . sort of have this theory," she said, "based on historical representations of mirrors in hauntings. I think we can use this mirror to see what, up until now, you haven't been able to. I think we can position this mirror to be a way in. To see who these ghosts are."

I could tell she was speaking the way she had when Adelaide was here, trying to present her ideas and philosophies cautiously enough for us to accept them, but I wanted to tell her no such care was needed; Callum and I had seen enough to believe whatever she said.

"Ghosts can do as little as reflect emotions, fears, desires, and secrets," Morgan continued. "And when that's the case, they're mere phantoms, coming to us in dreams, as shadows in our periphery, a smell or taste or memory. But sometimes, and more frighteningly, ghosts are real, and I mean *really* real, corporeal, tangible, not mere hallucinations, mental projections, or even the apparently purposeless phantom." She paused again, looking apologetic. "And when ghosts are real, they can do terrible, irreparable—if unspecified—harm. They have it in their power to change the course of a life . . ." Her voice dropped so low I struggled to hear her. "They have the ability to seal fates, maybe even to kill."

"So what are you suggesting we do?" Callum asked gruffly. He'd hardly said a word since I'd spoken of the abortion.

Morgan held up the mirror again, a small smile on her face. "Like I said, we start by figuring out the actual identity of these ghosts. If they're real, like you say, they're bound to have some sort of agenda, maybe a nefarious one. But we can't fight back until we know who they are and where they came from." She nodded in the direction of the foyer. "I believe, or at least, I hope, that if we hold up this mirror"—she waved the mirror in her hands—"to one of the broken ones and look at where the apparitions came from through a reflection, we might be able to see their real faces." She paused, looking hard first at me, then at Callum. "Are you ready for that?"

"Oh," I said, which was decidedly not an answer. Beside me, Callum gulped.

But Morgan must have been satisfied; she held up the gold-framed mirror and raised an eyebrow in supplication.

"Let's start in the upstairs bathroom."

∞

Five minutes later, I stared into the prismatic remains of Callum's bathroom mirror. My head ached from nonstop adrenaline, and frissons of panic kept radiating through my gut. *For Beatrix*, I kept reminding myself. We had to figure out who or what was haunting us if Beatrix was ever going to come back.

Callum held the gold-framed mirror while Joe and Morgan prepared their equipment. I could see by the way he kept readjusting his grip that his fingers were slick with sweat. I wasn't sure how Callum was sweating. Every inch of me was ice-cold, my fingers numb, my arms and neck prickling with gooseflesh.

I pushed down waves of panic and examined what I could see of my reflection in the shattered mirror. There were a few intact shards at the bottom, clinging to the wood. Or, at least, I thought they were intact; when I looked more closely, I saw that my reflection went on forever in a ghastly funhouse effect.

"Are you ready?" Morgan asked. She and Joe were in the open doorframe, Joe with a video recorder and electromagnetic field meter at the ready.

I nodded, but that was a lie. I wasn't ready. Not at all. Still, I stepped up beside Callum and took a breath.

"All right, so on the count of three, Callum will raise the mirror he's holding to the broken one on the wall." Morgan's voice was calm, but did the air suddenly feel different? Heavy and throbbing? Or was I imagining it, letting my fear get the best of me? Allowing the last twenty-four hours to prime me for chaos?

"Do I raise it on three or after three?" Callum asked.

Joe gave a little laugh. "Either one. I'll be ready." He held up the camcorder.

"All right, then," Morgan said again, but did she sound less certain than she had a moment ago? Less convinced everything would be fine? If so, it didn't matter, because the next word out of her mouth was the start of the count. "One..."

I blinked. *The air is not hazy, the air is not hazy*... Callum adjusted his fingers, almost losing his grasp on the mirror.

"Two..."

My stomach lurched. I shuffled to the side a half step, to better see into the mirror when Callum raised it.

"Three!" Morgan shouted.

Callum grimaced and lifted his arms. Joe aimed the camcorder. I looked into the gold-framed mirror, expecting to see one of the shimmery-faced ghosts made visible. Made far more terrible.

What I saw was the same broken mirror that hung on the wall. There was no ghost. No illuminated reflection. No question made known.

"Nothing happened," Callum said. I resisted the urge to respond, *No shit.*

I turned to Morgan. She and Joe were whispering to one another. "It's okay," she said to me and Callum a moment later. "I sort of expected that to happen."

"You did?" Callum's tone was suspicious.

"The ghosts have come and gone twice. Since they're not staying perpetually in your home, it stands to reason they wouldn't be present in the mirrors all the time either."

"It stands to reason, huh?" Callum said. "What part of this is 'reasonable' to you, lady?" I shot Callum a look, but neither Joe nor Morgan seemed to mind his little outburst.

"What do we do now?" I asked. My headache had worsened with this latest instance of receding adrenaline.

"We go on to the next mirror," Morgan said matter-of-factly.

We moved ourselves and the equipment to Beatrix's room and followed the same process. After another anxiety-spiking countdown, Callum raised his arms to reveal the same broken mirror we could see with the naked eye.

The same scenario unfolded three more times—in Bea's bathroom, in the downstairs bathroom, and, to my great surprise, in the foyer. I'd thought that since the foyer mirror was the first point of ingress, it might be the ghosts' main portal.

"What now?" Callum asked.

Morgan started to respond, but I interrupted, clearing my throat.

"Sorry?" Morgan said. "What was that?"

Fear clenched my insides, but I knew it had to be said. I grimaced, pushing images of the tortured creature from my mind, swallowing against the smell of burning flesh. My eyes flicked toward the living room.

"It's just that . . . there's one more mirror."

Chapter 51

"Oh?" Morgan asked. "Where is it?"

Callum looked confused, but then realization dawned on his face. He groaned. "No," he said, voice cracking. "Not that one. No, no, no." I could see that he, too, was remembering everything that had happened after the long-broken mirror had been rediscovered.

"Where is it?" Morgan said again, her tone making it clear she wouldn't be letting this go.

"Behind the couch," I responded. "It's broken too, but it didn't happen last night. This one broke six years ago. By accident," I added when I saw Morgan's curious expression.

The Tallows followed us into the living room. I tried not to look too carefully at the damage. There was a gaping hole in the front of the house from where the tree branch had fallen through. The floor was dotted with puddles, and the bats had taken over one corner of the ceiling for roosting. *Maybe insurance will cover this?* I thought. Hopefully our policy had a clause about ghosts.

Callum and I stared at the couch, neither of us wanting to reach back there. What if the ghosts returned right then? What if, this time, the corpse specter came from the shattered glass instead of the tortured wraith?

"So, this mirror was broken before?" Morgan asked.

"Yes," Callum and I said in unison.

"I'll grab it," Joe said, sensing our unease. He leaned over the back of the couch, then slid the mirror sideways until its frame became visible on one side. Morgan took over, sliding the mirror out the rest of the way before lifting it, struggling a little with its weight.

"Got it," said Joe, grabbing the other side. "Let's put it here."

They placed it dead center on the cushions. The only thing visible in the broken pieces were the stones of the fireplace across from the couch.

Joe grabbed the camcorder from the coffee table. Morgan handed Callum the gold-framed mirror. I stepped up beside Callum, my heart in my throat.

"Remind me again what to do if we see something," I said.

Morgan nodded as if this was a good question, though she'd gone over it several times. "If something shows up in the intact mirror, it will be important to have a clear view. So, Lainey, help Callum keep the mirror steady. Joe will be recording, so we can study the image later. I'll be using these"—she lifted the belt around her waist hung with various thermometers and readers—"to check for cold spots, random shadows, radiation spikes, disruptions in electromagnetic waves, changes in radio frequencies." She paused, sensing this wasn't what I needed to hear.

"The important thing is to stay calm," she added. "Joe and I are here. We won't let anything happen."

For the first time since they'd arrived, I saw Joe's neutral armor crack, and he rolled his eyes. I knew he didn't believe in any of this; he'd said as much at our last meeting. But his skepticism helped ground me.

Here was a man who'd been ghost hunting with his wife for over a decade and had never seen anything that convinced him of the supernatural. If we held up this mirror and it showed our ghosts, Joe would be faced with irrefutable evidence of them, as Callum and I had been last night and earlier today. The odds of Joe not only seeing ghosts for the very first time, but seeing ghosts bent on violence and destruction, seemed low. I took another breath.

"All right," I said, "let's do this."

Again, Joe lifted the camcorder. Again, Morgan counted.

Again, on three, nothing happened.

Until it did.

The mirror in Callum's hand shimmered. As we watched, the pieces of the broken mirror put themselves back together. The glass rippled and pulsed, and with each outward bubbling, the form materializing in the mirror appeared more corporeal. With one final pulse, we were staring at Lady Macbeth.

Her hood was up, her head tilted down. She was wringing hands coated with blood, crimson in some places, threaded with blackish-red clots in others. A sink, I realized. She was washing her hands over a sink. It felt strange to stare into a reflection within a reflection within a reflection within a reflection. Like I was standing over a bottomless precipice, about to fall in. I watched, mesmerized, as Lady Macbeth scrubbed furiously. A moment later, she started to mutter.

"No-no-no-no-no."

The hair on the back of my neck stood up. I'd heard this muttering before. In the yard last night as Lady Macbeth dug. But before then too. Seven months before. Last November. Standing over a sink.

Callum faltered with the mirror, and the image dipped. I tore my eyes away from the crimson and black and saw Joe's eyes, wide with disbelief.

"Hold it steady!" Morgan gasped. "Lainey, help him!"

But I couldn't help. Couldn't do anything but watch.

Lady Macbeth scrubbed and scrubbed. I found that my own hands were up, wringing in a mirror image of the specter's. "No-no-no-no-no," I whispered.

As if she'd heard, Lady Macbeth stopped. The muttering ceased. The blood, aside from a pale-pink tinge, had been washed from her hands. She looked up.

I found myself staring into my own pale face.

I stumbled backward, my heels hitting the fireplace, and though I went down onto the stone, my eyes remained locked on the image.

On me, out of my mind with a horror I'd been prepared to repress after the voluntary procedure, until the pregnancy had ended not with pink-tinged water in the toilet, as the doctor had told me to expect, but with grayish-white tissue and a mass of blood in my palms, which the internet informed me was not necessarily problematic but was wildly atypical. Me, scrubbing my hands, something I'd had to do again and again, for the blood hadn't stopped coming. Me, walking through the house with the eleven-week-old fetus, stopping to grab one of Bea's little-used teddy bears from the shelf, because if I were having an impromptu funeral, the bear seemed the very fucking least I could do. Me, burying everything in the backyard in the dead of night. Me, returning to the house from the grave, a string of muttered appeals on my lips. Me, lying in bed that night but feeling myself go through every one of the motions again and again.

It was me, knowing I hadn't made a mistake, but filled with horror over the experience, the secrecy, the shame of it, all the same. "Put it down," I said. My voice was hoarse, like something dug up from the dirt. "Please. Put the mirror down." But Callum didn't. Couldn't. Because inside the mirror, the image was starting to change.

Now it was Callum, the night of the housewarming. Metal candleholder in his hand. *The blunt object,* I realized. Inside the mirror, he swayed, drunk, eyes roving, dragging the metal across the wall. Across the mirror. In it, he saw something.

This, I realized. *He saw this.* Himself, looking at himself.

Looking at himself.

The Past-Callum lifted the candleholder above his head and smashed it into the mirror. It shattered, not only in the past, but in the present. I covered my face with one arm, turning away from the explosion. But the sound of glass showering the floor, the coffee table, never came. It was merely an echo. An illusion. When I looked up, the mirror atop the couch appeared exactly the same as it had before Callum had lifted the gold-framed counterpart to it.

I stared. Unable to move. Unable to think.

"What—" Callum started, but couldn't finish. Joe was no longer looking through the camcorder, but he also hadn't lowered it. He stared at the mirror in Callum's hands with a strange, shocked expression on his face. Morgan had one hand to her mouth, her eyes as big as the camcorder's lens.

I stared at the couch beneath the mirror. I'd been sitting in that exact place when Adelaide had first told me her idea for the haunting, and I'd responded with derision: *This place is twenty-five hundred square feet. It's not some gothic mansion. We're not on a cursed burial ground. There wasn't a murder here. And we built it, remember? There's no body beneath the floorboards.*

How badly I'd misunderstood. How blind I had been. I'd thought Callum wouldn't believe that the house was haunted because of its lack of history, and then, even when the actual ghosts had appeared, I'd been confused; this wasn't one of the Newport Mansions where I worked. This was a house untouched by history or hardship.

But I had missed something fundamental with that belief. It wasn't bad bones that caused a house to be haunted; it was its guts, what it consumed, what lived within it. We *had* built this house, Callum and I—the concrete foundation, the wood scaffolding, the plaster walls, and everything in between them. Then we'd embodied it, filling it with broken dreams, unfulfilled promises, expectations that turned into disappointment, fear, resentment, blame. We'd poisoned it so thoroughly that we'd *turned* it bad, as opposed to stumbling on something that'd been bad to begin with. We'd been parasites, transforming the constitution of our host.

"Oh my god," I said to the room, unaware of the tears trickling down my cheeks until I tasted them. "We haunted ourselves. *We're haunting* ourselves."

Chapter 52

It was starting to get dark. Callum and Joe were at the kitchen table, drinking coffee. Morgan was standing against the sink, asking if I wanted her to put on the water for tea.

"That's okay," I said.

"Are you sure?"

"Yeah. I . . ." I what? Needed a second? More like a lifetime to make sense of the past two days.

"I'm so sorry this is happening," Morgan said. I looked into her face. I didn't even recognize her as the woman who used to lobby the Preservation Society to bring ghost tours to the mansions. She was wholly new to me in this posthaunting world, where the ghosts of one's past haunted their present so hard that it affected the future.

I moaned, unsure what to do. It occurred to me that I hadn't called my parents since that morning. "I need to find my phone," I said. "To check on Beatrix."

Morgan nodded and turned to the stove, intent on making tea anyway. I went to the charging station and pulled my phone off the cord. The moment I lifted it, I knew something was wrong. Twenty-seven missed calls and almost as many texts. They were split in terms of caller; about half from my mother, the other half from Adelaide.

"Shit," I said, panicked.

"Everything okay?" Morgan asked.

I didn't answer, just opened the text messages from my mother. The last one she'd sent caused a lump of terror to well up my throat:

> Not sure why you're not answering, but the ambulance has arrived for your father. It's his heart. He's conscious, but I need to follow him to the hospital. I was going to leave Bea with Francine next door, but Adelaide called. She's been looking for you too. I told her what's going on, and she picked up Beatrix. They're on their way to you now.

My heart thundered in my chest. I checked the time stamp on the message. Twenty minutes ago. I looked up, horrified, just as Callum said, "Someone's pulling in."

I didn't bother with shoes but, on mothering autopilot, grabbed Bea's iPad and headphones, then ran out the door and down the front walkway. I met them at the edge of the drive, my heart soaring and then plummeting at Beatrix's happy-go-lucky skips across the pavement, the purple cast—and Love, the koala—held to her chest, the ecstatic expression on her face.

"Mommy, Mommy!" she cried. "I missed you! My head feels all better, but Papa is sick. Gram went to the hospital."

I scooped Bea into a hug. She smelled like honeysuckle and laundry detergent, and I wanted to hold her forever. Over Bea's shoulder, I caught Adelaide's eye. "Did you talk to my mom? Is my dad okay?"

Adelaide's face was pale against the fuchsia waves of her hair. "I'm not sure," she admitted. "They're hoping it was minor. He was stable before they transported him." Her eyes darted up to the house. "Why didn't you answer our calls? I haven't heard from you since last night, when you left me that super-weird voicemail." She widened her eyes as if to say, *You know, the one we shouldn't talk about in front of your daughter?*

Adelaide's attention wavered. "Is that Joe and Morgan's truck?" Her eyes narrowed. "What are they doing here?" She looked at the house again. "Lainey, what the fuck happened to all the windows?"

"Language, Auntie Adelaide," I said, and she rolled her eyes.

I set Beatrix down and she looked up at me. "Can I go on my swing set?"

"No!" I cried, but she took off running anyway.

I spun on Adelaide. "She *cannot* stay," I exclaimed, and held out the iPad and headphones, but she didn't take them. "I need you to take Bea somewhere—anywhere but here!"

Adelaide opened her mouth but was cut off by a shout from Beatrix. "What's wrong with the yard?" she cried, darting in and around the holes.

"Woodchucks," I called back. "They wanted to move into your fairy garden, but there was no room; they got mad and dug up the grass."

I turned back to Adelaide; her mouth was open, and she was staring at the yard in dismay.

"What *is* wrong with the yard?" she demanded. "And the windows? And that voicemail? What is wrong with every-fucking-thing right now, Lainey? Start talking!"

It flooded out of me in a pressurized deluge of words, everything from discovering Chris was the blackmailer to the revelation that Callum and I were being haunted by ourselves.

"But what about the other two ghosts?" Adelaide asked. "Neither of you have ever been a corpse or dragged your mangled body out of wreckage." It was just like Adelaide to accept everything I'd said at face value and go right for the plot holes.

"I'm not sure," I admitted, "but they're terrifying in different ways."

Adelaide stared up at the house. "So . . .what now?"

I was about to respond when I heard the door to the house open in the garage. Morgan poked her head out. "Um, hi, Adelaide. Nice to see you. Uhh, Lainey, we need you in here. Now." There was urgency in her voice.

I stared at Adelaide, wild-eyed. "Take her somewhere?" I pleaded.

"Where?" she asked.

"Your house?"

"I guess I could—" Her eyes fell on the playhouse at the top of the swing set. "What about there?" she asked.

I looked in time to see Beatrix disappear through the door of her fortress. "Pinecone House?"

"It's far enough from the main house, don't you think? And no ghosts have incorporated a trip down the slide into their wanderings. At least, not yet."

I frowned at her bad joke. "I don't know—"

"I'm worried about you. What if I need to be here? To help somehow?"

"Lainey?" Morgan called. She was back in the doorway again. "We need you in here." The urgency had climbed up a notch.

"Arghh!" I shouted in frustration. "I can't think straight. I don't know what to do." I took off toward the swing set, and Adelaide followed. At the bottom of the ladder, I turned. "Give me a minute," I said.

"Of course," Adelaide replied.

I climbed up and knocked. When there was no answer, I pushed open the door. *Bea's gone,* my brain screamed. *The ghosts got to her somehow! The house swallowed her whole!* Then I realized Bea was surrounded by blankets and stuffed animals at the center of the snug space. I smiled and held out the headphones.

Her face lit up. "Shows in the playhouse? I've never done that before!"

"I know, right? It'll be fun." She took them while I propped the iPad on a pillow shaped like a whale. My stomach twisted. She was so sweet, so innocent. How had this gone so wrong? How was my daughter, whom I'd wanted to protect more than anyone, thrust into this madness? I looked at her. The cat ears of the headphones poked out from between several plush horses and a second whale pillow. I pressed play, and cartoon dogs twirled on a swing while a smiling Dad-dog looked on with affection.

Despite the holes in the yard and my terror at what would come next, despite the malevolent chaos in my house—and my relationship—the image of Bea watching her favorite show, the show I usually made an exception for, putting down whatever work or household chore needed finishing to indulge in the delightful program with my daughter, injected something like hope into my heart. I paused the show and lifted one side of Bea's headphones from her ear.

"Which episode is this?" I cooed.

"'Double Babysitter,'" Bea squealed. I swore that whenever she watched the show, her voice took on the higher-pitched notes of the titular character.

"I love this one," I said. Beatrix reached for the iPad to restart it, but I put a hand on her arm. "Sweetheart?" I asked. She blinked her large gray-gold eyes at me. "Can we pretend it's like the babysitter episode tonight, and Adelaide is like Frisky, and Mommy has to go do something for a bit but will be back very soon?"

She thought this over. "Where are you going?" she asked.

I forced myself to appear calm, to keep up the facade that things were normal. "Nowhere. But I still need you to stay in here with Adelaide, no matter what. Just for a bit, okay? Do you have to go to the bathroom?"

Beatrix shook her head.

"Good, so you stay here with Adelaide, watch your show, and I'll come back shortly."

"Okay, Mommy." Bea reached for the iPad again.

"One more thing, 'kay, sweetheart?" I leaned forward and rubbed Bea's cheek with my own, then kissed her several times, my heart aching more fiercely with each kiss. "I love you. So, so much."

I replaced the headphones and pushed play. A moment later, Bea's laughter, infectious and more real than anything, rang out. I shut the door and climbed down from the fort. Adelaide was staring at me. "You okay?" she asked.

"No," I said. "Not at all. Take care of her while I'm in there, okay?"

"I promise."

I held her gaze. Who would have known her batshit plan to make my life better would have brought us here? As terrifying as it was, I felt like we belonged in this moment. When you realized you'd been haunting yourself, that meant things really needed to change.

Tell her thank you! a voice in my head howled. *Tell her how much you appreciate her! You suck at showing your emotions. It's okay to be vulnerable!* And this time, instead of letting the moment pass, I grabbed her and pulled her into a hug.

"Thank you," I said. "For all your help. For everything."

Adelaide held me a moment, then pulled away. As she did, I felt a lump in my pocket. I slipped my hand inside and pulled out the knife I'd brought with me into the tent.

"Here," I said. "I know, it's absurd. A knife against a ghost. But it would make me feel better if you had it."

She nodded and gave me a gentle shove. "Don't come out here again until you fix whatever's going on in there."

I nodded and started toward the house. I tried to look unafraid, in case anything was watching from the broken windows, but I was a mess of swirling terror and uncertainty.

"Hey," Adelaide called.

I stopped, looked back.

"Remember my advice."

"What advice is that?"

She winked. "Serial killer confidence, baby. Don't let those ghosts know how scared you really are."

Chapter 53

I entered the house from the back deck, turning away from the spot where Bea had fallen, the splintered wood of the rail leering at me like fangs. The playroom was empty and quiet, but I heard voices up ahead.

"What do you mean, we have to do it again?" Callum was demanding. I crossed the hallway, stopping a few steps back from the kitchen. Joe stood across from Callum at the island. Morgan was by the table.

"We can't get them to leave until we know who they are," Morgan said, her tone patient but firm.

"We *know* who they are!" Callum cried, banging his fists on the marble. "Somehow, some-fucking-way, they're us! Lainey and me. Some fucked-up echo from the past!"

I walked into the room. Everyone turned to look at me, and the conversation changed direction.

"Why is that pink-haired bitch here?" Callum growled. "And why does she have Beatrix?"

I filled them in on my father's heart attack and my mother dropping Bea with Adelaide to follow him to the hospital.

Callum peered through the open maw that used to be the kitchen window. "But they're gone, right? You sent them away?"

"I . . . didn't," I admitted. "I tried, but Adelaide thinks she should be here. In case she needs to help."

Callum let out a loud, bitter laugh and paced the kitchen. "What the hell is *she* going to do?" he said. "I don't like it. And having Beatrix here is a really bad idea. It's not safe."

Black spots popped at the corners of my eyes, and rage as sour as bile welled up my throat. "I don't think you're in any position to comment on Beatrix's safety."

"I'm not the one who brought her to a goddamned haunted house—"

"I didn't bring her here! My father's in the *hospital* and—"

"That stupid clubhouse isn't going to protect—"

"It's not the house that's haunted, you jackass, it's us!"

"All right, all right!" Joe said loudly. He put up his hands. "Can we get back to the main issue here?"

"Which is?" I asked, still unsure what they'd been discussing when I'd walked in a minute earlier.

"That we need to uncover the identities of the other two apparitions."

"Oh," I said, and sighed. "As long as it's only that." I sank into a nearby chair.

Morgan smiled weakly at me. "While you were outside, the ghost with blood on her hands—"

"Me," I interjected. "We might as well call them what they are. I was calling her Lady Macbeth in my head, before I realized . . ." I trailed off, then refocused on Morgan. "Anyway, yes, the ghost with blood on her hands is past-me . . . Past-Lainey."

"Right, okay, so, while you were outside, Past-Lainey and Past-Callum reappeared and went through the motions of their respective loops several times." Morgan tilted her head, something occurring to her. "Did you see your, um, past self out there when you were talking to Adelaide?"

I shook my head.

"Remarkable," Morgan mused. "When inside the house, you can see the ghosts when they step out of it. But when outside the house, you see nothing. They're invisible."

"Not true," Callum said from the island. "Those goddamn holes in the yard are certainly visible."

"Anyway," Morgan continued, "when the past ghosts reappeared, they retained their"—she winced—"er, *your* faces." She looked back and forth between Callum and me excitedly. When we only stared, she added, "Don't you see? Using the unbroken mirror to reveal their identities stuck. They no longer have the nonfaces they initially presented with. They're exposed, and therefore ready to be dealt with. But there are four ghosts, not two. So we need to uncover the faces of the others. Then we can figure out how to banish them all."

"But we held your mirror up to all the broken mirrors in the house," I pointed out. "It only revealed the identities of Lady Macbeth and the staircase specter. I mean, Past-Lainey and Past-Callum." I grunted in exasperation.

"That's true," Morgan admitted. She looked across the room to her husband and smiled. "But there are other ways to get what we want."

∞

Ten minutes later, Callum and I stood in the living room, watching as Morgan and Joe wound yarn—borrowed from Bea's craft supplies—around one end of the gold-framed mirror. Joe threw the ball of yarn over the chandelier directly above them and fashioned a noose-like knot through which he threaded the other end of the yarn. When he was done, the mirror hung flat in the air above the coffee table, to be raised or lowered as needed.

Morgan threw a black towel over the mirror's surface. "Do you have something wide and low we could fill with water?" she asked. "Like an oven tray, but big enough for the mirror to fit into?"

Callum stared blankly, but I knew just the thing. "There's a plastic tray of Bea's in the playroom. It keeps her Play-Doh and clay from getting everywhere. Would that work?"

Morgan said it would, so I went to fill it with water before handing it carefully over. She placed it on the coffee table below the mirror.

"Okay," Morgan said. "Let's form a circle." She removed a bundle of herbs and twigs from a satchel by her feet.

Callum narrowed his eyes. "So, are you a ghost hunter or a witch?" he asked.

She didn't answer.

"What are we doing exactly?" Callum pressed.

"Catoptromancy," Morgan said.

"And that is?"

"Divination using a mirror as the tool." She yanked the black towel off the mirror with a flourish like a magician pulling a scarf off the top of a hat to reveal a rabbit. "We're going to turn the lights off, and while we're visualizing what we want to see—the identities of the corpse specter and tortured wraith—we'll lower the mirror toward the table until its base is resting on the surface of the water. When that happens, we should see something in the mirror. An image. An explanation. Something that illuminates the answer to our question.

"Or, we'll see nothing at all." She shrugged. "This is far from a science, but I'm optimistic, since the last instance of using mirrors to fight mirror ghosts worked." She walked to the wall and flipped the switch, plunging us into relative darkness. The broken bay window let a fair amount of moonlight into the room, but Morgan looked satisfied.

"And if one of the ghosts reaches up and pulls us into the mirror with it?" Callum asks. "Then what?"

"I don't foresee that happening," Morgan said.

"You didn't foresee the ghosts being violent," Callum pointed out. "Or this"—he gave the gold-framed mirror a push, sending it swinging on the yarn—"showing that two of the ghosts have our own damn faces." He looked over at me as if expecting backup, but I rolled my eyes.

"She's trying to help," I said. "Can you keep an open mind?"

He grumbled something, but I ignored him and stepped up to the coffee table. Joe and Morgan stepped to either side of me. Callum was left to walk around to the other side and face me.

"Okay," Morgan said. "Joe, you want to grab the yarn?"

Joe complied.

"Raise it a bit."

Joe raised the mirror so it was a little above eye level for all of us.

Morgan held a lighter to the smudge stick until a small flame licked up from its end. When she blew it out, smoke curled from it in a steady stream. She moved her hand back and forth above the coffee table, the smoke rising and encompassing the mirror in its haze.

"Callum, I'd like you to envision the corpse specter," she began.

"What?" Callum's voice was shrill. "Why me? That thing clearly has it in for—"

He quieted when he saw the look Morgan was giving him. "Fine," he grumbled, and shut his eyes.

"Lainey, I'd like you to envision the ghost we've been referring to as the tortured wraith. Envision her pain. Try to feel it. Think of what she might have lost. Think of what might have happened prior to her crawling out of the mirror and through your living room."

I did as I was told, and while it wasn't hard, it wasn't pleasant. The smell of heather and basil gave way to gasoline and the sharp sting of alcohol. Along with charred flesh, I smelled blood, which I hadn't realized had been there in the wraith's presence before. I imagined the wretched thing collapsing to the ground, wailing in an agony that was more than physical, that was existential and all-encompassing. As if, besides the pain, she had lost everything . . . and been the cause of it.

"Good," Morgan said. "Now, move your focus from what you've seen of the apparitions to what you haven't seen. Couldn't see. Think about their faces." Then, more quietly, she said, "Joe, lower the mirror."

I heard the lighter click again. A fresh wave of smoke filled the room.

"Imagine the swirling, shifting, immovable nature of their faces becoming still," Morgan said. Her voice was calm, gentle. "Imagine the abstraction smoothing out. And as you do, open your eyes."

I thought of the wraith in the moment she'd stood before me, when it felt like she'd seen me despite her lack of eyes. I opened mine. The mirror was about six inches from the water and still lowering.

"Stare into the mirror," Morgan said softly. "And see the face of your specter reveal itself to you."

I stared into the mirror. With the smoke swirling around it, it wasn't hard to superimpose the mental image of the ghost into its reflection. It occurred to me that I should be seeing the reflection of the chandelier, the ceiling, in the mirror's surface. But nothing was there. It was merely a black, roiling depth.

Until it wasn't.

Chapter 54

Joe lowered the mirror until its base rested in the water. It floated there, and for a moment, I swore I could see the water *through* the mirror, the way its surface became liquid, a rippling pond, its secrets unknowable in the darkness. But then it was neither mirror nor water. It was water pooling on a sheet of glass, and beyond that, a vast expanse of night air.

The mirror was the windshield of a car.

Rain drummed against it, making everything beyond it reflective and disorienting. My hands were no longer dangling at my sides but curled around a steering wheel. I felt the strain of trying to see the road through the rain-pummeled windshield, and something else too . . . the dizziness of it. The gleeful reveling in the feel of being slightly out of control. With a jolt, I realized that, in whatever vision I was having, I was drunk.

"How was it?" My mouth produced the words, and someone from the back seat answered me.

"Fine." The voice of a girl.

"Did you dance with anyone?" I asked. "Luca McAllister, maybe?"

"Ugh, Mom, no. It's eighth grade, not high school. No one actually dances with anyone they like. I hung out with my friends."

"So, you like Luca?"

"Jesus, Mom, no. Can you just, like, drive? Why were you so late picking me up anyway?"

I didn't answer her, but I knew, despite feeling my feet on the floor of my living room while my four-year-old daughter watched an iPad in her backyard playhouse, that I would one day have a fourteen-year-old daughter who had a crush on a boy named Luca from her class. And that on the night of her eighth-grade Winter Ball, I would be late picking her up because I'd been at the office. Not headquarters for the Preservation Society of Newport County, but a rinky-dink office for a rinky-dink museum I'd gone to after the Preservation Society had proven too time consuming and high-stakes as Bea had gotten older.

I knew, the way I knew Joe, Morgan, and Callum surrounded me, that I'd informed the rinky-dink museum caterers to leave the extra champagne in my office at the end of a gallery showing and proceeded to drink all of it before closing up. I knew drinking to intoxication was not new in this future life of mine, but rather a common escape from the doubts and insecurities of being a single parent. I knew it was a way to anesthetize myself after recently losing my father to a heart attack. I knew it was something I did but did not analyze and hardly even acknowledged, and that while the recycling bin did not overflow with wine bottles every week, it was certainly full by the time the truck came for it every two weeks.

I didn't know, but *I saw* Beatrix, and I started to argue as I drove faster and faster in the rain. I saw her yell and kick the seat in front of her. I saw myself jerk the car into the other lane, rage tingling in my fingers and inflaming my tongue into angry words and accusations. A rage that I understood had been buried upon marrying Callum and ignored even further after embarking on a crazy plan with my best friend ten years earlier to haunt him into oblivion. We'd forced him to leave because I believed things would be better, that everything would be in my control, that I'd have the power to direct the future. To ensure Beatrix's safety. Her happiness. Her fulfillment.

But nothing was in my control. Least of all the car as it slid on the rain-slicked highway across two lanes. It hit the median with a tortured screech of glass and metal and flipped down the embankment. I saw the car's interior brighten as the windshield faced the sky, then darken as it plummeted toward the earth. I saw the approaching trees, the unforgiving rocks. And then, for the briefest of moments, I saw my daughter's face in the rearview mirror as she would look at fourteen, beautiful and grown-up, but also stark and stretched with terror. I heard the horrific crunch of metal anew and the unfathomable twist of steel. I heard the screams. Mine and hers. Then I heard nothing. Saw nothing but darkness.

No, not darkness. Thin light through the slit of an eyelid. I smelled gasoline leaking out of the wreckage. The alcohol in the acridity of my vomit. The blood. So much blood. Every ounce of my beautiful daughter's blood laid bare, exposed to the air. There was no question as to whether the life had gone out of her. She was still, empty. I heard the guttural wail of agony as I fractured with the knowledge of it, the pain that was more than pain. The pain that was a true and unending hell.

I felt the physical pain too. The pain of injuries sustained and, surprisingly, the lack thereof. The bottom half of my body was numb. My hips, legs, and feet as twisted as the hissing, steaming steel. Bones pulverized. Connections between essential aspects of myself severed like frayed marionette strings.

I felt the bite of the glass shards still clinging to the window as I dragged myself from the ruined vehicle, the lightless cocoon that might as well have been a barren womb, for my daughter had ceased to be while inside it. And how had that happened? How had she gone from me, from this world? Someone who was whimsy and effervescence?

Me, I thought, both now, where I stood, trembling, and in the future, utterly leveled and eternally damned. The "how" was because of me. She died because of me. Not Callum. *Not Callum.* All this time, I thought I needed to get her away from him. But I'd had no idea of the horrors the future could hold. The horrors I could *allow* it to hold, if I lost myself in this moment in my living room, surrounded by my alcoholic husband and a pair of ghost hunters and staring into a haunted mirror, and never found myself again.

I stayed in the vision long enough to feel the heat of the explosion and smell the burning flesh, long enough to hope for death without absolution.

I felt myself pull back from the vision, from the mirror, with a gasp so violent it knocked me backward. I hit the couch and rolled onto the floor, where I lay, sucking in air. Morgan knelt beside me.

"Lainey, are you okay? What did you see?" She stood. "Joe, is he okay? Can you get him on the couch?"

I didn't need to look up, to question Callum, to know what our catoptromancy session had shown him. If the tortured wraith was me, from the future, then the corpse specter was the ghost of the Future-Callum. It was absurd, how unsurprising it was, when you came right down to what the mirror must have shown him: If Callum didn't stop drinking, he would die.

I curled onto my side, gasping like a fish, my body humming with the memory of the pain, my mind recalibrated from the knowledge. There was only one final consideration, one more question I needed to ask, a question that had been posed before, albeit in fiction, when it came to ghosts:

Were these the shadows of the things that Will be, or were they shadows of the things that May be, only? Was the tortured spirit my fate, or could I still do something to avoid becoming her? To avoid causing the death of my daughter?

Chapter 55

"What the fuck do we do now?"

Callum was pushing away the mug Joe held out to him, repeating the same question over and over again. He was sitting on the opposite end of the couch, with Joe fretting over him the way Morgan was fretting over me. I'd managed a small sip of water but hadn't quelled my body's violent trembling.

Neither Joe nor Morgan had seen anything in the mirror once it had touched the surface of the water, but they'd agreed that both Callum's and my reactions—eyes rolled back in our heads, joints rigid, muscles seizing—were deeply indicative of not just an overwhelming experience but an out-of-body one.

"Can you tell me what you saw?" Morgan asked me gently.

I stared straight ahead, still unable to speak. But Callum must have recovered enough to be able to convert his vision into words.

"Cirrhosis," he choked out. He stared past Joe, past the walls of the house, reliving the vision. "That's how I die. And the lead-up is prolonged and painful. And—"

He stopped and looked across the room, catching my eye, then looked away.

"I'm alone at the end," he said, so quietly it was hard to hear him. "All alone. In some sort of disgusting end-of-life care home. No one was there. Not you." He gave me a look that was both embarrassed and accusatory. "Not Beatrix. Not even my mother."

He glanced warily at the mirror. "The corpse. It's me. My fate." He let out a strangled cry and turned to Morgan. "What do I do?" His tone was desperate. "How do I keep this from happening?"

I wanted to scoff, to tell him the best way to avoid dying from alcoholic liver cirrhosis was to quit drinking alcohol, but at that exact moment, the house began to shake. The rumbling was low but rose quickly. The small colony of bats that'd been hanging in the corner screeched and took flight, swooping wildly over our heads. Shards of glass still clinging to windowpanes clattered to the floor. The candles and planters hanging from the ceiling shook like boughs in a hurricane. The rumbling became so pronounced that my teeth chattered in my head.

"What's happening?" I managed to cry, but the words were lost to the roar. Just when I thought I'd go deaf from the sound of it, the rumbling stopped.

And all four ghosts burst into the room at once.

Lady Macbeth came in from the French doors, wringing her hands—*my* hands—so violently blood splattered the walls and floor, the *no-no-no-no-no* on her lips—*my* lips—frenzied and animalistic. The presence from the staircase lurched in through the main entrance, wielding its twisted hunk of metal like a weapon and groaning incoherently. Its resemblance to Callum the night of the housewarming six years prior was so exact, it was more memory than haunting.

From the place on the floor where, earlier, we'd thoughtlessly laid the broken mirror, the tortured wraith rose like a zombie from a black-and-white horror picture, pulling itself forward on hands embedded with glass. Its ragged voice rose in a howl that turned my blood to ice. When it lifted its head, I saw my own face.

The world went black, then came hurtling back in horrifically saturated Technicolor. I screamed, and as I did, I realized Morgan was yelling too, yelling and scrambling to reach Joe. When she did, they held each other, their eyes dark pools of horror as they took in the ghosts and the madness.

I turned to Callum, but his attention was fixed over my shoulder, his mouth a rictus of terror and revulsion. I knew the corpse specter must be behind me, but before I could turn, a rush of moldering cloth and rotting flesh darted past me and launched itself at Callum, gripping the wrist that, up until now, I'd forgotten had already been injured by the horrible, lumbering thing. Callum screamed, and his corpse, his own mouth, roared back at him not three inches from his face.

I felt the thing's rage. But something else too. I felt its desperation, the urgency of it. It may have been dead, but that didn't mean it wasn't almost out of time.

How do I keep this from happening? Callum had asked—begged, really—right before the house and its ghosts had gone apoplectic. I looked to where the staircase specter, Past-Callum, swayed and rallied, and was shocked to find that its attention was as focused on the battle between the Present- and Future-Callums as mine, Joe's, and Morgan's was.

His fate has already come to pass, I marveled. *There's nothing for him to do but remind and cause regret.* But Future-Callum's fate was uncertain. And this particular Future-Callum's fate was tied entirely to Callum remaining on his current path. The path of alcoholism, maybe even insanity. The path I'd been committed to keeping Callum on by infiltrating his psyche and haunting our house.

"Callum!" I screamed. The corpse didn't pause in its assault, but the other three ghosts snapped to attention. I didn't like the way the Future-Lainey eyed me, eyed the fight between the Present- and Future-Callums. If I voiced what I was thinking, I'd be alerting my own future specter to the fact that I knew what it wanted, opening myself up to danger. But I didn't have a choice, couldn't help but believe Future-Callum and Future-Lainey were inextricably linked.

"Callum!" I screamed again. "The only way for it to exist is if you remain on your current path! You can't die of alcoholism if you don't drink, and the only way to not be an alcoholic is to admit you're one!"

From beneath the heft of the macabre threat, I saw Callum pause, take in my words. The corpse had its hands around Cal's throat, but it wasn't choking him. It didn't want Callum dead; it wanted him traumatized. Demoralized and defeated. It wanted him to leave this haunting never having really left it.

"Do you hear me, Callum?" I screamed. "You can defeat it by admitting you're an alcoholic." I was crying, tears streaming down my cheeks, soaking my neck and hair. I thought of standing over him in the hospital as he slept, holding Beatrix to my chest and dreaming about the future. I thought of how the years had changed him, the ways the last month had changed him, solidifying the haunted expression on his face, the set of resignation to his mouth and chin. If things had changed so much in one direction, perhaps they could change back.

"This doesn't have to be the way it always is!"

This last utterance flipped some switch within him, and as the corpse specter raised its fist, Callum took the opportunity to roll away. He scrambled out from under the monster and took off toward the kitchen. Joe and Morgan and I ran to follow. A horrible, frenzied screeching engulfed me as all four apparitions responded to Callum's desertion. I felt, more than heard, the undead beast's footsteps on the floor behind me.

I rounded the corner into the kitchen to find Callum pulling bottle after bottle from the cabinet above the refrigerator. When he'd pulled the last bottle out, he began unscrewing caps and dumping them into the sink two at a time. Something twinged in my chest. It was heartbreaking, watching Callum resort to that most clichéd of actions an alcoholic with fresh resolve could take. I knew what he was going for, but I didn't know if it would be enough.

The corpse specter, too, was unimpressed. It flew into the kitchen like a ghostly train, all gray smoke and keening wails. It tackled Callum, knocking the bottle of vodka to the floor where it shattered, and dragged him away. Callum pummeled the thing with his fists, scratched at its eyes, but to no avail.

I turned to look for the others; Joe was at the table, throwing things out of the duffel bag like a madman, no doubt looking for something that would help. Morgan was holding a pendant around her neck she'd removed from beneath the collar of her shirt, her lips moving in silent prayer.

The cadaver continued dragging Callum, whose hands scrabbled for purchase on the edge of the counter, the leg of the coffee bar, the floor itself, the corner of the hallway. As he was about to disappear around the corner, I jumped forward.

"Here!" I yelled, and kicked the broken vodka bottle his way. It spun across the hardwood, and for a moment, I thought its trajectory was too wide and that it wouldn't reach him. But at the last second, Callum shot out an arm and intercepted it.

He lifted the jagged mouth of the bottle and stared, calculating, then brought it to the floor, breaking off one side and leaving himself with a single line of jagged glass. He raised the bottle and set his jaw.

"I've had enough of this shit," he growled. "Enough of you, enough of myself, enough of the drinking. I am an alcoholic, but I'm not"—he stuck the bottle in the side of the thing's neck—"going"—he dragged it across its throat—"to die one!" He yanked the bottle the final few inches, and the corpse jerked back, raising its fingers to the ragged mouth of its throat. It tried to swallow, but something black and viscous glugged out from the wound like oil, pouring onto Callum. Callum pulled himself out from under it and backed away, stopping when he hit the wall.

We watched as untold horrors poured from the thing: black blood and putrid tissue and bugs and chemicals and dirt. When it seemed nothing else could possibly be inside it, the corpse closed its eyes with a groan and slumped to the floor. Slowly, steam rising from its moldering remains, it sunk into the floorboards, like a series of time-lapse photographs of animal remains putrefying. A heartbeat later, the corpse specter had disappeared.

Callum and I stared at one another, our expressions mirror images of horror and relief. I sensed Joe and Morgan coming up behind me, and I started to turn, but my attention was diverted by movement at the other end of the hall.

Callum's annihilation of a future in which he died alone had been witnessed by more than the two ghost hunters and me. Lady Macbeth hovered and wrung her hands, fear on her face, her muttered exhalations more frenzied than ever. The staircase specter dropped the candleholder as he swayed. With wailing cries, their bodies spun into hazy tornadoes of ghostly material. They spun, faster and faster. Then, like smoke whooshing up a chimney, they vanished.

In their wake, one remained. The tortured wraith . . . the Future-Me, face twisted into an expression I hadn't seen before but, to my horror, could read: Outrage. Hatred. Bitterness and determination. In an instant, I saw that my Future-Self would not go as easily as the Future-Callum.

I thought of raising my hands, stepping toward her, trying to reason with her the way one did a spooked animal or irrational child. The thought was ridiculous, and she wasted no time proving she wouldn't make the same mistakes as the corpse specter. She let out a vengeful screech and scuttled forward on her mangled hands with a speed both horrifying in its unexpectedness and devastating in its singularity of purpose. Toward the hall and the sliding door to the backyard, then onward, to the playhouse.

Toward my unsuspecting daughter and best friend inside it.

Chapter 56

I sprinted forward, whipping around the corner of the living room and bounding through the French doors in two long leaps. From the far side of the playroom, I saw the wraith approach the slider, broken glass like the entrance to a carnival ride, stretched and menacing. It passed through it . . .

And disappeared.

I burst out after her, spinning in circles on the deck as I searched for her mangled form, but I saw nothing. Joe and Morgan ran out a moment later, both breathing hard.

"Where'd it go?" I demanded. I turned to Morgan. "It disappeared. Where the fuck did it go?"

She didn't answer, but she didn't have to. I followed her gaze to the yard. All three of us watched the thing's progression across the yard, invisible but for the disruption of loose soil as she dragged herself across the holes Lady Macbeth had dug over the last twenty-four hours.

"Oh my god." The words were a literal supplication rather than a pronouncement of disbelief. "Oh my god, no. Don't let her. No."

I heard Joe ask, "What's happening?" but I had already sprinted off the deck.

The second my foot hit tilled earth, my vision went black. A second later, colors and images exploded in my brain. My ears pricked. My fingers tingled. My view of the yard came back for a moment, flickered, then faded to black.

I saw the windshield of a car. Endless rain. Bloodred brake lights and disorienting reflections.

"No-no-no-no," I muttered helplessly.

I tried to clear the vision, blinking and rubbing my eyes, but nothing happened. I tried to run but tripped and fell. Beneath my hands was both the grittiness of dirt and the smooth, oily leather of a steering wheel. I shook my head again, but remained blind to everything but the vision. The future. "Morgan, Joe, please! Help me!" I cried, and started to crawl forward. Again, the future assailed me.

Dizziness. Drunkenness. Conversation. Anger.

From behind me, someone reached down and wrapped their arms around my chest. "Come on," a voice next to my ear said. "Come on, I'll help you. I don't know what's going on, but I'll help."

It was Callum. One step at a time, he dragged me forward, over the destruction in the earth, as images assailed me and the tortured wraith did her best to ensure my—and her—fate.

The car in my mind went faster. Callum and I struggled to cross the yard. I felt the kick to the back of my seat the same way I felt a jolt whenever my foot plunged into another hole. I felt the rage, both now and in the future. Rage at my helplessness, at how little I could control.

When the car in my mind slid across the rain-slicked highway and hit the median, Callum's hands were ripped from my body.

"Hey," I heard him cry.

I pitched forward, catching myself on hands and knees. At the same instant, my vision cleared like fog blowing off the ocean. I saw the bottom rung of the ladder to Pinecone House up ahead. The screech of glass and crunch of metal faded from my ears.

But I still heard the screams. Beatrix.

No, *not* Beatrix's screams. And not mine.

Adelaide's.

I watched in horror as the door to Pinecone House swung open and Adelaide was thrown from the platform as violently as if she'd hit a tree going eighty and been ejected through the windshield. Her body hit the ground and crumbled like one of Bea's dolls, all splayed limbs and fanned-out fuchsia hair.

This time I did scream. Screamed and rushed to my friend. She was conscious but only barely. She blinked and brought her hands to her face. Her fingernails were painted in an alternating pattern of marigold orange and rose pink. I held one of her hands, but Morgan and Joe were already there, running their hands along Adelaide's body, asking her if she was okay.

"I will be," she whispered. "My back hurts a little. And my leg. But Bea . . . get Bea. I had . . ." She coughed, winced. "I'd gotten her to fall asleep."

I turned and stared into the open door of Pinecone House in time to see the wraith materialize, no longer invisible despite being outside. It must have been Pinecone House that granted her corporeality, by virtue of Beatrix's understanding of what the word *home* entailed, expanding the wraith's territory beyond the confines of the house. She was standing now, her legs and feet a swirling mass of silvery smoke. The implications of her no longer having to drag herself made me dizzy.

I watched as the tortured wraith, that unyielding bitch who thought she had everything figured out, lifted my daughter. She held Bea to her blood-streaked face and nuzzled her. All the air left my body. Bea stirred. I jerked forward and felt something hard hit my hand. I winced, thinking no wonder Adelaide's leg hurt, that she'd broken the bone and it was protruding from her skin. But it wasn't bone. It was metal.

I slipped my hand into the slim side pocket of Adelaide's leggings and pulled out my knife. I raised it. Flicked it open. If Callum had slit the throat of his own unsought future, maybe I could do the same. Hoping to employ the wraith's same surprise tactic of unexpected speed, I ran for the ladder and propelled myself up it with one hand, the other aiming the knife at the left side of the wraith's neck, the opposite side from where she held Beatrix to her face.

A shimmering wall, like a mirror unspooling—or a reflective shield—cut down like the blade of a guillotine, the force of it throwing me off the ladder and onto my back in the dirt. I lay, dazed, struggling for breath, until rough hands thrust me upward.

Callum.

"Are you okay?" he shouted, eyes on Pinecone House. Already the barrier wall had shimmered out of existence, but the wraith stared down at me, triumphant, and I knew she would merely use the same trick again. I watched as Beatrix stirred again, blinking sleepy eyes. My helplessness threatened to devour me. Slowly, the ghost turned to the east-facing wall until her back was to me and both her and Beatrix's faces were framed by the mirror I'd hung for Bea myself, its intricately patterned border resembling the scales and prickles of a pinecone.

The wraith jerked forward, toward the mirror. Its surface shimmered, and the ghost, too, suddenly seemed less corporeal than she had a moment earlier.

It doesn't matter how she gets it, I realized sickly. *If she can't have my soul annihilated from grief and regret in the future, she'll take my soul annihilated now.* Same destination, different route. Could she take Beatrix through the mirror? I didn't think so. But I also thought the attempt might kill my daughter, or come close to it.

The realization that I couldn't stop what was about to happen was one I'd had before, as the car flipped over the median and the world became alternating patterns of dark and light.

Dark.

The wraith moved closer to the mirror.

Light.

My hand tightened around the knife.

Dark.

A screech of triumph rose from her mouth, the sound curling visibly and joining the growing chaos of her form.

Light.

I took two lurching steps forward.

Dark.

The thing's form—along with Beatrix's—became grayer and gauzier by the second.

Light.

I raised the blade.

Dark.

Like Lady Macbeth outside the living room, the wraith's form began to dissolve into a vortex, starting at her mangled legs and rising up to her neck. In an instant, both she and Beatrix were eclipsed by the swirling smoke storm.

Light.

I closed my eyes. I thought of the softness of my daughter's cheeks. The smell of her skin in the morning. The tight grip of her warm, trusting hand. I thought of games at the kitchen table and snuggling close as I told her stories. I thought of the sweet birdlike kisses she gave me when I helped her onto the toilet, or the way she asked me the most insightful questions in the last few minutes before she fell asleep. I thought of how the last four years were a tower of memories, each one stacked on the last to form our bond, and how the next ten years would be a void where new memories should have been made.

Dark.

And with that final thought, I plunged the blade into the soft part of my wrist, pressed down hard, and dragged it vertically from hand to elbow, forging a line the way a child might draw the start of a mirror with a silver crayon. Even as blood glugged from the wound, I dragged the blade across the other wrist, through the stitches, so deep and hard that the pain was like swallowing a dying star only to have it expand and contract inside me.

The effect was immediate and dizzying, a speeding train in reverse, sparks shooting from the tracks. The vision sped backward, memories I didn't actually have peeling back like bark from a diseased tree. The fiery wreckage. The glint of the embankment. An argument. Champagne in a sparkling glass. More glasses. Bottles. Avoiding my reflection in the mirror. A new job. New problems. New me.

Until every aspect of that one potential future was gone, and I was *me*, the old me, the rotten seeds so recently planted by the ghost of my future self, by the haunting—no, by *my*self, by the *staged* haunting—dug up and thrown to the wind. And more important, the old Beatrix, safe, if not happy, with no possibility of a mother who could do the unthinkable, who could set off a chain of dominoes that would cause her death. I could be happy, at least, in the knowledge that I'd saved her.

I dropped to my knees. Kept my eyes open long enough to see the wraith spin from the mirror like a tempest. She dropped my daughter and howled down at me with inhuman hatred and rage. My vision swam. I thought I saw her get sucked toward the mirror. I saw Morgan reach up the ladder and snatch Beatrix away from the swirl of gray and silver and carry her to the side, away from the swing set.

The blood ran down my arms like rivers, coating my fingers and hands, dropping onto the earth. Soaking into the holes, reddening the ground until dirt became clay. I thought of scrubbing my hands, of wringing them. But I didn't have to. Not now. Not ever. I'd done what I needed to. What I had to do. And I would do it again.

Because a good mother did what was best for her child, no matter the circumstances.

Somehow, night was becoming day. I lay on my back and stared at the sky. I watched it turn from black to blue. Blue to red. Red to gold.

Or perhaps I didn't. Perhaps I was already somewhere else, had already returned.

"Do you wanna play Favorite Thing?" Beatrix always asked me.

I had been playing, I realized. All along. It had all been my favorite thing.

Chapter 57

Dark.

    I stood at the center of a long black tunnel, unsure of which direction I should go. I turned left, walked for what seemed like ages, spurred forward by the distant night sky. But when I reached the tunnel's end, I found the sky was merely a mirror, reflecting back the long passage through which I'd come. The passage in the mirror appeared featureless, unknowable, which meant the tunnel must go on forever in the opposite direction. I turned. The darkness was obscene. Intimate. I didn't want to step forward, but I didn't have a choice.

    Light.

    A flicker. A metal box. The back of a vehicle? Longer than it was wide. Bright flashes of white. Gauze. Starched shirt. The bite of rubbing alcohol in my nostrils with no ensuing sting. "We need to stabilize," someone shouted. "Too deep!" and "severed tendons" and "surgery." I smelled blood like I'd never smelled blood before. Not after the abortion. Not during my visions of the future. This was blood as proof of life. Proof of existence. *My* existence.

    Dark.

    In the tunnel of my mind, I walked. One foot in front of the other, arms held out like a child balancing on a curb. I braced for the walls to close in on me. For the darkness to seep into my skin. Waited, breathless, for something to drag me back to the yawning black hole of a mirror. For something to devour me in the dark. But nothing came.

Except...

This time the way ahead *did* seem lit by stars, twinkling like a million tiny mirrors against a midnight sky. I could keep walking—*would* keep walking—and make it out of the darkness.

Light.

I opened my eyes. There was so much color. Not merely the sun streaming through the blinds, but the flowers. Pink roses and orange daylilies. Garnet irises, their satiny petals beautiful enough to pacify even the staunchest detractors of the color red. I could smell them too. Fresh, like sunlight itself.

I turned. Beside the flowers, beside the windows, there were chairs. Empty ones.

But Beatrix was not sitting. She was standing. At my opened eyes, she leaned over the bed. Her face was light and love and safety and happiness. A tiny mirrored image of my own.

"Mommy, Mommy!" she squealed. "You're up! I missed you so much!"

When she leaned down to hug me, I caught our reflection in the tempered glass of the hospital windows.

I caught our reflection, and smiled.

After

Two years later

For the second time since opening it, I read the email from the Rhode Island Historical Society. It seemed that a recent documentary had renewed fervor for the gravesite of Mercy Lena Brown, known as "the last New England vampire." After Mercy's death in 1892, residents of Exeter accused her of draining her brother's life force, and subsequently exhumed her body. The exhumation revealed blood in her heart and liver, confirming the townsfolk's suspicions: Mercy was a vampire.

The Historical Society frequently dealt with legend trippers who tried to make off with Mercy's headstone, and now they were proposing I take Mercy's headstone for the exhibit I was curating; I couldn't type my return email accepting their proposition fast enough.

I spun from my desk and checked the clock. Twenty minutes until I had to meet Adelaide for lunch. I was about to dive into the next email when someone knocked on the office door behind me.

I turned to find Callum in the doorway. "Hey," I said, a jolt of anxiety zagging through me. "Is Beatrix okay?"

"Yes, of course, sorry. I'm picking her up from your mom's this afternoon. I was thinking of taking her to that art and animals exhibit at Rosecliff . . . Wild Imagination, right?" He arched an eyebrow. "If that's all right with you?"

I laughed. "It's fine. Just because I don't work for the Preservation Society anymore doesn't mean I don't want to support their programming. I love the idea of you guys going to Wild Imagination. Let me know how it is."

"Okay." He nodded, more to himself than at me, as if pumped he'd gotten the courage to ask. "Okay, sweet. And yeah, I'll definitely let you know. Though you know Beatrix . . ."

"I know Beatrix," I agreed. "I'm sure she'll tell me about it in painstaking detail."

We both laughed before falling silent. It still felt strange sometimes, even two years later, talking with Callum. *Really* talking. Though perhaps strangest of all was how quickly the channels of communication had started flowing after the divorce. It was as if, by finalizing our agreement, we could finally move forward, finally separate from one another, extricate ourselves from the codependence. It was also probably no coincidence that our divorce was made final right around the five-month anniversary of Callum's sobriety.

Callum's gaze dropped, and I realized I was flexing my wrists the way I did when they were bothering me. I'd spent longer at the computer than I'd planned to.

"How are they?" he asked, nodding at my arms.

"All healed up after the last surgery. Dr. Cohen is a miracle worker, truly. No long-term tendon or nerve damage, and no motor or sensory dysfunction." I shrugged. "I just have to be sure not to overdo it."

Callum was silent again, and I knew what he was thinking. I'd been lucky. Lucky not only to survive my injuries but with regards to convincing the doctors it had all been a huge misunderstanding. That I *hadn't* tried to kill myself. That we'd been working on staging a haunting, almost like a play, and I'd dragged what I'd thought was a prop knife down my wrist so hard and fast that the pain hadn't registered before I'd done the same thing to the other wrist. It was a bonkers story, but with four witnesses all attesting to the same thing, they'd had no choice but to believe me.

I'd been endlessly grateful for the others' support. I'd had enough to deal with in my recovery without having to convince a psychiatrist I wasn't a danger to myself or an unfit mother to Beatrix. Especially because, in the beginning, I thought that was how Rosalie Taylor would try to spin things.

"How's everything with you?" I asked. "How's work?"

"It's good." He cleared his throat. He seemed nervous.

"Meetings going well?"

He shifted from one foot to the other. "That's sort of what I came to talk to you about."

Another jolt of anxiety. Had Callum relapsed? Flashbacks from two years ago assailed me. Callum standing shit-faced in the living room, railing about moving furniture. Callum pouring a drink the morning of Flypocalypse. Callum holding the end of a straw, staring me in the eyes, and bending it . . .

"It's my two-year anniversary on Friday," he said. "I'm speaking at the seven o'clock meeting. Will you come?"

Relief coursed through me, mixed with overwhelming joy. "Of course!" I exclaimed. "Of course. Nothing would make me happier."

"Great," he said. "That's so great. My sponsor, Wally, will be there. And Monty."

I let out a small laugh. "I have to say, I never would have thought Monty had it in him. Who would've expected your former drinking-buddy-in-arms would be such an ardent supporter of your recovery?"

Callum nodded in agreement, but I could tell something was still bothering him.

"How about your family?" I asked. "Is your mom going to be there?"

He sighed, and I knew I'd hit on the source of discomfort. "I don't know," he admitted. "She still says she doesn't get it. Doesn't understand any of it. Why I quit drinking. Why I stood by you after your injury. Why I agreed to the divorce. Why I didn't fight you on sharing custody with Beatrix."

I crossed the room and put a hand on his arm. "And she probably never will. But you don't need her to."

He stared at my hand on his arm, then nodded. "You're right. You're always right."

"No," I said. "I'm not. And that's okay."

He nodded again. We stared at each other. I opened my mouth to say something else, but a commotion came from outside my office.

"You're busy," Callum said. "I'll let you go."

"It's the afternoon tour getting back. They'll be going through the museum now to see the exhibits. But I am meeting Adelaide for lunch soon."

Callum put a hand in his pocket and took out his keys. "Tell her I said hi," he said generously. "And Lainey?" He gestured around us. "I'm really glad this is going so well. The tours. The museum. All of it."

I smiled. "Thanks," I said. "I'm glad too."

I watched him walk out. He crossed in front of the windows as he made his way to his car. Again, the urge to say something, to call after him, came over me. *It's okay,* I told myself. *You don't have to tell him everything right now.* That was the best part of our new reality. Whenever I needed to talk to Callum, to tell him something, he listened.

I left my office, heading toward the main part of the museum. I crossed the foyer and opened the heavy wood door, peeking into the cavernous room on the other side of it. A group of ten sat on the long bench, listening in rapt attention. Morgan stood at the room's center, regaling the tour-goers with the story behind each haunted artifact on display behind her. Joe was in the corner, preparing a selection of ghost-hunting equipment for demonstration.

I tried to close the door without being seen, but the hinges creaked, and everyone's attention shot to me. One woman yelped. Another brought a hand to her heart, thoroughly startled.

"Don't worry," I said. "I'm not a ghost. I'm real."

The tour-goers laughed.

"I'm sorry to have interrupted you." I met Morgan's eye. "I'm heading out to meet Adelaide. I'll let you know as soon as I'm back if we're any closer to procuring Bathsheba Sherman's gravestone for the fall exhibit."

She grinned and nodded. "Sounds good." She turned to the group. "Ladies and gentlemen, do not let her fool you with unnecessary apologies. This is Lainey Taylor! Another founder, along with myself, Joe, and Adelaide Benson, and the one who secured this historic Newport property. But she's also the director of museum affairs and chief curator of Newport's first—and only—Museum of the Supernatural and Gilded Age Occultism."

The tour-goers clapped raucously.

I blushed. "Thank you very much. Enjoy the rest of your tour." I returned Joe's nod from the corner and shut the door.

I headed for the exit, passing alcove after alcove, admiring each artifact as I sailed down the hallway: a ghost doll from the General Nathanael Greene Homestead; a section of the terrazzo floor from the reception hall in Belcourt Castle; a portrait of Angela O'Leary from the Providence Art Club, where she'd committed suicide; the wooden coffin pendant that'd belonged to the poet Sarah Helen Whitman.

I stopped before the final artifact—or, series of artifacts. A wall of mirrors. Mostly broken ones. Five, to be exact. The fifth, and only intact, mirror was a gorgeous gold thing, small and rectangular, reminiscent of one that hung above the mantelpiece in Marble House's ballroom. Its intricately patterned border resembled the scales and prickles of a pinecone.

I stood to the side of the mirror, hesitating. Something was inside it. I could feel it. But then I stepped in front of it. Stared into the silver. Smiled.

I wasn't afraid of mirrors. And I wasn't afraid of my reflection. Not now. Not anymore.

I stepped into the bright summer sun, pulled the heavy door shut behind me, and walked down the stone path. I was already thinking ahead to lunch with Adelaide. Thinking of the wildly colored dress she'd be wearing, the turquoise hair. The feather earrings and multicolored nails. Likely, she'd have leads on all sorts of haunted artifacts she wanted to pursue across Rhode Island. Throughout New England. She'd want to bring Gothic lecturers into the museum. Stage plays. Maybe hire an illusionist to put on performative séances.

And I would listen. Consider all of it. Nod and reflect and ask questions.

Because crazy or not, that girl had some really great ideas.

ACKNOWLEDGMENTS

How to Fake a Haunting would not have been possible without my trusted circle of second readers: Thank you to Belicia Rhea, Tom Deady, Larry Hinkle, and Allan Patch for their lightning-fast turnarounds and scalpel-sharp insight. This book was very much its own type of misbehaving poltergeist, a crafty trickster that refused to conform to my initial expectations of a peaceful writing experience. In the end, though, like most personal hauntings, it taught me something I didn't realize I needed to learn, and my second readers were there to help shepherd that lesson along.

Thank you to my editor, Gabino Iglesias, together with whom I shared many barks of laughter (sorry, I just couldn't resist). His painstaking attention to everything from rhythm to word choice, pacing to paranormal creep-factor, made this novel what it is. Working with him was a highlight of my writing career to date, and I'm eternally grateful for that experience.

Thank you to Gracie Doyle for her even-keeled and commonsense approach to editing what is now our third novel together; and to the entire team at Thomas & Mercer for their direction, passion, and support. Thanks as well to my agent, Jill Marr; I'm always most excited to share my latest ideas with her, and her enthusiastic response to a novel about a staged haunting that goes a little bit (at least, as initially pitched) off the rails was no exception. I look forward to presenting her with the next exciting—and potentially bonkers—literary lightning rod.

Thank you to my friends and fellow writers who acted like lighthouses in the storm of this tempestuous and capricious novel: Elissa Sweet, Lauren Daniels, Jessica Wick, Joshua Rex, Mary Robles. And to Claire Cooney for organizing innumerable Google Meet writing sessions so that we could be alone with our difficult writing projects together. A thanks, as well, to Andrew Morenzoni for detailing the myriad complications that would arise from attempting to plumb blood into a residential waterline.

Thank you to my parents, Jeanne and Rick Quattromani, for their confidence, love, and unending encouragement. And to my sister, Lauren Forenza, and all my extended family members, especially Christine Granfield, for their unconditional support of each new project.

A special thanks to my husband, John Beauchamp, who's fallen victim once or twice to my horror film–inspired pranks. One October night several years back, after he'd fallen asleep on the couch, I took a picture of him sleeping there using his own phone, texted it to my cell, then pretended to have gone to bed and been woken by the incoming photo. "Why did you send this to me?" I demanded, until my earnestness convinced him *someone* had taken the photo and sent it. If not him, who? Who could have known that his confusion and—dare I say?—fear would be the basis for the conception of *How to Fake a Haunting*? And while I apologize to him yet again for having a little fun, what's the point of being married to another horror-loving soul if you can't pretend there are nefarious forces at work in your home? Especially when that pretending might occasionally lead to a novel?

And finally, thank you, as always, to my daughter, Eleanor, my partner in crime when it comes to scaring Daddy (pretending she could see a spirit that followed him home after a visit to Lafayette Cemetery was a particularly impressive touch); and my partner in life for every adventure, challenge, and new experience I ever hope to have. She's my favorite thing, every time, all the time, whether giggling together on a mundane Tuesday or hunting for seashells on a white-sand beach, in the real world and across the inside-out, upside-down Wonderland-esque landscape of my dreams.

ABOUT THE AUTHOR

Photo © Joshua Behan

Christa Carmen is the author of *Beneath the Poet's House*; *The Daughters of Block Island*, winner of the Bram Stoker Award and a Shirley Jackson Award finalist; *Something Borrowed, Something Blood-Soaked*, an Indie Horror Book Award winner; and numerous short stories, including the Bram Stoker Award–nominated "Through the Looking Glass and Straight into Hell." She has a BA from the University of Pennsylvania, an MA from Boston College, and an MFA from the University of Southern Maine. Christa lives in Rhode Island with her husband, daughter, and bloodhound–golden retriever mix. When she's not writing, Christa keeps chickens and uses a Ouija board to ghost-hug her dear, departed beagle. Most of her work comes from gazing upon the ghosts of the past or else into the dark corners of nature, those places where whorls of bark become owl eyes, and deer step through tunnels of hanging leaves and creeping briars only to disappear. For more information, visit www.christacarmen.com.